Fiji

A Novel

Also by Lance & James Morcan:

The Ninth Orphan

Fiji

A Novel

Lance & James
MORCAN

Sterling Gate Books

Fiji: A Novel

Published by:
Sterling Gate Books
52 Aranui Drive,
Papamoa 3118,
Bay of Plenty,
New Zealand
sterlinggatebooks@gmail.com

Cover Painting: Mathwalta, Venua Levu Vitisa, Fiji, c.1840
Artist: Titian Ramsay Peale (1799-1885)

National Library of New Zealand publication data:

Morcan, Lance 1948-
Morcan, James 1978-
Title: Fiji: A Novel
Edition: First ed.
Format: Trade Paperback
Publisher: Sterling Gate Books
ISBN: 978-0-473-19471-0

Dedicated to the loving memory of:

Bernard George Morcan
&
Herbert George Fletcher

Part One

SHORES OF CONFLICT

PROLOGUE

A Fijian maiden stooped to pick up a shell as she walked along a white sand beach at Momi Bay, on the western side of Fiji's main island of Viti Levu. Sina had a natural island beauty. Lithe and graceful, her dark skin glistened in the tropical sun. She wore a traditional grass skirt and shawl made from tapa, or bark cloth.

The beach was bordered by a grove of coconut trees and the turquoise waters of the bay. Tropical birds filled the sky—among them Kingfishers that dived into the sea, competing for fish.

At one end of the beach, a distinctive headland protruded out into the Pacific. It accommodated a village whose entrance was marked by defensive fortifications in the form of bamboo palisades. The village was home to the Qopa, the region's predominant mataqali, or clan.

Out in the bay, Qopa fishermen speared fish and cast nets from their canoes. Beyond them, foaming surf marked the reef that ringed much of Viti Levu. The constant sound of waves crashing against the reef was like the boom of distant thunder.

Several miles beyond the reef, a ship sailed by, her sails billowing as she was pushed along ahead of a light southerly. Sina and the other villagers paid scant attention to the vessel: they'd become used to the comings and goings of the white man's ships.

The maiden noticed the shadows were lengthening. It was time to think about returning to the village. She smiled as squealing village children playing at the water's edge splashed one another, white teeth sparkling against their black skin. Like all Fijian children, they seemed to wear permanent smiles.

Sina stopped to pick up another shell, dropping it into a woven flax bag hanging from her shoulder. Humming a traditional lullaby to herself, she was unaware a tall, muscular warrior was watching her impassively from the shadows of the coconut grove. Standing motionless, the sinister warrior held a musket in one hand. Only his coal-black eyes moved—his heavily tattooed, battle-scarred face adding to his air of silent menace.

This was Rambuka, also known as the Outcast, the charismatic leader of a tribe of cannibals feared by villagers up and down the coast. Rambuka's eyes subconsciously widened as he studied Sina. He liked what he saw. Finally, he moved, gliding soundlessly among the palm trees like a spirit as he stalked his prey.

Still singing, Sina bent down to study an unusual shell. A sudden movement to her left caught her eye and she looked up to see Rambuka rushing toward her, musket in hand. She recognized him immediately. Screaming, she turned to flee, but had barely taken a step before her assailant was onto her, dragging her back to the trees. Startled by her screams, the children ran toward the village, shouting.

Terrified, Sina lashed out and twisted around, trying to bite her attacker. Rambuka slapped her hard, momentarily stunning her. Everything started spinning and Sina felt as if she might faint. Effortlessly hoisting her over his shoulder, the Outcast began running inland.

Behind them, Qopa warriors came running from the nearby village, alerted by the children's screams. Most carried clubs or spears, while some had tomahawks they'd acquired from white traders. Nearly all were tattooed about the arms, legs and torso. The warriors were led by Joeli, son of the village ratu, or chief.

A big, powerful man, Joeli's proud bearing and intelligent eyes were clues to his royal bloodlines. Bone earrings hung from his ears and a huge, intricately-carved, whale bone club dangled from a cord around his waist, a dozen human teeth inlaid around its head testament to how many men he'd killed in battle. Most striking, however, was his massive hairstyle. Nearly two feet high and even wider across, it was dyed blue with yellow stripes through it. Earlier treatment with burnt lime juice would ensure it remained stiffened in place for a few more days at least.

Some of Joeli's warriors wore equally flamboyant hairstyles—many dyed a bright color and some even multi-colored; several sported hairstyles of a geometric shape while the orange-dyed hair atop one proud warrior was all of six feet in circumference. Such weird and wonderful styles could be seen on men throughout Fiji and were worn as a symbol of masculinity and social standing.

The frightened children all talked at once and pointed down the beach. Joeli led his warriors to the spot the children had indicated and there two sets of tracks were immediately visible in the sand. He turned, grim-faced, to his warriors. "It could only be the Outcast," he decreed.

A fine-looking young warrior with a distinctive birthmark on his forehead and a zany, geometric hairstyle asked, "Who has he taken?" This was Waisale, a close friend of Joeli's.

Joeli looked down, avoiding his friend's eyes. He suspected that Rambuka had abducted Sina, but didn't want to say as much until it was confirmed. It was common knowledge Waisale and Sina were lovers.

A sense of foreboding suddenly came over Waisale as he studied the footprints that Rambuka and his captive had left behind. "Sina!" he murmured. Without another word, Waisale sprinted into the coconut grove, following the tracks into the dense rainforest beyond. The others ran hard on his heels.

#

Dusk was approaching and Sina was near exhaustion when the Outcast finally stopped running, allowing her to briefly rest and drink from a shallow stream. Their flight had taken them into the forest-covered hills above Momi Bay.

Scratches and bruises covered Sina's face and body, and she winced as she splashed water over her face. Aware of Rambuka's reputation and knowing what fate awaited her, she looked frantically around, her mind racing, desperate to find a way out of her predicament.

Rambuka grabbed her by the arm. Sina shrank back, expecting to be raped. Instead, she was dragged into the water. Her heart sank as the Outcast began pulling her along upstream, leaving no tracks for anyone to follow. The realization was setting in that Rambuka wasn't merely intending to rape her—he was abducting her. Her skin crawled at the thought.

A quarter of a mile behind, Joeli and his warriors followed their quarries' tracks. With night approaching, they knew they were running out of time. Waisale led the chase, desperate to save Sina. However, as Rambuka had intended, the tracks ended at the stream. In the fading light, Waisale ran up and down the bank, frustrated at the dearth of signs to follow.

Joeli shook his head. "The Outcast is taking her to the Land of Red Rain," he said simply. His tone suggested the dye was cast; there was no saving Sina now. Joeli and the others reluctantly turned and began retracing their steps back to the village.

Waisale stayed behind, looking east toward the highlands of the interior. He knew the land Joeli had referred to lay beyond those same highlands. Exactly where the outcasts were hiding wasn't known. They moved around constantly, using various hideouts. Many a raiding party had set out from Momi Bay to try to find their enemies in the past, but the land was rugged and the outcasts hid their tracks well.

Pain and anger rose up like bile in Waisale's throat. He vowed he'd go to the Land of Red Rain and rescue Sina.

1

Three months after Sina's abduction, the sun's first rays pierced the clouds, heralding the start of a new day for the occupants of the small Fijian settlement of Levuka, on picturesque Ovalau Island, to the east of the main island of Viti Levu. The clouds and oppressive humidity served as a reminder to the island's residents that the wet season was approaching.

Fiji's capital of the day was built around a busy harbor that accommodated sailing ships and indigenous craft of all descriptions. Despite the early hour, the level of activity on and off the water immediately signified to newcomers that this was a lively and bustling settlement.

Several horse-drawn carts laden with European visitors and their wares were already traveling the short distance up a narrow, palm tree-lined track linking Levuka's wharf with the township. The visitors were traders and merchants from two of the newly-arrived ships anchored offshore. Along the way, they passed Fijian fishermen meandering down to the waterfront where their waiting canoes would carry them to the bountiful fishing grounds beyond the reef that surrounded their island. The fishermen greeted the visitors with broad smiles as the carts trundled by.

Europeans were almost as numerous in Levuka as the local

natives. They included settlers, sailors, whalers, sealers, adventurers, escaped convicts and a variety of other colorful characters—as was the case elsewhere throughout the islands of the South Pacific. For most, Levuka would not be a final destination. Rather, it would serve as a temporary base from which they could conduct their trading or other entrepreneurial activities until such time as profits began waning, as they inevitably would.

On this, the last day of October, in the year 1848, profits were the last thing on the mind of twenty-two-year-old Susannah Drake. The young Englishwoman, recently arrived in Levuka after an eventful six-month voyage out from London, had been awake most of the night. Something had made her restless, but she wasn't sure what exactly.

The sound of her father snoring through the paper-thin wall separating his bedroom from hers reminded her where she was: in a two-bedroom guest cottage on the spacious grounds of Levuka's Wesley Methodist Mission Station. The cottage was situated on a rise above the town.

Susannah pulled back the drapes and looked out her bedroom window. She could see the town's residents were stirring. Merchants were preparing to open their stores in readiness for another day's trading and revelers from the night before were weaving their way back to their respective lodgings, looking somewhat worse for wear.

The young woman turned away from the window and eased her tired limbs out of bed. Stretching, she walked over to a dressing table, sat down and began brushing her long, red hair. In the soft morning light, her hair shone like gold and framed a face that was angelic yet determined—and undeniably beautiful; the modest night-dress she wore couldn't hide her shapely figure, but her most amazing feature was her hazel eyes, which were flecked and which sparkled like diamonds.

Looking at her reflection, Susannah marveled at the chain of events that had brought her to this point in her life. She and her father, the Reverend Brian Drake, had come to Fiji as missionaries. They were en route to Momi Bay, an isolated settlement on the west coast of Viti Levu, where they would run a fledgling mission station.

For no apparent reason, as she often did, Susannah suddenly thought of her late mother. Jeanette Drake had passed away when her daughter was twelve, yet it seemed like only yesterday. While her passing had hit Susannah hard, she knew it had affected her father the worst. Drake Senior had been like a lost soul since the death of his dear wife.

When the good Reverend had announced to his parishioners one year ago that he had a calling to spread God's Word to the natives of Fiji, Susannah hadn't hesitated to volunteer to accompany him. While she, too, wanted to do her bit for the church, she couldn't bear the thought of letting her father travel to the other end of the world alone. He'd opposed it at first, but Susannah finally got her way, as she usually did.

Susannah finished brushing her hair then picked up her copy of *The English Bible* and flopped back down on the bed. This particular version of the scriptures had been translated from Hebrew in 1583. It was dog-eared, having been handed down to Susannah from her deceased mother and from her mother before that.

As she often did, Susannah opened the Bible randomly and began reading from whatever page it opened at. On this occasion, it fell open at the Book of Judges, chapter 16, which described the tumultuous love affair between Samson and Delilah.

Reading about the events surrounding the tale of the doomed lovers, other images soon began invading Susannah's mind. She thought of the young, golden-haired rigger who had caught her eye aboard the ship on the voyage out from England. Lithe and handsome, he'd tried every trick known to man, to bed her. She'd resisted his advances, being the good Christian girl she was, but now wondered if she'd made the right decision. Try as she may, she couldn't forget him, or his chiseled body.

Erotic images came to mind as Susannah imagined how Delilah must have felt being ravaged by Samson. The images gradually blurred. When they came back into focus, she was Delilah and the rigger was Samson; he was disrobing her and she wasn't resisting.

Susannah immediately felt guilty. In an attempt to rationalize her feelings, she came to the conclusion it was the overwhelming masculinity of men like Samson and the golden-haired rigger that excited her. Yet she was frightened by the intensity of her feelings also.

At her father's rectory in London, Susannah had had a few suitors over the years. All were God-fearing men and most would have made faithful husbands and good fathers. The problem was all were predictable and boring. None of the young Christian suitors who had received Drake Senior's tick of approval had that dangerous persona that most attracted her. As much as she hated to admit it, she was attracted to men who were the antithesis of her father.

As Susannah continued reading, the forbidden thoughts returned. This time they were even more intense and exciting. Her pulse raced and her breathing became labored as she imagined strong hands caressing her body. She shook her head to try to dispel the fantasy, but she was too aroused to quash it.

Feeling more guilty than ever, she prayed to God to expel the sinful thoughts from her mind—to no avail. It was useless. Whatever she tried, failed.

Before she knew it, the fantasy completely took over her mind. Susannah imagined herself lying naked with Samson, or perhaps it was the rigger, and feeling him explore her naked body. The fantasy was so vivid she could almost feel his lips on her breasts and his fingers between her legs.

A sudden knock on the bedroom door snapped Susannah out of her reverie. She dropped her Bible on the floor.

"Are you decent?"

It was her father. Susannah had been so preoccupied she hadn't realized he'd surfaced. She picked up her Bible from the floor. "Yes, Papa. Come in."

Drake Senior entered the room. The clergyman-turned missionary was as stern-looking and forbidding as his daughter was fetching. Tall and angular, he bore a closer resemblance to an undertaker than a missionary. His piercing eyes softened at the sight of his daughter and only child reading her Bible. So feminine and radiant was she, Susannah reminded him of his deceased wife who also had an angelic appearance. "Good morning, my dear," he said affectionately.

Suppressing her sexual self and reverting to the prim and proper young woman she knew her father expected her to be, she responded brightly, "Good morning, Papa."

The good Reverend took a quick look out the window then turned to his daughter. "We should give thanks to the Lord for this splendid day."

"Yes, Papa."

They both knelt down beside the bed and began reciting the Lord's Prayer. "Our Father who art in heaven, hallowed be thy name. Thy kingdom come, thy will be done, on earth as it is in heaven."

As she prayed, Susannah's thoughts began to stray once more. The sexual images that had invaded her mind minutes earlier returned and began waging war against her spiritual self. She feared she was fighting a losing battle.

#

Less than a quarter of a mile away, as Susannah and her father prayed, a young American emerged from one of the numerous brothels on Levuka's dusty main street.

Adventurer Nathan Johnson was one of the more interesting characters who happened to be passing through Levuka. Recently arrived after a three-month voyage from his home port of San Francisco, the young man was here to trade muskets for the Fijians' highly prized beche-de-mer, or sea slugs. He then intended shipping the exotic sea slugs to China where they would fetch exorbitant prices, thereby adding to his not inconsiderable wealth.

Nathan was feeling considerably older than his twenty six years. Little wonder, he admonished himself, as he'd just spent the night gambling and drinking before falling asleep in the arms of a prostitute.

Now, standing outside the brothel, studying his reflection in a window, he didn't like what he saw. Bloodshot eyes stared back at him and his long, dark hair framed a face, which, although undeniably handsome, was paradoxically youthful and world-weary at the same time.

The youthfulness, he knew, came from his pretty mother who had died giving birth to him and whose face he'd only ever seen in a portrait painting; his world-weariness came from the life he'd led since fleeing home as a boy to escape a violent father. Since then, in the course of traveling the world, he'd already seen and done more than most men would in two lifetimes.

Shaking his head as if to dispel painful memories, Nathan set off down the street toward the boardinghouse he was staying at. Striding out, he found even this light exertion caused him to sweat profusely, such was the humidity. Tall and athletic, he had the look of someone who knew how to look after himself, and his fine attire, although somewhat crumpled after a night on the town, left no doubt he was a man of means.

His short journey took him past a motley collection of ramshackle buildings that made up the town center. Many were drinking establishments while others served as brothels. They were quiet now, but Nathan knew as the day progressed they'd all be doing a roaring trade.

Nearing his boardinghouse, he was confronted by two drunken sailors staggering arm in arm toward him. They immediately stepped aside to make way for the imposing, broad-shouldered stranger. There was something about him that told them he wouldn't hesitate to use the Bowie knife that rested easily in its sheath on his hip. Nathan passed them without breaking stride.

Nathan's rakish good looks attracted admiring glances from a group of shy Fijian girls sitting in the shade of a cluster of palm trees. They giggled and whispered excitedly among themselves. Ignoring them, Nathan stopped to admire the handiwork of an elderly Fijian man sitting cross-legged, carving an intricate design into a length of Fijian kauri.

The old man smiled, revealing several missing teeth. "Bula," he said, offering the traditional island greeting.

"Bula," Nathan responded coldly. The young American had little time for indigenous people and he wasn't bashful about showing his disdain for them. In his experience, the natives of every land he'd ever visited were ungrateful for the economic prosperity and civilized customs Europeans brought to their shores. It was the same with the Native Americans of his homeland and he was sure the natives of Fiji were no different. Behind their welcoming smiles, he sensed resentment.

Notwithstanding his bias, Nathan was astute enough to recognize the Fijians—like all Pacific Islanders—were extremely resourceful people. Collectively, they'd explored and settled much of the vast Pacific.

Looking into the eyes of the old Fijian, Nathan reminded himself he was looking at the end result of thousands of earlier generations. He wondered what claims to fame the old man's forebears had.

As he continued on his way, Nathan recalled what he knew about Fiji and its South Sea neighbors. During the voyage out from San Francisco, he'd had plenty of time to study the history of the region. He'd learned that as the pharaohs of ancient Egypt were building their pyramids, and Chinese civilization was developing under the

Shang Dynasty, adventurous seafarers from Southeast Asia began settling the far-flung islands of the South Pacific. Then, several centuries later, the archipelago of Fiji had been discovered and settled. Comprised of some three hundred or so islands spanning nearly six thousand square miles of ocean between the Equator and the Tropic of Capricorn, Fiji remained hidden from the outside world for centuries. Successive invasions, first by other islanders then more recently by Europeans, had changed all that.

Nathan understood it was Dutch explorer Abel Tasman's *discovery* of the archipelago in 1643 that had heralded the beginning of the end for Fiji as Fijians knew it. Traders and missionaries had soon followed and now the settlers were arriving. Everything he'd heard told him that nineteenth-century Fiji was a melting pot of warring tribes, European adventurers, mutineers, escaped convicts, beachcombers and all manner of undesirables.

The young American was well aware of Fiji's reputation for being a South Sea paradise and a place where a pretty penny could be made. It was now the trading center of the South Pacific. Variously referred to as the Feejee Islands, the Friendly Islands, and the Cannibal Isles, he guessed it was the latter description that was probably the most deserving. He'd been told cannibalism was not only practised by the fierce Fijians, it was rife—as many a white man and the occasional white woman had found to their cost. It hadn't surprised him to learn that Fijians were constantly at war, and defeated enemies invariably ended up consigned to the cooking pot or, at best, to a lifetime of slavery.

Understanding the bloody history of Fiji had convinced Nathan his latest trading venture couldn't help but succeed. He knew these natives, like those of North America, lusted after muskets. He'd read that when the musket was introduced, not so long ago, the nature of warfare in Fiji had changed almost overnight, as it had in nearby New Zealand and, indeed, in his homeland. Centuries-old grudges between tribes were being settled once and for all as those who had muskets wreaked vengeance on those who had none; skirmishes in which a few warriors died were being replaced by full-scale battles where hundreds were slaughtered.

On reaching the well-presented, main street boardinghouse that served as his temporary home, Nathan hurried inside, anxious to take a bath and catch up on some much-needed sleep.

2

At dusk, Nathan emerged from his boardinghouse feeling somewhat refreshed. He looked dashing in his evening attire, which included a white muslin shirt tucked into cotton breeches. The outfit was complemented by fashionable dress boots he'd purchased in San Francisco.

Pausing outside his lodgings, Nathan surveyed his surroundings. His startling blue eyes—no longer bloodshot—missed nothing. He noted Levuka was coming alive, as it did every evening. The bars and taverns were already full, and men were starting to queue unashamedly outside the brothels. *Levuka is at its basic best*, he mused.

Setting off along the street, he had to step around a large pig rooting about in a pile of horse manure. Nearby, roosters strutted around raising little puffs of dust as they fought over food scraps that had been tossed into the street from an eating establishment.

Nathan paused briefly to watch a fight between two sailors who were trying to bash the living daylights out of each other. They were being egged on by a small crowd of men baying for blood. There was no sign of any law enforcement. Nathan judged Levuka to rival Kororareka, a port settlement in the far north of New Zealand, as the most lawless town he'd ever visited. As was his habit, he allowed the palm of his right hand to brush the handle of his Bowie knife. The feel of it against his skin, together with the knowledge that he knew how to use it to deadly effect, never failed to bring him comfort.

The young American was heading for Levuka's community hall, the venue for a much-talked-about dance. He'd heard the evening would be the social occasion of the year. Never one to shy away from a good shindig, Nathan was looking forward to kicking his heels up one more time before getting down to the serious and often dangerous business of trading muskets.

Although the sun had all but vanished, it was still hot and humid, and Nathan was sweating by the time he reached the hall. Situated on a hillside, it had splendid sea views. Music and laughter came from within and a *Welcome* banner hanging above the front door served notice that Levuka and the island of Ovalau welcomed the European traders, entrepreneurs, and settlers who had begun arriving in droves.

Inside, couples danced as musicians played an Irish jig, while other guests were conversing and drinking at trestle tables set up around the outside of the dance floor. The guests, who were exclusively European, were being waited on by Fijian servants. Lighting was provided by lanterns hanging from the walls and by flickering candles resting in their holders on each tabletop.

Among those seated were Susannah Drake and her father. In her innocence, Susannah wasn't aware that, as by far the prettiest woman in the hall, she was attracting admiring glances from all the eligible bachelors and from some of the married men as well.

The Reverend Drake, looking as forbidding as ever, was none too impressed by the attention his daughter was attracting from the menfolk. Nor was he impressed by the dancing. He considered that pastime a little too licentious. When a Fijian waitress arrived at his table with a trayful of alcoholic beverages, Drake Senior disdainfully waved her away, leaving her in no doubt he considered drink an evil. Instead, he leaned over and grabbed two glasses of pineapple juice from an adjoining table, giving one to his daughter.

Susannah did not fully share her father's strict attitudes, but she loved and respected him, so tolerated his puritanical ways. She always felt out of place at such events and would have preferred an early night, but had agreed to keep her father company. He'd insisted the outing would do her good. The irony was neither wanted to be here; each was here only to please the other.

The young Englishwoman was feeling bored. Inevitably, her thoughts strayed—as they did at times like this—to the golden-haired rigger whose attentions she had, to her eternal regret, discouraged.

Susannah looked up just as Nathan sauntered through the hall's front door. In spite of herself, she felt her pulse quicken. Nathan looked positively striking in his fashionable outfit. Susannah couldn't help but observe that the handsome young man's arrival had also been noticed by most of the women in the hall.

For his part, Nathan was pleasantly surprised to find there were a good number of women at the function. He assumed, correctly, that most were wives of the men in attendance.

It took him a few moments to spot Susannah. He could see at a glance she was the most attractive woman in the hall. In fact, he deduced she was the most attractive woman he'd seen in quite some time.

As soon as she realized Nathan was staring at her, Susannah quickly turned her head, pretending she hadn't seen him.

Also observing Nathan was Eric Foley, first mate off the *Rendezvous*, the schooner that would transport the young American and his muskets to his next destination the following day.

Foley, a middle-aged, rough-and-ready, bearded Irishman whom Nathan had met the previous day, was at the Drakes' table and, to their consternation, was noisily chewing beef jerky while simultaneously drinking rum. He was draining his third glass and was already decidedly merry. Foley was in the company of a younger English crewmate whom he affectionately referred to as Lightning Rod, a highly strung simpleton who couldn't sit still for a second and whose fresh-faced features were marred by an angry scar that ran down the side of his face.

Foley's craggy face creased into a grin when he caught Nathan's eye, his grin revealing a set of tobacco-stained teeth. He beckoned to the younger man. "Top o' the evenin' to ye, Nathan Johnson," he shouted in the strongest of Irish accents.

Nathan was pleased to observe that Foley was sharing a table with the stunning woman he'd spotted and immediately walked over to join him. "Good evening, Mr. Foley."

"Eric'll do," Foley growled. "Glad ye could make it," he smiled, clasping Nathan's hand and pumping it firmly.

"Wouldn't have missed it for the world," Nathan said. Although addressing the Irishman, he was looking at Susannah, who was still pretending not to have seen him. Nathan was momentarily distracted by Lightning Rod who was humming tunelessly to himself. The simpleton seemed to be in a world of his own.

Foley was genuinely pleased to have Nathan's company. He liked the young American and although they'd not long met, already considered him a friend. The feeling wasn't mutual: Nathan simply viewed people like Foley as someone to use—to get what he wanted. While he was invariably agreeable, in all his travels and in his numerous business dealings he'd never returned the warmth or friendship others, like Foley, had extended to him. As a consequence, he literally hadn't a friend in the world – only acquaintances. He recognized this, but it didn't bother him. His eye was on what he considered a bigger prize: material wealth. Friends could come later.

Right now, Nathan was more interested in others at Foley's table—in particular, the beautiful redhead who at that precise moment was still looking the other way and didn't seem even remotely aware that Nathan existed even though he was standing only a few paces from her.

It was then he noticed Drake Senior. Nathan guessed the older man was the young lady's father and, by the way he was glaring at him, could see he was none too happy about the interest being shown in his daughter.

Foley gestured toward the Drakes. "Nathan, these are the missionaries I told ye about yesterday."

Drake Senior stood and extended his hand to Nathan.

Foley added, "Reverend Drake, this is Nathan Johnson."

The two shook hands. The missionary didn't release Nathan's hand immediately. Nathan thought he seemed to be assessing him. He couldn't help but be impressed by the strength of the older man's grip and instinctively increased the pressure of his own. The two stared each other down for several drawn-out moments.

Looking into Drake Senior's piercing eyes, Nathan recalled the conversation he'd had with Foley the previous day. The Irishman had told him the Drakes would be traveling with him aboard the *Rendezvous* to Momi Bay, on the big island of Viti Levu. There, they'd take over the Wesley Methodist Mission Station and continue the mission's work in bringing the Word of God to the natives.

Nathan considered it ironic that while the Drakes were spreading God's Word, he'd be supplying their flock with the white man's weapons. He wondered if Drake Senior knew about his plans to trade muskets to the residents of Momi Bay. Judging by the disdainful look on his opposite's face, he did.

Sensing tension between the two men, Foley turned toward Susannah. "And this is the good reverend's lovely daughter, Susannah."

Only now did Drake Senior release Nathan's hand and only now did Susannah look at the young American.

"How do you do, Mister Johnson," Susannah said formally, extending her hand.

Taking her hand gently in his, Nathan observed she spoke with the same cultured English accent as her father. "My pleasure, ma'am."

Susannah smiled coolly then quickly withdrew her hand.

After an awkward silence, Drake Senior asked, "What business do you have in Momi Bay, Mister Johnson?"

Before Nathan could answer, they were interrupted by Lightning Rod, who had clearly had too much to drink. The simpleton lurched over to Susannah and stooped to address her, his face only an inch from hers. Slurring his words, he asked, "Would you like to dance, m'lady?"

Susannah turned her face away to avoid the whisky fumes Lightning Rod was breathing over her. "No, thank you," she said politely. "I don't know how to dance." She wasn't lying. Not completely anyway. Because of her strict upbringing, she had attended very few dances so lacked confidence on the dance floor.

"Please, Miss . . . just one dance," Lightning Rod persisted.

Foley went to intervene, but Drake Senior beat him to it. The missionary leaned over and placed his hand on Lightning Rod's shoulder, giving him a hard stare. "My daughter said no."

Lightning Rod got the message and turned away, humming to himself again.

Foley turned to Susannah. "You'll have to excuse poor old Rodney." The Irishman pointed to the long, pinkish scar on his companion's face. "He was struck by lightning and hasn't been the same since."

Susannah's manner softened as she observed the scar. Realizing

16

Lightning Rod was a simpleton and not just a boorish drunk, she smiled understandingly. Susannah suddenly became aware Nathan was staring at her and ceased smiling immediately, determined not to offer him any encouragement.

Drake Senior looked at Foley's crewmate incredulously. "Struck by lightning? My word."

Foley shrugged. "Well, sir, 'tis actually quite a common occurrence at sea. On almost every voyage, crewmen have close shaves with lightning. However, old Rodney seems to attract lightning somehow," he chuckled. "That's why we call him Lightning Rod!" Foley laughed heartily into his beard.

Listening in, Lightning Rod burst out laughing even though he didn't comprehend the joke was on him. The Drakes failed to see the humor, but nevertheless smiled politely. Sensing the English pair weren't amused, Nathan assumed a serious expression.

Warming up to his task, Foley decided to use his Irish charm to entertain his small audience. He quickly grabbed Lightning Rod by the arm, steered him onto the dance floor and twirled the simpleton around in a comical rendition of the waltz. "Old Rod here's English and I'm Irish," he shouted back at the bemused onlookers. "We should be permanently at war with each other, you know, but Rod'n me are different to most other English-Irish collaborations. Truth be known, we keep each other warm at night!" Foley winked at Nathan conspiringly.

The Drakes looked aghast when they caught on to Foley's meaning. Noting they'd fallen for his blarney, the Irishman quickly waved one hand dismissively. "Only joking!" he assured them.

Standing to one side, Nathan surreptitiously observed Susannah and her father. The thought of traveling to Momi Bay in their company filled him with a degree of trepidation. He'd met their kind before—God's disciples intent on spreading His Word to the heathens. Never in all his travels had he seen anyone else risk so much for so little, if anything, in return.

Although he admired their courage, he viewed the Drakes and other missionaries as fools, or at best, deluded martyrs. He just hoped they wouldn't oppose his trading plans. Twice in the recent past—once when trading muskets to Maoris in New Zealand and again when trading tomahawks to American Indians back home—missionaries had nearly sabotaged his trading activities. They'd made it very clear they viewed trading weapons as highly immoral and counter to their efforts.

As a nonbeliever, Nathan knew he would have to hold his tongue regarding Christian morals. He decided for the moment he'd let the Drakes think he was a Christian. Fortunately, pretending to be something he wasn't to get what he wanted was a skill he'd mastered in his boyhood. He'd long since learned if he could convince others he shared their views, dealings usually went smoothly. While he knew some would consider that deceitful, he preferred to think of it simply as good business. After all, his end goal was the attainment of riches.

With his goal in mind, Nathan turned to Drake Senior. "May I teach your daughter some dance steps, Reverend Drake?"

The older man seemed taken aback at Nathan's boldness. He looked at Susannah, who surreptitiously shook her head, indicating her disapproval of Nathan. After a moment's hesitation, Drake Senior motioned to his daughter to stand up. "Go on, my dear," he smiled. As much as he hated to admit it, he knew it was time for Susannah to start mingling with the opposite sex. Even though he didn't like the look of Nathan one bit, he reasoned that one dance couldn't hurt.

Susannah glared at her father, but did as he bade. Nathan led her by the arm to the center of the crowded dance floor as the band played a slow waltz. He was suddenly very aware of her closeness and of the warmth that emanated from her body. Placing his arm around her slender waist, he began leading her around the floor.

After a minute or two, Susannah loosened up a little and allowed herself to smile at her dance partner. Their eyes met and she had to look away. She was sure his startling blue eyes could see right into her soul.

Susannah looked back to find his eyes still fixed on her. As before, she felt her pulse quicken. This worldly young man had an effect on her she had no control over. His thigh brushed hers and she felt a delicious warmth spread through her veins. She tried to fight the feeling, but the more she fought it, the less control she had. Susannah felt her cheeks redden.

For his part, Nathan was also trying to fight the feelings of lust he felt for Susannah as he guided her around the floor. Her red hair gave her an underlying air of sexuality and her femininity filled his nostrils as he breathed her in; her hand in his felt cool yet so hot it was almost painful. No stranger to women, he marveled at the effect Susannah was having on him. He desperately wanted to bed her and it took all his control not to pull her tight against him and kiss her. That was all he wanted—nothing more. The truth was he had never actually been in love. Unlike Susannah, he'd had many opportunities to fall in love, but had always opted for short-term, physical relationships ahead of anything more meaningful. One miffed lover had said he couldn't commit because that would mean loving someone more than he loved himself. He'd laughed it off, but, on reflection, had admitted to his inner self there may have been some truth to that.

Nathan returned his full attention to Susannah. Although certainly beautiful, she was the type of woman he despised. How he would have loved to erase the moral superiority he imagined was written all over her face. If not for the fact that she and her father would be his traveling companions over the next couple of days, or that Drake Senior was close by, he'd have been tempted to rip her pretty, white cotton dress off and have his way with her then and there.

As the band played on, Nathan continued staring at Susannah. The young woman was feeling unnerved by Nathan's forward manner. But more than that, she was afraid he'd realize the effect he was having on her.

Dear Lord, forgive me for feeling like this.

Susannah avoided Nathan's eyes for the remainder of the dance.

3

Early next morning, a horse-drawn cart carried the Drakes the short distance from their temporary lodgings at the mission station to the waterfront. The cart was groaning beneath the weight of bags and boxes containing their personal effects.

Gone were the clouds of the previous day; the sun had the sky to itself, forecasting another hot day ahead.

Susannah and her father were both filled with a sense of excitement knowing they were about to embark on the final leg of a journey that had started in England. Out on the harbor, they could see the *Rendezvous*, the schooner that would deliver them to their final destination, the mission station at Momi Bay. Sailors could be seen clambering over her decks, readying her for the voyage ahead.

Susannah wondered idly if Nathan was already on board. She had no way of knowing that he was, at that very moment, observing her through a telescope he'd borrowed from the Irish first mate, Eric Foley.

Despite the early hour, the track they followed was clogged with hundreds of Fijians who, like them, were heading down to the waterfront. It seemed the entire native population was on the move. The local people were chattering away and seemed excited about something.

"I wonder what the occasion is, Papa?" Susannah asked.

"Perhaps they are coming to wave us off, my dear," Drake Senior suggested.

"I doubt that," Susannah smiled.

They arrived at Levuka's waterfront to find access to the wharf partially blocked by the crowds. The Fijians were singing a traditional song. Their harmonies echoed hauntingly in the still morning air.

"Must be some kind of ceremony," Drake Senior ventured. He looked to the cart's Fijian driver for some explanation, but the man seemed strangely noncommittal, mumbling something incoherent.

With difficulty, the cart weaved through the crowd and finally trundled onto the wharf where the *Rendezvous*'s longboat was waiting to take the Drakes out to the schooner. Willing hands lowered the Drakes and their possessions down into the longboat, and in no time the craft was moving away from the wharf.

As the longboat closed with the *Rendezvous*, the Drakes observed the Fijians on the sandy foreshore. Behind the assembled throng, they could see a massive drua, or double-hulled sailing craft, resting high and dry on the sand. The drua was all of forty yards long and comprised hundreds of wooden components knitted together to form its deck and hull. A smaller hull was joined to the main hull by a myriad of crossbeams to provide strength and flexibility.

Pointing toward the drua, Drake Senior said, "It appears they may be going to launch that vessel."

"Why such a fuss about it, I wonder?" Susannah mused aloud.

The oarsmen knew the answer to that question, but remained silent as they bent their backs and concentrated on their rowing. They knew that throughout the islands and waterways of Fiji, the mighty drua—or craft similar to this one—inspired dread and awe. The result of major building programs and human sacrifice, the sacred, double-hulled craft could carry as many as three hundred warriors at close to twenty knots. The oarsmen also suspected, in keeping with tradition, the launching of this particular drua would be accompanied by human sacrifice on a large scale. They just hoped the *Rendezvous* set sail before the missionary couple could witness such an awful spectacle.

When the longboat nudged up against the schooner's side, Nathan joined crewmen in assisting the Drakes aboard. "Good morning, Miss Drake," he smiled, extending a helping hand to

Susannah as she reached the deck by way of a ladder attached to the rail.

Taking the hand of a nearby sailor in preference to Nathan's, an unsmiling Susannah said, "Good morning, Mr. Johnson."

Nathan noted the young Englishwoman seemed far from pleased to see him—and her father completely ignored him.

Also on deck to greet the Drakes was the ship's master, Captain Billy McTavish, a grizzled old sea dog with the thickest of Scottish burrs. A friendly Scotsman, he made them feel immediately at ease—as did first mate Eric Foley, who was considerably more sober than the last time he saw the missionary couple.

Lightning Rod hovered around behind Foley and looked delighted when Susannah beamed a warm smile his way.

While the Drakes' personal effects were being lifted aboard, Captain McTavish had a quiet word with one of his crew. The crewman nodded grimly and immediately escorted the missionary couple to their quarters below deck. Negotiating the steerage steps that would take them to their quarters, they had to momentarily brace themselves as the anchor was hastily raised, the sails were hoisted and the *Rendezvous* began sailing out of Levuka's harbor.

The Drakes were blissfully unaware that the crewman who accompanied them was under orders to find some excuse to detain them below deck so they would not witness what was already beginning to unfold on shore.

By now, the Fijians' numbers on Levuka's foreshore had grown to several thousand. Despite their numbers, they were strangely quiet. There was an air of tension. The ratu, or chief, overseeing proceedings stepped forward to address the assembled. A huge man even by Fijian standards, he raised his hand skyward. Two hundred naked warriors fell to their knees before him. He ordered them to their feet. They stood and the ratu circulated among them, offering words of encouragement.

Like the ratu, many of his warriors sported hairstyles similar to those of the warriors of Momi Bay. Some hairstyles were two feet high or more, while others were almost that wide, and many were brightly colored. Their owners wore them proudly while, to any European looking on, the effect was comical.

The warriors' faces shone with pride at the great honor they believed awaited them. Their ratu reminded them of the rewards in store for them in the Spirit World. He then raised his hand a second time and the warriors turned and solemnly began walking up to the drua. The crowd parted to make way for them.

All two hundred warriors lay down in two rows that extended from the drua's bow to the water's edge. It was evident to Nathan and the others watching aboard the *Rendezvous* that the warriors were about to be sacrificed as human rollers. Other warriors grabbed hold of ropes dangling from the drua's deck. The onlookers began singing while those holding the ropes began pulling. The drua held firm in the sand.

As more natives pulled on the ropes, it slowly inched forward. When its hull rolled over the first of the naked warriors, it gathered speed. Screams of agony and grunts of pain rang out as the nearest warriors were crushed to death in this centuries-old tradition.

Now moving at walking pace, the mighty drua rolled inexorably down toward the sea. Beneath her hull, more sacrificial warriors were crushed. Their mangled bodies were left half-buried in the sand behind her. Miraculously, one or two survived, albeit badly injured. They were quickly finished off by club-wielding natives.

As the death toll rose, the singing was replaced by the wailing and chanting of loved ones. Their loss was assuaged slightly by the knowledge their dearly departed were already on their way to a better place.

Now only a few paces from the water's edge, the drua gathered momentum. One of the last warriors in the sacrificial line-up, a teenage boy, suddenly lost his nerve and rolled out of the way. An armed warrior ready for such incidents clubbed him unconscious and rolled him back into position. The boy disappeared beneath the hull as the drua finally slid into the water.

Behind the vessel, two lines of broken, mangled bodies marked its bloody passage to the sea.

A huge cheer erupted from the onlookers. After several years of effort, and many, many sacrifices, their sacred drua was now afloat.

More natives appeared carrying a mighty mast and sails. These were hoisted on board, and still more men were sacrificed as the mast was assembled and the sails rigged. These sacrificial volunteers were killed by spear-wielding warriors who expertly stabbed them through the chest or back, killing them quickly.

The sea around the drua was soon red with blood. It wasn't long before the sinister fins of ocean predators appeared.

Aboard the *Rendezvous,* the crewman assigned to the Drakes was working hard to ensure the couple remained below deck. He maintained a steady patter as he insisted on giving the missionaries a guided tour of the galley, the dining room and even the hold once they'd familiarized themselves with their quarters. They remained mercifully ignorant of the bloodshed onshore.

However, Nathan didn't escape the sickening sight. He was standing at the stern rail as the schooner sailed out of the harbor. With the aid of his borrowed telescope, he saw every ghastly detail of the launching of the drua.

The young American was sorely tempted to bring the event to the attention of the Drakes. He thought the bloodshed may change their view of the *noble* Fijians whose souls they were so intent on saving. But he resisted the temptation.

#

Nathan was still on deck when the Drakes finally emerged from below for one last look at the picturesque island of Ovalau. The island was growing steadily smaller as the schooner continued west toward Viti Levu.

As before, the Drakes ignored Nathan as if he wasn't there, preferring to talk to the captain and first mate. The young American was beginning to wonder if he was invisible. He had no way of knowing Susannah was very aware of his presence.

Nearby, Lightning Rod emptied a bucket of slops over the schooner's side. Nathan noticed the simpleton kept looking nervously skyward. He wondered whether he was looking at the riggers scrambling about in the rigging high above or at the cloudless sky beyond.

Noticing Nathan's interest in Lightning Rod, Foley wandered over to him. "Don't worry about Rod," Foley explained. "He's just looking for the next lightning bolt."

"Doesn't he know lightning never strikes twice?"

"He's been struck five times that I know of, has poor old Rod."

"Well, I'll be damned." Nathan shook his head in disbelief, turning back to study Lightning Rod. Foley walked away chuckling.

Looking over at Susannah, Nathan noted she was still studiously ignoring him. Taking the hint, he retired below deck, intent on checking his valuable cargo in the schooner's hold.

Down in the hold, he soon found what he was looking for: five caskets. They contained the muskets he'd acquired for his forthcoming trading venture.

Prizing open the lid of the nearest casket, he could hardly contain his delight at the sight of twenty brand-new, gleaming muskets. The caskets were part of a larger consignment of muskets he'd brought with him from San Francisco; the balance of muskets were stored under lock and key back in Levuka.

Nathan wondered how his plans to trade muskets to the Fijians would pan out. He knew there was a lot to consider. The problem was Susannah kept intruding on his thoughts.

Damn that woman!

He forced himself to focus on his trading plans.

#

Later that day, Susannah sat on the deck reading Fijian words aloud from a text book. Behind her, to starboard, was the big island of Viti Levu. "Nau-rari," she said hesitantly, struggling to get her tongue around yet another strange place name. "Nau-sori. Nausori. Sigatoka. Lautoka."

Further along the deck, but within earshot, Nathan was studying Viti Levu's Coral Coast through a telescope. As he surveyed the coastline he remembered he'd read that Viti Levu translated as *Great Land*. He sneaked the occasional glance at Susannah, who remained engrossed in her studies.

Nathan was joined by Foley. To the younger man's chagrin, the hard-case Irishman continued where he'd left off over breakfast, relating his life story to his new friend.

"As I was saying," Foley began rambling, "Foley comes from the Gaelic O'Foghladh, which means I'm from a long line of plunderers! I concede 'tis fair to say we Foleys all have a touch of the blarney, also."

Nathan, who could barely understand Foley's thick Irish accent at the best of times, wasn't listening. His attention was fully on the young Englishwoman. He hated how she was dominating his thoughts.

"We Foleys sure have the blarney alright," Foley said, continuing his ramblings, "but me ma also taught me that a man's gotta earn his bacon. And that's what I tell the men under me. Earn your bacon. Even it if means squealin' like a pig." The eccentric Irishman scrunched up his weatherbeaten face and proceeded to squeal like a piglet. He stopped when he realized Nathan wasn't amused.

Ignoring the men, Susannah continued reciting aloud, "Malololailai, Namuka-i-Lau. Namenalala." She had been studying Fijian since departing England. Only now was the language starting to make sense to her. She continued, "Natovi, Waya Waya Lailai."

Listening to her, Nathan shook his head. Turning to Foley, he whispered, "Does she really think those natives are gonna give a damn about the Word of God?"

The Irishman shrugged. "Buggered if I know," he muttered. "Seems to me, the bloody English are determined to convert the heathen masses regardless of whether they wanna be converted or not." Shaking his head, he wandered off.

Nathan returned his attention to the distant coastline. Aptly named the Coral Coast, breakers crashed over the coral reef that lay off Viti Levu's southern shores. White foam marked the reef's location, and Nathan could hear the faint but constant boom of breakers against the coral. Beyond it, the bure huts, or thatched, tropical dwellings, of some unnamed village could be seen among the lush groves of palm trees that lined the coast.

4

That night, in his cabin aboard the *Rendezvous*, Nathan combed his hair in front of a mirror then paused to glance out a porthole. Under a full moon, the Coral Coast's distant shoreline looked romantically exotic.

Leaving his quarters, he walked along a passageway and entered the schooner's dining cabin. Here, he found Captain McTavish and Foley entertaining guests at the captain's table. The guests included Susannah and her father, an Italian artist who, by all accounts, made his living painting seascapes, and an English whale-spotter who had been contracted to undertake a whale count in Fiji's western whaling grounds.

McTavish was in the act of pouring champagne when he saw Nathan. "Ah, Mr. Johnson, please join us."

Nathan looked around. Acknowledging the others, he said, "Good evening, gentlemen." He then looked directly at Susannah. "And ladies."

Susannah nodded perfunctorily in his direction. Sitting down, Nathan noted neither Susannah nor her father was drinking the champagne that was on offer, preferring the fresh orange juice, which was also in plentiful supply. Catching Susannah's eye, he asked, "You don't drink?" Nathan immediately cursed himself for being so crass. He'd been so anxious to engage the missionaries in conversation and get on their good side that he'd said the first thing that had come into his mind.

"Why, does that offend you, Mr. Johnson?" Susannah asked.

"No, not at all." Nathan was about to apologize for asking so pointed a question when Susannah abruptly turned away and began conversing with her father.

"Champagne, Mr. Johnson?" McTavish asked, holding out the champagne bottle.

"Thank you, captain," Nathan said.

As the Scotsman topped up Nathan's glass, Susannah surreptitiously studied the American. In spite of herself, she had to admit he looked more dashing than ever. She fought against the familiar feelings that rose up inside her. The fact that such a worldly and by all accounts ungodly young man could affect her so, annoyed her. She felt a flash of anger toward Nathan then immediately felt guilty for allowing him to affect her this way.

A Filipino cook entered the cabin holding a large pan piled high with grilled fish. He was followed by none other than Lightning Rod who was holding a tray of steaming vegetables. The simpleton appeared close to spilling the tray's contents and was humming to himself as usual.

"Please excuse the help tonight," Captain McTavish apologized. "Cook's assistant is unwell and Rodney here was recruited to stand in for him at the last moment."

Lightning Rod beamed with pride at the sound of his name being mentioned and began humming more loudly than ever, causing the captain to visibly cringe. To ease Captain McTavish's embarrassment, the Italian artist commented on the food's presentation, saying it would have done justice to the finest restaurant in the civilized world.

"Here, here," Drake Senior added supportively.

The dining cabin fell silent as the diners started on their first course. The only sound came from a jittery Lightning Rod, who continued humming while hovering close to Foley. In a world of his own, he seemed unsure what was expected of him and began talking to himself, attracting sideways glances from the passengers. Foley was so used to Lightning Rod, he ignored him.

As the food was devoured, Nathan observed Susannah, who

28

continued to avoid his gaze. She looked even more ravishing than he remembered. Her soft, red hair framed her beautiful face and contrasted spectacularly with her smooth, pale skin.

And as for those eyes!

Her hazel eyes seemed to flash whenever she looked at him. He felt like he was drowning whenever he gazed into them.

Drake Senior was unhappy at the attention Nathan was paying Susannah. "You say you have some business in Momi Bay, Mr. Johnson?" the missionary asked, breaking the silence.

Nathan tore his eyes away from Susannah. "Yes," he answered. "I intend trading there with the natives."

Foley suddenly burped loudly, albeit unintentionally. Susannah glanced disapprovingly at the crude seaman. Totally unaware he'd interrupted the conversation, the Irishman enthusiastically resumed eating. He speared a large slab of beef with his hunting knife and shoveled it unceremoniously into his mouth. As he gnawed away at the beef, gravy dripped down his beard. To the disgust of the other diners, Foley didn't bother to wipe the gravy away.

From the far end of the table, the Italian artist asked, "What take you to Momi Bay, signore?" He spoke in not-quite-perfect, heavily accented English. "I hear there are only savages there."

The Drakes tensed at the use of the word savages.

"Savages!" Lightning Rod interjected.

Ignoring the simpleton, Nathan said, "Well, according to my research, the Fijians at Momi Bay have been educated by the missionaries." The young American glanced at the Drakes, hoping he was impressing them. He had deliberately avoided referring to the Fijians as savages. "I expect it will be safe to trade there."

"Them Fijians, they all savages!" Lightning Rod said, leaning close to Nathan.

Frowning at Lightning Rod, Foley held his forefinger to his lips, indicating he should remain silent. Sulking, the simpleton began pacing up and down behind the diners.

Susannah asked, "What is it they have at Momi Bay that you wish to acquire, Mr. Johnson?"

"Beche-de-mer."

Susannah and the other guests looked bemused. She enquired, "Beche-de-mer?"

"Dried sea slugs."

Susannah looked none the wiser. Nathan had come prepared. He reached into his jacket pocket and pulled out a dried sea slug sample. It resembled a blackened banana. He handed it to Susannah. Aghast, she took the sample from him and quickly dropped it onto the tabletop.

"What on earth?"

"Also known as sea cucumber," Nathan explained, noting he now had Susannah's full attention. "The Chinese can't get enough of the stuff. They say it's an aphrodisiac."

Drake Senior asked, "And is it?"

Nathan grinned. "Well, there's no shortage of Chinese, so I guess it must work."

Foley and McTavish burst out laughing while Susannah did her best to hide a smile. Her father was not amused. Nathan inwardly cursed. Remembering his past struggles with missionaries, he really didn't want to offend the Drakes, but it was always tricky having to tip-toe over the moral high ground they occupied.

Recovering her composure, Susannah looked back at Nathan. "And just how do you hope to get this . . . sea slug?"

Nathan suddenly realized the Drakes weren't aware he was a musket trader. He could sense another moral judgment coming up. "I hear there's increasing unrest on that side of the island," he said, choosing his words carefully. "The natives at Momi Bay require muskets to defend themselves against their enemies, so I intend to trade muskets to them."

The Drakes looked at Nathan as if they'd suddenly noticed horns growing out of his head. After a pregnant pause, Susannah asked, "Is that a wise thing to do, Mr. Johnson?"

"I see no harm in it, Miss Drake. Anyway, the natives are unlikely to trouble you missionaries. It's their own kind they have most problems with."

Susannah's eyes flashed with anger. "That's hardly the point, Mr. Johnson. They could exterminate each other."

McTavish ventured, "Some would say that may not be a bad thing, ma'am."

Susannah shot an angry glance at the captain then turned back to Nathan. "Have you no conscience, Mr. Johnson?"

"Well, I . . ."

"Don't be too hard on Mr. Johnson, Susannah," Drake Senior

said, gently admonishing his daughter. "It's not for us to judge him." He frowned at Nathan. "Only God can do that."

There was another awkward silence. The other guests could see there was tension in the room and felt it prudent to refrain from contributing to the conversation at this point. To a man, they sensed it was safer to remain silent.

Foley attempted to come to Nathan's rescue. Speaking with his mouth full of food, he pointedly ignored Drake Senior and waved his fork at Nathan. "Watch out for those Momi Bay savages," he warned. "They'd just as soon eat ye as do business with ye!"

Lightning Rod leaned forward, repeating his catch-cry, "Fijians, them cannibals!" Foley finally lost patience with his simple crewmate and clipped him over the ear. Lightning Rod clasped his reddened ear. "Ouch!"

Foley turned back to Nathan. "Rod's dead right," he said. "The Fijians are all bloody cannibals."

The Drakes took immediate exception to this, and Drake Senior eyeballed the Irishman. "Mr. Foley, cannibalism is no longer practiced at Momi Bay. If it were, the Wesley Methodists would not have a mission station there and I would not risk taking my daughter there."

Foley shrugged and focused on clearing the last of his food from his plate. Conversation again lapsed into an uncomfortable silence.

Nathan looked down at his glass and absentmindedly swirled the champagne it held. *This ain't going at all well,* he told himself. Bubbles rose to the champagne's surface. He momentarily became lost in them, remembering back to when he'd also had idealistic attitudes about the world. They weren't dissimilar to the attitudes Susannah, and to some extent her father, had.

Attending a Catholic-run school in Eureka, California, Nathan had been taught by the priests and nuns that all people were equal in the eyes of God.

His experiences in the real world, however, had made him shed such naive beliefs. Ever since running away to sea at the tender age of twelve, he'd seen firsthand the wide gulf that separated the civilized world from the barbaric cultures of native peoples. He'd also stopped believing in God long ago.

"Nathan, are you with us?" McTavish's commanding voice woke Nathan from his reverie.

The young man looked up to see everyone at the captain's table was staring at him. "Sorry," he mumbled.

The captain was in the middle of proposing a toast. McTavish raised his wine glass. "As I was saying, here's to success at Momi Bay for everyone concerned."

Foley and the whale-spotter responded in unison with, "Hear, hear."

"Amen to that," Nathan said.

The Drakes both fixed Nathan with a cold stare, unimpressed by his casual use of the biblical expression.

Nathan took the hint. After draining his glass, he prepared to retire to his cabin. "Well, if you'll excuse me, I have a big day tomorrow." He looked at Susannah, but she avoided his gaze even more determinedly than ever.

"Good night, Mr. Johnson," McTavish said.

"Kill them bloody cannibals!" Lightning Rod shouted in a shrill voice. He flinched when Foley shaped up to smack him again. "Else them eat ya for dinner," he mumbled.

Nathan and Foley chuckled, amused by Lightning Rod's comments. The simpleton chuckled, too, even though he didn't have a clue why. Soon, everyone except the Drakes was laughing aloud.

As the laughter subsided, Nathan left the dining cabin. He could feel the critical eyes of the missionaries on his back as he departed.

5

Lying in the dark on the bottom bunk of her cabin, listening to the schooner's timbers creak as the *Rendezvous* plowed steadily westward through the night, Susannah tensed when the cabin door suddenly opened.

He did come!

The young Englishwoman had sensed Nathan would come to her. The chemistry between them in the dining room earlier had been unmistakable. She'd locked and unlocked her cabin door a dozen times since then. Now that he'd arrived, she was pleased she'd finally decided to leave it unlocked. "Is that you?" she asked timidly.

"Of course," Nathan chuckled as he locked the door behind him.

Nathan's deep voice thrilled Susannah to the core. The very thought of the American being alone with her in her cabin thrilled her, too. And it scared her. She'd never made love before, and the prospect was as frightening as it was thrilling. Much as she wanted to feel Nathan's hands on her, she instinctively pulled the top sheet up over her naked body as the young man approached the bunk. She held her breath and watched wide-eyed as the shadowy figure began undressing only an arm's length away.

Finally, he finished undressing and stood looking down at her. In the dark, Susannah sensed rather than saw that he was naked. Nathan reached down and tried to pull the sheet away from her. Susannah held the top of the sheet tight under her chin for a moment before releasing her grip and allowing Nathan to pull it down around her ankles.

Before she knew it, he was lying next to her. He made no move for a moment or two, but, pressed up against her on the narrow bunk. Susannah knew for sure that he was naked. The knowledge of what was to come was almost too much for her. She felt overcome with desire before he'd even laid a hand on her.

Unable to control herself any longer, she threw herself on top of him and began kissing him passionately. Nathan wrapped his strong arms around her and expertly rolled her onto her back. Opening her legs, she wrapped them around him and arched her back as he entered her. Moaning, she felt strong hands shaking her.

"Susannah! Wake up! Wake up!" The voice was her father's. "You're having a nightmare."

Susannah opened her eyes and had to close them immediately, so bright was the morning sunlight that flooded through the porthole of the cabin she shared with Drake Senior. She immediately realized the lovemaking was only a dream.

"You were groaning in your sleep," Drake Senior advised her.

"Did I wake you?" Susannah asked. She immediately looked down and was relieved to find she was wearing her nightgown and the top sheet was covering her.

"No, child," Drake Senior smiled. "I have been up since dawn." He retired behind the curtain that effectively separated their cabin into two compartments, giving each a semblance of privacy at least. "You were tired so I let you sleep on."

Lying on her bunk staring up at the underside of the bunk above her, Susannah felt guilty that she was capable of such vivid and erotic dreams. She immediately blamed Nathan for giving her such sinful thoughts and making her feel as she did.

Why did you have to come along?

\#

Later that morning, having enjoyed breakfast with her father and Captain McTavish, Susannah ventured above deck. Leaning over the port-side rail, she looked down at the sea's foaming surface as the *Rendezvous* sliced through the water ahead of a brisk easterly.

The sight of the foam, the smell of the salt air and the feel of wind in her hair took her back to the long, arduous voyage she and her father had endured coming out from England. They had traveled in the company of other missionaries who were also being posted to newly established missions in Australia, New Zealand and elsewhere throughout the New World.

That eventful journey, which had seen them suffer all manner of deprivations including starvation and nearly sinking—not to mention being pursued by pirates—had reinforced in Susannah's mind why she had agreed to come to Fiji. While the other missionaries on board had all been godly people, they were far too smug and predictable for Susannah's liking. She'd known their kind all her life and desperately wanted to interact with people from different cultures and backgrounds. If she didn't do that soon, she was afraid she would die of boredom.

A sudden gust of wind brought her back to the present. As the wind strengthened, she noticed the sea was running higher. She studied the waves. They reminded her of paintings she'd seen of rolling desert sands and wondered if there was any truth to the theory that the world's deserts were once oceans. She speculated on how long ago that would have been and decided it was probably back in the days of Ancient Greece or even earlier.

For no apparent reason, the image of a Greek god came to mind. Chiseled from white marble, the god was frozen in a naked pose; his face morphed into Nathan's. Susannah imagined the American was making love to her—as he had in her recent dream.

The young Englishwoman tried to put Nathan out of her mind. Thinking about him unleashed a myriad of feelings. She felt excited, frightened, happy, confused, aroused, and sinful—all at once. Above all, she felt angry. Angry because it was his fault she was engaged in this internal war between her spiritual self and her sexual self. Despite herself, she wondered how his lips would feel against hers.

While she continued to fantasize, Susannah would have been mortified to know that the real Nathan was observing her at that very moment. The American was further along the deck, partially concealed behind blankets crewmen had hung up on a makeshift clothesline. He was admiring Susannah's curvaceous figure, which was accentuated by the figure-hugging summer dress and top she wore. The view was especially alluring from behind.

Nathan was annoyed for allowing himself to be distracted. He'd ventured above deck to psyche himself up for the trading he was planning to do when they arrived in Momi Bay later in the day. He knew from experience he'd need to be in business mode when he stepped ashore. Susannah was distracting him from that. He turned his back on her and tried to put her out of his mind, but it was no use: she was pervading his mind and his thoughts.

The young man gave up trying to ignore Susannah and, after making sure her father was nowhere in sight, walked along the deck toward her. Knowing she was unaware of his presence, he decided to indulge himself a moment longer and just stood there, gawking at Susannah's shapely backside. "Good morning, Miss Drake," he finally ventured.

Susannah, who thought she was alone, spun around. She immediately felt guilty and wondered for a moment if Nathan somehow knew she'd been fantasizing about him.

"Sorry, I didn't mean to frighten you," Nathan added.

Susannah quickly gathered her composure. "Good morning, Mr. Johnson."

"Did you have a good night's sleep, ma'am?"

The guilt Susannah had felt moments earlier suddenly returned tenfold as she remembered the erotic dream she'd had. She quickly nodded, to indicate she'd slept well before diverting her eyes from Nathan's and looking toward the shore. It was then she noticed giant sand dunes along the shoreline. She gasped at the sight of them. They seemed to be reaching for the sky.

Noting the object of her interest, Nathan said, "Those are the famous sand dunes of Sigatoka." He added, "I saw them on my arrival in Fiji."

"How wonderful," Susannah enthused, momentarily forgetting her antagonism toward Nathan.

Susannah wasn't the only one fascinated by the mighty dunes. The Italian artist was frantically setting up his easel further along the deck, anxious to capture the scene on canvas before it disappeared from view.

As the passengers admired the dunes, a deserted Fijian village came into view. Its bure huts had recently been smashed and burned to the ground. Smoke rose from the still-smoldering ruins, and there was no sign of life.

A Welsh deckhand sidled up to the young couple. He nodded toward the village. "That'll be the handiwork of Rambuka," he proffered with some certainty.

Susannah studied the distant village then glanced at the Welshman. "Rambuka?"

"Aye. His warriors are the scourge of this coastline. They call them the outcasts." The deckhand pointed toward Viti Levu's distant highlands. "They live up there somewhere." Nathan and Susannah studied the highlands. Dark storm clouds hung ominously over them. "Cannibals, all of 'em," the deckhand added before wandering off.

Alone again, Nathan smiled at Susannah. In her usual haughty manner, she gave him a quick glance before looking back at the shoreline. Nathan asked himself why he was persisting with such a young woman who, he could see, was clearly on a different planet to himself. Try as he may, he couldn't come up with a sensible answer.

"I do not envy the task you and your father have set yourselves here in Fiji," Nathan said probingly. Susannah looked at him sharply. Pleased to see he had her attention, he continued. "I fear you may be facing an uphill battle."

"Oh? And why is that?"

"Well," Nathan paused, thinking on his feet as he went. "Fiji ain't called the Cannibal Isles for nothing. From what I've seen, these Fijians are some of the most savage people on earth."

"As my father told you last night, the Fijians at Momi Bay no longer practice cannibalism," Susannah retorted. "That is testimony to the effectiveness of the Wesley Methodist Mission and the power of Christianity."

"You may be right, but there are many tribes on the island of Viti Levu and not all are civilized."

"Well, if the mission has succeeded with one tribe, I see no reason why we cannot eventually convert all Fijians to Christianity."

"I admire your courage, but there's been many a good Christian killed by savages." Susannah looked skeptical. Nathan continued, "I've seen a priest dismembered and eaten by Indians in South America, and in Africa I once met a female missionary, not much older than you, who ended up being burned alive by Zulus."

"Your point is?"

"My point is some peoples cannot be civilized. I've dealt with natives all over the world and they are not like us. No matter how much you try to educate them and no matter how many missionaries try to convert them, the native races never seem to evolve."

Susannah looked perceptively into Nathan's eyes. Her intuition told her that he was a racist. She reminded herself she'd met many such bigots back in England. "All people are equal in God's eyes, Mr. Johnson," she said.

Nathan couldn't believe how naive she was. He chose to keep that observation to himself, though. He'd already said enough.

Without another word, Susannah turned and walked away. Nathan was about to follow when Drake Senior suddenly appeared on deck. The two men nodded briefly to each other before the missionary joined Susannah at the far rail.

Father and daughter engaged in earnest conversation. At one point they both looked back at Nathan. The American pretended not to notice. He could imagine what they were saying about him.

6

A rare storm was threatening as the *Rendezvous* sailed north along Viti Levu's western shoreline toward Momi Bay. Rare because this was the dry side of the island where the climate was usually hot and the sun scorched all before it—unlike the soggy eastern side whose rainfall regularly topped one hundred inches a year. Even so, the archipelago was officially entering its wet season, so the odd storm or tropical cyclone could be expected even here in the west.

On the schooner's deck, Lightning Rod jumped when a clap of thunder boomed out. He ran below deck, almost colliding with Nathan, who was venturing outside at that very moment, drawn by the growing din of waves crashing on the reef.

"Careful, Rod!" Nathan cautioned.

The simpleton wasn't stopping. He always shot below deck at the first sign of a storm.

Nathan strolled to the bow just as the *Rendezvous* entered the narrow passageway that would take it through the reef and deliver it safely into Momi Bay.

Aware that reefs were the main cause of shipwrecks in these waters, he found he was holding his breath as the *Rendezvous* negotiated a gap that seemed barely wider than the vessel. The noise of waves smashing against the reef was deafening.

In no time, the schooner was through the reef and into calmer waters. Nathan breathed a sigh of relief.

Sailing into Momi Bay, a village came into view directly ahead. Nathan guessed it was home to the tribe he'd come to do business with. He noted it was located atop a distinctive headland at the northern end of the bay.

A long, sandy beach extended for some distance from the village. Halfway along the beach, a pile of rocks rose straight up out of the sand, like some crude memorial. Nathan had no way of knowing he was looking at the very spot where Rambuka, the Outcast, had abducted Sina from. The rock pile was a memorial. It had been erected in Sina's honor by her grief-stricken lover, Waisale, who even now, three months after the event, spent most of his time searching the highlands of the interior for his beloved.

The distant beating of drums announced the *Rendezvous*'s arrival in the bay. The drums could only just be heard above the sound of the crashing waves.

"Quite a sight, ain't it?"

Nathan turned to see he'd been joined by Foley. "Sure is," the American agreed.

Pointing at the village, Foley shouted, "That's the village of the Qopa."

Studying the village, Nathan could see the Qopa were going about their everyday lives. Like the Fijians back at Levuka, these people, with their distinctive frizzy hair, were impressive specimens and appeared to be even more warlike than their eastern cousins. The men carried clubs or spears, and armed lookouts were in evidence, guarding all approaches to the village.

Nathan turned to Foley. "Are they expecting trouble?"

"They're always expecting trouble," the Irishman chuckled. "These people are constantly at war with someone."

Nathan studied the warriors' weapons. He was relieved to see there wasn't a musket in sight. That augured well for what he had in mind.

The Drakes emerged from below deck, anxious to see the place that was soon to become their new home. Excited, they hurried to the near rail to take in the view. Neither acknowledged Nathan even though he was standing only a few feet away.

Drake Senior pointed to the Wesley Mission Station. Nathan

noticed it for the first time. Comprised of a modest house and separate chapel, it enjoyed splendid sea views and was located a couple of hundred yards from the village—just short of the rock memorial. Laughing children were playing inside the white picket fence that surrounded the station.

No sooner had the schooner anchored than a canoe laden with fresh fish and other trade items approached from shore. Qopa villagers maneuvered the canoe alongside the *Rendezvous*. A sailor threw a rope ladder over the schooner's side, and in no time a dozen smiling, half-naked men and women were scrambling aboard, carrying their trade items with them. Crew members took special note of the women, several of whom were very pleasing on the eye.

Nathan couldn't help noticing how lax security was aboard the *Rendezvous* compared to other vessels he'd sailed on. He just hoped the captain knew what he was about.

The other thing he noticed was the amazing hairstyles some of the Qopa men sported. He'd seen similar styles worn by the warriors back in Levuka, but seeing them up close and personal like this was something else. He smiled at the sight of one particularly short individual who had such a mass of hair atop his head that it gave the illusion he consisted solely of a pair of bare legs protruding from beneath a giant puffball. A younger man's hair was streaked with almost every color of the rainbow.

Bartering began immediately. Tomahawks, tools, and blankets were traded for fresh fish, yams, and coconuts. One enterprising sailor traded a large piece of bright yellow cloth for some quiet time with a curvy maiden. His crewmates jeered and whistled as he escorted her below deck.

The Drakes looked on disapprovingly. Drake Senior complained to McTavish, claiming the sailor's behavior set a bad precedent, but the captain could see no harm in his crewman's actions, and he assured the missionary the precedent for such conduct had been set long ago.

Susannah surreptitiously studied Nathan, who was standing alone toward the stern. The American looked so strong and virile. As much as she despised what he stood for, she couldn't tear her eyes away from him. His form drew her to him like a magnet. She adored everything about his looks—the waviness of his long, dark hair, his tanned skin, and his handsome face, but most of all it was his startling blue eyes that aroused her the most. Susannah inwardly chided God for putting such a perfect specimen of a man right in front of her. She knew nothing could ever happen between them, but that didn't make things any easier. In fact, it made things harder.

Nathan finally noticed Susannah staring at him. Embarrassed, she quickly looked away.

A short time later, giggling alerted those on deck to the return of the maiden and the sailor who had traded cloth for time alone with her. They were hand in hand and she was proudly wearing her newly acquired yellow cloth as a shawl. The pair were greeted with loud guffaws from the other sailors. Only the Drakes seemed unamused.

When the trading finally ran its course aboard the *Rendezvous*, the villagers began returning to the waiting canoe that would take them and their new possessions back to shore.

#

Nathan watched as the schooner's longboat was lowered over the side in readiness for the Drakes, who, like him, were preparing to go ashore. He then assisted crewmen to lower the couple's luggage and possessions, and his own carry-bag, into the longboat before climbing down a rope ladder to take his place in the craft. Not one to take unnecessary chances, he carried a musket over one shoulder and wore a pistol tucked into his belt.

Below deck, the Drakes were gathering the last of their belongings. Both were feeling relieved and excited to have reached their final destination. Drake Senior watched his daughter proudly as she collected her things. Over the past six months, she'd proven herself a woman to be reckoned with, surviving a journey that had tested the most adventurous of men. Yet still he worried about her.

Susannah noticed the concern on his face. "What is it, Papa?" she asked.

Drake Senior stood before Susannah and grasped her by both shoulders. "My dear, are you sure this is what you really want?"

Susannah knew, as well as fearing for her safety, her father worried that this was not the life she'd have voluntarily chosen for herself. She desperately wanted to say something that would satisfy him, but couldn't find the right words. *Is this really the life I want?* she asked herself. Susannah knew it probably wasn't. Smiling brightly, she said, "Don't worry about me, Papa. I am happy being with you."

Drake Senior hugged her affectionately. "If only your mother could see you now," he murmured. The thought of her dear mother almost brought a tear to Susannah's eye. Drake Senior finally released her and, forcing an optimistic smile, said, "Onwards and upwards, my dear. The Qopa of Momi Bay are waiting to be educated in the ways of the Lord!" Without further ado, he led the way up to the deck where they found McTavish and Foley waiting for them.

"All set?" the captain asked.

"We are indeed, captain," Drake Senior said.

"Very good, the longboat is waiting." McTavish led them to the rope ladder and motioned to two sailors to assist the Drakes.

As the pair began climbing down into the longboat, Susannah was annoyed to see Nathan waiting in the craft. She'd hoped she wouldn't have to be around him much longer for the temptation was becoming too great. In no time, the missionaries found themselves safely seated opposite the American.

Susannah looked disapprovingly at the musket resting next to Nathan. When she noticed the pistol tucked into his belt, she felt she had to say something. "Are those really necessary, Mr. Johnson?" she asked, staring pointedly at the weapons.

"I'd say so, ma'am, considering we are so far from civilization," Nathan replied.

Voices from above distracted them. They looked up to see McTavish, Foley, and Lightning Rod staring down at them from the schooner's rail.

McTavish called down to the Drakes, saying, "I wish you both luck at the mission."

"Thank you, captain," Drake Senior responded.

McTavish looked at Nathan. "We sail at first light tomorrow, Mr. Johnson. You have until then to finish your business."

"That will be plenty of time," Nathan assured him.

Lightning Rod waved at the American. "Goodbye, Nathan. Have a nice life!"

"It's not goodbye, Rod. I'll be returning to the ship tonight."

"Goodbye, Miss Drake," Lightning Rod called to Susannah. "Watch out for them savages."

Foley clipped Lightning Rod over the ear as if to knock some sense into him. The simpleton burst into tears. Immediately regretting his actions, Foley ruffled his crewmate's unruly hair. Placated, Lightning Rod stopped blubbering and beamed a huge smile. He and Foley then waved cheerfully to Susannah and the others below.

The oarsmen pushed off and began rowing toward shore. As they rowed, Nathan found himself staring at Susannah yet again. She avoided his eyes, preferring to study the shore.

Drake Senior was more displeased than ever at the interest Nathan was taking in his daughter. Determined to take every opportunity to make it clear he disapproved of Nathan and his kind, he said, "You know, I think the Fijians have more to fear from we Europeans than we do from them."

Sensing he was about to receive another lecture, Nathan cautiously asked, "Oh, why is that, Reverend?"

"As has happened everywhere else Britain and America have ventured, we seem intent on plundering the indigenous natives' bounty and dispossessing them of their valuable resources." Nathan had heard this view point many times before. He was about to respond when Drake Senior continued, "First there was James Cook and the other explorers who took the Fijians' hospitality and accepted the sexual favors of the women, in return for what?" The missionary answered his own question. "For syphilis and other deadly diseases."

"I'm sure Mr. Johnson has heard this before, Father," Susannah interrupted.

Ignoring his daughter, Drake Senior said, "Then came the whalers and sealers, plundering the ocean of its animal life and depriving the Fijians of a valuable food source. And then came the traders who felled the mighty forests of sandalwood that once covered these islands." Drake Senior eyed Nathan accusingly. "And now come men like you, intent on trading muskets to these people. And for what? Sea slugs!"

The missionary was getting himself worked up. He was only too aware that the impact of Europeans on Fiji had been enormous: the white invaders had imposed and were continuing to impose their greed, depravities, and diseases on indigenous Fijians. He asked, "What price a human life, Mr. Johnson?"

"From what I know of these people, Reverend Drake, we Europeans are their best chance of survival, or of becoming civilized at least," Nathan countered. "They were intent on wiping each other out. Cannibalism was, or still is, rife, so maybe the white man has something to offer them."

Drake Senior was about to respond when Susannah placed her hand on his arm. She shook her head, indicating he should remain silent. To Nathan's relief, Drake Senior took his daughter's advice.

As the longboat neared shore, the passengers turned their attention to the mission station. Its tiny chapel and adjoining European style dwelling were now clearly visible.

Determined not to part from the Drakes on bad terms, Nathan looked at Drake Senior and asked, "What success do you think you will have converting these people, Reverend?"

"My understanding is the natives here are hungry for the Word of God," Drake Senior pontificated.

Susannah added, "Our task has been made easier by the Smiths. They set the mission post up a few years ago."

"Are they still here?" Nathan asked

"No. The Smiths returned to England last month."

Nathan looked concerned. "So you'll be here alone?"

Drake Senior smiled patiently. "Well, not quite alone," he said, placing an arm around Susannah. "We have each other . . . and we have God."

A dubious Nathan looked away. As the longboat nosed up into the shallows, he jumped out and turned to assist Susannah from the craft. She refused his offer, preferring to wait for one of the oarsmen to assist her. Becoming used to her rebuffs, Nathan busied himself helping to unload the Drakes' possessions.

A score or more friendly villagers descended on the Drakes and greeted them respectfully. It was clear they were expecting the couple.

Smiling children ran up to inspect the new arrivals, their gleeful laughter echoing around the bay. The children took a shine to Nathan and vied for his attention. Susannah pretended not to notice.

Several young Qopa men collected the Drakes' possessions and began carrying them up to the nearby station. Susannah followed them. To Nathan's disappointment, she didn't look back.

Drake Senior debated whether to farewell the young American. Finally, he extended his hand. "Good luck, Mr. Johnson. May the good Lord be with you."

The two shook hands. "I wish you and your daughter well, sir," Nathan said sincerely.

Something in Nathan's voice told the missionary he actually

meant what he said. Drake Senior nodded to Nathan, flashed a grimace that almost resembled a smile, then followed Susannah up the beach.

Nathan retrieved his carry-bag and musket from the longboat, slung them over his shoulders, and began striding toward the Qopa village. The children followed close on his heels, shouting and vying for the tall American's attention. Behind them, Nathan didn't see Susannah quickly glance back in his direction.

#

Nearing the village, Nathan observed palisades of bamboo poles lined up in strategically placed rows. He could see they would allow defenders to retreat to the next row of palisades should the preceding row be overrun in battle. They presented a formidable barrier to any would-be enemy. It was obvious to Nathan that these people were well organized.

A deep ditch in front of the outer palisades presented another obstacle for invaders to overcome. Long planks, tied together to resemble a walkway, spanned the ditch, affording easy access for the villagers and visitors. Nathan was in no doubt the planks would be removed if the village was under attack.

Still with his escort of children, he walked unchallenged across the ditch and into the village via an opening between the palisades. Here, more children rushed forward to greet him, and the adults stopped what they were doing to look at him. This told him that white visitors were still something of a novelty in these parts.

Nearby, a master carver was busy instructing his young charges in the age-old art of carving. Under his guidance, kauri posts were being transformed into works of art as the apprentices labored away with hammer and chisel. Much of their work would adorn the exteriors of the villagers' homes—often as decorative archways over the front entrances to their bures, or huts. Many of the bures were so adorned.

Nathan noted the carvings had a Polynesian influence. He identified similarities between these carvings and those he'd seen in Samoa and elsewhere in the Pacific during his voyage out from San Francisco. The young man knew the carvings told a story, or had some special significance, but looking at them he couldn't even begin to guess what that could be.

The village accommodated dozens of bures of various sizes.

They surrounded a large meeting house, which was the focal point of the village and which featured the largest and most spectacular carvings of all. Many of the carvings were inlaid with shell and bone.

It was from the meeting house that Joeli, the ratu's strapping son, and Waisale, his handsome young friend with the distinctive birthmark on his forehead, suddenly emerged. Waisale had just returned from the highlands of the interior after yet another unsuccessful search for his beloved Sina, the maiden abducted by the Outcast. Their proud bearing alluded to their royal bloodlines, but it was their hairdos that really set them apart from other warriors. Joeli's massive hairstyle, now dyed orange, was even wider and higher than it was three months earlier, while Waisale's zany, geometric hairstyle was uniquely colored what could only be described as *shocking pink*.

Waisale jealously guarded the secret ingredients that made up this color for it was widely believed he was the only Fijian in the entire archipelago with pink hair. The young warrior had promised he'd divulge the ingredients as soon as he found Sina. This ensured he at least had the support of every vain man in the village.

Joeli and Waisale saw Nathan and headed straight for him. The American noted the huge club Joeli carried. He noted, too, the human teeth inlaid around its head. The teeth numbered thirteen now, indicating Joeli had killed another man in the past few months.

Nathan couldn't take his eyes off the incredible hairstyles worn by the two otherwise macho-looking warriors. It took all his control not to burst out laughing. He knew that would be construed as an insult and was afraid he'd end up in a cooking pot.

Joeli stopped a foot from Nathan and, in Fijian, said, "White-Face is not welcome here." Nathan looked blank. Joeli switched to pigeon English. "What White-Face want?"

Nathan disliked dealing with native peoples at the best of times, more so in circumstances like these when they insisted on flexing their muscles on their home turf. Having to go through all their longwinded rituals in order to trade, like some pathetic rite of passage, was akin to pulling teeth for the American. He'd found from experience the only way he could endure it was to keep his mind focused on his ultimate goal. He constantly reminded himself of the profits he would make if the trade was successful. Nathan unslung his musket and held it toward Joeli. "I have come to trade muskets."

Joeli took the weapon from him and studied it. A movement behind him announced the arrival of Joeli's elderly father, Iremaia, who was the Qopas' ratu, or chief. Iremaia was resplendent in a ceremonial tapa cloak and turban. He was a man of great mana, or spiritual strength. As was the custom, villagers in his path prostrated themselves before him to demonstrate their total subservience to their ruler.

At the sight of the musket, the ratu hurried to his son's side and took the weapon from him. Looking from the musket to Nathan, Iremaia fired questions at Joeli in his native tongue. Joeli answered his father respectfully. As father and son talked, Nathan's eyes were drawn to a striking whale bone pendant hanging around the ratu's neck.

Joeli turned back to Nathan. "This is Iremaia, great ratu over all of Momi Bay."

Nathan extended his hand to Iremaia. "Nathan Johnson, from America."

Iremaia ignored Nathan's outstretched hand and addressed him in halting English. "Na-than John-son?" The young American nodded. The old ratu continued, "You have musket to trade?"

"Yes. One hundred muskets."

On hearing this, Iremaia's eyes lit up. Returning his attention to the musket in his hands, he cradled it lovingly for a few seconds longer before handing it back to Nathan.

Nathan shook his head. "That is my gift to you." He'd learned firsthand that natives of all lands loved receiving gifts—especially gifts that *appeared* to come with no strings attached. Of course, there were strings attached: Nathan was looking to use the Qopa, just as he used everyone who came within his orbit.

Iremaia's wrinkled face creased into a smile. He clasped the musket to his chest as a mother would a child. His unsmiling son looked on, unimpressed. Waisale appeared more receptive and studied the musket with interest.

The men would have been perturbed to know that, at that very moment, on a scrub-covered hill overlooking Momi Bay, the Outcast, Rambuka, was watching them. Half a dozen fellow outcasts lay on either side of him. Wearing grass skirts, their only concession to modern ways was that they all carried muskets. Bones and sticks inserted through apertures in their noses and ears added to their savage appearance, as did the tattoos that covered their faces as well as their bodies.

Unlike the Qopa, they shunned outrageous hairstyles, preferring to wear their hair short or shaggy. Behind them, fifty more musket-bearing warriors lay in wait. They'd been there since first light. Like Rambuka, their attention was focused on the four men below who were still deep in conversation.

7

Rambuka stretched his long, muscular frame in the grass as he positioned himself for a better view. His fierce, battle-scarred, tattooed face was a picture of concentration and his coal-black eyes burned with hate as he studied Iremaia and the ratu's son, Joeli, in the village below.

He had scores to settle with those two.

The Outcast turned his attention to Nathan. He wondered if the white man was related to the beautiful white woman he'd seen arriving at the mission station a short time earlier.

Watching Nathan conversing with Iremaia and Joeli, Rambuka wished he knew what they were talking about. The Outcast guessed the conversation involved trade, and he speculated whether the white man had more muskets like the one he'd just handed to the old ratu.

Rambuka switched his attention from the men to an enclosed storage structure perched atop four tall poles near the village meeting house. He looked longingly at the structure for he knew what it contained. The warriors on either side of him were looking at it, too. Like him, they lusted after its contents. After all, that was what had brought them to Momi Bay. Each took note of the two huge warriors currently guarding the structure.

For Rambuka, this village held many memories for him. After all, it was once his home; Iremaia was his father and Joeli his half-brother. Rambuka had lived at Momi Bay until he'd been cast out of the Qopa mataqali, or clan, and forced to make his own way in the world.

Memories of his past life flashed before his eyes. He took himself back five years to when he was a fully fledged member of the mataqali.

Until Joeli was born, Rambuka had been first in line to become ratu. Unfortunately for him, his mother was not of royal bloodlines. As soon as Joeli had entered the world, everything changed. As the son of Akanisi, Iremaia's senior wife, Joeli was destined to inherit his father's title and ever since Joeli arrived on the scene, Rambuka had been planning his demise. He got his chance on a hunting trip when he'd speared Joeli and left him for dead. Unfortunately for him, Joeli had survived and returned to the village.

The village council had ordained that death was too good for Rambuka. Its members branded him an outcast and placed a tabu, or curse, on him. This meant that bad luck would befall anyone who offered him shelter or extended the hand of friendship to him. As a final insult, a bitter Rambuka was confined to a life of slavery.

As the seasons went by, he'd grown ever more bitter. His hatred for Iremaia and Joeli, and indeed for all the Qopa, grew by the day. He dreamed of wreaking vengeance on them. When an opportunity to escape presented itself, he took it along with a handful of fellow slaves. So began Rambuka's campaign of terror against his old village and against other villages up and down the coast.

Despite his failings as a human being, Rambuka had always been a charismatic character. His numbers had grown as more disenchanted warriors joined him. Widely known as *the outcasts,* they wreaked havoc throughout much of Viti Levu. Their influence increased as they acquired muskets. Rambuka's followers were also made up of a few non-Fijians, including Tongans and Samoans, who had ended up in Fiji either as a result of inter-island warfare or the healthy slave trade that existed between the islands.

Rambuka's favorite past-time was abducting attractive maidens. As well as keeping him and his men amused, there was a more sinister reason behind this: to impregnate the women and so increase the outcasts' numbers in order to eventually create a new tribe. It was rumored Rambuka kept the women as sex slaves at his inland hideouts.

Women up and down the coast lived in fear of the dreaded Rambuka and his fellow outcasts. Hunting parties had tried in vain to find the outcasts' hideouts, but the cunning Rambuka had a number of encampments at his disposal and frequently relocated his followers from one to the other. Fear of reprisals ensured that tribes in the vicinity did not reveal the whereabouts of these encampments.

Forcing himself to focus on the present, Rambuka eyed the musket Iremaia was holding. Muskets were the big advantage the outcasts had over the Qopa. He didn't want to lose that advantage. Rambuka knew he needed to act quickly.

Down in the village, unaware he was being observed, Iremaia questioned Nathan. "What you want trade for muskets?"

"Sea slugs."

"Sea . . . slug?"

Nathan displayed the sea slug sample he carried with him. Joeli snatched it from him and studied it for a second then looked at his father. "Ah, trepang."

Iremaia studied Nathan intently for several long moments then announced, "We trade."

Nathan flashed a broad grin. While he was genuinely pleased trading was to commence, his grin hid the frustration he always felt when dealing with native peoples. He knew they wanted his muskets and would trade just about anything to get their hands on them. Why they insisted on this masquerade of pretending they didn't care whether they acquired muskets or not, he never could work out. In this respect, he decided, all natives were the same whether they were Native American, Zulu, Maori, Aboriginal, or Fijian. The irony was, he could see through their apparent disinterest so easily it was laughable.

The American and Iremaia then negotiated the terms for the forthcoming trade. It was agreed half the muskets in the *Rendezvous*'s hold would serve as a down payment on the sea slugs. Nathan would unload the muskets before the schooner sailed the following day, and he would stay in the village as Iremaia's guest until the *Rendezvous* returned from the western whaling grounds two weeks later. This would allow sufficient time for the harvesting of enough sea slugs to complete the transaction. On the *Rendezvous*'s return, the balance of muskets would be unloaded. Then Nathan would ship the sea slugs to Levuka and from there to China where they'd fetch extraordinary prices.

As the terms of trade were confirmed, Nathan could hardly contain his excitement. Iremaia had agreed to part with double the quantity of sea slugs Nathan had been willing to settle for. Already a man of means, he was aware he would soon be wealthy enough to retire. Not that he planned to. His dream was to build a trading empire using his own fleet of ships to transport the products acquired in the course of his trading ventures around the world.

"You eat with Iremaia tonight," the old ratu insisted.

"Thank you, great ratu." Nathan forced a smile. Even though socializing with Iremaia was the last thing he wanted to do, Nathan knew it would be taken as a slight if he refused the offer of hospitality.

Just deal with these bastards a little longer, he told himself, *and the world is yours.*

Iremaia motioned to Nathan to follow him. The ratu and Joeli then began walking toward the meeting house. Their guest followed, wondering what Iremaia had in mind.

Approaching the meeting house, Nathan noticed the same enclosed structure perched atop four tall poles that Rambuka had been studying earlier. He guessed, correctly, it was used for storing something. Just what, he couldn't imagine though he knew it must be of value to warrant two warriors guarding it. There seemed to be no means of access to the structure.

Another huge warrior stood guard at the entrance to the meeting house. He bowed respectfully as Iremaia escorted his guest inside.

The meeting house was unoccupied as they entered, but it quickly filled as matagali, or tribal elders, filed into it. There were no women present and the mood was solemn. Iremaia and Joeli sat down, cross-legged, on a pandanus mat, and the ratu motioned to Nathan to sit on his left. As soon as he was seated, the matagali sat down in a semicircle opposite. Nathan noticed a large kava bowl half full of kava on the ground nearby.

Speaking in his native tongue, Iremaia then welcomed Nathan and explained to the assembled why the vulagi, or visitor, was here. The speech seemed to go on forever. Nathan was learning that, as with the natives he'd begrudgingly traded with elsewhere in the world, the Fijians took pride in their abilities as orators. He hid his impatience.

Don't you people know time is money?

Among native peoples, he knew, simple introductions could, and often would, take hours.

Nathan's attention strayed to the shrunken heads and skulls of former enemies adorning the meeting house walls. The young man eyed them nervously. He thought he heard Iremaia mention his name and quickly looked back at the ratu. As before, his attention was drawn to the whale bone pendant around Iremaia's neck. Five inches long, its dagger-like base tapered to a sharp point. The carvings along its length were so lifelike they almost seemed real.

A boy slave suddenly appeared holding a small bowl. Unlike cannibalism, slavery was something missionaries hadn't managed to convince the Qopa to dispense with. Slaves were such an integral part of life at Momi Bay. For centuries, they had eased their masters' workload and had provided the mana, or prestige, the ratu's position demanded. Nathan guessed banning slavery would be one of the major challenges facing the Drakes.

The slave boy dipped the small bowl into the kava bowl and handed it to Iremaia. The ratu clapped his hands together three times before taking the bowl and draining its contents. He handed the bowl back to the boy then clapped three times again.

Nathan stared at the wooden kava bowl half full of the distinctive, muddy-looking kava that was so popular with Fijian men. Staring at the vile-looking liquid, Nathan realized he was about to have his first experience of drinking it. He'd heard that kava, made from the sacred kava root, featured at every ceremonial occasion throughout the Fiji islands.

The boy filled the bowl again then held it out to Nathan. The American looked at Iremaia, who nodded encouragingly. Nathan tentatively clapped three times then took the bowl in both hands. He studied its contents unenthusiastically. Aware every eye was on him, he gulped down the kava, handed back the bowl and clapped three times again. All except Joeli seemed impressed.

Nathan struggled to keep his composure as the delayed effects of the kava struck him. The vile liquid he'd just drunk reminded him of camel's piss, or how he imagined camel's piss would taste.

#

While Nathan was pretending to be enjoying Fijian hospitality, Susannah and her father were settling into their new quarters in the mission station further along the beach. The modest cottage they now called home would be their base for at least the next year, so they were determined to make it as homely as they could.

As they unpacked the possessions they'd brought out from England, Drake Senior told his daughter of his strategies for converting and educating the Qopa. Susannah was crucial to his plans for, despite her tender age, she was an experienced teacher, having taught first-year pupils in a London school for several years. The good reverend was aware Susannah's colleagues considered her a teacher in the truest sense, in that she inspired her pupils to learn all they could about any and everything.

Drake Senior firmly believed one of the best long-term ways to Christianize native peoples was to educate the children. That was primarily why, after much soul-searching and inner torment, he'd finally relented and allowed Susannah to accompany him to such an ungodly part of the world.

A portrait painting of his late wife caught his eye in one of his travel bags. He retrieved it and stared at the beautiful face in the painting. A shadow fell over the canvas, alerting Drake Senior to the presence of his daughter.

At the sight of her dear mother, a tear came to Susannah's eye. Looking at Drake Senior, she whispered, "Oh, Papa, how I wish she could be here."

"She's here in spirit, my child," Drake Senior smiled, placing an arm around his daughter.

#

Later that afternoon, feeling excited and more than a little nervous, Susannah wandered alone along the Momi Bay foreshore. She still couldn't believe she'd ended up on the other side of the world in such an exotic location—somewhere that was totally different from England. It was what she'd always longed for.

Looking around, Susannah took everything in: the palm trees swaying above her, the white sand beneath her feet, the foreign smells, the constant boom of waves crashing on the reef, the exotic birdlife, the majestic, blue hues of the sea on one side and the contrasting lush greenery of the foliage on the other.

The young Englishwoman was suddenly distracted by a dragonfly that hovered in front of her face. She'd seen dragonflies before, but could hardly believe the size of this one. It was all of five inches long.

Up ahead, a man-made pile of rocks rising up out of the sand caught her eye. Then she saw a shock of pink hair behind it. The hair belonged to Waisale, of course, though Susannah wasn't to know that. He was paying homage to the memory of Sina. Waisale suddenly saw Susannah. The two stared at each other for several moments before Waisale turned on his heel and jogged off back to the village.

Susannah followed at a more sedate pace. She marveled at the zany hairstyle worn by the handsome young man and wondered what he'd been doing at the rock pile. So taken was she by his pink hair, she'd hardly noticed the birthmark on his forehead.

Nearing the village, the sound of traditional Fijian singing and chanting could be heard above the thunder of the distant waves. Susannah saw a large crowd was gathering in the village and wandered over to investigate. The Qopa appeared to be preparing to celebrate something.

As she approached, Susannah studied the villagers. Like all Fijians, the adults were impressive in stature. Tall and heavily muscled, most wore traditional grass skirts and little else. Those related to Iremaia, or who had royal bloodlines, wore tapa, or bark cloth robes and shawls or capes made from the bark of the mulberry tree. The cloth was decorated with symbols in charcoal black and ochre red. Headmen wore robes and turbans made of the same material. The warriors were never without their traditional weapons. Many of the men were tattooed. Susannah deduced they'd make fearsome enemies.

The children ran about naked while the teenage boys and girls wore similar grass skirts to the adults. Susannah was surprised to see even the teenagers were tattooed. She noticed the tattoos had strong sexual connotations—pornographic even. The lewd artwork made her blush.

Entering the village, every child in the immediate vicinity gathered around her, vying for her attention. Susannah was immediately enchanted by their unrestrained joy and welcoming smiles. The children ran excitedly alongside the beautiful white woman, their ranks swelling with every passing moment.

Looking around her, Susannah noticed the children's enthusiasm for her presence didn't appear to be matched by the men, who seemed to be glaring at her. She suddenly found her way barred by several strapping warriors. They made it clear that as a vulagi, or foreigner, she wasn't welcome here. Mystified, she turned to go when Iremaia's first wife, Akanisi, who was effectively the Queen of the village, appeared at her side.

Speaking in her native tongue, the old woman berated the warriors, saying, "Let her pass, she is speaking for the new god and is here to help us."

The warriors hesitated then stood aside to allow Akanisi to lead Susannah through. Akanisi led her by the hand into the midst of the gathering.

As they pushed through to the front ranks, Susannah saw the villagers were indeed preparing for a ceremony. An old man was addressing the assembled. Susannah turned to Akanisi for an explanation.

"High priest bless this place for new meeting house," Akanisi whispered in halting English. The old woman told Susannah the corner posts for the meeting house were about to be erected. She wanted to explain that this act had great significance in Fijian society and always warranted a ceremony such as this, but could not express that in English. Instead, she pointed to four large kauri posts that lay on the ground close to the area that had been staked out to accommodate the new structure.

Susannah noted the posts were in fact trees that had been stripped of their bark and branches and cut to equal length. She estimated each one must be fifty feet long. The chanting intensified.

As women began wailing, Susannah noticed Nathan among the onlookers. He'd already spotted her and nodded in her direction.

Susannah quickly averted her eyes, hoping he wasn't aware she'd seen him. It seemed whatever she did these days, the American was always there, as if trying to tempt her.

Nathan, who had been escorted to the ceremony by Iremaia, smiled to himself. He knew Susannah had seen him.

The two vulagi looked on as four naked warriors stepped out from the villagers' ranks. The warriors held themselves proudly as they allowed friends and family members to lead them to deep postholes that had been dug to accommodate the posts. The warriors were then lowered one at a time into the holes until they disappeared from view.

Susannah looked to Akanisi again for an explanation of what was happening.

"Our warriors receive great honor," Akanisi said gravely. Struggling to find the right words, she lapsed into her native tongue. "They have been chosen to support the corner posts to keep them straight," she explained.

Susannah was pleasantly surprised to find she could at least partially understand Fijian as spoken by a native. Her study of the language was beginning to pay off. However, she was so gripped by the drama unfolding in front of her she didn't even acknowledge what Akanisi was saying.

As villagers lowered the posts down into the same holes the warriors now occupied, the realization of what was about to happen suddenly struck Susannah. She left Akanisi's side and pushed her way through the onlookers to look down into the nearest hole where she saw the warrior who occupied it was standing a good ten feet beneath her. All she could see of him was the top of his frizzy hair; his arms were wrapped around the pole, as if to hold it straight. There was barely room for him and the pole.

To Susannah's horror, chanting villagers began shoveling dirt down on top of the warrior until he was concealed. "Dear God, no!" she cried. Until she was finally pushed aside, Susannah noted the doomed warrior appeared to accept his fate calmly.

The same routine was repeated at the other three postholes. Unable to watch the macabre spectacle any more, Susannah turned away.

Sensing the young woman's discomfort, Akanisi hurried to her side. She could see Susannah was shaking like a leaf. "What wrong?" Akanisi asked in English. "That is ancient custom." Reverting to her native tongue, she added, "It is a great honor for a warrior to be a sacrifice."

Susannah shook her head. It was too much for her to take in. Later, she would learn such human sacrifices were common throughout the archipelago and, indeed, throughout the Pacific Islands. Here, it was deemed an honor for a warrior to be chosen to be buried alive supporting the corner posts of a meeting house or any other sacred structure. Such an unselfish gesture ensured the warrior would be rewarded in the Afterlife he believed awaited him in the Spirit Land.

The chanting and wailing had now reached fever pitch. Susannah felt like her head was going to explode. Witnessing these human sacrifices was making her question for a moment just what she'd gotten herself in to. She was aware she shouldn't judge what she couldn't fully understand, but she instinctively knew such disregard for the sanctity of human life was heathen in the extreme.

Susannah suddenly wanted to be with her father back in the *safety* of the mission station. She turned and began pushing her way through the crowd. Behind her, Akanisi watched, mystified, as the young woman fled.

Breaking free of the crowd, Susannah began running. She only managed a few steps before she collapsed onto all fours, sobbing.

What have I got myself into, Lord?

Finally, recovering her composure, she slowly pushed herself to her feet and began trudging toward home. *Home.* This place didn't feel like home to her.

As she walked, Susannah became aware she was being followed. Before she even turned around, she knew who it was.

"So now you see these people are animals."

Nathan's words stopped her in her tracks. Susannah slowly turned around to face him. A hundred different responses swirled about in her head, but when she did respond, it was from the heart. "No. What I see is a people in need of our assistance." Nathan smirked. At that moment, Susannah hated him. "Is everything a joke to you, Mr. Johnson?"

"Not at all. It's just that life is cheap to these savages." Nathan paused for a moment. Looking at Susannah, he couldn't help thinking she looked more radiant than ever. At the same time, he became aware he was getting some kind of perverse enjoyment seeing her angry and emotional like this. "Having just witnessed what you have, doesn't it make you question why you are here?"

Susannah shook her head angrily. He'd touched a nerve, but she wasn't going to give him the satisfaction of knowing that. "To the contrary, it gives me even more determination to enlighten these peoples in the ways of God. Christianity is the light." Nathan was about to respond when the feisty Englishwoman cut him off. "You are a deceitful man, Mr. Johnson. I've been watching how you interact with these people. You treat them like your friends, but secretly you despise them. Your only god is money, and you will sell your soul to the devil in order to get it."

With that, Susannah turned her back on Nathan and continued on her way.

The American didn't know why, and he certainly didn't show it, but deep down he was cut by her words. He quickly shook his head in disbelief, as if to shake off the affect her words had on him.

Why do I care what a naive young missionary thinks?

Nathan watched Susannah until she reached the mission station where her father was waiting for her. Drake Senior had been watching them for a while. He looked straight at the young American. Nathan noted there was no friendly wave, not even a nod of acknowledgment.

When the Drakes disappeared inside their cottage, Nathan turned and strode back toward the village where he would continue to ingratiate himself with the Qopa. And why not? After all, big riches awaited him.

8

As the day drew to a close at Momi Bay, Nathan wandered around the village observing the Qopa preparing their evening meals. Aware he was a guest of their ratu, the villagers greeted him with smiles. Their greetings were genuine. Word had already spread that the vulagi was bringing muskets to their village.

Nathan forced himself to respond in friendly fashion to the villagers. He viewed this pre-trading time simply as a charade he had to endure.

The American flinched involuntarily as he watched two young men barbecuing a large leatherback turtle over an open fire. Writhing and hissing futilely, the turtle struggled until it finally succumbed to the heat. Nearby, family members roasted a pig in a lovo, an underground oven comprised of heated stones. Nathan noticed an old man tending the pig was using a large bone that looked suspiciously like a human femur.

Nearby, teenage boys expertly split coconut shells on the sharpened end of a stake in the ground. Their mother rebuked them, slapping the oldest on his bare back when some of the milk spilled out of the shells.

Looking around, Nathan observed armed lookouts patrolling the village perimeters. Above them, rain clouds threatened, reminding him the wet season was approaching. Again, he studied the strange structure that sat atop four high poles near the meeting house and wondered what it contained that was so valuable it needed guarding around the clock. A new guard paced up and down in front of it, spear in hand.

Glancing at the nearby mission station, Nathan's thoughts strayed to Susannah. Apart from a flickering light that shone from the mission house windows, the station was already in darkness. He wondered how Susannah and her father were passing their time and what they'd be talking about.

Iremaia suddenly appeared in the open doorway of his large bure. Seeing Nathan, he beckoned to him to join him. Nathan hurried over and followed the old ratu inside. There, he found a cooking fire crackling in the center of the gloomy, smoke-filled bure. Its flames lit up the faces of Iremaia's clan, who included his four wives and an assortment of relatives of all ages.

The unwelcoming Joeli was among them. Akanisi, the ratu's first wife and mother of Joeli, supervised two slave girls who were tending the fire. There was so much laughter and chatter nobody could hear themselves speak. Nathan was greeted with welcoming smiles from all except Joeli. It was almost as if the ratu's son sensed the true intentions that lay behind Nathan's ready smile. The American worried that Joeli was going to be an obstacle to his forthcoming trade.

Looking around, Nathan saw that, even here, there was evidence of past conflicts. Several shrunken heads hung from the thatched roof and traditional weapons of various descriptions lay scattered around.

Iremaia motioned to Nathan to sit next to him. Sitting down, he noted the dirt floor was covered in mats woven from pandanus leaves. Marveling at their beautiful colors, he would learn later the effect was achieved by burying the leaves in mud and laboriously boiling them with other plants. Parrot feathers lined the outsides, adding to the colorful effect.

Generous helpings of steaming hot yams, sweet potatoes, and shellfish were carried in by slaves from the lovo outside. Diced raw fish was added and coconut cream was poured over the food, adding to its tantalizing appearance and aroma.

Selaima, a fetching slave girl who looked about sixteen but was in fact twenty, served the food in wooden bowls carved from the timber of some of the numerous varieties of trees that flourished in the region. She served Iremaia first, then Nathan, smiling openly at him as she did so.

After dinner, the men drank kava while Selaima and several other girls entertained them by performing a meke, or traditional dance. Wearing only grass skirts, their nubile bodies gleamed in the firelight as they danced to the beat of a hollowed-out log that served as a drum. The accompaniment was provided by two men who, using the palms of their hands, expertly pounded out an ancient rhythm.

Nathan watched, entranced, as the smiling dancers performed. Glancing at his companions, he saw they, too, were entranced. To a man, they appeared to have eyes only for Selaima. Studying the slave girl, he could understand why: she was very easy on the eye— especially while performing an erotic dance as she was now.

The American was beginning to feel the effects of the kava he'd been drinking. He'd forced himself to partake of the vile liquid in order not to offend Iremaia. Already his lips were numb and his brain felt like it was going the same way.

The rain that threatened earlier arrived with a vengeance as it only can in the tropics. It beat a steady tattoo on the bure's roof, threatening to drown out the sound of drumming. The drummers responded by intensifying their efforts and the dancing became frenetic as the dancers tried to keep pace.

Watching the semi-naked girls dancing, Nathan's thoughts strayed to Susannah and he wondered what her naked form looked like.

#

At the mission station less than a quarter of a mile away, the Drakes were about to start on the first course of their first-ever dinner in the surprisingly comfortable dining room of their cottage. Susannah placed a bowl of soup on the table in front of her father then sat down opposite him. A Bible lay open between them. Father and daughter closed their eyes and bowed their heads.

Drake Senior prayed, "Lord God, we thank thee for this sustenance. We thank thee also for delivering us safely to Momi Bay and pray that we may find many converts among our Fijian brothers and sisters whose souls we have come to save."

Together, they said, "Amen."

Drake Senior smiled at his daughter and they proceeded to drink their soup.

Over the course of the meal, the reverend told his daughter of his long-term goal of converting the more uncivilized Fijians in Viti Levu's unexplored interior.

Susannah had immediate misgivings. She interrupted her father, saying, "But Nathan . . ." Drake Senior looked sternly at his daughter. Susannah quickly corrected herself. "Ah . . . Mr. Johnson tells me the tribes of the interior are still cannibals."

Drake Senior studied his daughter carefully for a moment, before nodding. "What Mr. Johnson says is true. Not that he knows much about anything. He is the devil's instrument, that man." The reverend looked intensely into Susannah's eyes as if to drive home his point.

"Yes, I know, Papa."

Drake Senior then went on to lay out his ambitious plans for eventually converting the whole of Viti Levu by working in with other missionaries. "There is safety in numbers," he reminded Susannah, "and in the Christians' armor." He patted the open Bible in front of him to emphasize his point.

What he didn't say was that Susannah did not feature in his plans to spread the gospel to the warlike tribes of the interior. While he was prepared to accept the risks involved, he had no intention of placing his daughter in harm's way. He would leave her to continue the good work the mission was doing at Momi Bay. But his plans for the interior would have to wait. There was much to do here first.

As he spoke, Drake Senior thought he had Susannah's undivided attention. He wasn't to know her mind was on other things. At that very moment, she was wondering what Nathan was doing.

Outside, the rain momentarily eased. The pair finished their soup in silence. The only sound other than the clink of spoons on soup bowls was the distant thunder of waves crashing on the offshore reef.

In the sudden stillness of night, the sound seemed magnified. Then the rain returned harder than before, drowning out the sound of the waves.

After bidding her father goodnight, Susannah retired to her bedroom. By the light of a candle, she read a few passages of her Bible before kneeling in prayer to thank God for delivering her and her father safely to Momi Bay. She then blew the candle out and climbed into bed.

Lying there in the darkness, her mind whirled with all the events of the day. She recalled the pornographic tattoos she'd seen on the young Qopa men at the sacrificial ceremony. Susannah tried to block the images from her mind, but they wouldn't go away. Soon, she was imagining herself in the sexual positions of some of the women featured in those tattoos.

As she finally slipped into unconsciousness, the sexual fantasies took on a life of their own. She dreamed she was alone in a bure with a man. It was dark so his identity was a mystery to her. He was slowly disrobing her; she was becoming impatient and urging him on. His hands greedily devoured her breasts and then explored the rest of her body.

Finally, he lay on top of her. As he prepared to enter her, Susannah saw the man's face.

It's Nathan!

Susannah woke with a gasp. She discovered her hand was on her vagina, which was deliciously wet with desire. Feelings of guilt were accompanied by relief that she'd only been dreaming and was still a virgin. She immediately began to pray to God that he would give her the strength to resist the temptation of having sex before marriage.

Though she believed in the power of prayer, Susannah knew she was in danger of being overwhelmed by the intensity of her sexual fantasies. Her forbidden desires were like demons she couldn't exorcize, no matter how many biblical versus she recited. They kept coming like waves in an ocean.

#

By the flickering light of a fire stick protruding from one interior wall, Nathan took in his new surroundings. He was standing in a small bure on the village outskirts. Moments earlier, one of Iremaia's servants had escorted him to it and, before departing, had indicated this was where he was to spend the night. At a glance, he could see it consisted of one bare room. An unused cooking pot rested in front of a makeshift fireplace. Worn pandanus mats only partly covered the dirt floor, leaving exposed areas muddy on the rare occasions it rained—as was the case this night.

Two old, worn blankets folded on a mat by the near wall indicated that was where he'd be sleeping. The blankets looked out of place. They were obviously the result of some long-forgotten trade.

Nathan removed the pistol he carried in his belt. It had been concealed by his shirt, which he wore over his trousers. Then, slipping out of his wet clothes, he picked up one of the blankets and used it to dry himself down. Naked, he doused the flame on the end of the fire stick, lay down on the mat, and pulled the other blanket over him. Even without a pillow, it was surprisingly comfortable.

Staring up into the darkness, listening to the driving rain, Nathan began to fantasize about Susannah. He felt his manhood harden as he imagined himself caressing her shapely body. He drifted off, dreaming he was having his way with the beautiful young missionary.

#

Nathan awoke with a start and sat bolt upright. He was sure a woman had just been kissing him. Looking around, he saw that he was alone. The rain had eased and moonlight was now shining through gaps in the clouds, piercing the darkness and lighting the bure's interior.

Aware he'd been dreaming, he lay back down and replayed the dream in his mind, trying to determine who it was who had been kissing him. Susannah's beautiful face filled his mind. He drifted off to sleep, dreaming of her again.

9

When dawn arrived at Momi Bay, mist blanketed the sea and the surrounding hills. The mist was so dense it was like cotton wool, obscuring all that it covered. Nathan was sleeping soundly—as were the Drakes and most of the villagers.

The only sign of life came from the Qopa lookouts. Among them was Babitu, a one-eyed warrior who was patrolling the headland behind the village. He followed a well worn trail near the cliff edge, a traditional conch, or sea shell horn, hanging from a cord over one shoulder.

The mist always made Babitu nervous because not even his keen hunter's eye could pierce its denseness. So he was relieved when it began to lift.

Out in the bay, the gray outline of the *Rendezvous* was now visible where moments earlier there had only been mist.

A movement beyond the schooner caught Babitu's attention. He tensed as the sail of an outrigger canoe appeared out of the mist. The mist parted momentarily to reveal thirty musket-bearing warriors sailing the craft at speed toward the beach below the village. Two more war canoes suddenly appeared close behind.

"The outcasts!" Babitu said to himself. Although he couldn't identify the warrior in the bow of the nearest canoe, he knew instinctively it was Rambuka. Babitu lowered his spear and raised the conch to his mouth, blowing into it for all he was worth.

The blare of the conch echoed throughout the bay, immediately waking its sleeping residents.

After several long blasts on the conch, Babitu raced back to the village, shouting, "The outcasts are coming!"

Villagers emerged from their bures, alarmed by the sudden commotion. The men and some of the women carried weapons. They knew full well what the blare of the conch signified. Behind them, children stumbled out into the open air, looking confused and frightened.

Nathan awoke at the same moment. Still half asleep, he quickly dressed and emerged from his bure in time to see the one-eyed Babitu talking to Iremaia and Joeli. Babitu was pointing at the bay. Nathan looked to where he was pointing, but saw nothing. The mist had descended again, hiding any sign of the approaching danger.

An alarmed Iremaia led his warriors down to the beach, carrying the musket Nathan had gifted to him. Unsure what was going on, Nathan retrieved his pistol from his bure and followed them.

On the beach, he caught up to Iremaia, who was staring into the mist. The ratu saw Nathan approach and turned to him. "Rambuka's outcasts come," he said simply.

Nathan followed Iremaia's gaze, but saw only mist. Moments later, the mist parted to reveal three outriggers spearing in toward the beach. The American estimated they were less than three hundred yards distant and traveling fast. He knew little about the outcasts, but recalled they lived in the interior of Viti Levu. Nathan wondered how they'd come to acquire oceangoing craft. He wasn't to know they'd seized the outriggers after ransacking the village whose smoldering ruins he'd seen from the *Rendezvous* the previous day.

"Back to the village!" Iremaia ordered his warriors. "Prepare to give our guests a welcome they will not forget!" He hurried back toward the village with his warriors close behind.

Only Nathan and Joeli hung back. The ratu's son wanted Rambuka to see him.

Looking on, Nathan could see the hatred in Joeli's eyes. He wondered what had caused the bad blood between him and Rambuka.

In the lead outrigger, Rambuka recognized Joeli. The half-brothers locked eyes and held each other's gaze for several moments as Rambuka's craft approached the shallows.

Joeli turned to go. "We must hurry!" he said to Nathan.

Nathan's only thought was for his own safety. He didn't care about what happened to the Qopa because he knew Fijians were always at war. That was their way of life.

Life and death are nothing to these people, so I'm damned if I'm gonna risk my life to help them.

Nathan turned and looked out to into the bay where the *Rendezvous* was anchored about half a mile offshore. He considered swimming to the schooner, but figured he would probably be shot or captured before he reached it. Nathan then looked behind him at the rainforest that fringed the village. He considered it offered the best chance for escape.

It was then the American suddenly remembered Susannah and her father. He cursed when he realized this complication was likely to put him in danger. For a moment he considered leaving the missionaries to their own resources, but the thought of Susannah being raped, or worse, changed his mind.

Nathan ran after Joeli. "What about them?" he asked, pointing toward the mission station.

Joeli simply shrugged, indicating he didn't have time to worry about the missionary couple, and continued running toward the village.

Nathan reluctantly sprinted toward the mission station. As he neared it, he saw the Drakes had already emerged onto the veranda of their cottage. Despite the early hour, they were fully dressed. By their expressions, Nathan could see they were obviously still trying to work out what the commotion was all about.

Waving his arms as he ran, Nathan shouted, "Hurry! Get to the village!"

The couple looked at Nathan in bewilderment. Neither moved.

Leaping the rail onto the cottage veranda, Nathan glanced over his shoulder and saw the outcasts had almost reached shore. "Quickly," he urged, "we don't have much time!"

Drake Senior asked, "What's all this about?"

"No time to explain! Just worry about getting yourself and your daughter to safety."

Only now did Drake Senior notice the outcasts. Turning to Susannah, he said, "You go with Mr. Johnson, my dear. I have to get something."

"No, Papa!" Susannah implored. "We must go." She, too, had seen the outcasts.

Turning to Nathan, Drake Senior said, "Take her."

Nathan took Susannah firmly by the arm and began pulling her toward the village. As he ran, he noticed some of Iremaia's warriors doubling back toward the mission station. Evidently, the ratu had sent them back to provide an escort for the Drakes. Nathan wasn't aware it was, in fact, Joeli who had sent the warriors back.

The ratu's son had had second thoughts about the welfare of the missionaries who had come to spread God's Word. Although he wouldn't admit it, Joeli had a grudging admiration for the Drakes and their kind—even though he couldn't relate to their god. Nathan, however, was something else; Joeli couldn't care less about his welfare.

Looking behind her as she ran, Susannah saw her father had disappeared inside the cottage. She was relieved to see him reemerge almost immediately, clutching a Bible in one hand and a pistol in the other. He began running after them.

The sight of a pistol in Drake Senior's hand came as a shock to Susannah. She hadn't known her father possessed such a thing. While it was a shock to her, it was only mildly surprising to Nathan. He'd suspected the reverend had steel in his spine and would not be content to leave the safety of his daughter entirely in the good Lord's hands.

Down on the beach, Rambuka's outrigger canoe was the first to reach shore. The Outcast and his followers jumped out and pulled the craft up onto the sand just as the other two outriggers arrived.

At the same time, on board the *Rendezvous*, Lightning Rod was on watch. As always, the simpleton was looking nervously skyward as he paced the deck. The mist finally lifted and early morning sunlight bathed the bay. Lightning Rod did a double-take when he saw the armed outcasts on the beach. He rang the schooner's bell to raise the alarm. "Savages! Savages!" he stammered. Soon, the deck was crawling with armed crewmen.

Lightning Rod was still ringing the bell when Nathan and the Drakes reached the safety of the village. As soon as the trio had crossed the ditch in front of the outer palisades, warriors withdrew the plank walkway, leaving no easy access to the village.

Inside the first line of palisades, the Drakes were greeted by two large women who each had babies strapped to their backs. The women took Susannah and Drake Senior by the hand and led them away to where the other villagers had assembled, on the headland behind the village. As Susannah was being led away, she looked back at Nathan and mouthed her thanks.

Looking around, Nathan observed Iremaia and his warriors had taken up defensive positions behind the palisades. Several female warriors were among them.

The American strode toward the ratu. He was feeling angry and frustrated.

This ain't my fight!

However, he knew in a sense it was his fight, for now there was no chance for escape—and there was Susannah to think about it. Like it or not, he knew he couldn't leave her to fend for herself.

Fortunately, Nathan had been involved in many skirmishes around the world, and he'd lost count of the number of men he'd shot with his trusty musket or stabbed with his Bowie knife, so the prospect of one more skirmish didn't affect him as it would some.

Glancing behind him, he noticed two warriors were escorting the women, children, and elderly toward a rocky outcrop at the far end of the headland. Susannah and her father were among them.

The American joined Iremaia on a wide plank that served as a platform behind the palisades. The vantage point offered a commanding view of the approaches to the village. Nathan was alarmed to see the outcasts were now less than a hundred yards away. A quick head count told him there were ninety or more of them. Led by Rambuka, they were coming at a fast trot, their muskets held high. Their grotesque nose bones and other facial adornments added to their sinister appearance.

Iremaia pointed at Rambuka. In Fijian, he said, "Treacherous dog. He must die. I will personally cut out his heart and eat his flesh." The ratu spat in Rambuka's direction.

Nathan could never have guessed Iremaia's hatred was directed at his own son. He looked around at the defenders. Brandishing their primitive weapons, the Qopa appeared staunch and ready for battle, but Nathan feared they'd be no match for an enemy armed with muskets. Apart from his pistol and Iremaia's musket, firearms were conspicuous by their absence.

As if they'd read his mind, the outcasts opened fire. Nathan observed their shooting was pretty accurate considering they were firing and reloading as they ran. *This ain't looking good,* he told himself.

The boom of musket fire was deafening. Crouched behind the palisades, the Qopa could only wait until their enemies were within range of their spears.

The outcasts' attack was slowed by the deep, strategically placed ditch that ran along the full length of the first line of palisades. Once in the ditch, the outcasts had to climb up the other side. At this point they were at the mercy of Iremaia's warriors, who rained spears and rocks and other missiles down on them. Despite having the advantage of cover, half a dozen Qopa were shot dead by sharp-shooting outcasts.

Nathan used his pistol to good effect, killing two outcasts. He suddenly noticed two defenders waiting with axes held high at the far end of the ditch. They were looking back at Iremaia. At the ratu's signal, they began hacking at posts supporting a wooden barrier that was acting as a dam, preventing water from flooding into the ditch from a river just beyond the headland. Most of the outcasts in the ditch saw the danger too late. As the last post was smashed aside, the barrier collapsed and water swept along the ditch, turning it into a raging torrent.

Behind the palisades, Iremaia's warriors cheered as those in the ditch were swept down its full length. Several outcasts drowned. Unfortunately, Rambuka wasn't among them. Some sixth sense had alerted him and he'd just managed to clamber out before the torrent reached him.

As the torrent subsided and the water settled, the ditch now resembled a moat, presenting a new obstacle for the outcasts to overcome.

Nathan was surprised how sophisticated the Qopas' defenses were. He'd never seen technologies like these used before by natives.

Momentarily stymied, Rambuka led his men back beyond the range of his enemies' spears. There, he called a council of war, surrounding himself with his senior warriors.

During the lull, Nathan considered his situation. Until now, he'd been keeping an ace up his sleeve—his muskets. He'd known all along that if he could somehow signal to the *Rendezvous*'s crew to transfer muskets to the village, then Iremaia's warriors would stand a better chance. Still he hesitated: the muskets were needed to trade to the Qopa. If the muskets ended up prematurely in the Qopas' hands, he doubted he'd ever see them again. Nor would he see the sea slugs he'd been promised. That would put his trading plans back weeks or even months. Even though his own life was in grave danger, the lust for riches consumed him.

It was only when he looked back at Rambuka and saw the ruthless expression on his face that Nathan realized this was do or die. Rambuka and his outcasts clearly weren't going anywhere, and if the Qopa couldn't fight fire with fire then Nathan knew he and Susannah would be killed—and probably eaten—along with everyone else.

The American picked that moment to approach Iremaia. "We can't hold out against their muskets," he said bluntly. The old ratu nodded, having already reached this conclusion. Nathan pointed to the *Rendezvous* out in the bay. "I have muskets," he reminded him.

Iremaia shook his head sadly. "Not bring musket ashore . . . enemy between us and ship."

Nathan looked at the outcasts and knew Iremaia was right. Access to the beach was impossible. It was then he heard the ringing of axes against timber. The outcasts had begun felling trees from the nearby rainforest. As each tree fell, other outcasts began dragging them close to the flooded ditch. It was obvious they planned to use these to bridge the obstacle.

#

After a brief respite, a shout alerted Iremaia's warriors that the outcasts were coming again. Carrying the six trees they'd felled, the outcasts extended them across the ditch, forming makeshift bridges. Then, at a signal from Rambuka, they began attempting the tricky crossing.

Despite the spears and other missiles being rained down on them, most of the outcasts managed to get across. Their ranks quickly swelled as more crossed over.

After several failed attempts to scale the palisades, half a dozen outcasts managed to break through. One came straight at Nathan, swinging his musket, which he was holding like a club. The

American ducked beneath his assailant's weapon and shot him at point-blank range.

Nearby, Joeli was proving equally useful. Holding his huge club in his right hand and a tomahawk in his left, the ratu's son dispatched two outcasts with deadly efficiency. Fighting alongside Joeli, the handsome young Waisale and the one-eyed Babitu were just as deadly, dispatching three outcasts between them.

The expansive and colorful hairdos worn by many of the Qopa made them readily identifiable—especially Waisale, whose shocking pink hair set him apart from everyone else and, unfortunately for him, also made him a target. Several outcasts lined him up in their sights, but amazingly none found their mark.

Waisale would claim later his hair created magic that protected him. His friends would argue the marksmen were blinded by the brightness of his hair.

As the invaders kept coming, Nathan's thoughts returned to his muskets. While he was still reluctant to risk losing them, he knew they represented his only way out of his present predicament. He looked at the *Rendezvous* out in the bay and at the headland behind him. An idea came to him and he hurried over to Joeli. "We need muskets!" he shouted. Joeli grunted his reluctant agreement. "I have muskets," Nathan reminded him. Joeli looked directly at the *Rendezvous* and then back to the young American. Nathan continued, "My friends on board could bring the muskets to the cliffs." He pointed back at the headland behind them. "We could haul them up the cliff face."

Joeli considered this, then gave the briefest of nods. Nathan immediately turned and ran back to the bure he'd spent the night in. Inside, he retrieved a small mirror from his carry-bag, dashed back outside, and ran along the headland toward the cliff edge. There, he used the mirror to reflect sunlight and flash a message to the schooner.

On board the *Rendezvous*, McTavish and first mate Foley had been arguing as they watched events unfold on shore. Knowing that Nathan and the Drakes were in danger, Foley had wanted to lead an armed party ashore to help the Qopa repel the outcasts. The captain had opposed this on the grounds it was too dangerous. Flashes of sunlight coming from the headland suddenly caught their attention.

McTavish said, "I'm guessing that's Mr. Johnson."

"Aye and I'm guessing he wants his muskets, sir," Foley added, looking at the captain expectantly.

McTavish weighed up the pros and cons then, relenting, said, "You and a dozen armed men can take the muskets ashore in the longboat, Mr. Foley." The Irishman turned to leave, but the captain restrained him, saying, "But the men are to take no part in the fighting. Just deliver the muskets to the foot of the cliffs and get back to the ship quick as you can."

"But sir—"

"I will not risk my men in some intertribal skirmish, Mr. Foley," McTavish interjected.

"Aye, sir." Foley turned on his heel and hurried off. "You two," he shouted at two nearby crewmen, "launch the longboat." Rounding up half a dozen others, he said, "Load three caskets of the American's muskets into the longboat."

The crewmen hurried to carry out their orders while Foley hand-picked twelve men to accompany him ashore.

#

While Nathan awaited the arrival of his muskets, Susannah and her father were circulating among the villagers who had taken refuge on the rocky outcrop at the end of the peninsular.

The missionaries comforted the frightened women, children, and elderly, offering words of encouragement and ministering to them with prayer. Although the couple's knowledge of the Fijian language was basic at best, they at least made themselves understood and their efforts were appreciated by all.

Susannah noticed a young mother who was trying her best to comfort her three infants. The infants were crying for their father who was involved in the hostilities less than a hundred yards from where they were sheltering. Susannah hurried over to comfort the small group.

Engaging the young mother in conversation, she quickly learned the woman's husband was among the defenders. "Let me pray for your husband," Susannah suggested in hesitant Fijian. The woman nodded eagerly, her eyes bright with hope. "What is his name?" Susannah asked.

"Kafoa," the woman said softly.

Praying aloud, Susannah said, "Dear Lord, I pray you will watch over Kafoa and keep him safe in the coming battle. Protect him so that he will return unharmed to the arms of his loving wife and children. I pray also for the welfare of the other Qopa warriors and all the people of Momi Bay."

Opening her eyes, Susannah saw Nathan. He had his back to her and was still signaling the *Rendezvous* from the cliff edge.

Susannah resumed praying. "I pray also for Mr. Johnson and ask that you keep him safe from harm . . ." She suddenly stopped praying. It came as a surprise to her that she had mentioned Nathan in her prayer. The realization dawned on her that she didn't despise him as much as she thought she did.

Suddenly aware the young mother and her children were looking at her, Susannah, closed her eyes and said, "Amen."

Susannah had no way of knowing she wasn't the only one thinking of Nathan at that moment. Selaima, the seductive slave girl, had been thinking of the American from the moment she first saw him in Iremaia's bure the previous evening. She hadn't been able to get him out of her mind, and now, as Selaima watched him at the cliff edge, she vowed she wouldn't rest until he shared her bed mat.

10

Watching the *Rendezvous* from the cliff top, Nathan was relieved to see the schooner's longboat being launched. He hoped the craft would be used to bring his muskets ashore. Sure enough, one casket of his muskets appeared from below deck promptly followed by two more.

Nathan quickly did the math: sixty muskets. He thought that should be enough. Again, he wondered if he was doing the right thing.

I can't believe I'm doing this to save these bastards.

The American reminded himself the muskets were needed to save his own skin—and Susannah's. He glanced back at the battle raging behind him and could see the defenders' situation was becoming desperate. Rambuka and his outcasts were now pouring through gaps they'd smashed in the palisades and were engaging Iremaia's warriors in vicious hand-to-hand fighting.

Nathan looked back at the longboat and its crew and willed them to hurry. He knew the Qopa couldn't hold out much longer.

Rambuka was sensing victory. The Outcast saw Iremaia, aimed his musket at him, and pulled the trigger. The musket malfunctioned with a hollow click. Rambuka cursed and began priming his musket for a second attempt. He was interrupted by a female defender who was coming at him with a spear. Using his musket as a club, he smashed her to the ground. The Outcast then dropped his musket, grabbed a throwing club hanging from his waist, and threw it at Iremaia.

The old ratu saw the club spinning end over end toward him and ducked just in time. The weapon's blade lodged between the eyes of a tall warrior standing directly behind him, the force of the blow hurling the victim backward. More outcasts poured through the gaps in the palisades.

Realizing his warriors were about to be overrun, Iremaia shouted, "Fall back! Fall back!" The Qopa retreated to the second line of palisades, where possible carrying their dead and wounded with them.

Faced with another line of defense, Rambuka thought it prudent to delay the final assault until all options had been considered. He signaled to his followers to fall back beyond the range of the defenders' spears. They, too, carried their dead and wounded with them.

Out of danger for the moment, Iremaia took stock of his situation. It didn't look good. At least ten defenders had been killed and twice that number wounded. Rambuka had lost a similar number, but at least the remaining outcasts were armed with muskets. Iremaia knew it was only a matter of time before his Qopa warriors were overrun.

Villagers not involved in the fighting were still huddled together on the rocky outcrop at the end of the headland. The children's crying and the groans of the wounded mingled with wailing and chanting for the dead.

Susannah and her father were helping tend the wounded. Using some of the nursing skills she'd acquired on the voyage out from England, Susannah was busy stitching up a nasty gash in a warrior's thigh while her father bandaged the arm of another warrior.

The Drakes were too preoccupied to notice the *Rendezvous'* longboat nosing into the foot of the cliffs below them, but Nathan wasn't. He'd been watching the craft since it had set out for the headland. Foley was at the helm. The Irishman had twelve armed crewmen with him. Lightning Rod and three others manned the oars.

Nathan wasn't the only one watching the longboat. Rambuka had noticed it, also. Ten of his followers had launched one of their out-riggers and were sailing out from the beach to investigate. Nearing the longboat, they were met by a volley of musket fire from the sailors.

The shooting was accurate: one outcast was killed and another wounded.

The outrigger promptly turned back. As it sailed away, an outcast in the stern fired a parting shot. It hit Lightning Rod between the eyes, killing him instantly. He fell back into the longboat.

Foley rushed to Lightning Rod's aid. "Rod!" Distraught, he cradled his young crewmate in his arms as the other sailors jumped onto rocks at the foot of the cliff. "Not you, Rod," he whispered. "Not you."

The Irishman could only watch as a reception party of four teenage boys from the besieged village helped unload the three caskets of muskets and a crate of ammunition from the boat then secure the cargo to long ropes hanging down from the cliff top. Still holding Lightning Rod in his arms, Foley glanced up and spotted Nathan looking down from the cliff top a hundred feet above. The two nodded gravely to each other. Moments later, Nathan's precious cargo was being pulled up the cliff face.

On the cliff top, Nathan could see that some misfortune had befallen Lightning Rod, but right now he had too much on his mind to worry about him. Joeli and Waisale suddenly appeared at his side and began assisting the dozen or so men who were pulling on the ropes. As soon as the caskets were safely on terra firma, the warriors rushed to open two of them and distribute the muskets and ammunition.

Nathan grabbed two muskets for himself. He and the others then hurried back to reinforce the defenders barricaded behind the second line of palisades. Four warriors brought the third casket of muskets and spare ammunition with them.

Waiting behind the palisades, Iremaia could only watch as the outcasts razed bures on the village outskirts. Smoke from a dozen fires curled skyward. Rambuka stood among the ruins, staring insolently at his enemies. He turned and strode back to his men, rallying them for another attack.

Iremaia and his warriors welcomed the arrival of Nathan's muskets. In no time, every spare musket was accounted for. This presented a new set of problems as most of the warriors were handling a musket for the first time. The bemused Qopa grappled with loading their newly acquired weapons. The results would have been comical if it weren't for the severity of the situation. The one-eyed Babitu accidentally discharged his musket, shooting a hole through the foot of the hapless warrior next to him. The wounded Qopa fell down, holding his foot and bellowing in pain. There were several other near misses as other muskets were accidentally discharged.

Nathan ran frantically from one warrior to the next, teaching them how to prime their muskets, fire and reload. Shaking his head in frustration, he sought out Joeli, complaining, "Never mind your enemies. Your own men are gonna wipe each other out!"

The ratu's son looked at Nathan with a look that said *that's your problem*. He simply said, "You teach, White-Face."

It was then Nathan noticed Joeli didn't have a musket. He offered his spare musket to him. Joeli looked at Nathan with disdain, pointing to the club he was holding and the tomahawk hanging at his side.

Nathan took the hint and hurried off to provide what instruction he could to other warriors who were more receptive to using the white man's weapons.

While Nathan was helping the warriors master the use of their muskets, Joeli and Iremaia discussed tactics. There wasn't a lot to talk about as their options were limited. Essentially, they had to hold off their enemies for as long as they could before retreating to the next line of palisades. Their final stand would be made at the rocky outcrop where the villagers had gathered at the end of the headland. If all else failed, in the time-honored tradition survivors would jump over the cliff rather than face capture.

A lookout shouted out, drawing the defenders' attention to the outcasts who were gathering around a cooking fire they'd lit. Looking on, Nathan saw they were roasting the body of a man on a make-shift spit they'd placed over the fire. Rambuka himself was overseeing the gruesome ritual as two of his men turned the spit.

Joeli identified the body as that of his cousin. "It is Solomone," he murmured.

Iremaia nodded grimly as he watched Rambuka prod the carcass with a stick. Satisfied it was tender, Rambuka then carved off a morsel of cooked flesh, which he held up high for all to see.

The Outcast yelled, "Rambuka eats the flesh of his enemies!" He then devoured the flesh.

Shouting chilling war cries, Rambuka's followers then attacked the body, using knives and tomahawks to carve off flesh for themselves.

The Qopa watched, grim-faced, as one of their own was eaten before their very eyes.

The outcasts then began massing to resume their attack on the village. At a signal from Rambuka, they came, firing as they ran. This time they were met with a crescendo of musket fire from the defenders. Most of the shots went high or wide, but some found their mark.

Several outcasts fell. The worst damage was inflicted by Nathan, who proved he was a fine marksman, shooting dead three outcasts with his first three shots.

Still the outcasts kept coming. Leading the way, Rambuka broke through the palisades. He was closely followed by a dozen others. Fierce hand-to-hand fighting followed. As he fought, Rambuka eyed the storage hut perched atop four high poles that he and the others had been studying earlier. The Outcast disengaged from the fighting and led seven of his men toward the hut. Four of them carried axes. When they reached the structure, the axemen began hacking at the poles while Rambuka and the other three stood guard, ready to repel any villagers who came at them.

Iremaia and Joeli were so engrossed in the fighting, they didn't notice Rambuka's men chopping down the storage hut. A dozen mighty axe blows was all it took for the first pole to topple. The others followed almost immediately and the whole structure fell to the ground.

Only then did Joeli notice what Rambuka was up to. Unfortunately, he was powerless to stop him: Joeli had been baled up by three outcasts and was fighting for his very survival.

Rambuka wasted no time in smashing open the storage hut. He looked in and smiled. There, unscathed, was his prize: a whale's tooth known throughout Fiji as the golden tabua. Extracted from the lower jaw of a sperm whale, its golden color had been achieved by staining with tumeric after polishing with the leaves of the masi ni tabua tree. A plaited cord of pandanus leaf was attached to each end of the tooth.

Traditionally the most valued possession within Fijian culture, the golden tabua was the ultimate symbol of respect among all the tribes. It was certainly the most sacred possession of the Qopa and had a mana, or status, all of its own.

Rambuka reached in and plucked out the sacred tooth. He held it up before his eyes and marveled at how its golden sheen sparkled in the sunlight.

Joeli could only watch from afar as his half-brother lay claim to the golden tabua. He knew better than most how much the sacred object meant to his people. It played an important role in the very fabric of everyday life, keeping the Fijian culture alive. It featured in births, deaths, sealing interclan and intertribal alliances, and was even used to settle grievances.

Joeli's heart sank when he saw Rambuka drop the golden tabua into a pouch that hung from his waist. He vowed he'd kill Rambuka and retrieve the prized possession before this day was out. Right now, he had more pressing problems. Wielding his trusty club and tomahawk, he'd dispatched two of the three outcasts who had baled him up, but their places had been immediately taken by two more. One of them, a huge man, was proving a real handful and Joeli had to backpeddle rapidly to avoid the big man's swinging club.

Seeing Joeli's plight, Nathan shot the huge outcast dead with his musket then shot another with his pistol. Joeli made short work of the third outcast, cleaving his head in two with his tomahawk. He barely had time to acknowledge Nathan's life-saving actions with a nod before he was confronted by another two outcasts.

A Samoan outcast broke through the last line of defenders and began running up the hill toward the villagers huddled on the rocky outcrop. He carried a musket in each hand and shot a club-wielding villager who tried to intercept him.

On the rocky outcrop, the Drakes were working feverishly to save the life of a wounded boy warrior. They looked up just in time to see the Samoan climbing over the rocks, not five yards away. Susannah screamed. The outcast stood atop the rocks, legs astride, and raised one of his muskets toward Drake Senior. The missionary drew his pistol from his belt, aimed it, and fired. His aim was true. The Samoan fell on top of Susannah, winding her. Terrified, she screamed again and pushed the dead man off her.

Drake Senior looked at the smoking barrel of his pistol. "Forgive me, Lord," he whispered. Turning to Susannah, he asked, "Are you alright?"

Shocked, Susannah nodded and turned her attention back to the boy warrior whose life they were trying to save. She knew she had to stay busy. As the sounds of battle grew closer, she feared she'd flee in panic if she took any notice of what was happening further along the headland.

To take her mind off the mayhem around her, Susannah allowed her thoughts to stray to Nathan, whom she observed had rejoined the battle. She was starting to think she may have misjudged the American. After all, he had risked his life coming back to alert her and her father to the outcasts' arrival, and now he was using his own muskets to help the Qopa fight off their enemies.

Almost as quickly, she put Nathan out of her mind, telling herself he was ungodly and worldly to a fault. *A leopard can't change its spots,* she reminded herself.

Behind the second line of palisades, the defenders were sustaining horrific casualties. Iremaia found himself face-to-face with his outcast son, Rambuka, who had rejoined the fray since uplifting the golden tabua. As the old chief struggled to reload his musket, Rambuka smiled cruelly and raised his tomahawk. Thirty yards away, Joeli looked on powerless to help his father as, seemingly in slow motion, Rambuka brought the sharp blade of his tomahawk down on Iremaia's skull, splitting it in two. The Outcast then raised his blood-stained weapon above his head and looked skyward, shouting, "Vengeance!"

Joeli sprinted to intercept his half-brother. Rambuka saw him coming and aimed his musket at him. He failed to see that Nathan already had him in his sights.

Nathan fired his musket. Unfortunately, his shot was hurried and for once his aim was off. The musket ball struck Rambuka, but not where Nathan had intended. The Outcast fell to the ground, clutching his wounded shoulder.

As Joeli neared his fallen enemy, he found his path blocked by several outcasts intent on protecting their leader. He slashed and hacked at them with his tomahawk and club, so desperate was he to avenge his father's death as well as to retrieve the golden tabua he knew Rambuka had on him. The outcasts fell back before him, unable to combat his fury.

The sight of their fallen leader was a blow to the outcasts. They began to lose heart and were soon retreating to the beach. Several managed to form a protective ring around Rambuka and they dragged him with them as they went.

Joeli cried out to his warriors, "Rambuka has the golden tabua. Stop him!"

Try as they may, the Qopa warriors couldn't break through the protective ring. The outcasts effectively shielded Rambuka as they executed a fighting retreat. They were followed by the Qopa, with Nathan in tow, all the way down to the beach. Several outcasts were shot before they could reach their waiting outriggers. Stragglers and wounded outcasts were quickly dispatched with.

On the beach, the surviving outcasts launched their outriggers and sailed off as fast as they could. As they headed out into the bay, Nathan noticed the numbers aboard each craft were considerably less than when they'd arrived. He estimated they'd lost as many as thirty men, or a third of their number.

Iremaia's warriors jeered their departing enemies, taunting them with ancient insults before shouldering their arms and returning to the village. Trailing along behind them, Nathan could see at a glance the village had suffered terrible casualties. Scores of Qopa had been killed, others wounded. Bodies lay strewn about everywhere. From what Nathan could ascertain, only some twenty or so able-bodied Qopa warriors remained.

Back in the village, he found Joeli cradling Iremaia's body in his arms and uttering a prayer to the Spirit World. Looking on, the American had no way of knowing that Joeli was promising the spirits he would avenge his father's death and recover the golden tabua Rambuka had stolen.

When he finished chanting, Joeli removed the whale bone pendant hanging around his father's neck and placed it around his own. As the ratu's oldest son and soon-to-be leader of the Qopa people, the pendant was now rightfully his.

11

Dazed villagers wandered among the remains of their bures, inspecting the damage and tending the wounded, while others were still making their way down from the rocky outcrop above what was left of their village. In the village center, the dead had been laid out in rows on the ground; the haunting sound of wailing combined eerily with the tormented cries of the wounded.

Death and destruction were not the only reasons for their grief: they were also mourning the loss of their sacred golden tabua. Without it, their hopes for the future had evaporated.

The Drakes worked feverishly alongside village healers helping those whose wounds were life-threatening. They did this as much for their own benefit as for those they were trying to help: both father and daughter were still traumatized by the day's events and felt they had to do something to keep their minds off the carnage they'd witnessed.

Susannah, in particular, was in a state of shock. As she stitched up a warrior's wound, she looked around for Nathan. She was becoming increasingly worried for him, having not seen him since the outcasts had been sent packing.

Where are you? Are you still alive?

Finally she saw him. He was on the other side of the village, circulating among the villagers. Susannah immediately relaxed. Feelings of relief flooded through her. She was momentarily embarrassed to think she'd been concerned for Nathan's welfare and quickly tried to put him out of her mind. Looking toward the distant mission station, she saw the cottage and outbuildings had been destroyed by the outcasts, but noted the chapel had survived unscathed. Drawing her father's attention to it, she asked, "Why didn't they destroy the chapel, too, Papa?"

Drake Senior studied the chapel. "Even heathens have respect for the House of God, my dear."

Susannah smiled. "Amen to that."

Nearby, Joeli was walking among his people, offering them encouragement, just as his father would have were he still alive. The villagers greeted him with greater respect than ever, knowing that he would soon be their new ratu. As usual, the strapping warrior hid his feelings, trying to portray strength and confidence. Beneath the facade he felt empty. The loss of his father and so many friends had left him feeling shattered—the loss of the golden tabua even more so.

Looking around, Joeli couldn't help but notice how few ablebodied warriors remained. Even with muskets, he knew they'd be a pushover if the village was attacked again.

This was a common story throughout Fiji and, indeed, throughout the Pacific Islands. Fortunes constantly ebbed and flowed among these warlike people. The Qopa were no different. At certain times in their history they'd reigned over much of western Viti Levu and over many of the offshore islands. Now, with their numbers of fighting men greatly diminished, and the golden tabua gone, their fortunes were at an all-time low.

Ever a realist, Joeli knew his people's future was up to the gods. The only thing they had going for them now was they had muskets—and he knew they had Nathan to thank for that. The original terms of trade still stood, but Nathan had advised, albeit against his better judgment, he was prepared to wait for the villagers to keep their side of the bargain. The American understood that right now they had more pressing matters to attend to.

Joeli approached his grief-stricken mother, Akanisi. She was crying out for her departed husband whose body she was lying over. Joeli placed a loving hand on her shoulder.

Akanisi looked up at him through tear-filled eyes. "Joeli, strangle me so that I can be with my husband in the Afterlife," she implored him. Joeli shook his head sadly and turned away from her. "Joeli!" she shouted after him. Her son walked away and did not look back.

Thus rejected, Iremaia's senior and most cherished wife slowly stood up and began walking resolutely toward the cliff edge. All eyes were on her—except for Joeli's. He'd seen enough death for one day.

Susannah looked on, horrified, as Akanisi approached the cliff edge. She was equally horrified that none of the villagers seemed interested in stopping the elderly woman from taking her life and could only watch as Akanisi stepped out into space and disappeared from sight. Susannah screamed. It was a long and despairing cry.

Drake Senior pulled her to him and held her close. Susannah was shaking and sobbing at the same time.

"It is the way of these people," Drake Senior explained. "The wife of a departed husband believes she must accompany her husband's spirit to the Spirit World."

Distraught, Susannah looked up at her father. "But why?"

"Only they can answer that, my dear." Drake Senior looked around at other grieving women. "There will be more such deaths before this day is out."

#

As the villagers set about getting their lives back in order, no one noticed a wounded outcast hiding behind a still-burning bure on the village outskirts. He had a spear lodged in his thigh. Grimacing, he pulled it out. Too incapacitated to try to flee, he chose to remain hidden until after dark and then try his luck.

Meanwhile, Nathan continued circulating among the villagers. As he did, a movement behind the still-burning bure caught his eye. He walked over to investigate.

Behind the bure, the wounded outcast picked up the spear he'd just discarded and held it tight as Nathan approached. Knowing he was about to be discovered, he stepped out from his hiding place and hurled the spear at Nathan. Its point caught the unsuspecting American in the chest. Nathan fell to the ground, writhing in agony.

The outcast tried to flee, but his leg wound prevented him from running and he was reduced to hopping.

The attack on Nathan had been witnessed by Waisale. Running

to intercept the outcast, the handsome young warrior quickly over-
took him and clubbed him to the ground. On his back and writhing
in pain, the outcast lashed out at his attacker with his good leg.
Waisale clubbed him again, killing him, then returned to help
Nathan, who was groaning. The spear was still lodged in his chest.
As Waisale removed it, Nathan lapsed into unconsciousness.

Joeli and Babitu, the one-eyed warrior, arrived in time to help
Waisale carry Nathan toward one of the few bures still standing in
the village. As they neared it, Joeli called, "Inoki! Inoki!" An elderly
healer emerged from the bure and hurried to Joeli's side as fast as
his old legs would allow. Joeli told Inoki, "Your healing powers are
needed, old man."

The healer nodded as Waisale and Babitu carried Nathan into the
bure. Inoki went to follow, but was restrained by Joeli.

"Summon the powers of the great Spirit Healer," Joeli commanded. "Pray for the health of the White-Face." Almost as an
afterthought, he added, "I lost my parents and many good friends
today. I do not want to lose the White-Face."

Inoki bowed to Joeli and hurried inside the bure.

#

On a rocky beach at the far end of Momi Bay, Rambuka's defeated outcasts were resting and treating their wounded. Their outrigger
canoes bobbed about in the shallows nearby.

A long-haired outcast was using a knife to dig the musket ball out
of Rambuka's shoulder. Rambuka gritted his teeth against the pain.
As the musket ball was extracted and an herbal plant dressing was
applied to his shoulder, he looked back at the headland that was the
cause of his current misery.

Although Rambuka had tasted defeat, he had the golden tabua.
Remembering the sacred object, he lifted it from his pouch and held
it up for his men to see. Their eyes opened wide at the sight of it.
Rambuka shouted, "The golden tabua is ours. Now the good
fortune the Qopa dogs have had will be ours, too."

The outcasts cheered their leader's words. To a man they knew
the significance of having the golden tabua in their possession.
From this moment, only good luck would come their way and only
bad luck could befall its previous owners—for to lose the sacred
object was to invite disaster.

Rambuka returned the golden tabua to his pouch and looked

across Momi Bay at the headland that was once his home. He made a promise to himself. Thinking aloud, he said, "I killed our father today, Joeli. Next time we meet I will eat your heart."

#

While the outcasts were recovering, Susannah was helping Inoki try to save Nathan's life. She'd only learned of the attack on Nathan after the event and had hurried to the healer's bure the moment she received the news.

By the light of a log fire burning in the middle of his compact dwelling, Inoki was using a variety of herbs and other natural cures to try to reduce Nathan's fever. A concerned Susannah assisted him, sponging sweat from Nathan's brow, while Selaima, the slave girl, was heating a pot of water over the fire. Nathan was falling in and out of consciousness. Leaves covered his chest wound.

A stern-looking Joeli looked on. Inoki was very aware of the future ratu's presence and worked even more fervidly to save Nathan. The old healer was relieved when Joeli eventually left the bure.

Outside, Joeli noticed crewmen from the *Rendezvous* had come ashore and were now mingling with the villagers. McTavish and Foley were among them, offering comfort where they could. Joeli saw Waisale nearby and hurried over to him. "Are the lookouts in place?" he asked. Waisale nodded. "Good," Joeli continued, "we must be prepared for a counterattack. Our enemies will know we are vulnerable."

"At least we have muskets now," Waisale said.

"We still need to master their use. At present, they are of more danger to us than to our enemies."

Waisale smiled grimly. "How is the White-Face?"

Joeli shook his head as if to say he didn't hold out much hope for Nathan's recovery.

The two turned their attention back to the *Rendezvous* crewmen, who were now dispensing medicine and dressings to the wounded.

Joeli looked scathingly in their direction. "Look at the White-Faces. Where were they when we needed them?"

"They delivered Nathan Johnson's muskets to us," Waisale reminded him.

Joeli shook his head. "The White-Faces were slow to arrive—like sea turtles."

"They lost a man helping us," Waisale said. "And Nathan Johnson may have to pay with his life."

Joeli knew Waisale was right. The whites had paid a price today. He subconsciously looked back at Inoki's bure where he knew Nathan was fighting for his life at that very moment.

Wailing and chanting came from the meeting house, which, like Inoki's bure, was one of the few structures still standing in the village. Joeli hurried toward it. Inside, family members were gathered around the bodies of their loved ones. The chanting was hauntingly disturbing.

At the sight of their future ratu in their midst, the villagers fell to their knees and prostrated themselves at Joeli's feet.

Joeli had eyes only for his father. Iremaia's body, resplendent in a ceremonial cloak, was resting in state on a raised platform in the middle of the meeting house. The old ratu's youngest wife, Adi, held her dead husband's hand while she and Iremaia's other surviving wives rocked and chanted beside him. Joeli went to Adi's side and stared down at his father. He was struck by how peaceful Iremaia looked in death.

Adi, a striking young woman with fine features, looked up at Joeli through anguished eyes. She released Iremaia's hand and reached out for Joeli's. "Please help me," she implored. "I wish to die so that my husband will not be alone on his journey to the Spirit Land."

By now all chanting had ceased in the meeting house and every eye was on the grief-stricken Adi. Joeli looked down at her, his face devoid of emotion.

Adi continued, "Strangle me so that I may join my husband to ease his loneliness."

"My mother, Akanisi, has already gone to be with my father," Joeli reminded her.

"She chose death by taking the long drop," Adi said, referring to Akanisi's jump from the cliff top. "Her journey to your father's side will be slower than mine. If I am strangled, I will be by his side in the Afterlife immediately."

Joeli stood, unmoving, for a long time. He knew there was truth in Adi's words: the priests maintained that the spirit of a wife who died by strangulation was united with the spirit of her dead husband in the blink of an eye. Whereas the journey to the Afterlife was a lot slower if death were by any other means. So, Joeli knew, in all likelihood his father's spirit was still alone at this very moment. He could not bear the thought of Iremaia being lonely in death. Added to Joeli's woes was the fact that his mother's body had not been found. After Akanisi's fall, the sea had taken her and, so far, had not given her back despite an extensive search by the villagers.

Joeli wrestled with his emotions. Finally, he looked at Adi and nodded. Relief and gratitude passed over her face. She fell to her knees before Joeli and kissed his feet. Joeli bent down and pulled her to her feet. "You know what you must do," he told her.

Excited by what lay ahead, Adi hurried to join a nearby group of women whose number included her two sisters and an aunt. Knowing what was in store for Adi, they quickly bathed her and dressed her in fine garments. Adi then said her goodbyes to the women. They shed simultaneous tears of joy and of sadness. Ready now, she returned to Joeli's side. He escorted her to the far end of the meeting house, away from the others. Looking around, he motioned to Adi's older brother, Manasa, who immediately recruited the services of three other men. Linking arms, they approached Adi.

Having witnessed this ritual many times over the years, Adi knew exactly what she must do next. She sat down facing the far wall, her back to the others. This was the signal for the villagers to begin singing a haunting melody. Adi sang along quietly, a slight tremor the only betrayal of any trepidation over what was about to happen. Overall, she appeared calm, even happy. Her calmness reflected the overriding joy she felt knowing she would soon be with her husband.

The singing intensified as Joeli tore a length of tapa cloth and wound it tight so it resembled a cord. Winding the cord once around Adi's neck, he handed the other end of the cord to Manasa.

Just then, Drake Senior appeared in the open doorway. The singing had caught his attention and he'd come to investigate. Sensing something was happening, he pushed his way through the assembled villagers until he reached Joeli's side. His gaze rested on Adi.

Adi's aunt stepped forward and, placing her hand on the back of her niece's neck, gently pushed Adi's head forward so that her chin rested on her chest. Joeli looked into the eyes of Manasa. As Adi's nearest blood relative, it was up to him to make the next move. Without any hesitation, Manasa began pulling his end of the cord while Joeli took up the resistance at his end. The cord immediately tightened, cutting off Adi's air supply. Her face reddened and her eyes bulged as the cord tightened.

Horrified, Drake Senior rushed to Adi's assistance. "Dear God, no!" he cried.

Two robust men grabbed him and pulled him back. Drake Senior could only look on as the gruesome ritual continued.

The three other men Manasa had recruited immediately lent their assistance and began pulling on the cord. Their arm muscles bulged as they engaged in this deadly tug-of-war. At the same time Adi's aunt, a big woman, clamped one hand over her niece's mouth and nose.

The singing intensified.

As Adi was starved of air, she began convulsing and throwing her arms about. Unable to watch, Drake Senior turned his head away. After a struggle that seemed to go on interminably but in fact was only a short while, Adi slumped forward, dead. The singing immediately ceased and was replaced by chanting and wailing. Drake Senior returned his gaze to Adi and began reciting the Lord's Prayer aloud.

Joeli and the others i67y7fgmmediately released the cord. Manasa removed it from around his sister's neck and carried her body over to where Iremaia lay. There, he lay her body down beside Iremaia's. A high priest then offered up a prayer, seeking a safe journey to the Spirit World for the souls of the deceased. The other villagers gathered around, offering up prayers of their own.

Drake Senior had seen enough. He felt sick to his stomach. Disgusted by the display he'd just witnessed, he strode toward the doorway, pushing villagers out of his way. Outside, he doubled over, dry retching. When he recovered, he straightened up to find himself face to face with Joeli. Glaring at him, Drake Senior asked, "Why?"

"It is the way of our people."

Then your people will burn in hell, Drake Senior thought, turning his back on Joeli.

The future ratu watched impassively as the missionary walked away.

#

That night, sponging Nathan's forehead in Inoki's bure, Susannah felt exhausted by the day's events. Still in shock, she desperately wanted to sleep, but dared not leave Nathan unattended. Inoki and

Selaima had been helping her until they'd succumbed to their tiredness and fallen asleep on floor mats nearby.

Nathan was no better. He was feverish, tossing and turning and crying out in his sleep. Fresh bandages around his chest were already blood-stained.

Susannah studied his face. It was lit by the embers of the fire that had been burning in the middle of the bure until a few moments earlier. Susannah didn't have the energy to keep it going and tend to Nathan.

Drake Senior suddenly entered the bure. He looked down at Susannah. "How is he?"

"Not good, Papa. He has a fever."

Drake Senior was actually more concerned for his daughter's wellbeing than for the American's. "You should get some rest now."

Susannah shook her head, indicating she wouldn't be leaving Nathan's side. Drake Senior said, "We need to talk."

Sensing her father had something important on his mind, Susannah slowly pushed herself to her feet and allowed him to lead her from the bure.

Outside, Drake Senior came straight to the point. "I made a terrible mistake bringing you here," he murmured. "This place is far too dangerous for a lady."

"No, Papa. I—"

"Hush, my child. I have already reached a decision. When we have finished nursing the wounded here and helped them begin to rebuild their lives, I will be sending you home."

Susannah shook her head stubbornly. "Papa, you said yourself the good Lord will protect us."

Drake Senior drew himself up to his full height and looked sternly at his daughter. "I have made my decision," he growled, turning away. Without another word, he began walking brusquely toward the mission station.

Susannah watched him depart then she reentered Inoki's bure to keep her vigil over Nathan. She arrived to find Selaima awake and wiping sweat from Nathan's forehead with a damp cloth. Smiling at the slave girl, Susannah took over from her. She was alarmed to see Nathan was perspiring more than ever despite the cool night air.

Live, damn you.

A worried Susannah sponged Nathan's face, determined to

combat his fever and keep him alive. Nathan cried out in his sleep as the fever held him in its grip.

Susannah was so preoccupied, she didn't notice the look on Selaima's face. The slave girl didn't like playing second fiddle to the Englishwoman. She wanted to care for the handsome American herself.

Selaima wasn't as worried about Nathan as Susannah was because she knew something Susannah didn't: she knew Nathan would live. Just how she knew, not even she could explain. She had powers that, as far as she was aware, only she knew about.

The slave girl had what the other members of her distant Bauan clan referred to as *the gift*. The gift couldn't easily be explained. Unique to the Bauans, it surfaced in one member of the clan, on average, once every ten or so summers. Whoever inherited the gift inherited amazing powers of healing and prophecy. They could also cast spells, which primarily accounted for why others held them in awe and often feared them.

In Selaima's case, she hadn't become aware of her powers until very recently. For some reason not even she completely understood, she'd chosen—for the moment at least—to keep her powers to herself.

Now, watching Susannah care for Nathan, Selaima thought about using her powers to help the wounded American. But she wouldn't stop at that: she'd also use her powers to ensure the Englishwoman kept well away from the man she knew they both lusted after.

12

Susannah woke to the sounds of labor coming from outside. Although the sun had not long risen, it was evident to her the villagers were already up and about. The young Englishwoman felt refreshed even though she'd been up half the night attending to Nathan.

Suddenly remembering where she was, Susannah rolled over and found herself looking into Nathan's face, not an arm's length away. He was sleeping peacefully. Beyond him, the old healer, Inoki, and the slave girl, Selaima, were also sleeping. Susannah allowed her gaze to return to Nathan's face, taking in his handsome features. She found herself memorizing every feature, every line on his face.

Nathan suddenly stirred, jolting Susannah out of her reverie. She waited to see if he'd woken. He remained fast asleep. Sitting up, Susannah leaned over to check Nathan's dressings. Satisfied they were all right, she then placed the palm of her hand on his forehead to check his temperature. *Still too hot.* His forehead felt clammy. Knowing the best thing she could do for him was to let him sleep, she slowly pushed herself to her feet and walked toward the bure's open doorway.

Outside, she yawned as she observed her surroundings. Villagers were attending to the task of rebuilding their bures and defenses. Joeli was down near the beach supervising the relief of lookouts who had spent the night guarding the approaches to the village. The future ratu was about to lead a small group of warriors out to patrol the surrounding hills. All except Joeli carried muskets. He still stubbornly preferred the tried and tested traditional weapons of his forefathers.

Susannah looked beyond the warriors to the mission station. The unscathed chapel stood out like a beacon amid the destruction around it. The mission house and a small building that had served as a workshop and laundry had been razed to the ground by the outcasts.

Susannah began walking toward the mission station. As she walked, she steeled herself for the inevitable confrontation ahead: she knew her father would be raising the subject of sending her home.

At the mission station, Susannah found Drake Senior already up and about. He had converted the unscathed chapel into a temporary abode, complete with two beds and a makeshift table. Susannah noticed he'd already prepared breakfast for two.

"Good morning, Papa," Susannah said.

"Good morning," an unsmiling Drake Senior responded. "Breakfast is ready," he said, nodding toward the table.

Father and daughter ate in silence. The tension of the previous evening—when Drake Senior had insisted Susannah must return to England—was still in the air.

Looking through the chapel window at the *Rendezvous* anchored out in the bay, Drake Senior said, "The *Rendezvous* sails for the western whaling grounds today." Susannah said nothing. The reverend continued, "I have arranged with Captain McTavish to take you back to Levuka when the ship returns this way in a couple of weeks."

"Papa, I told you—"

"It is not safe for you here."

"My place is here—"

"Enough!" Drake Senior thumped the tabletop with his fist, causing Susannah to jump. "You already have my decision," he said.

Close to tears, Susannah stood up and ran outside.

"Susannah!" Drake Senior called.

She ignored him and kept running down to the beach.

Susannah reached the beach as the *Rendezvous*'s longboat was approaching the shore. In it were the familiar figures of Captain McTavish and Eric Foley as well as two sailors who were manning the oars. Susannah walked down to the water's edge to greet them.

McTavish and Foley saw her coming. They climbed out of the craft and approached her. The captain asked, "How is Mr. Johnson, Miss Drake?"

"He seems a little better this morning, thank you, captain."

"That's good to hear."

Susannah remembered Lightning Rod. She looked sympathetically at the Irish first mate, saying, "I was sorry to learn of Rodney's death, Mr. Foley."

"Thank ye, Miss," Foley mumbled. There was an awkward moment of silence. Foley looked at the captain then back to Susannah. "Ah, Miss . . . I understand ye'll be leaving this place soon," he ventured.

Susannah feigned surprised. "Why would you assume that, Mr. Foley?"

"Well, Miss, your father is concerned for your safety. You've already seen 'ow dangerous it is here. Those cannibals could return."

"Our lives are in the good Lord's hands," Susannah responded. She turned and pointed to the mission station chapel. "You will have noted the outcasts did not touch the chapel."

The two seamen looked at each other, unsure how to respond. Finally, McTavish said, "Ah, I'm afraid we can't delay our departure for the Mamanucas any longer."

"But what about Mr. Johnson?" Susannah asked.

"He's better off here with you."

Susannah looked to Foley.

"Unfortunately, we have to leave him 'ere, Miss," Foley apologized. "We must get to the western whaling grounds before the cyclone season begins."

"Oh, I see."

McTavish hurriedly added, "The whalers are relying on us to deliver urgent provisions, but we'll be back this way in a fortnight. So we can check on Mr. Johnson then."

The two seamen seemed embarrassed they couldn't be of more assistance. McTavish doffed his cap. "Good luck to you and your father."

Foley added, "And to Nathan."

"Thank you." Susannah smiled. "May God be with you." She watched as the seamen returned to the longboat and were rowed back toward the *Rendezvous* before walking slowly up to the village. As she walked, her thoughts returned to Nathan. She wondered how he was faring. Without realizing it, she quickened her pace.

Striding through the village toward Inoki's bure, she was pleased to see that life was slowly returning to a semblance of normality. The villagers were making steady progress rebuilding their bures, children were running around, and laughter could be heard for the first time since the carnage of the previous day. Looking back at the mission station, she saw work was now underway there, too. Having finished breakfast alone, Drake Senior had begun rebuilding the mission house. He was being assisted by two strapping young men he'd recruited from the village.

Susannah paused outside Inoki's bure to watch the *Rendezvous* up anchor and sail out of Momi Bay. The schooner was rapidly pushed westward ahead of a stiff easterly. Susannah knew her father would be expecting her to board the schooner when it next called in. Putting that out of her mind, she entered the bure to find Nathan was still sleeping. Inoki and Selaima were now awake and watching over him. The old healer was hovering over his patient, chanting, while the slave girl sat nearby, singing softly.

Susannah went straight to Nathan and knelt down beside him. Placing her hand on his forehead, she checked his temperature again.

Good!

She nodded, encouraged by what she found: Nathan's temperature had come down since she'd left him earlier.

Selaima smiled to herself as she watched Susannah fuss over Nathan. Initially, she'd wondered what the relationship was between the Englishwoman and the handsome American. It had always been clear to her the woman had feelings for him, but just how deep those feelings ran she could only guess. Since Nathan had been wounded, it had become very clear to her just how much Susannah cared for him.

It irked Selaima that Susannah thought it was because of her own efforts and her foreign healing methods that Nathan was now out of danger. She longed to inform her that his recovery was because of the magic herbal potion she'd administered while alone with him.

Selaima also longed to inform Susannah that she would soon be ill as a result of a spell she'd woven. Not ill enough to die, but ill enough to keep her apart from Nathan for a while at least.

Nathan slept for the remainder of the day and most of the night, waking only to drink fluids that Susannah forced into him at regular intervals. This had the desired effect and his temperature gradually normalized. The downside was that he frequently urinated where he lay. Susannah thought, if Nathan were lucid, he'd agree that urinating in his sleep was a small price to pay for his life.

#

The following morning, Nathan woke to find he was alone with Inoki, who, at that moment, was hovering above him, chanting and waving a smoldering stick over his head.

Looking at his clothes, the young American realized they'd been changed; he was wearing someone else's trousers and someone had bathed him. He wondered who had been responsible for that, not realizing that Susannah and Selaima had taken turns caring for him through the night.

Nathan racked his brains trying to recall what had happened to him and how he'd ended up here. His chest hurt like hell. Slowly, the memory of being speared by the wounded outcast he'd stumbled onto after the attack on the village came to him.

When was that? Yesterday? Last week?

Then details of the battle came flooding back to him, like small explosions in his brain.

Inoki suddenly held the smoldering stick under Nathan's nose and began chanting more loudly. Not wanting to offend the elderly healer, Nathan resisted the urge to turn his head away to escape the smoke, which was threatening to choke him. When Nathan felt he could bear it no more, Inoki mercifully removed the stick and lapsed into silence.

Observing the old man, Nathan thought back to how he'd almost left the villagers alone to fend for themselves. The fact that he'd even considered so cowardly an act made him feel ashamed— especially as the people he'd been ready to forsake were now the very people who were keeping him alive in their village. For one of the few times in his life, he actually felt his conscience stirring.

Nathan suddenly thought of Susannah and wondered where she was. The thought occurred she may have left Momi Bay. His fears were allayed when, moments later, Susannah entered the bure holding a jar. Nathan imagined he caught a look of pleasant surprise on her face, but couldn't be certain. The two stared at each other in silence.

At last, Susannah said, "Nathan . . . ah . . . Mr. Johnson. How are you?"

"Nathan will do," he said, gingerly trying to sit up. "I've been better."

Susannah went to him and helped him to sit up. Then, opening the jar, she said, "These are healing herbs we brought out from England. They might help." With that, she gently removed Nathan's bandages and sprinkled crushed herbs over his chest.

Nathan watched her as she proceeded to rub the herbs into his wound. Finally, he asked, "Since when did you start worrying about me?"

Susannah blushed. "This is the least I can do after what you did for us . . . and for this village."

This only served to remind Nathan how he'd nearly deserted Susannah and her father. Casting guilty thoughts from his mind, he studied Susannah's beautiful face and lustrous red hair as she worked on him. Their faces were only inches apart. Neither said another word, but still the pair somehow seemed to communicate. An unseen energy flowing between them.

Suddenly mindful of her close proximity to Nathan, Susannah abruptly stood up, embarrassed, and prepared to leave, saying, "I will pray for your health."

Nathan was about to ask her to stay a while, but couldn't find the words. The young Englishwoman had that effect on him.

Susannah paused in the doorway. Looking back, she said, "Oh, by the way, the *Rendezvous* left this morning."

Nathan frowned but said nothing. He remembered the balance of his muskets were still in the schooner's hold and wondered if he'd ever see them again. Strangely though, Susannah dominated his mind more than the potential profits from his pending trade. He couldn't believe how mesmerized he was by the redheaded missionary. She had cast a spell over him, which Nathan put down to his feverish state.

13

Wailing and chanting woke Nathan from a deep sleep. Sunlight streamed in through the open doorway of Inoki's bure, hurting his eyes. He closed them momentarily to shield them from the light.

Alone in the bure, Nathan took a few moments to remember where he was. Since being wounded, he'd spent much of the past week sleeping and had not risen from his bed mat other than to attend to his personal needs, so weak was he.

As the wailing grew louder, he forced himself to his feet and stumbled to the doorway. Swaying unsteadily on his feet, he leaned against it and noticed a steady stream of mourners descending on the village. He deduced they must have traveled from surrounding villages to pay their respects to Iremaia and, judging by the ceremonial attire of some, he could see there were ratus and headmen among them. Beneath their turbans, they looked splendid in their tapa robes and their colorful mulberry bark capes and shawls.

Some mourners were arriving by canoe, others materialized on foot out of the nearby rainforest. Many had traveled long distances—such was the esteem they had for Iremaia and their Qopa allies. Nathan could see that all carried gifts and food; some even brought slaves as gifts.

The mourners, who now numbered in their hundreds, were

assembling outside the village meeting house, some fifty yards from where Nathan was standing. Iremaia had lain there in state since his death.

One by one, the mourners sat down, cross-legged on the ground, facing the meeting house. There was an expectant hum of conversation that carried faintly to Nathan above the distant thunder of waves crashing onto the offshore reef. Children scampered around on the fringes of the crowd.

Nathan didn't realize the occasion was also to be an acknowledgment of Joeli's new status within the Qopa clan. As Iremaia's oldest son born of Akanisi, Joeli was about to be proclaimed ratu.

The young American studied the mourners, hoping to catch a glimpse of Susannah. He was secretly disappointed he hadn't seen her for the past few days. What he didn't know was she had developed a mysterious rash which, until today, had forced her to remain indoors at the mission station in case it was contagious. The strange thing was it had disappeared as quickly as it had occurred. Of course, Susannah wasn't to know the rash was a result of the spell Selaima had placed on her to keep her out of circulation for a while.

Nathan sensed Susannah had developed feelings for him, which he thought could explain why she had been avoiding him. *That's probably wishful thinking,* he cautioned himself. To be fair, given the severity of his wound, his progress over the past week had been remarkable and he was rapidly improving. Even so, he was far from his old self.

Just venturing outside unaided was an effort and his chest was painful to touch.

Nathan suddenly caught sight of Susannah. She was sitting with her father in the midst of the other mourners. They had their backs to him. He debated whether to walk over to join them, but felt he wouldn't make it. Just standing was proving difficult. He was beginning to feel faint so he sat down on the grass, his back against the wall of the bure.

The American was unaware that while he was looking at Susannah, he was being observed from afar by Selaima. The slave girl was biding her time, planning her next move to seduce him.

Looking around him, Nathan was amazed how industrious the Qopa had been since he'd been out of commission. The razed bures and destroyed defenses had been rebuilt so that the village looked almost as it had before the battle with the outcasts. All that was missing—aside from warriors who were notable by their absence—was the storehouse that had once rested atop four poles in the center of the village. As before, Nathan wondered what the storehouse had held.

Looking along the beach at the nearby mission station, he could see that Drake Senior had been industrious, too. The wooden framing of the new mission house appeared to be near completion.

Beyond the mission station, Nathan could see the now-familiar storm clouds gathering above the Nausori Highlands of the interior. He guessed the wet season had arrived there and wondered when it was going to arrive in Momi Bay. By all accounts, its arrival in the western regions of Viti Levu was overdue.

Nathan couldn't see inside the meeting house, but at that moment all the members of Iremaia's extended family were gathered around the bodies of Iremaia and Adi, his youngest wife. The old ratu's remaining wives were among them, as was Joeli, who was proudly wearing the whale bone pendant he'd inherited from his father.

The future ratu looked more imposing than ever adorned as he was in the same ceremonial turban and mulberry bark cloak his father had once worn. In keeping with tradition, the cloak featured eye-catching charcoal black and ochre red designs.

Joeli suddenly withdrew from the others. It was time. Straightening his cloak and squaring his broad shoulders, he walked toward the doorway.

Outside, the crowd quietened as Joeli emerged from the meeting house. He sat down facing the assembled then signaled for the formalities to begin.

Village matagali, or elders, proceeded to welcome the visitors. One by one, they delivered their lengthy speeches, paying homage to Iremaia. Like islanders throughout the Pacific, they considered themselves wonderful orators and could not be hurried. Their speeches inevitably began with a summary of their clan's history and finished with a recital of their genealogy dating back to the earliest known Fijian ratus. These were interspersed with imaginative accounts of their personal heroism in countless battles with their numerous enemies.

In some cases, the enemies they referred to were in attendance.

Insults, and imagined insults, were duly noted and would no doubt be avenged at some future date—such was the way things worked in Fiji.

#

After several hours of oratory, many of the children were asleep in their parents' arms and the adults were becoming restless. Fifty yards away, sitting on the grass outside Inoki's hut, Nathan had long since fallen asleep.

Finally, the crowd fell silent when the elderly Kamisese, a respected toreni koro, or village headman, stood to speak. "Bula. This is a sad occasion and a happy one," Kamisese proclaimed. "Today, we farewell a great ratu and we welcome another." The crowd cheered Kamisese's eloquence. The old man held his hands up for silence. He looked directly at Joeli. "Joeli, descended from Iremaia, descended from Naikelekele . . . your warrior bloodlines can be traced all the way back to the great Umbari. May their blood run through your veins and give you the strength to lead your people to greatness."

A huge cheer erupted, waking Nathan. Rubbing sleep from his eyes, the young American looked on as Joeli stood to acknowledge his supporters. A hundred warriors from neighboring villages lined up in rows three deep to hail the Qopa's new ratu. Chanting and stamping their feet in unison, the warriors gave thanks to the war spirits.

Joeli's few remaining able-bodied warriors joined them, proudly brandishing their new muskets. The sight of over a hundred fierce warriors paying homage to the spirits sent a thrill through everyone present.

Watching the impressive display, Nathan found his mind wandering. He wondered what the future held for him—and whether Susannah could possibly feature in that future.

What on earth are you thinking, Nathan chastised himself. *It's an impossible romance, so forget it. A classy woman like that would never want to end up with a rough diamond like you!*

Nathan wished he could banish Susannah from his mind. He wanted to get as far away from her and as quickly possible for she was distracting him from his mission in the Pacific. He only hoped that once she was out of sight, she would also be out of mind, but he knew he couldn't be sure of that. All he knew for sure was such a sophisticated, not to mention religious, woman was well out of his league. Still though, she dominated his thoughts like nothing else.

The young American had never been in love before, so he didn't have a clue what it felt like and whether this was it. Truth be told, up until now he didn't actually believe in the idea of love—only lust— but, as much as he hated to acknowledge it, there was definitely some bizarre feeling inside him that wouldn't go away. It was like some dizzy combination of seasickness and ecstasy. It was so intense, he'd completely lost his appetite. As much as he tried, however much he reasoned with himself, the desire to be with Susannah wouldn't go away.

This was totally different to how he'd felt toward any other woman. As he pondered this, Nathan had an inkling as to why Susannah had infiltrated the prison of his mind when all other women had failed: it was her demeanor and zest for life. Life sparkled in her eyes in a way that he'd never seen in any of the numerous women he'd bedded, regardless of their beauty.

Pondering his future once more, the American decided it wouldn't be a bad thing if he were to spend the remainder of his life with Susannah.

Nathan realized he was being foolish. He reminded himself it was an impossible romance. For starters, Drake Senior would never allow it.

#

Later, after Iremaia had been buried in the tribe's nearby burial cave and the mourners had departed, Joeli stood alone with his thoughts on the headland overlooking Momi Bay. He was staring out to sea, thinking of his dear departed parents and preparing himself mentally for a future without them. Joeli knew now how his father must have felt. As ratu, the responsibility for the village and its people was his alone. It was a big responsibility and it weighed heavily on him.

A noise told him someone was approaching. Joeli turned to see Nathan and Inoki walking slowly toward him from the village below. It was obvious to him the American was in pain: he was walking slowly and leaning heavily on the old healer for support. As they neared, Joeli motioned to Inoki to leave them. The healer wandered off, leaving the young men alone.

Nathan attempted to walk the last few paces to Joeli unaided.

Such was the effort, he stumbled and fell to his knees. Joeli offered no assistance, believing Nathan would lose face if he did. Nathan doggedly pushed himself to his feet and finally reached Joeli's side. The two men looked intensely at each other for several moments.

Nathan nodded. "Bula, Joeli."

The young ratu stepped forward until their faces were only inches apart. "Bula, Nathan Johnson." Joeli reached out with his right hand and clasped Nathan's left shoulder. With his other hand he removed the whale bone pendant from around his neck and held it out to Nathan. He wanted him to have it.

Nathan was taken aback. He knew how much the heirloom meant to Joeli. "I cannot accept this. It was your father's. He would want you to have it."

The young ratu looked wistfully at the treasured heirloom then back to Nathan. "My father would want you to have. You help defeat our enemies." Not prepared to debate the issue, Joeli firmly placed the pendant around Nathan's neck. "It where belong. Now I give to you, cannot take back."

Nathan reluctantly accepted the pendant. Again, the two young men stared long and hard at each other. There was a new respect in the eyes of each. Joeli said, "Joeli thank Nathan Johnson for helping my people."

Nathan nodded, accepting the other's gratitude, but behind his calm exterior he was troubled by his conscience, which had returned even stronger than before. His guilt stemmed from the knowledge that Joeli didn't realize Nathan had only been looking after his own interests during the battle. He'd never even considered the Qopas' interests and yet here they were giving him shelter and caring for him. For the first time in his life, he was becoming aware just how selfish an individual he really was.

Joeli looked out to sea for a moment and then back at Nathan. "My people will collect trepang in return for muskets." Nathan looked puzzled. "Trepang . . . sea slugs," Joeli translated in hesitant English.

"Ah."

"It ready by time ship return," he said, referring to the *Rendezvous*.

The American marveled at Joeli's sincerity. It was obvious he intended to honor the terms of the agreement his father had reached with Nathan.

In all his travels, Nathan had never allowed himself to get close to a native, or even to get to know one, like he was beginning to with Joeli. He was surprised at the level of respect he was beginning to feel toward the young ratu, but more than that, he was surprised by the realization that he felt as he did.

The two began walking back down to the village. Joeli walked slowly to allow Nathan to keep up.

Nathan suddenly asked, "Will your enemies return?"

Joeli smiled a rare smile. "Our enemies always return." The young ratu turned and pointed east toward the distant highlands of Viti Levu's interior. He said, "Out there . . . somewhere . . . where our enemies come from." Nathan observed the highlands for the second time that day. Joeli continued, "Rambuka, the Outcast, live there. In . . . jungle . . ." Joeli searched for the correct English word. Eventually, he lost patience and resorted to sign language. Nathan watched him curiously.

With his hand, Joeli simulated rain falling from the sky.

"Rain?" Nathan asked.

"Ah . . . rain." Joeli looked back at the highlands. "Where outcasts live. It rain there, sometimes red rain . . . rain of death."

Nathan looked puzzled. "Red rain?"

Joeli nodded. "Yes . . . red rain." He turned to Nathan, his expression fiercely determined, then addressed him in his native tongue. "Joeli, son of Iremaia, ratu of our people, will never allow our enemies to take this land from us."

Nathan nodded to acknowledge his understanding of Joeli's sentiments, if not the words. Suddenly tired, he headed back to his hut, leaving Joeli alone with his thoughts.

#

Next day, makeshift walking stick in hand, Nathan shuffled slowly along a forest trail in the hills behind Momi Bay. His chest wound still caused him some pain and he gritted his teeth as he forced himself to keep moving.

Narrow shafts of sunlight broke through gaps in the trees, illuminating patches of foliage and giving the tropical forest a cathedral-like atmosphere.

As he paused to rest, the sounds of women's laughter and singing carried to him on a gentle breeze from a nearby valley. He went to investigate, pulling up sharply when he saw Susannah and three village women bathing naked in a stream below. Hidden from view, Nathan stood transfixed, watching.

Floating on her back, Susannah was using her shapely legs to propel her sensuous body through the water. Her pert, rounded breasts gleamed as the water washed over them. Unaware that Nathan was close by, she floated like a starfish, her eyes shut tight to avoid the glare of the bright sun.

Nathan felt a stirring in his loins.

My God, she's exquisite!

His fingers strayed to the whalebone pendant Joeli had given him and, without even realizing it, he began caressing the sacred heirloom. He looked at Susannah longingly for some time before a feeling of guilt overcame him. Tearing his eyes away from her, he reluctantly resumed his walk.

Nathan wasn't aware that while he'd been observing Susannah, he'd been under observation himself—and still was. Selaima had followed him from the village. She'd been about to show herself to him when Nathan had become distracted by the Englishwoman. Watching the way he studied Susannah sent a stab of pain through the slave girl's heart. At that moment, she hated Susannah as much as she loved Nathan.

In the stream, Susannah's companions sang a song that was often heard throughout western Viti Levu. Its joyous melody carried up and down the valley. Despite the trauma of recent events, Susannah was at last feeling at peace. Lulled by her companions' singing and the feeling of weightlessness as she floated in the cool stream, she hadn't a care in the world right at that moment. Her nakedness and the feeling of the sun on her face suddenly took her back to her childhood in England.

The young Englishwoman was transported back to another sunny day in London's Hyde Park, near the Drake family home in the Borough of Kensington. She was fifteen and in love for the first time. In fact, that was the only time in her life she had been in love. The boy was a sixteen-year-old Cockney who was an apprentice chimney sweeper. Susannah would secretly meet him whenever her father was busy with parish duties.

That day in Hyde Park was the last time she saw the boy. He was killed shortly after in a work-related accident at an East End foundry. The boy's death, on top of the earlier passing of Susannah's beloved mother, had served to teach the young woman how fickle life could be and how abruptly loved ones could be taken from her. That hard lesson, she suspected, accounted for her reluctance to allow herself to fall in love again.

A cloud cast a brief shadow over Susannah, ending her day-dreaming. She swam over to rejoin the Qopa women who were sunning themselves on a rock. Climbing out of the stream, she joined them on the rock to dry off just as the sun conveniently reemerged. She tilted her face toward it, luxuriating in its warmth.

Susannah marveled at how she could feel so relaxed and at peace after the awful recent events at Momi Bay. At the same time, she knew her current state of mind wouldn't last.

Of late, she'd been questioning her motives in coming to Fiji, finally admitting to herself that, unlike her father, she had not been motivated by any overwhelming need to spread God's Word to the natives. Rather, she had come to escape England's gray skies, to get over the sadness of her youth and to make her father proud of her.

If she were honest with herself, after only a few weeks in Fiji she was feeling dissatisfied. About what, she couldn't be sure and this irked her.

Not for the first time that day, her thoughts turned to Nathan. Like him, though, she figured theirs was an impossible relationship. She tried to banish him from her mind, but the harder she tried the more she thought about him. Despite his ungodly ways, something about the American intrigued her.

As always, whenever she thought of him, she experienced a fluttering in her lower tummy. It was a delicious feeling.

14

On the surface at least, life had returned to normal at Momi Bay. In the twelve days since the village had come under attack, the bures had been rebuilt, the defenses repaired, and the dead buried; the wounded were recovering, the Qopas' slaves were tending the crops, and fishermen were out casting their nets and spearing fish.

The sun was shining too, although that wasn't especially normal for the wet season was usually here by now.

Watching his people trying to piece their lives back together, Joeli knew that for many life would never be the same again. Women had lost husbands or sons in the recent battle and children had lost fathers.

The young ratu's fighting force had been decimated, and he knew it would take years to rebuild it. Joeli realized he needed to forge alliances with other tribes—and quickly.

Children were playing nearby, their gay laughter a clue to the ease with which, like children everywhere, they were able to put the past behind them and live in the moment. Joeli knew most of the children by name and was aware some had been orphaned as a result of losing a father in battle and then losing a mother who had taken the appropriate action to join her husband in the Afterlife. Yet they appeared not to have a care in the world.

Looking over at the mission station, Joeli could see the rebuilding program was progressing nicely under Drake Senior's supervision. The cottage was well on the way to completion, and Susannah had already resumed leading daily Bible classes and singing lessons for the village children. While Joeli had no interest in the white man's god, he respected the missionary couple who had risked their lives for his people when the outcasts had struck.

Beyond the mission station, Joeli noticed Nathan walking along the beach. The American was now moving freely and appeared almost fully recovered—testimony to his natural strength and fitness levels.

In the village center, villagers were watching two muscular warriors who were about to engage in a wrestling match. Joeli wandered over to watch. Wrestling was a favorite pastime among the Qopa. The villagers cheered for their favorite as the bout got underway. It was a close contest. Finally, the bigger of the two combatants began to dominate his opponent. Showing surprising agility for a big man, he got behind his opposite and threw him to the ground, thereby winning the contest according to village rules. The onlookers cheered. There was much laughter as the loser's wife berated her husband for losing. Hitting him with a stick, she marched the henpecked man back to their bure where, according to tradition, he'd have to pleasure her to win her forgiveness.

Joeli suddenly spotted Waisale running up from the beach, the geometric masterpiece of shocking pink hair atop his head bobbing up and down as he ran. Joeli quickly walked to intercept him.

Breathless, Waisale ran up to him, saying, "Our neighbors, the Mamanucans, say the Great White Shark has returned to these waters!"

Joeli looked surprised. "Are you sure? It is too early in the season."

"Early or not, the Mamanucans say the Great White is here."

Joeli considered this. "This is good. It has been a long time since the Great White blessed our waters." He looked keenly at Waisale. "We need the Shark Caller."

Waisale nodded and hurried to his hut to gather up supplies for the brief ocean voyage he knew was ahead of him. Behind him, Joeli saw Nathan walking up the beach toward him. He waited for the American to reach him.

Nathan noticed Joeli was looking at the whale bone pendant he'd given him. The American now wore it permanently around his neck.

After an awkward pause, Joeli said, "Waisale goes to fetch Shark Caller. You go with him."

Nathan didn't know what Joeli was talking about. Nor was he sure whether he was being ordered or invited to go somewhere. He asked, "What is a shark caller?"

Joeli smiled. "You see." Turning, he saw Waisale returning from the village with a large bag over his shoulder. He knew the bag contained food supplies and drinking water. Turning back to Nathan, he said, "You wait." He then hurried to intercept Waisale.

Nathan looked on as Joeli had a discussion with Waisale. He wasn't to know the ratu was telling the engaging young warrior that Nathan would be accompanying him on his voyage.

\#

Nathan still wasn't sure what was going on as he helped Joeli and Waisale push a small outrigger canoe into the water. Before he knew it, Waisale had jumped on board and was pulling him up after him. Nathan didn't resist, thinking they were going on a leisurely sail around the bay. In no time at all, the canoe was skimming across the water toward the open sea.

\#

Later, out of sight of land, Nathan realized this was no joy ride. They were headed somewhere else, and he had no way of finding out where. He'd discovered early in the voyage his likable companion with the pink hair didn't speak a word of English. That didn't stop Waisale talking to him. The young warrior chatted nonstop in his native tongue and didn't seem fazed that Nathan couldn't understand him.

Wisely, Nathan decided to sit back and enjoy the trip. He watched as Waisale used the traditional methods of South Seas navigators to stay on course as he single-handedly sailed his outrigger due west from Momi Bay. Occasionally, he motioned to Nathan to assist, but the American sensed it was more out of giving him something to do than needing assistance.

Holding onto the tiller, Waisale made tiny adjustments to ensure their course remained true. He was constantly noting the position of the sun and the direction of ocean currents as well as studying the ever-so-slight variations in the ocean swells.

Nathan knew enough about sailing to realize that Waisale was one hell of a sailor.

#

It was almost nightfall when the outrigger canoe approached a tiny atoll—a mere dot in the ocean. Little bigger than a football field, the atoll accommodated a single bure hut.

As the canoe neared the atoll, Nathan saw an elderly bearded native emerge from the bure. He'd learn later, this was the one referred to as *the Shark Caller*. Originally from the Lau Group, far to the east, he looked quite different to Waisale and the other Fijians of Viti Levu with his straight hair and aquiline features.

Waisale beached the canoe and jumped out on to the sand.

Smiling, the Shark Caller greeted him. "Bula. I see you, young friend."

Waisale responded, "Bula. I see you, old friend." The Shark Caller then looked inquiringly at Nathan, who was now standing in the shallows. "This is Nathan Johnson," Waisale explained. "He is an American."

"Why is he here?"

"I don't know. The ratu said he should come."

The Shark Caller scowled in Nathan's direction then, with his arm around Waisale's shoulder, he escorted him up to his bure. Nathan followed, feeling like an intruder.

Nathan's discomfort didn't last long. On arriving at the Shark Caller's bure, he was invited to join the other two in a kava ceremony. After several hours of drinking kava, the three became good friends even though Nathan couldn't understand them and they couldn't understand him.

After dark, their insides warmed by kava, the trio boarded Waisale's canoe and set sail for Momi Bay. They sailed through the night. As his forefathers had done before him, Waisale used the stars as his guide.

#

Next day, hundreds of Fijians lined the foreshore at Momi Bay. The local villagers had been joined by the residents of neighboring villages. Everyone was in a high state of excitement.

Drawn by the large gathering, Nathan looked around, trying to work out what the occasion was. Every now and then, he was approached by warriors who greeted him by firmly clasping his left shoulder with their right hand and staring solemnly at him before walking off. This had become a daily occurrence. It had unnerved him at first—until he realized they were paying their respects to him. His standing in the village almost rivaled that of Joeli's since he and his muskets had helped repel Rambuka's outcasts.

Further along the beach, Susannah was sitting alone on a log. She, too, had been drawn by the large gathering. Unlike the others, she was not excited or happy. She felt melancholy for some reason. It was as if a dark cloud had descended over her.

Wild cheering from the multitude gathered on the beach brought Susannah back to the present. She tried to focus on what was happening, but try as she may, she couldn't stem the flow of tears that began coursing down her cheeks. She didn't know what was making her so emotional. All she knew was there was something missing in her life. No longer did she feel satisfied with half a life, which, if she was honest with herself, was all the missionary's life she'd chosen could ever be.

Within the crowd, Nathan watched with interest as the onlookers' ranks suddenly parted to reveal the Shark Caller being escorted from the village to the beach by Joeli.

The onlookers dropped to all fours and bowed their heads as their respected ratu and the equally esteemed Shark Caller approached.

Pausing to adjust a pennant-like piece of masi, or tapa cloth, attached to a post, the Shark Caller then waded out into the sea. The old man stopped only when the water reached his neck then he began chanting. It was a shrill, haunting chant unlike any Nathan had heard. The onlookers watched this ancient ceremony in awe.

Nathan looked on, bemused, when he suddenly noticed Susannah sitting alone further down the beach. Even from a distance, her shapely body was very evident in the cotton dress she wore. The strong feelings Nathan had felt when he saw her naked in the stream returned. Taking a deep breath, he set off toward her.

As he approached Susannah, he felt increasingly nervous. Again, he couldn't believe the effect she had on him. He who had traveled the world, fought many a battle, and gained a substantial fortune. Yet here was a virginal woman—of that he was certain—making his knees tremble and his brow sweat.

Susannah was still crying when she saw Nathan approaching.

Quickly drying her eyes, she forced a smile and called out, "It's good to see you looking so healthy."

Nathan smiled and sat down beside her. "That's thanks to you." He looked closely at her. It was clear she was upset about something. "Are you all right, Susannah?"

Susannah's eyes widened for a moment. This was the first time he'd called her by her Christian name. Susannah thought she detected a fondness in his deep, rich voice when he used her name. She liked that. Not that she let on. Instead, she deflected the question by pointing at the Shark Caller. "The shark calling has begun."

Nathan looked out into the bay where the Shark Caller continued to chant. He asked, "Shark calling?"

Susannah nodded. Looking at the Shark Caller, she explained, "The villagers tell me they call him the Shark Caller. He is supposedly possessed of magical powers that enable him to communicate with sharks." Nathan looked skeptical. Susannah continued, "I've never seen it before, but I've heard some amazing stories."

Nathan offered no comment. He looked at the beautiful young woman, willing her to keep talking. Her cultured English accent excited him.

Susannah blushed. She chastised herself for letting Nathan have this effect on her. Anxious not to betray her feelings, she started rambling. "I hear the Qopa believe the Shark Caller and his kind also have the power to stop the sun," she blurted out.

Now Nathan looked even more skeptical, but he quickly camouflaged his skepticism with a smile and willed her to continue. Even though Susannah wasn't talking about personal things, it was as if there was a subtext behind her words and she was actually revealing her deepest, most private thoughts and her true inner self. Nathan could have listened to her all day. He wanted to reach out and stroke her gorgeous red hair. Instead, he just looked into her hazel eyes. Despite himself, he soon found himself drowning in their depths. They sparkled like diamonds, just as they did the first time he met her.

Blushing alarmingly, Susannah said, "The Qopa believe if they are late getting home and need a little extra daylight, all they need to do is pick a certain kind of reed, hide it from the light, and call out to the sun. That way they can postpone the darkness until they get home safely . . ."

Fearing she was making a fool of herself, Susannah's voice trailed off. She glanced at Nathan, certain he'd be laughing at her. Instead, she found him staring at her intently. He was absentmindedly fingering the whale bone pendant around his neck. Still, his eyes never left hers.

On a sudden impulse, Nathan jumped to his feet and, looking down at Susannah, suggested, "Let's go for a walk."

Momentarily taken aback, Susannah hesitantly allowed Nathan to help her to her feet. The two walked side by side along the beach. They waved at a lookout lounging against a nearby palm tree. The lookout waved back.

Nathan and Susannah walked close together, their hands almost touching. So engrossed were they in each other, neither noticed Selaima, who followed them from within the grove of palm trees that bordered the beach. Keeping to the shadows, she never took her eye off the couple.

The Shark Caller's chants faded as the couple continued along the beach. Nathan picked up a flat stone and threw it out to sea. The stone skipped across the water's surface.

Susannah noted his new vigor. "I see you are back to full health. How much longer do you expect to be here?"

"Why, are you going to miss me?" Nathan smiled mischievously.

Embarrassed, Susannah looked away. Nathan came to her aid immediately, saying, "The *Rendezvous* should be back soon to take me and my shipment of sea slugs back to Levuka."

"Then where will you go?"

"Then I sail to China."

"I see."

Nathan noted that Susannah was suddenly quiet. He looked into her eyes. "You know, this really is no place for a woman. What kind of a future can you expect in a place like this?"

Nathan had touched a raw nerve.

Susannah rounded on him. "Do you think this is what I want?" she challenged. "This is the last place on earth I want to be!" Nathan was taken aback by the emotional outburst. Susannah continued, "But sometimes God's will comes first. This is what he has chosen for me."

Nathan raised his eyes to the heavens. "And you really believe that drivel?"

Susannah looked away for a moment, angry. "You don't believe in anything do you, Nathan?" Her tone was accusing. At the same time, she felt ashamed. Nathan had unwittingly forced her to confront her own misgivings over her suitability to carry out God's work. Her anger was partially directed at herself, but of course Nathan couldn't know that.

The American reached beneath his shirt and pulled his pistol from his belt. "I believe in this," he said, waving the weapon under her nose.

Susannah looked at the pistol and shook her head. "I thought you were different. I thought maybe, just maybe, somewhere beneath your hard exterior, you were compassionate."

"This is a savage land, Susannah. Lofty ideals like compassion will only get a man killed." Susannah appeared deeply offended. Pointing back down the beach, Nathan said, "Just look around you. These people, or people just like them, are eating one another, for Christ's sake!"

Susannah was disappointed with Nathan. "I should be getting back," she said turning to go.

Aware he'd spoiled the mood, Nathan said, "Wait." Susannah composed herself and looked back at him. Nathan lost himself for a moment as he looked into her shimmering, hazel eyes. He wanted to tell her he had feelings for her, but the words refused to come. It was as if his tongue had frozen.

Susannah looked back at him defiantly. She was feeling confused, unsure whether to love or hate the man standing before him. The only thing she was certain of was he affected her like no man ever had.

Does he want me like I want him?

Nathan thought he saw something in her eyes. He desperately wanted to kiss her, but found himself rooted to the spot, suddenly paralyzed.

Do something, man!

Unsure exactly what he should do or say next, Nathan was saved from further embarrassment by a little girl who ran up to them. Stopping in front of the couple, she proudly displayed a handful of colorful pebbles. "Bula," she said shyly.

Susannah and Nathan looked at the girl and laughed. Their laughter was somewhat forced. The little girl joined in the laughter.

Taking her by one hand each, they began walking back along the beach to rejoin the crowd. Still they didn't notice Selaima tracking them.

As they neared the assembled Fijians, the Shark Caller's chants grew louder. The girl ran off to play with friends, leaving the young couple alone. The Shark Caller hadn't moved since wading out into the sea. Still up to his neck in water, he continued his high-pitched chanting.

Ever skeptical, Nathan turned to Susannah. "How long is this meant to take?"

Susannah frowned at him. "Be patient."

The chanting continued for so long Nathan was ready to return to the village. Then it suddenly stopped. The onlookers collectively gasped as a huge fin sliced through the water toward the Shark Caller.

Pointing the fin out to Nathan, Susannah whispered, "That will be the Great White."

Nathan couldn't take his eyes off the drama unfolding out in the bay. The fin veered away only yards short of the Shark Caller. The old man resumed chanting as the shark began circling him. More fins appeared, smaller than the Great White's. They, too, circled the Shark Caller, who appeared oblivious to the danger. Wild cheering broke out among the onlookers. Nathan could hardly believe his eyes.

Susannah, shouting to be heard, said, "The Great White answers the call of the Shark Caller. It brings other sharks with it."

Men waiting aboard canoes in the shallows began paddling furiously out from the beach to intercept the sharks. In the lead canoe, Joeli and Waisale reached down and hauled the still-chanting Shark Caller from the water. The crews of the other canoes set about killing as many sharks as they could. They used nets to snare the sharks and then they speared them, but they were careful not to harm the Great White. The sea in the immediate vicinity quickly turned red with blood. A feeding frenzy followed as sharks turned on one another.

One of the men in Joeli's canoe fell overboard. Willing hands hauled him back on board just before the sharks could reach him.

On the beach, the onlookers were cheering and sea shell horns blared out as the men aboard the canoes began towing their catches back to shore. Despite the danger still posed by live sharks, villagers waded out to greet them. They helped pull the captured sharks up onto the beach, taking care to avoid their gnashing teeth.

Before long, the carcasses of thirty or more sharks had been lined up in rows on the sand. Smiling villagers used hunting knives to carve strips of flesh from them while others cut off the highly valued fins. Slaves carried the spoils back up to the village.

A beaming Joeli surveyed the scene proudly. He announced, "Tonight, my people eat well!"

His warriors cheered and performed a joyous dance. Young boys emulated them. Joeli noticed Nathan and Susannah looking on. He nodded toward them.

Susannah suddenly saw her father. Drake Senior was staring directly at her and Nathan. He seemed displeased to see her with the American. "I must go now," she said, hurrying away to join her father.

Nathan wanted to call out, *When can I see you?* But he was once again momentarily struck dumb. As Susannah and her father were swallowed up by the crowd, he found he was missing her already.

The American's body language and demeanor were easily read by Selaima, who was still observing him from the cover of the palm trees. It was clear to her that Nathan was obsessed with Susannah. Her animosity toward the Englishwoman intensified. Feelings of jealousy were rapidly turning to hate.

Nathan turned his attention back to the scene on the beach. Beyond the villagers he saw the Shark Caller. The old man was now further down the beach, away from the others. He was kneeling beside a lone shark carcass.

Nathan approached the Shark Caller. As he neared, he heard the old man chanting softly while looking into the eye of the dead shark.

"Great hunter of the sea, you have lived a noble life," the Shark Caller intoned in his native tongue. "You have served your purpose. Now you will perform one last act. You will give me your eye so that I can see all things as you do."

Although the words were foreign to him, Nathan felt he understood what the Shark Caller was saying. He looked on as the old man used a shell to cut out the shark's eye. The Shark Caller held it up, offered another chant, then popped the eye into his mouth and swallowed it whole.

15

As dusk fell, the Qopa enjoyed the day's spoils. Cooking pots brimmed full of the prized shark fin soup and shark flesh was grilled over cooking fires or baked in lovos throughout the village.

Nathan had been invited to dine with Joeli and his extended family in their bure. He arrived as the young ratu was about to share shark fin soup with family and friends around an open fire. Children were among the happy group, and there was much laughter and gaiety.

The American was welcomed and invited to sit on Joeli's right. Waisale was already seated on his left. Nathan noticed a number of fetching young maidens were present, and they seemed to be paying a lot of attention to Joeli. To his knowledge, Joeli wasn't married, but he guessed it would only be a matter of time before the young ratu took the first of many wives—as was the tradition.

After he'd had his fill of soup, Nathan watched as Selaima and other slave girls served portions of baked shark covered in coconut cream. As they carried out their tasks, he couldn't help but notice that Selaima was making eye contact with him at every opportunity—as she had been since their first meeting. For a moment he was seriously tempted to give her some clue that he was interested in whatever it was she had in mind. There was no denying she was a seductive and beautiful young woman. Only the thought of Susannah prevented him from giving into temptation.

The realization that his feelings for a missionary were preventing him from having his way with the temptress now before him was a watershed moment for Nathan. He knew he'd changed. The Nathan of old would never have let a relationship with one woman stand in the way of a relationship with another. Not that he could claim to have a real relationship with Susannah. If he were honest, it was more a longing on his part than a relationship. And he didn't even know how Susannah felt about him.

You must be getting old, Johnson.

As always, the ratu was served first and, as a mark of respect, everyone waited for him to begin eating. Holding a steaming slither of shark flesh, Joeli mischievously waited for several drawn-out moments. The younger children became restless, and their parents had to physically restrain them from eating before Joeli had his first mouthful. Chuckling to himself, he pretended to put the slither into his mouth. His stalling tactics attracted groans from family members. Finally, he stuffed it into his mouth. Laughing, the others gratefully followed suit.

An elderly woman shook her head as if to reprimand Joeli for his teasing.

The laughter and conversation faded as the food was devoured. Nathan ate heartily like the others.

Joeli noted the American's liking for the shark's flesh and nodded with satisfaction. "Nathan Johnson," he said, "it is good you healthy now. Healthy good."

Nathan smiled and kept chewing.

Waisale leaned over to Joeli. Speaking Fijian, he said, "What is this thing between Nathan Johnson and the white woman?"

Joeli looked at Nathan mischievously. Speaking English, he said, "Waisale ask, what happen between you and missionary woman?"

Nathan feigned innocence. By now all eyes were on him. "What do you mean?"

Joeli turned to the others. Speaking in Fijian again, he said, "Nathan Johnson claims there is nothing between him and the woman."

Waisale chuckled and said, "And I am the ratu of all of Viti Levu!"

This provoked widespread laughter from all except Selaima. Nathan looked to Joeli for an explanation.

Reverting to English, Joeli said, "Waisale say Nathan Johnson love white woman."

Nathan raised his hands in mock surrender. "All right! I do like her a little."

Lapsing back into Fijian, Joeli told the others, "He loves her . . . a lot."

This provoked more laughter. Waisale asked Joeli, "What does Nathan Johnson plan to do next with the white woman?"

Translating, accurately this time for Nathan's benefit, Joeli said, "Waisale ask what next move with white woman?"

"I thought perhaps I'd take her a bunch of flowers."

When Joeli relayed this to the others, they shook with laughter, demonstrating their ignorance of this European courting custom.

Waisale told Joeli, "Tell Nathan Johnson no woman will open her legs for someone as ugly as him if that is all he gives her."

Joeli turned to Nathan and said, "Waisale say you have no chance. Better to send him in your place."

Nathan looked at Waisale and shook his head good-naturedly, provoking yet more mirth. Waisale slapped Nathan on the back, prompting him to join in the laughter.

Sitting there, laughing and drinking kava with his newfound Fijian friends, Nathan was coming to the realization that the prejudices and feelings of superiority he'd harbored toward native peoples in the past were vanishing as quickly as the level of kava in his drinking bowl was dropping. Despite the external and cultural differences, their warmth and humor had melted his icy heart and he'd become very fond of them.

He now recognized they were not so different to him. Less sophisticated in European terms perhaps, but they shared many of the same likes and dislikes, hopes and dreams, fears and passions that he did.

The American now understood that all the beliefs he once held were just that: beliefs. He'd judged the Fijians—and probably all native peoples—before giving them a chance.

Nathan suddenly felt ashamed for his previous attitudes yet he sensed these Fijians were totally forgiving. They now accepted Nathan almost as if he were a member of their clan.

This only served to make him feel more ashamed than ever. He vowed then and there, he'd at least try to treat all people of all creeds and colors as equals.

After the meal, Nathan accompanied Joeli as he did the rounds of the village. This was a routine the young ratu followed every night. They stopped every so often to check the rebuilt fortifications and talk to the lookouts.

As they walked, Nathan commented, "You have a good friend in Waisale."

Joeli nodded. "He is a brother to me."

"He has a zest for life." The ratu looked at him blankly, not understanding. They walked a few more paces in silence. Nathan said, "But I sense an inner sadness in Waisale."

Joeli stopped by a rock and indicated they should sit down. When they were seated, he said, "Waisale once . . . love my cousin Sina. She so beautiful I would have her myself if not related."

Joeli could remember the day Sina and Waisale became a couple as if it were only yesterday. Waisale had been pursuing Sina, unsuccessfully, for weeks. Finally, she'd relented and allowed him to make love to her on the beach, in full view of the village and of fishermen out in the bay. The villagers had smiled at the sight of two of their own consummating their love for each other. From that day on, until her abduction by Rambuka, the couple had rarely been apart. The families of each were delighted by the union and had planned a wedding feast to formalize the love match.

"What happened?" Nathan asked, bringing Joeli back to the present.

"Rambuka take her. It happen one moon before wedding feast take place. Children see the Outcast take her. That was early in dry season. No see her since." Joeli got to his feet and resumed walking.

Nathan followed. He asked, "Has anyone looked for her?"

"Trackers search for days," Joeli responded defensively, "but Rambuka cunning dog. He hide tracks well."

"Where's his hideout?"

Joeli shrugged. "In mountains somewhere." He added, "Waisale still search for her to this day, but Viti Levu is big island."

The pair stopped outside Nathan's bure. They bade each other good night and Nathan retired. Inside, he lay down and reviewed the day's events. As always, his thoughts turned to Susannah. He wondered what she was doing right now.

As sleep approached, a faint noise in the doorway alerted Nathan to the arrival of someone. He looked up and saw it was Selaima. To his surprise, the seductive slave girl smiled and began disrobing.

Nathan shook his head. Getting to his feet he said, "No." By now, Selaima had slipped out of her grass skirt and was standing before him naked. "No," Nathan repeated. The girl looked confused. Nathan picked up her skirt and handed it to her. "I'm sorry."

Selaima nodded to indicate she understood. Nathan's actions confirmed what she'd suspected: the American had given his heart to the white woman. Dressing quickly, she smiled to hide her disappointment and departed.

Nathan lay down and stared at the ceiling.

What the hell's come over you?

He knew it wasn't like him to turn away an available woman—especially not a seductive one like Selaima. Deep down though, he understood. He was consumed by Susannah. There was no room in his life for anyone else. He drifted off to sleep thinking about the Englishwoman, subconsciously caressing the whalebone pendant resting on his chest.

#

On her bed mat in the female slaves' quarters on the other side of the village, Selaima couldn't sleep. After her rejection by the American earlier that evening, sleep was the last thing on her mind.

She wanted revenge—not against Nathan, but against the woman who was keeping him from her.

Rolling lithely to her feet, she crept out of the hut she shared with a dozen other slaves and walked quickly toward the rainforest beyond the village outskirts, taking care as she went not to stumble into any of the Qopa lookouts she knew would be in the vicinity. As she walked, she checked the contents of a small flax bag she carried.

Reaching the edge of the forest, she skirted around it until she found a track, which she then followed for half a mile or so inland. The track led her to a well-concealed cave entrance, which she crawled through. Inside, the cave opened up into a large cavern. A small opening in its roof allowed moonlight through, giving the cavern a cathedral-like quality. This suited Selaima for what she had in mind.

Using two sticks and some dry grass she'd collected outside the cave, she proceeded to rub the sticks together and, in the tradition of her forefathers, made a fire. Then, retrieving special herbs and potions from her bag, she sprinkled them over the flames. The fire erupted into life, its flames leaping skyward as if propelled by gas or some other fuel. Selaima breathed in the resulting aromas, soon falling into a trance.

In her trance-like state, she then began chanting, summoning the darker spirits to fill the void she believed existed around her. Although her eyes were closed, she could see the spirits. They appeared as bat-like creatures, always moving too fast to see clearly.

Selaima was working herself into a state. Her chanting quickly degenerated into grunts and she began frothing at the mouth. A feeling of faintness descended on her. She knew from experience she'd soon lose consciousness and so had to hurry if she were to achieve what she'd set out to do.

Screaming at the spirits, she shouted, "Keep the missionary woman and Nathan Johnson apart!" She imagined she saw the spirits react violently at the mention of *missionary woman*, but couldn't be sure. Nearly out of it, she added, "Remove her out of the way of temptation so that Nathan Johnson has eyes only for me."

With that, Selaima lost consciousness and fell forward into the fire, its heat scorching the flesh from her face, neck, and arms. She would wake when sunlight replaced the moonlight that presently shone through the opening in the cavern roof above her. When she did, the skin on her face, neck, and arms would be unmarked, completely free of even the tiniest blemish.

Selaima didn't understand *the gift*, but she trusted it. It gave her magical powers and those powers protected her just as she knew they would protect Nathan.

16

Squawking seagulls attacked the decaying remains of shark carcasses as Nathan walked along the beach. The carcasses were all that was left of the sharks after the villagers had finished with them following the miracle the Shark Caller had performed.

Above the squawking gulls and the distant thunder of waves on the reef, the sound of children singing reached Nathan. Looking over at the nearby mission station, he could see Susannah leading a dozen Qopa children in singing a hymn in English. The strains of "The Lord Is My Shepherd" carried to him on a gentle breeze.

Nathan watched Susannah intently. He thought back to the previous day and silently cursed, knowing how close he'd come to kissing her near the very spot he was now standing. Susannah finally saw him and waved. He waved back and resumed his walk, leaving the young woman to continue leading the children in song.

Further along the beach, Nathan found Drake Senior chopping up a length of driftwood for firewood. On the sand beside him, Nathan could see the missionary's trusty pistol lay on top of his Bible. *Covering his bets both ways,* Nathan thought. The good reverend was clearly taking no chances following the recent raid.

Drake Senior didn't acknowledge Nathan. The younger man wasn't surprised. He was under no illusions: Susannah's father didn't approve of him and nothing he did was likely to change that.

Just beyond Drake Senior, Nathan stopped at the rock memorial that Waisale had built in memory of his beloved Sina. Nathan wondered if Waisale would ever find her. From what Joeli had told him, he knew that was unlikely. To find Sina, Waisale would have to find the outcasts' hideout. The villagers had been hunting Rambuka and his outcasts for years without success.

Nathan had a sudden urge to test his fitness. His chest wound was healing nicely, but he hadn't really put it to the test. Checking that he was out of sight of the mission station, he stripped off and ran naked into the sea. As soon as he was waist-deep in the water, he began swimming parallel to the shore.

Nathan swam hard for a hundred yards or so then turned and swam back to where he'd started. He finished feeling surprisingly strong and vowed he'd swim further tomorrow.

#

Later, keeping to their daily routine, Drake Senior and Susannah walked up to the village. There, they circulated among small groups of villagers, praying over them and reading excerpts aloud from their Bibles. Some villagers were receptive while others looked bemused as the father-and-daughter missionary team tried to explain, in faltering Fijian, how the son of their god had died nailed to a cross for their sins and how it was evil to worship stone idols.

"Why do you worship the son of a god who is nailed to a wooden cross?" a young mother asked, pointing to an image of the crucifixion on the cover of Drake Senior's Bible.

"Because he died for my sins . . . and yours," Drake Senior answered patiently.

"When did he do this?" the woman's husband asked.

"Many centuries ago."

"Why would the son of your god die for our sins before we were even born?" the young mother asked.

As Drake Senior battled with the Fijian language to try to get through to his bemused audience, Susannah found her attention was wandering. She couldn't help thinking how peaceful Momi Bay looked. Along the shore, fishermen were standing, waist-deep in the water, casting nets while others, with spears at the ready, were stalking fish in the shallows. Among the rocks, women and children searched for mussels and other shellfish.

Susannah noticed a young couple walking hand in hand through the village. They had eyes only for each other. She couldn't help thinking what a handsome couple they made. Watching them took her back to her teenage years and the innocent relationship between her and her first love, the handsome Cockney lad. She looked wistfully at the youthful Fijian couple as they disappeared into a bure. They clearly had plans that didn't involve anyone else.

Susannah suddenly noticed Nathan walking through the village. He was heading toward the bure he'd been allocated.

The young Englishwoman pretended not to see him. Moments later, she sneaked a glance at him only to find he was staring directly at her. They smiled fleetingly at each other just before he disappeared into his bure.

Susannah found she was breathing faster than usual and her pulse was racing. Aware her father had observed her looking at Nathan, she quickly pulled herself together and tried to focus on what Drake Senior was saying to their growing audience.

Shouts from a lookout alerted everyone to the arrival of a foreign craft in the bay. Susannah looked up to see a huge drua, or sacred canoe, rounding the headland. The villagers stopped what they were doing and gestured excitedly toward the vessel. It belonged to a friendly tribe from the Mamanucas island group and was laden with items of trade.

Nathan emerged from his bure, attracted by the shouting. He immediately saw the drua. It reminded him of the craft he saw being launched back in Levuka. The young man wondered if the launching of this drua had been accompanied by the same number of human sacrifices.

Led by Joeli, the villagers walked down to the beach to greet the Mamanucans. Susannah and her father joined them and quickly found themselves being carried along by the throng of excited people. Nathan casually followed along behind.

By the time the villagers reached the beach, the drua was rapidly closing with the shore. In the bow of the vessel was Lemeki, the Mamanucans' ratu. A large scar down one side of his face spoiled his otherwise fine features. However, his most notable feature was his hairstyle. Three feet across and at least that high, it was even more massive than Joeli's—and brighter, too. It was dyed red with blue stripes running through it.

Lemeki spotted Joeli on the beach and nodded toward him. Joeli stared back sullenly. Although Lemeki was an old friend and long-time ally of the Qopa, Joeli wasn't at all happy about the other's hair. As the ratu of Momi Bay, he prided himself on having the most magnificent hairstyle and didn't like playing second string to any-one—especially someone from another clan.

When the drua reached the shallows, the strong and agile Lemeki jumped onto the sand and strode up to Joeli. The Mamanucan smiled inwardly as he noticed Joeli couldn't take his eyes off his hair.

Despite his jealousy, Joeli put on a brave face and smiled. "Bula," he said. "You look well today, my brother."

Lemeki responded, "Bula, it has been too many seasons, my brother." He suddenly assumed a grave expression. "I received news of your father's death only recently. Iremaia was a great ratu." Lemeki suddenly smiled and slapped Joeli on the back. "Now the Qopa have another great ratu."

Momentarily forgetting Lemeki's hairstyle, Joeli glanced at the vegetables, fruit, live turtles, and other trade items in the drua. He asked, "What is it you hope to trade those for?"

Lemeki looked pointedly at the remains of the beached shark carcasses. "We, the Mamanucans, would be happy to relieve you of what is left of those."

Joeli laughed and embraced Lemeki. "I knew the smell of shark would soon bring the hungry Mamanucans here."

Still laughing, Joeli led Lemeki up to the village. The other Mamanucans followed with their slaves, who carried their trade items. They chattered animatedly with the local villagers as old friendships were renewed.

Following along, Nathan noted that the visitors' slaves, who he'd learn later were from another island group, were of such noble appearance they appeared more like royalty than slaves. He looked out for Susannah and her father, but couldn't see them in the crowd.

In the village, the Mamanucans exchanged their goods for dried shark meat and fins. There was plenty to go round. All parties appeared satisfied with the trade.

Nathan finally saw Susannah. He was disappointed to see she was still with her father. Taking a deep breath, he wandered over to join them. "Hello, Susannah," he smiled. He was happy to see that Susannah looked genuinely pleased to see him.

"Hello, Nathan."

Nathan looked at Drake Senior and immediately noted the man did not look at all pleased to see him.

He knows I lust after his daughter.

Steeling himself, Nathan said, "Good afternoon, Reverend."

"Mr. Johnson," Drake Senior mumbled.

The three turned their attention back to the proceedings. Nathan and Susannah pretended to take keen interest in what was going on, but their body language suggested they had other things on their mind. Their interest in each other was not lost on Susannah's father.

Drake Senior took Susannah by the arm and addressed Nathan sternly. "Excuse us. We have more of the Lord's work to do." He then began escorting Susannah back toward the mission station. Walking away, Susannah glanced back at Nathan, who flashed her a quick smile.

#

That night, the villagers and their guests watched as the Mamanucans' slaves tended a strip of heated rocks in the ground. There was an air of excitement.

The two ratus, Joeli and Lemeki, were sitting side by side on a raised platform overlooking the heated rocks. Joeli was barely recognizable. Since the Mamanucans' arrival, Joeli had received a makeover. Cloak upon cloak had been draped over his beefy frame so that he looked considerably bigger than usual, and he wore a pearl necklace, bracelets, and bangles he'd acquired in recent trades. But his most outstanding feature was his hairstyle. No longer resembling a huge orange puffball, his hair had been dyed bright yellow and elongated so that it rose even higher than Lemeki's.

Now it was Lemeki's turn to be sullen. The look on his face told everyone he wasn't happy about being upstaged.

A dapper-looking Nathan sauntered over to see what was happening. He noticed Susannah and her father in the crowd and debated whether to join them. He'd had enough of the cold shoulder treatment he'd been receiving from Drake Senior, but like a moth drawn to a flame, he found himself drawn to Susannah. Sidling up to her, he said, "Good evening."

Susannah disguised her pleasure at seeing Nathan behind a polite smile, but her heart was racing. "Good evening, Nathan," she murmured.

Nathan nodded to Drake Senior, who responded with the briefest of nods. "What's going on here?" the young man asked feigning interest in the proceedings.

"The Mamanucans' slaves are about to give a firewalking demonstration," Susannah explained, knowing full well that Nathan's interest lay elsewhere.

None the wiser, Nathan was about to question her further when a roar went up from the assembled. He looked around to see half a dozen slaves, all men, emerging from a small hut. Seemingly in a trance, they chanted as they walked toward the heated rocks. The rocks were so hot they glowed red. A large slave then dropped a piece of tapa, or bark cloth, onto the nearest rocks and it immediately burst into flames. The chanting continued as the slave stepped barefoot onto the rocks and started walking across them. Nathan noted he showed no sign of discomfort let alone pain. The other slaves followed, trancelike, in single file. Nathan and the Drakes looked on in disbelief.

Susannah turned to Drake Senior. "How on earth do they do that, Papa?"

Drake Senior shrugged. He was as mystified as her. The crowd voiced its admiration as the slaves retraced their steps across the hot rocks. "I hear the firewalkers are all of the Tui Sawau tribe, from an island south of here," Drake Senior said.

As the missionary talked, the back of Nathan's hand brushed against Susannah's. To each, the other's touch seemed as hot as the red-hot coals before them.

Susannah was tempted to leave the back of her hand resting against his, but she reflexively withdrew it. She immediately regretted this as his touch had thrilled her so.

For his part, Nathan wanted to reach across and grab her hand, but he wasn't sure how she'd react. The speed with which she'd removed her hand from his suggested she wasn't receptive to his advances.

They glanced at each other fleetingly. Each hid their feelings from the other, but the emotions of each were in full flight. Susannah suddenly felt giddy. She knew she should walk away now, but lacked the will.

Unaware of the mini-drama occurring next to him, Drake Senior said, "They are the only people in all of Fiji who can do this. The common belief is a spirit god has given them a supernatural immunity to fire."

Nathan and Susannah pretended to be interested in Drake Senior's explanation, but their minds were elsewhere. Susannah was sure her face must be bright red and prayed her father wouldn't notice.

Drake Senior didn't notice, but Selaima did. Hidden in the crowd opposite, her eyes never left Susannah's face. The jealous slave girl searched Susannah's face for some outward sign of the curse she knew would soon befall her. Just how that curse would manifest itself, and when, she wasn't sure. What she was sure of was the spirits would ensure that the missionary woman was placed beyond the reach of Nathan—for that is what her curse demanded and her curses always came about.

The firewalkers finally finished their ritual and dispersed to the cheers of the crowd.

Sensing something was up between the Nathan and Susannah, Drake Senior racked his brains for a solution to a problem he'd known had been brewing for some time. While he trusted his daughter and knew she'd eventually recognize the ungodly American adventurer was unworthy of her, he didn't want to see her get hurt in the meantime.

What to do?

The answer came to him in a flash of intuition. Turning to Nathan, he said, "Mr. Johnson, perhaps you would like to join us for supper tomorrow evening?"

Nathan couldn't believe his ears. Neither could Susannah. Nathan stammered, "Well, I—"

"Good," Drake Senior said quickly. "That's settled then." The reverend then marched off, pulling Susannah with him.

Susannah looked back at Nathan. Her expression told him she was as mystified as he was as to why her father had invited him to supper. Needless to say, Nathan was secretly delighted—and so was Susannah.

Walking toward the mission station, Drake Senior prayed he'd done the right thing. Reviewing his rationale, he believed if Susannah spent long enough in the company of the American, talking to him and hearing his selfish viewpoints on life, she'd come to realize he was the egotistical, ungodly, unholy bastard the good reverend knew him to be. *Familiarity breeds contempt*, he reminded himself.

17

The following morning, villagers assembled on the beach to farewell their good friends, the Mamanucans, who at that moment were readying their drua for the return voyage to their island. Hosts and guests alike were highly satisfied with the outcome of the visit: the trading had been successful, old friendships had been strengthened, and new liaisons forged.

As the drua sailed away from the shore, the Mamanucans' ratu, Lemeki, looked directly at Joeli, who was standing in the shallows. The two nodded gravely to each other. Despite their competitiveness, the respect each had for the other was obvious to all.

Nathan watched from the village as the Mamanucans sailed out of the bay, then turned his attention back to the village. He was hoping to see Susannah, but was disappointed to find she'd returned to the mission station. Nathan knew he'd be on tenterhooks until he saw her that night at the supper engagement her father had invited him to. He was looking forward to that, even if he wasn't sure what Drake Senior was up to.

#

Later, as he wandered along the village outskirts, Nathan noticed Joeli approaching, or, more correctly, he saw his high, bright yellow hair approaching. "Bula," he called out.

"Bula, Nathan Johnson," Joeli responded. "You look well today, my brother." The ratu stopped before Nathan. "Tomorrow, we collect trepang to complete our trade."

Nathan smiled at the thought of taking delivery of his precious sea slugs. "How long do you expect that to take?"

"Few days. You have them before ship return," he said, referring to the *Rendezvous*'s scheduled return.

The boom of a musket being discharged behind the village caused Nathan to jump. Joeli smiled as two more shots rang out. "My warriors practice killing." He motioned to Nathan. "Come."

Nathan followed Joeli to a valley behind the mission station. There, they found all the village's able-bodied warriors assembled. Waisale was among them. As always, his pink hair set him apart from the others. The Qopa were practicing priming, firing, and reloading the muskets Nathan had supplied. Their technique had improved little since they'd fought off Rambuka's outcasts. Muskets were going off in all directions, and the valley was already a haze of gunsmoke. No thought was being given to safety.

A warrior dropped to the ground when he saw a musket being aimed at his belly at point-blank range. Its owner was trying to load it, not aware it was already loaded. The musket suddenly discharged, its shot flying just over the head of the warrior who was now lying face-down in the dirt. The lucky warrior immediately jumped up and berated the man who had nearly killed him.

Joeli looked on with misplaced pride as he watched his warriors practice. Turning to Nathan, he was bemused to find the young American was rocking with laughter. Joeli scowled.

Realizing he risked offending Joeli, Nathan assumed a serious expression. "Their technique is wrong," he said seriously. "They're more likely to kill each other than their enemies if they keep doing what they're doing."

Joeli looked aggrieved. "You teach?"

Without another word, Nathan walked down and joined the warriors. He proceeded to show them how to use their new weapons correctly. Joeli looked on, impressed.

Also looking on, unobserved, was Drake Senior. He was far from impressed at the sight of Nathan teaching members of his flock how to use the white man's weapon of death.

#

As night approached at Momi Bay, Nathan left the village and walked toward the mission station. In his white muslin shirt, fashionable cotton breeches, and dress boots—the same outfit he'd worn to the dance in Levuka several weeks earlier—he looked every inch the debonair gentleman, albeit somewhat nervous. He self-consciously rearranged a bunch of flowers he was holding as he walked.

Behind him, the sky was turning a dramatic orange and pink as the sun set. Still the long-awaited wet season hadn't arrived at Momi Bay. *Any day now,* the villagers had promised.

A hundred yards ahead, Nathan could see Drake Senior chopping firewood outside the newly rebuilt mission house. A lantern burning inside the house cast a warm glow in the fading light.

Fifty yards from the mission house, Nathan saw Susannah appear in the open doorway. She was framed by the light behind her. Even from a distance, with her hair up and dressed as she was in a white cotton dress, she looked especially beautiful. She smiled and waved when she saw Nathan then retreated back inside to attend to the meal she'd been preparing. Her father continued chopping wood.

In the gloom, Nathan suddenly stumbled when he caught his foot on something concealed in the long grass. He saw immediately it was the body of one of the village lookouts. The lookout lay on his back, a tomahawk protruding from his skull. His sightless eyes stared up, almost accusingly, at the startled young American.

Nathan dropped his flowers and pulled his pistol from his belt. He remained crouched down and looked around for the other lookouts who always patrolled the area between the mission station and the village at dusk.

Holy shit!

There was no sign of them. Nathan cursed himself for not noticing this earlier. He started running toward the mission station, shouting as he ran. "Reverend Drake! Susannah!"

Drake Senior looked up. At the same time, Susannah stepped outside to see what the commotion was about. Behind them, a sudden movement caught Nathan's eye. He saw the Outcast, Rambuka, looming up out of the shadows, knife in hand. Rambuka was flanked by two of his followers. None of them had muskets, only traditional weapons. Whatever it was they were planning to do, it was obvious to Nathan they planned to do it in silence.

The Drakes saw the danger too late. Susannah screamed as Drake Senior raised his axe to meet the sudden threat.

The nearest outcast, a tall, rangy man with a heavily tattooed face, threw his spear at the missionary. The weapon tore through Drake Senior's throat, its serrated point protruding out the back of his neck.

Susannah opened her mouth to scream again, but any sound was stifled by Rambuka, who clamped one hand over her mouth. She could only watch, horrified, as her father fought to draw a breath.

Choking, Drake Senior slowly toppled forward, gasping for air. Down on hands and knees, he died like that.

"No!" Nathan shouted. He couldn't believe what was happening. It seemed surreal—as if everything were occurring in slow motion.

In the rapidly fading light, Susannah struggled futilely in Rambuka's steel grip as the Outcast dragged her toward the nearby trees. Nathan sprinted toward them, determined to get to Susannah before the jungle and the darkness swallowed her up.

Noting his intentions, the other two outcasts moved to intercept him. Nathan aimed his pistol and fired, killing the nearest attacker, a big man with a missing ear. The tattooed outcast charged Nathan, club in hand. The two met head on. The outcast aimed his club for Nathan's head. With no time to reload his pistol, Nathan drew his Bowie knife and slashed the man's nose, almost cutting it off. The wounded outcast dropped his club and put both hands to his face, trying to stem the flow of blood. Using the butt of the pistol he was still holding in his other hand, Nathan savagely clubbed the outcast twice over the head, knocking him unconscious.

Looking around, he could see Rambuka had almost reached the cover of the trees twenty yards or so ahead. Nathan desperately tried to reload his pistol as he sprinted to save Susannah. Knowing he was running out of time, he aimed the unloaded weapon at Rambuka, shouting, "Stop!"

Believing the pistol was loaded, the Outcast pulled up, removed his hand from Susannah's mouth, and held the blade of his knife to her throat, making sure he kept his hostage between himself and Nathan.

Terrified, Susannah cried, "Nathan!"

Nathan knew he somehow had to delay Rambuka until reinforcements arrived. Behind him, he could hear villagers coming to investigate, alerted by the pistol shot. Rambuka was also aware of the threat. He began backing up toward the trees, keeping his knife at Susannah's throat. Nathan followed, pistol raised in the firing position.

As she was being dragged along, Susannah spoke to Rambuka in his native tongue. "Please," she pleaded, "don't hurt me." Susannah instinctively knew the man accosting her was the cannibal they called the Outcast. She recalled seeing him, or someone very like him, leading the attack on the village. More to the point, she was aware of Rambuka's reputation for abducting women.

Rambuka grinned sadistically at her then looked at Nathan. In pigeon English he warned, "Any closer White-Face, I cut her throat."

Nathan hesitated. Rambuka motioned to him to drop the pistol. Again Nathan hesitated. Knowing he didn't have long, Rambuka pricked Susannah's throat with the point of his knife. The young woman gasped as the knife's sharp tip drew a drop of blood.

Momentarily beaten, Nathan let his pistol fall to the ground.

Rambuka sneered, "She mine now, White-Face." The Outcast gave another sadistic smile and then dragged Susannah into the rainforest.

Susannah screamed, "Nathan! Help me!"

Nathan retrieved his pistol and chased after the pair. In the dark, he could hear them crashing through the undergrowth. Nathan tried to follow the sounds, but became disoriented as he charged blindly to left and right. The sounds of his quarry gradually faded. He looked around, desperate, but it was now too dark to see any tracks. Nathan shouted. "Susannah!" It was a long, despairing cry. He turned and ran back to recruit the assistance of the villagers.

Emerging from the rainforest, Nathan was relieved to see Joeli, Waisale, and a dozen other warriors running toward him. All except the young ratu carried muskets. Nathan shouted to them, "Hurry!"

Joeli saw the two outcasts and Drake Senior lying nearby as he ran up to Nathan. He asked, "What happen?"

"It was Rambuka," Nathan said breathlessly. "He took Susannah."

"How many?"

"I only saw Rambuka," Nathan said, "and these two." He motioned to the two outcasts on the ground. The tattooed outcast was starting to come round. The man's face was a bloody mess as a result of the knife wound he'd suffered. Nathan pointed to him, saying, "That one's still alive."

Joeli nodded to two warriors. They immediately grabbed the wounded outcast by the ankles and began dragging him back toward the village while Joeli translated what Nathan had told him for the benefit of the other warriors.

When Waisale heard what had happened, his heart went out to Nathan. Having lost his beloved Sina in near-identical circumstances, he knew what the American was going through at that very moment.

At a nod from Joeli, Nathan led them at a fast trot into the rainforest. The American ran as fast as the darkness and heavy undergrowth would allow. Joeli ran at his shoulder. Behind them, the other warriors fanned out, covering a wider area.

It soon dawned on Nathan he was running blind. He wasn't sure Susannah and her abductor had come this way. Truth be known, at that moment he didn't even know where north was. The deeper they plunged into the jungle, the more lost he became. Feelings of panic set in. *Please let me find her!* He grew more desperate, trying to find some sign of his beautiful Susannah.

Realizing Nathan was lost, Joeli grabbed him by the arm and held him fast.

"We have to keep going!" Nathan protested.

"Too dark!" Joeli said simply. The young ratu released his grip on Nathan then put his fingers to his lips and peeled off a shrill whistle. Turning to Nathan, he added, "We search in morning." He whistled twice more.

One by one, the other warriors materialized out of the darkness. Addressing them in Fijian, Joeli said, "We will begin the search at first light."

"We can't give up now!" Nathan complained. "He has Susannah."

Joeli remained firm. Shaking his head, he said, "We search in morning." He turned to return to the village.

"What about the outcast we captured? He'll know where Rambuka is taking Susannah."

For the first time, Joeli smiled. "He will be questioned." He began retracing his steps to the village. Nathan and the others followed.

Walking behind Nathan, Waisale looked sympathetically at the American's back. His thoughts went to his beloved Sina.

Although Susannah's abduction was tragic for those concerned, Waisale knew the wounded outcast could lead them to Rambuka's hideout—and to the women he'd abducted.

18

Beneath a full moon, a large crowd had gathered on the riverbank near the village to watch the interrogation of the wounded outcast. The captive was lying on his back, his hands tied behind him; what was left of his nose was covered in congealed blood, a legacy of the damage Nathan's Bowie knife had inflicted earlier that evening.

To the wild beating of drums, warriors performed a cibi, or war dance, to demonstrate their superiority over their captive. With clubs and spears raised high, they danced aggressively only inches away from him. He looked up at them fearlessly and laughed openly at their efforts. This incensed one warrior, who kicked him in the face, dazing him and drawing more blood. Another warrior urinated over him.

The drumming softened and the warriors were pushed aside by a dozen near-naked maidens who performed a wate, or dance, aimed at sexually humiliating their captive. To the cheers of the onlookers, the nubile maidens left nothing to the imagination as they simulated intercourse and performed other crude gestures in front of and over their captive. This age-old insult was too much even for him, and he closed his eyes to try to escape this ultimate disgrace.

The drumming ceased as Joeli arrived. He was accompanied by Nathan and Waisale. As one, the dancers and other villagers prostrated themselves before their ratu. Joeli nodded to his warriors, indicating the interrogation of the captive should begin.

A warrior tied a rope around the outcast's ankles and threw the other end of the rope over a branch that extended out over the river. Two husky men then retrieved the dangling rope end and began pulling on it. The captive was pulled feet-first and ended up hanging headfirst just above the water while the men supported his weight. The villagers cheered at his predicament.

Addressing the captive, Joeli asked, "Where is Rambuka's hideout?"

The captive spat in Joeli's direction. "Eat shit, you dog!"

Joeli nodded toward the two husky men, who immediately paid off the rope, lowering the captive into the river until his head and torso were submerged. Holding his breath, the captive thrashed about under water trying to free himself.

Nathan looked on impassively. His fingers strayed to the whale bone pendant he wore. His thoughts were with Susannah; concern for her consumed him. The present seemed like a living nightmare—more surreal than ever.

One who was taking more interest than most in the drama being played out was Selaima. The slave girl knew it was because of the curse she'd placed on Susannah that this was happening. Although she was delighted the Englishwoman had been taken from Nathan, she was afraid the captive would reveal the whereabouts of the outcasts' hideout.

This was something she hadn't foreseen and she wondered, momentarily, if the *gift* had let her down.

The captive's movements were becoming more desperate as he was starved of air. Joeli nodded and the men lifted the outcast out of the water. The ratu gave the captive a few moments to regain his breath then, once more, asked, "Where is your hideout?"

The captive shouted, "I will die before I tell you that, you miserable—"

Before he could finish the insult, the husky men lowered him into the water a second time. Again, he thrashed about. Joeli waited longer this time before motioning to his men to lift him up.

The captive emerged coughing and spluttering. This time, he was ready to talk. "Our hideout is at Tomanivi," he spluttered, "three days' march inland. Please! Don't let me drown!"

"Where exactly?" Joeli asked.

Looking on, Selaima willed the captive to remain silent.

"In the valley that runs north to south on this side of the mountain," the captive gasped.

Selaima's heart dropped. All she could hope for now was that Nathan wasn't so committed to the Englishwoman that he'd join the expedition that would most assuredly be mounted to rescue her. If he remained in the village, that's when she'd work her magic on him.

Satisfied, Joeli walked off. Nathan and Waisale followed. As they departed, Joeli briefly raised one hand. At this signal, his men lowered the captive into the river again, this time leaving him to drown.

Wanting confirmation the captive had revealed the whereabouts of Rambuka's hideout, Nathan hurried to Joeli's side. "Did he tell you what you needed to know?" he asked anxiously.

Joeli nodded briefly and kept walking. Neither he nor his two companions spared a second thought for the drowning outcast behind them. Joeli could only think of recovering the sacred golden tabua Rambuka had stolen from the village, while Nathan and Waisale could only think of rescuing the women Rambuka had taken from them.

The young ratu looked up as the moon disappeared behind clouds. "The wet season will arrive tomorrow." He spoke English for Nathan's benefit.

Nathan wasn't listening. He just wanted the night to end and the chase to begin.

Watching the three men from afar, Selaima was in no doubt that Joeli would go after Rambuka. She knew how much the golden tabua meant to him. What she didn't know was whether Nathan would accompany Joeli. She prayed to the spirits that he wouldn't for she knew that to venture into the outcasts' territory was to invite death.

In the village, Joeli paused outside his bure and turned to Nathan. He placed one hand on the American's shoulder. "We leave for Tomanivi early."

Nathan nodded and without a word walked on to his own bure. Inside it, he cleaned his musket and rammed food, spare clothing, and ammunition into a backpack in preparation for the early morning departure. Finally, he lay down and tried to sleep.

Sleep refused to come. Instead, a million thoughts coursed

through his mind. A picture of Susannah being raped by Rambuka and his followers kept coming to him.

Nathan gave up trying to sleep. Instead, he lay there, on his back staring up at his bure's thatched roof and thinking of the events that had brought him to this point in his life. It seemed like he'd been in Fiji for years, not weeks. He felt very little connectivity between the self-centered man he was when he arrived and the man he was now. And, he knew, that change was due entirely to Susannah. From the moment he'd first seen her, he'd been unable to think of anything or anyone else. She'd drawn out his real self from deep inside him—a side he never knew existed. Because of her, he felt more alive than ever before.

Before Susannah, all he'd cared about was attaining more wealth or buying more land so he could mingle in higher social circles. Material things suddenly seemed unimportant. All that mattered to him now was Susannah. Without her, life would be meaningless and empty.

For the first time ever, Nathan realized he cared for someone more than he cared for himself. He'd known that the instant Susannah was abducted. She was his whole world now.

Nathan knew he would do whatever it took, whatever the sacrifice, to rescue her—even if it meant giving his own life. He only hoped he could reach her before she was harmed.

\#

While Nathan was trying in vain to get to sleep, Susannah was having the same problem. Exhausted after her abduction earlier that night, she was now lying beneath a makeshift bivouac of branches and leaves that Rambuka had hastily assembled, trying to get to sleep.

The Outcast lay nearby, sleeping soundly despite the cold and the light rain that was now causing water to drip down onto him and his captive. Both were covered in scratches—a result of their headlong flight through the dense jungle earlier. A vine now linked them. Before going to sleep, Rambuka had tied one end of the vine to Susannah's wrist and the other end to his. It was now stretched tight, ensuring any movement by his captive would wake him.

After snatching Susannah from the mission station, Rambuka had dragged her a good six miles inland before stopping for the night. He knew the best trackers in the world couldn't follow his tracks in the dark, but had decided to put as much distance as he could between himself and his former tribesmen before stopping.

Rambuka knew Joeli and his warriors would be on his trail at first light. Quite apart from rescuing the Englishwoman, he knew his half-brother would want to recover the golden tabua he and his followers had taken from the village.

What Rambuka didn't know was whether his companions had survived the fight at the mission station. He was pretty sure one of them had been killed, but wasn't sure about the other. If one had survived, Rambuka knew Joeli would already know where his Tomanivi hideout was.

Right now, though, he had more pressing matters to attend to— such as reaching his hideout before his enemies overtook him. Normally, that wouldn't have been a problem, but having to drag a woman along with him complicated things somewhat.

Rather than be captured, Rambuka promised himself he'd kill the woman and flee on his own.

Lying close to her captor, Susannah was in shock. She had been ever since she'd seen her father choking to death with a spear through his neck. Even now, despite her predicament, she could think only of her father. The vision of his gruesome death filled her mind and try as she may, she couldn't dispel it.

Finally, Nathan forced his way into her mind. The realization struck her that she wanted to experience what it was like to make love and marry and have children. It struck her like a thunderbolt. And she knew she wanted all that with Nathan. Lying beside Rambuka, those dreams seemed so remote now.

Susannah wondered if Nathan would come looking for her. She was now in no doubt he lusted after her, as she did him, but was not at all sure he cared deeply enough for her to risk his life.

She wondered, too, whether her dear papa's assessment of Nathan was correct. The words *self-centered* and *ungodly* still rang in her ears.

When she weighed it all up, Susannah knew the only one she could rely on was God. With that, she immediately prayed that this nightmare would end.

Please, God, hear my prayers!

Part Two

THE LAND OF RED RAIN

1

Heavy rain on the thatched roof of Nathan's bure announced the arrival of the wet season in Viti Levu's western regions. It also woke Nathan from a fitful sleep. He'd been awake most of the night, thinking about Susannah. Every time he'd dozed off, terrifying images of the young woman being abused by Rambuka had forced themselves into his mind, waking him.

Still half asleep, Nathan was momentarily disorientated. Looking through his bure's open doorway, through the sheets of rain, he could see it was not yet dawn. Yet people were already moving about.

Rousing himself, he jumped up from his bed mat and quickly dressed. Then, slipping his pre-packed backpack over his shoulders, he tucked his pistol into his belt, grabbed his musket, and hurried outside.

Nathan fell in beside a handful of warriors who were making their way to the village outskirts where others had already assembled. Joeli was preparing to address them. In total, Nathan counted twenty men. Sadly, they represented virtually all that remained of the village's ablebodied warriors. Waisale and the one-eyed Babitu were among them.

All had muskets except for Joeli, who carried his preferred

tomahawk and whale bone club. Many carried traditional weapons as well.

Everyone ignored the rain, which was still pelting down.

Studying Joeli and the other warriors, Nathan immediately noticed a major difference from the last time he'd seen them: gone were the extravagant hairstyles. Overnight, the warriors had washed the dye out of their hair and cut their frizzy locks back to more manageable proportions. Nathan guessed this had been prompted by the need to be able to blend in with the terrain and vegetation in the days ahead. *After all,* he mused, *bright yellow or shocking pink hair would stand out like dog's balls in the greenery of a rainforest.* Nathan looked at Joeli and Waisale as if seeing them for the first time.

When Joeli was satisfied everyone had arrived, he announced, "We know where our enemies hide." Speaking in his native tongue, he had to shout to make himself heard above the driving rain. "The Outcast has our golden tabua and now he has two of our women," he said, referring to Susannah and Waisale's betrothed, Sina. Holding his huge club above his head, he shouted, "We will take back what is ours and send our enemies to the Underworld where they belong."

With that, the other warriors raised their muskets and broke out into a war chant.

Watching them, Nathan could only guess what Joeli had said to stir them up so. The American was becoming impatient. He wanted to start moving. To his way of thinking, this was not the time to stand around talking.

Joeli knew differently. He realized he was quite possibly about to lead his remaining warriors to their deaths, so it was important to remind them what they were about to put their lives on the line for.

Before they set off, villagers appeared out of the rain and began bestowing their best wishes on friends and loved ones. Selaima was among them, though she hung back, anxious not to attract attention.

The slave girl scanned the faces of the men who were with Joeli. Her heart sank when she saw Nathan. The sight of his musket and backpack immediately told her he was planning to accompany the others.

While Selaima was observing Nathan, she was unaware she herself was being observed. Inoki, the elderly healer who had helped nurse Nathan back to health, was watching her from afar. He'd suspected for some time she was up to no good, but he had no proof. So, rather than report his concerns, he'd decided to keep an eye on her.

Some of the villagers had misgivings about what Joeli and the others in his pathetically small raiding party were planning. Among them was Kamisese, the respected toreni koro, or village headman. He challenged Joeli, saying, "You could be walking into Rambuka's trap like a fish swimming into a net."

"I have considered that," Joeli shot back.

"It is dangerous for you to take all our fighting men with you. Rambuka's outcasts could be waiting to attack the village as soon as you have gone."

By now, the other villagers had fallen silent. They sensed there was truth in what the headman was saying.

"That is a risk I must take," Joeli countered. "As long as Rambuka is free to come and go as he likes, and steal from us, we lose respect. The dog must be punished. We are growing weaker by the day and Rambuka is growing stronger. It is now or never." He added, "You forget old man, Rambuka has the golden tabua. I must recover it and return it to its rightful place, here."

Acknowledging the wisdom in Joeli's words, Kamisese nodded, saying, "May the war spirits go with you then."

Joeli turned and led his warriors inland at a fast trot. Nathan followed, bringing up the rear. Behind them, the villagers offered up chants to the gods of war.

The villagers continued chanting until long after the departing warriors had been swallowed up by the rainforest. Then, singly or in pairs, they trudged back to the village.

Selaima remained behind, staring in the direction she knew the warriors were heading. She was feeling desolate. While her curse had effectively removed Susannah from Nathan's reach, it hadn't prevented the American from leaving to look for her. She decided it was time to call on the *gift* once more and conjure up another curse.

The slave girl entered the rainforest and quickly made her way to the same cave she usually went to when she needed privacy. So focused was she on what she was about to do, she didn't notice she was being followed.

Inoki had decided to follow Selaima as soon as she had struck off into the forest on her own. He was becoming more convinced she was up to no good. Now he was having trouble keeping up with the young woman. Battling the driving rain, and slipping and sliding in the mud underfoot, he had to force his old legs to move as fast as they could to keep up.

Peering through the rain, Inoki suddenly realized he could no longer see the slave girl. He wasn't to know she'd entered the cave via the concealed entrance only she knew about. The opening was so narrow, he missed it and walked on by. After a fruitless search, he gave up and headed back to the village.

Meanwhile, in the same cavern she'd used to cast a spell on Susannah previously, Selaima prepared to weave her magic once more. This time, she used different methods, shunning the need for a fire. Reaching into the small flax bag she carried, she withdrew a potent mix of herbs which she placed in her mouth and swallowed. Then she stripped naked and began dancing. Chanting while dancing in an ever-widening circle, she fell into a trance almost immediately.

Calling to the spirits, she chanted, "Bring Nathan Johnson home safely to me." Selaima repeated this over and over until all the words ran into one. It didn't occur to her to place another curse on Susannah because she considered the Englishwoman dead already. She believed Susannah would never be seen again.

Finally, Selaima became delirious and collapsed onto the rock floor.

#

Several miles to the east, the fleet-footed Qopa warriors were still maintaining a fast pace after two hours of steady running. They were following two wiry trackers who tirelessly criss-crossed the terrain ahead, looking for some sign of the Outcast and his hostage.

Behind them, slipping and sliding in the mud, Nathan was struggling to keep up. He couldn't believe how much fitness he'd lost. There was a time, not so long ago, when he could have maintained this pace all day and hardly raised a sweat. At the moment, his chest wound was hurting and he was already regretting his decision to carry a backpack. He noted his companions traveled light, carrying emergency rations in pouches that hung from their waists.

As he ran, Nathan's life flashed across his mind. It suddenly dawned on him that, until now, he'd never done anything worthwhile before. Certainly, he'd achieved much in terms of wealth, conquest, and landownership, but nothing that warmed his heart or that could remotely be considered noble. If honest with himself, he knew he'd lived a superficial existence that was dominated by the desire to *prove* to others that he was a man rather than simply *living* like a man. He knew now that Drake Senior had recognized that in him; it was no wonder he'd tried to come between him and Susannah.

You saw right through me, didn't you, Reverend?

Susannah was the one individual in his life he'd ever felt any true love for. As he thought of her, his imagination took on a life of its own. In his mind's eye he saw Rambuka's outcasts raping her repeatedly then feeding her broken body to the dogs.

Banishing the ghastly images from his mind, Nathan pushed himself harder to keep up with the Qopa warriors. Despite his best efforts, the thought that he may never be able to tell Susannah how he really felt about her wouldn't go away.

#

By the time the Qopa raiding party reached the Nausori Highlands, the pace had begun to slow. The men suddenly emerged from the jungle onto the crest of a hill.

To the east, the highlands continued all the way to a horizon that was hidden behind rain clouds.

The warriors knew Tomanivi lay in that direction. For most, this would be their first visit to the sacred mountain.

Surveying the highlands, Nathan noticed the rainforest was disrupted by pockets of stately Fijian kauri trees. A few miles distant, the vegetation almost completely gave way to entire forests of kauri. He studied them intently, knowing full well they concealed the whereabouts of Susannah and her abductor.

The men pressed on. They nibbled at their rations as they ran beneath a canopy of towering kauri, slowing only to ford streams which were rapidly turning into rivers as the driving rain continued unabated. Not wanting to advertise their presence to the locals, they avoided villages along the way.

#

At the same time, eight miles further east, Rambuka was making good time even though he was being slowed by Susannah. An early predawn start combined with the Outcast's superior knowledge of the highlands had enabled them to put an extra couple of miles on their pursuers. The rain was helping him, too, by washing away their tracks.

Rambuka was feeling confident he could reach his hideout before his pursuers caught up with him. The Outcast knew without a shadow of a doubt his half-brother was coming for him. He didn't need to see Joeli or his warriors to know that. They wanted what he had: their golden tabua and their women. He wondered whether the young white man was with them.

Beside him, Susannah was nearly out on her feet. Bruised, wet, tired, and hungry, she offered no resistance as Rambuka pulled her along after him. Her once-white cotton dress now hung from her in tatters. Like her, it was torn and covered in mud.

Susannah was living a nightmare. The shock of recent events had been replaced by a weary numbness. She felt like she was in someone else's body, being pulled along by some inexorable force. Exhaustion and weariness were taking over from the fear that had gripped her earlier.

While the memory of her father's death was still vivid in her mind, she was now more concerned about her own survival. *Papa is dead,* she reminded herself as Rambuka pulled her into a shallow mountain stream.

Papa would want me to fight to stay alive.

For the first time since her abduction, Susannah's thoughts turned to escape. Logic told her she couldn't escape from Rambuka. Not in her present state. *But I can slow him down.* She immediately began scheming.

Wading upstream in knee-deep water, she suddenly pretended to trip, falling headfirst into the stream. In a flash, her captor hauled her to her feet and grabbed her by the throat. He squeezed until she couldn't breathe. As she was starved of oxygen, she could feel herself losing consciousness. Finally, Rambuka released his vice-like grip. Susannah collapsed, gasping, and was only prevented from falling into the water again by her captor's strong arm.

Pulling her close to him, Rambuka threatened, "Next time I kill you." With that, he resumed wading upstream, pulling Susannah after him.

More despondent than ever, Susannah knew her abductor meant what he said. He'd kill her rather than risk being slowed down any more than he had been.

Thinking things through, she realized Rambuka was pushing hard because he believed they were being pursued. This gave her renewed hope. She wondered who exactly was coming after them and prayed that Nathan was with them.

More than anything else in the world, she wanted to see the American again.

2

As night approached, Joeli's trackers reached the stream at the same point their quarry had entered it earlier. The two trackers were scouting around searching in vain for tracks when the others caught up.

Nathan charged impatiently into the stream, anxious to keep going. He pulled up when he realized no one was following. Turning around, he saw Joeli conferring with the trackers. The ratu motioned to his warriors, indicating it was too dark to continue. They began preparing a campsite. Resigned to having to wait till morning to resume the search for Susannah, Nathan joined them.

Scouting around upstream, Waisale found a cave in the bank. The others agreed it would be a good place to overnight. They welcomed the shelter it would afford from the relentless rain.

Inside the cave, a fire was quickly lit. Everyone sat around it, drying out and eating some of their rations. The one-eyed Babitu spotted a large iguana, or native lizard, sitting motionless on a nearby rock. He stabbed it with his hunting knife, skewered it onto the end of a stick, and began barbecuing it over the fire. Once cooked, he sliced it into small pieces and shared it with his companions. Only Nathan abstained. He couldn't bring himself to eat it. Besides, he wasn't hungry.

The American sat apart from the others, his chin resting on his folded arms. Around him, some of the others talked in hushed tones while others went to sleep. In the firelight, the men's shadows danced on the rock walls and water glistened on the surface of the rocks. Soon, the crackle of the flames and the soft tinkle of the nearby stream were all that disturbed the silence.

Lost in thought, a bone-weary Nathan stared into the fire. He wondered how Susannah was faring at that very moment.

Are you still alive? Is he mistreating you?

Nathan became distressed just thinking about her. *What if I never find her?* he asked himself. He vowed he'd make the Outcast pay for what he'd done. Finally, he gave in to his weariness and lapsed into a deep sleep.

#

Further inland, Susannah and her abductor were also sheltering in a cave. Rambuka had chosen a small cave whose entrance was hidden behind dense vegetation and was effectively invisible to anyone who didn't know of its existence.

Susannah instinctively knew the fierce Outcast had used the cave previously. He seemed to know the land so well, and was so sure of himself, she seriously doubted she'd ever escape him or know freedom again.

For now though, Susannah's only concern was surviving the night with her virginity still intact. As she sat with her back against the far wall of the cave, she avoided making eye contact with Rambuka, who, at that moment, was sitting staring at her.

Against the cave wall, Rambuka was just a shadowy outline. In the darkness, only the whites of his eyes and, occasionally, his teeth could be seen.

Susannah closed her eyes and prayed to God. While she prayed, though, she sensed it was already a foregone conclusion. *Rape to an animal like Rambuka is nothing,* she thought. *He has probably raped hundreds of innocent women.*

The frightened young woman's concerns escalated when Rambuka suddenly stood up and walked over to her. Certain that she was about to be ravaged, she froze; her head felt numb and she realized, for the first time in her life, the hairs on the back of her neck were standing on end.

Oh my God, this is it!

Susannah wanted to flee, but she was too afraid even to move. All she could do was close her eyes.

To her surprise, Rambuka wrapped a wide strip of flax around her mouth, effectively gagging her, then he produced a length of vine which he used to tie her hands behind her back. He tied the other end of the vine to the branch of a tree that extended through the cave's opening, thereby preventing her from escaping.

What's he doing?

Susannah was even more fearful she was about to be raped, but wondered at the significance of being gagged. She guessed there was no one else within miles of them, and even if there were, they wouldn't hear her screams above the sound of the rain that was still beating down outside.

A few moments were all Rambuka needed to secure Susannah. Then, without a word, he scrambled out of the cave.

Alone, in the solitude of the cave, it slowly dawned on Susannah her abductor had left her to die. Rather than kill her outright, he'd elected to let her die slowly. The gag, she was convinced, was to ensure no one would hear her cries for help if they did happen to pass by close to the cave entrance.

The thought of dying alone, in a place her body would never be found, terrified her more than the thought of being raped. Panic welled up in her chest. Whimpering, she struggled to free herself. Her bonds held fast. Realizing it was hopeless, Susannah collapsed to her knees, sobbing.

#

The young Englishwoman didn't know how long Rambuka had been gone when she heard a faint noise at the entrance to the cave. When she saw the Outcast's shadowy figure enter the cave, she was momentarily relieved. She'd been convinced he'd left her to die.

Rambuka immediately untied Susannah and left her to remove the flax gag he'd tied around her mouth. This took a while for it was tied tight. As she struggled to untie it, she noticed Rambuka had brought something into the cave. It wasn't until he lit a fire on the dirt floor that she saw it was the carcass of a piglet. The Outcast had used his hunting skills to snare it. He was now skewering it with a sharpened stick. That done, he held the carcass over the flames, turning it slowly until its pink flesh began to turn a golden brown.

As Susannah watched the piglet being barbecued, her original fears returned. She was more convinced than ever her abductor intended to rape her.

When Rambuka adjudged the piglet was ready to eat, he drew his hunting knife and sliced tender portions of hot pork, which he devoured greedily. As an afterthought, he threw a portion to Susannah. It landed on the dirt at her feet. "Eat," he ordered.

Susannah had no appetite. She shook her head, indicating she had no intention of eating anything at the moment.

This infuriated Rambuka. Not used to being defied—especially by a woman—he pulled out the piglet's intestines, jumped to his feet, and strode over to where Susannah was sitting. Angrily grabbing her face with one hand, he forced the intestines into his captive's mouth. Then, using his fingers, he pushed the intestines down into Susannah's throat so that she was forced to swallow them. Satisfied, he returned to the fire where he ate the remaining portions of pork.

Susannah felt as though she'd been violated. She was gagging as the intestines worked their way down into her stomach. Her first instinct was to cry, but another instinct—far stronger—began to assert itself. She felt like rebelling. Rambuka may have taken away her freedom, but he hadn't broken her spirit.

The young woman knew it would be dangerous to infuriate Rambuka any more than she already had, but something made her react. Looking defiantly at her abductor, she stuck her fingers down her throat in an effort to make herself throw up. Almost immediately, she regurgitated the intestines, spewing them onto the floor.

Rambuka couldn't believe what he was seeing. His captive had openly defied him. More angry than ever, his anger was exceeded only by his surprise. Susannah was the most difficult woman he'd ever met.

The Outcast had never been this close to a white woman before, and this was a whole new experience for him. The countless Fijian women he'd abducted had almost immediately accepted their lot and resigned themselves to the life of sexual slavery that most assuredly awaited them. *Fijian women know their place,* he told himself.

Susannah was different. As much as she drove him crazy, Rambuka decided then and there he desired her more than he had any other woman in his entire life. He wanted to penetrate her—and soon. There was something about her smooth white skin and her fiery red hair that kept him permanently aroused. Rambuka forced himself to maintain self-control.

Observing the Outcast, Susannah was convinced he'd rape her now. She didn't know that even though Rambuka was a cannibal, he lived by a strangely puritanical code. Every one of the many women he'd abducted over the years had remained untouched, by him or any of his followers, for one full week—to allow his high priest to rid the women of evil spirits. Throughout that week, he and his followers would fast to purify their souls before planting their seed in the new addition to their flock. This, he was convinced, would ensure any offspring would be born pure. After the event, he and the others could then eat human flesh—an act that further purified their souls, or so he believed. This act was usually accompanied by an orgy.

To Susannah's amazement, Rambuka stretched out beside the fire and fell asleep almost immediately. Still she didn't relax. It wasn't until she heard Rambuka snoring that she finally breathed a sigh of relief.

Not for the first time since her horrific experience began, Susannah wondered whether she'd have the courage to attempt an escape. She looked longingly at the cave entrance, but Rambuka had positioned himself so that she would have to step over him to reach it.

Susannah couldn't help noticing that even in sleep Rambuka looked dangerous. His knife, which he held in his right hand, was resting on his chest while his left hand rested on the steel head of his tomahawk.

#

Before dawn, Nathan woke feeling refreshed after a surprisingly good night's sleep. Remarkably, he'd slept right through—despite his concern for Susannah. He immediately felt guilty that he could sleep at a time like this. His fingers caressed the whale bone pendant he wore as he pondered where Susannah was and what she was doing right now.

Nathan recalled a dream he'd had during the night. It came back to him in sharp flashes. He'd seen his future. He was an old man resting on a rocking chair, smoking a cigar on the porch of a mansion somewhere in rural America; he was rich and highly respected, but totally dissatisfied because he'd never married, had no children, and was alone in his twilight years.

Recalling the dream caused him to feel overwhelming sadness. He became convinced it was his destiny to end up like that old man unless he could grow as a human being. Nathan knew Susannah held the key to his future: she could help him evolve. He felt confident he could communicate his deepest feelings to her—something he hadn't been able to do to anyone else, not even himself.

I have to find her.

After Nathan and the others had eaten some rations, Joeli led them from the cave that had served them so well. Outside, they were relieved to find the heavy rain had been replaced by a light drizzle.

With the trackers leading the way, they set off along a rainforest trail at a steady jog. Nathan found it easier to keep up with his companions. Each day, he was feeling a little stronger.

#

Now deep in the Nausori Highlands, Joeli's raiding party occasionally stumbled across a remote village. As before, they gave the villages a wide berth. Joeli was mindful of the fact they were entering the outcasts' territory and Rambuka had eyes and ears everywhere.

Leading the way, the Qopa trackers had long since given up following their quarry's tracks. The rain had put paid to that. Their focus now was on ensuring they found the quickest route to Tomanivi. Always, they headed eastward.

Clambering over rocks alongside a rain-swollen river, Joeli and the others were greeted by a fine curtain of spray and a thunderous din as they neared a waterfall. They scrambled up a steep track beside the falls. Bringing up the rear but not falling behind as he had the previous day, Nathan tried not to look down. He never did like heights. Instead, he focused his attention on Joeli, who, as usual, was leading from the front.

Looking at the young ratu, Nathan could tell Joeli was already in war mode. His body language and single-minded determination told him that.

The American felt a flood of gratitude toward Joeli for risking the last of his warriors to rescue Susannah. Sure, Joeli wanted to rescue Waisale's woman, too, and he was desperate to recover the golden tabua, but it was Susannah's abduction that had prompted him to act.

Feelings of guilt resurfaced as Nathan remembered how, only a few weeks earlier, he'd been ready to betray the Qopa if it had meant securing a better deal for himself.

What Nathan didn't fully understand was Joeli had decided it was time to resolve matters once and for all with his treacherous half-brother. While the young ratu wasn't sure he could defeat Rambuka, he considered it more honorable to die trying than to allow the evil outcast to maintain his reign of terror and continue abducting women.

The track delivered Joeli's party to a hilltop above the tree line. Here, they paused to rest just as the drizzle cleared and a watery sun tried its best to pierce the clouds. To the east, kauri-forested hills extended as far as they could see. Mist Mountain was the only distinctive landmark. Its summit was appropriately shrouded in mist.

Nathan studied the mountain, wondering if that was their destination. He couldn't stop thinking about Susannah. The thought of the innocent young woman in Rambuka's hands was tearing him apart.

3

While Nathan was studying Mist Mountain, further to the east Susannah was about to get her first look at Tomanivi as Rambuka dragged her inexorably toward his hideout. Since dawn, the Outcast had been driving her so hard, the exhausted Englishwoman was beginning to think, for the first time, she may not last the journey.

Not that she knew where their destination was, for she hadn't been privy to the information Joeli's warriors had prized from the outcast they'd tortured back at Momi Bay. For all she knew, Rambuka could be taking her to the other side of Viti Levu.

Susannah had no idea how much time had elapsed since they'd set out from the cave they'd spent the night in. She wasn't even sure whether it was morning or afternoon, though she suspected it was still morning. Even though it had stopped raining, ever-present storm clouds ensured the sun remained well hidden.

As well as feeling exhausted, Susannah was experiencing hunger pains for the first time. She now regretted she hadn't accepted the food scraps Rambuka had offered her the previous night. Susannah slipped in the mud as she followed her abductor up a steep forest trail.

The increasingly impatient Rambuka grabbed her by the hair and pulled her to her feet. "Keep up!" he snapped.

Rambuka spoke so infrequently—and when he did he sounded so gruff—Susannah had trouble interpreting his words, as she did on this occasion. However, she got the drift. Ignoring her pain as best she could, she forced herself to move faster.

Susannah could see her abductor was showing signs of stress, or anxiety at least. Despite her exhaustion, she had the presence of mind to realize Rambuka suspected they were still being followed. As before, this gave her hope. And, as before, she wondered if Nathan was among those who were following them.

Mercifully, they reached the crest of the hill they were climbing and began descending on the other side. The going was suddenly easier, but this only prompted Rambuka to increase the pace.

Susannah bumped into the Outcast when he came to an abrupt halt. Looking around, she saw they'd emerged into a forest clearing. She glanced at Rambuka and noticed he was staring at something directly ahead. Following the direction of his gaze, she saw a distant mountain. She wasn't to know it was Tomanivi, the highest mountain on the island and their intended destination.

Just as Mist Mountain was covered in mist, the summit of Tomanivi was covered in cloud—as it usually was at this time of year.

As if on cue, the rain that had cleared earlier returned heavier than ever. Rambuka knew rain was a constant companion in the rainforests around Tomanivi, especially during the wet season. He also knew the closer they drew to the mountain, the heavier and more persistent the rain would become.

The sight of the sacred mountain spurred Rambuka on. He grabbed Susannah by the wrist and pulled her down the hillside after him. Only his firm grip prevented her from sprawling headfirst into the mud.

In a valley at the foot of the hill, they found their way barred by a swift-flowing stream. It came as no surprise to Susannah that Rambuka pulled her into the stream and, keeping close to the near bank, began wading upstream. Ever since he'd abducted her, he'd made use of many different waterways—be they streams, rivers, lakes, or swamps—in this fashion. It had taken Susannah a while to work out he did this to hide their tracks. Again, this reminded her that Rambuka believed there was a strong possibility they were being followed.

The stream led them to a waterfall. Without even pausing, Rambuka began pulling his captive up a rocky trail beside it.

Susannah was suddenly afraid for her life. She and Rambuka were both slipping on the slime-covered rocks and the path they followed was becoming increasingly treacherous, yet the Outcast seemed oblivious to the danger. Pulling her up after him, he shouted at her, urging her to keep moving. Susannah couldn't hear him above the thunder of the falls. She dared not look down.

Recognizing that Susannah wasn't coping, Rambuka dropped back behind her and began pushing her from below. Susannah found this helped. She couldn't help thinking it wasn't very ladylike having a cannibal place his big hand on her soft derriere and push her up the side of a cliff. *That's the least of your troubles,* she told herself.

At a point about halfway up the falls, Susannah suddenly realized Rambuka's hand was no longer on her ass. Looking down, she saw the Outcast had stopped to urinate into the falls. Quickly averting her eyes, she looked up to see how far she was from the top. She estimated it was about thirty feet.

Susannah suddenly thought she heard her father's voice calling to her above the thunder of the falls.

Papa!

Just as suddenly, she remembered he was dead. Thinking of her dear papa, she wondered what he'd do in her predicament. She recalled the advice he gave her back in her teenage days when she used to play chess at an exclusive all girls' school in London. *Never change a winning game, my dear,* he would say, *but always change a losing game.*

Susannah ceased her daydreaming when she felt Rambuka's hand on her ass. She immediately resumed climbing. As she climbed, her father's words kept coming to her. She knew she was losing whatever game she was playing right now.

What to do, Papa?

The young Englishwoman sensed they were nearing their destination. She remembered the look in Rambuka's eyes when he saw the big mountain.

Maybe that's where we are heading.

Susannah knew her chances of escape would reduce drastically once they'd reached Rambuka's hideout. Then she'd be up against him and his men, and not just him.

Your best chance of escaping is right now while it's just you and this animal.
But dear God, please show me how on earth I can ever escape from him. This is
his territory. He is bigger, stronger, and faster than me and he knows this land
like the back of his hand.

Reaching up for a handhold, Susannah dislodged a large rock.
Only by applying upward pressure with her hand did she prevent it
falling on top of her. Studying the rock, she estimated it to be about
the size of a soccer ball. Grasping it in both hands, she pulled it free
from the cliff face, turned, and looked down at Rambuka.

Please, Lord, give me the strength to do this thing and overpower this evil
man.

The look on Rambuka's face told her the Outcast knew immediately what she was planning to do.

As Susannah threw the rock down at her abductor, Rambuka
leaped to one side. The rock missed him, but he fell about ten feet,
landing heavily on a protruding boulder. He lay there unmoving.
Blood streamed from a nasty head wound.

Breathing heavily, Susannah studied Rambuka's motionless form
for several long moments. She was convinced he was dead.

The thought that she'd killed someone hit her like a sledgeham-
mer. Feelings of faintness threatened to engulf her, and she hugged
the surrounding rocks for fear she'd fall. The feelings passed. She
resumed climbing, anxious to put as much distance between her and
Rambuka—in case he wasn't dead.

Reaching the top of the falls, she looked back down for one last
look at her tormentor.

Dear God, no!

To her horror, she saw that Rambuka wasn't dead. He'd regained
consciousness and was already pushing himself to his feet. He
looked up, and Susannah pulled back out of sight before he could
see her.

Terrified, she began running along the cliff top, desperate to
escape.

Meanwhile, Rambuka was faced with a dilemma. He had no idea
how long he'd been unconscious, and he wasn't sure whether
Susannah had continued scaling the cliff face or had climbed back
down. The rain and the constant spray from the falls instantly
washed any tracks away, so there were none of the usual signs for
him to follow. He had to rely on instinct. Logic told him that,

although it would have been easier for her to continue to the top on her own, she'd have climbed down because that was the way home for her—and that's where her help was coming from. Rambuka immediately began retracing his steps down the cliff face. As he climbed down, he blinked continually to keep the blood out of his eyes.

At the foot of the cliff, Rambuka entered the rainforest and scouted around for special herbs and leaves, which he quickly located. Expertly combining them to form a poultice, he covered his head wound. Then, reaching into the small pouch that dangled from his waist, he fished out some more powerful herbs, which he popped into his mouth and began sucking. These, he knew, would ease his splitting headache. That done, he began searching for his quarry's tracks.

Above the falls, Susannah was running for her life. She was convinced Rambuka would kill her if he found her. Looking over her shoulder, she was amazed he hadn't appeared yet. The thought occurred he may have gone down the cliff face. *That's the only explanation,* she decided.

Realizing she may have bought herself some time, she stopped running and reassessed her options.

He'll soon realize I climbed to the top of the falls. I have to hide where he can't find me and hope he gives up looking for me.

She knew Rambuka would be mindful of the fact the Qopa—and possibly Nathan—would be coming after him, so he couldn't afford to spend too long looking for her.

Where to hide?

Looking behind her, her heart sank when she noticed her tracks in the soggy ground. They stood out like signposts. Susannah resumed running until she came across the next mountain stream. Then, taking a leaf out of Rambuka's book, she waded into the water.

Which way to go? Upstream or downstream?

This time, Susannah thought of home. She immediately headed downstream.

Behind her, in the valley beyond the falls, Rambuka quickly reached the conclusion Susannah hadn't retraced her steps.

Away from the spray of the waterfall, he could find no additional tracks, which indicated she'd climbed to the top of the falls, not the bottom. Cursing, he retraced his steps yet again and climbed up beside the falls. At the top, he immediately saw Susannah's tracks and followed them to the point where she'd entered the stream.

Rambuka was faced with yet another decision—whether to go up or downstream. Following his instinct, he headed downstream.

#

Susannah had been wading through the stream's shallows so long, her feet felt numb. She dared not allow herself to think she may have eluded Rambuka, but deep down she was beginning to feel a glimmer of hope.

Approaching a set of rapids, she finally climbed out of the stream. Only then did she become aware she was being followed. The sound of someone, or something, splashing through the water behind her told her she wasn't alone. Turning, she saw the familiar form of Rambuka charging after her. His bloodied face was a mask of rage as he closed in on her.

Screaming, Susannah began sprinting along the bank of the stream, looking around wildly for some avenue of escape. There was none.

The Outcast quickly overtook her, throwing her to the ground. He then cuffed her about the head and face with his open hand, bruising and cutting her, but taking care not to incapacitate her.

"No, please!" she cried out. Even in her distressed state, Susannah recognized that her abductor wasn't out to kill her. She instinctively knew he intended to keep her as his hostage.

Susannah's instincts were spot on. Rambuka wanted to keep her for himself, and he wasn't about to let her escape.

This realization chilled her to the bone. She decided then and there, when the opportunity presented itself, she'd kill herself rather than let Rambuka and the other outcasts have their way with her.

4.

Nathan walked directly behind Joeli as the young ratu led the raiding party through kauri forests en route to Mist Mountain and, theoretically at least, to the outcasts' hideout beyond it.

A colorful, squawking parrot perched in the branches of a towering Fijian kauri tree above them caught Joeli's attention. He stopped to study it. Nathan hovered impatiently at Joeli's shoulder, as if urging him to keep moving. It took the American a moment to realize the parrot's squawks could be a sign that Joeli had picked up on.

Watching Joeli study the parrot reminded Nathan of similar experiences he'd had hunting with members of the Ohlone tribe back in San Francisco. Like the Qopa, the Ohlone were at one with nature. While he'd once looked on them—and indeed all native peoples—as inferior to whites, he'd always admired their ability to read the signs of nature. Joeli, in particular, seemed to have a special ability. Generation upon generation of Qopa wilderness intelligence had been handed down to the young ratu. As was the case with all Fijians, it was in his blood and so instinctive he was hardly conscious of it. From the moment he'd learned to walk, he'd been taught how to read nature's signs. Now, studying the parrot, he knew something wasn't right.

Joeli had immediately identified the bird as a red shining parrot.

Its crimson-red plumage had given its breed away instantly as had its distinctive squawk. The fact that it was squawking at all alerted Joeli to the fact something was wrong. He knew the red shining parrot normally didn't draw attention to itself when people were in the vicinity—as if aware its bright plumage already made it a target for the hunter's spear. The fact that it was squawking now put him on high alert.

Moments later, it came as no surprise to Joeli when one of his trackers, Rewa, appeared, running as fast as his long legs could carry him. Joeli hurried forward to meet him.

Breathing hard, Rewa pointed back the way he'd come. "Outcasts!" he gasped.

Concerned, Joeli asked, "Did they see you?" Rewa shook his head, indicating they hadn't.

"Where is Penaia?" the ratu asked of the other tracker.

"He stayed to observe them. They are setting up camp."

"How many?"

"I counted ten men."

"Is Rambuka with them?"

"No, but they have two prisoners. One is a White-Face."

"The Englishwoman?"

"A man," Rewa said, shaking his head. "He looks familiar."

Listening to the conversation, Nathan knew something was up. Not for the first time, he wished he could speak Fijian. Joeli flashed hand signals to his warriors, indicating there was danger ahead. They immediately fell into single file behind him, muskets at the ready. Nathan joined them. The ratu then nodded to Rewa, who immediately struck off toward the outcasts' campsite.

A few moments later, the other tracker, Penaia, materialized out of the forest. He pointed behind him, indicating the outcasts' campsite was close by. At the same time, men's laughter could be heard coming from the site. The smell of smoke was in the air, too.

Joeli and the others crept forward to observe their enemies. Following close behind, Nathan stood on the branch of a fern, rustling its leaves. The others looked back at him, glaring. When they were satisfied their enemies hadn't heard anything, they resumed inching forward.

Soon, the campsite came into view. From the cover of trees and dense undergrowth, Nathan quickly identified the men as outcasts.

With bones and sticks inserted through apertures in their ears and noses, their primitive appearance made them instantly identifiable.

Nathan immediately thought of Susannah and wondered if Rambuka had brought her here. His eyes swept the campsite, searching for a sign of her. He could see the outcasts had begun roasting the carcass of some animal over a fire. Nathan assumed it was a wild pig as several other pig carcasses lay nearby—obviously the result of a successful hunt.

The outcasts were in jovial mood, joking around. Their muskets were stacked nearby, but they were obviously not expecting trouble as no guards appeared to have been posted.

Something caught Nathan's eye.

White skin!

He realized there was a European tied up next to the pig carcasses.

Please let it be Susannah.

Whoever it was, he'd missed seeing her, or him, earlier because an outcast had been standing in his line of sight. Now that the outcast had moved, Nathan had a clear view. Crushing disappointment set in when he realized it was a man. Short and stocky, the curly haired man looked to be in his early thirties. Another outcast stood in front of the man, blocking Nathan's view.

Looking over at Joeli, Nathan wondered if he and the others had seen the white captive. He noticed their attention seemed to be focused on something else. Nathan looked closer at the carcass the outcasts were roasting over the fire.

Jesus!

He suddenly realized it wasn't a pig they were roasting: it was a man.

Nathan looked back for another glimpse of the white man. The outcast who had been blocking his view conveniently moved, allowing him to observe the white captive more closely.

The man was Jack Halliday, a Cockney who had gained a reputation for himself as something of a legend up and down Fiji's Coral Coast. Shorter than average and not especially good looking, the curly haired Cockney nevertheless had a mischievous face which generally endeared him to all he came into contact with. Not on this occasion, however. In his current perilous position, he was feeling anything other than mischievous. His perceptive green eyes looked around desperately, and his mind was in turmoil as he processed his helpless situation.

Formerly a convict who had served time in New South Wales, in the fledgling British colony of Australia, Jack had escaped by stowing away on a Fiji-bound ship. After jumping ship and swimming ashore when the ship neared the village of Koroi, on the Coral Coast, he'd been adopted by the local villagers. That had been seven years ago.

In the intervening years, Jack had ended up marrying a Fijian maiden of royal blood and having children by her. Having a village headman as his father-in-law gave him a certain status. This status was enhanced after Jack's heroics saved the village from certain defeat when attacked by an enemy clan.

Never one to waste an opportunity, Jack had set about starting up a trading business, taking advantage of the opportunities presented by the sandalwood traders who frequented Fijian waters. Initially, he'd acted as an interpreter and a go-between, between the traders and the Fijians; later, he negotiated directly with the Fijians, buying the cutting rights to their coastal sandalwood plantations and selling those rights to the traders for profit. As one profitable venture followed another, Jack acquired a small arsenal of muskets, which he donated to the village that had adopted him. This further endeared him to the villagers, and he now enjoyed almost equal status to their ratu.

It wasn't only as a successful trader and provider that Jack Halliday had a reputation for: he was well known up and down the Coral Coast, and on many of the outlying islands, as a womanizer without peer. Although happily married, he took advantage of his frequent excursions away to bed the many village maidens who were only too pleased to give themselves to him. Jack wasn't fussed whether his concubines were single or married; as a result, he was offside with many angry husbands.

In recent months, the bottom had fallen out of the sandalwood trade as the once-precious sandalwood plantations had been all but wiped out by greedy Fijian landowners and even greedier European traders. As a result, Jack had turned his attention to securing cutting rights to the forests of Fijian kauri that were so prolific in Viti Levu's interior. It was this new venture that had seen him end up in his current predicament.

Jack and his Fijian guide had been captured earlier that morning while mapping the kauri forests located within the territory the Cockney had recently acquired cutting rights for. The day had started out like any other for Jack. Having enjoyed a night of lust with yet another Fijian woman at a local village, he and his guide had struck out early aboard his horse-drawn cart for the western boundary of the forested area he had cutting rights to. When the terrain had become too rugged for the horses, he and his guide had left them tethered and continued on foot. An hour later, they'd literally stumbled into the outcasts' campsite—apparently just in time to feature on the day's menu.

The outcasts had killed Jack's guide immediately, but had spared the Cockney for the moment. Trussed up like a turkey, Jack could only watch while his captors had made a human skewer out of his guide and proceeded to cook him over the fire. He'd been left in no doubt his captors were cannibals—and he was in no doubt he'd also be eaten before the day was out.

Now, watching his former guide's flesh melting in the flames that crackled not ten feet away, Jack asked himself what he'd done to deserve this fate.

Looking on from the cover of the trees, Nathan wondered what circumstances had brought the white man to this isolated corner of the world. He was suddenly anxious to talk to the man to learn if he'd seen Susannah or at least had any news of her. Inching forward, he squeezed between Joeli and Waisale. They were debating whether to ambush the outcasts and kill them or give them a wide berth and hope they could reach their destination without being detected.

Waisale favored the latter option. "If we fail to kill them all, the survivors would warn Rambuka we are coming," he whispered.

"He already knows . . . and if we try to go around them, they could find our tracks later," Joeli argued, "or we could still run into them on our return from Tomanivi."

Unable to follow the conversation, but anxious to express his opinion, Nathan said, "If we don't deal with this now, we'll probably have to deal with it on the way back. I say we hit 'em hard."

Joeli looked at Nathan for several long moments before making up his mind. Turning to Waisale, he said, "We attack now."

Waisale nodded and circulated among the others, relaying the ratu's orders. Nathan could see the Qopa were excited by the prospect of killing their enemies. The warriors knew what to do; they immediately disappeared into the surrounding trees and proceeded to encircle the campsite.

Nathan and Waisale stayed close to Joeli. Holding their weapons out in front of them, they began crawling on their bellies through the undergrowth to get closer to their enemies.

The American prayed the ambush would succeed. He knew if even one outcast escaped, Rambuka would be ready and waiting when they reached his hideout—*if* they ever found his hideout. The only chance they had of rescuing Susannah was to keep the element of surprise, he thought.

As they crawled closer, they were able to see all the outcasts and could hear their voices clearly. Nathan now had a clear view of the white captive. Apart from bruises and a split lip, he seemed okay. At one stage, the man's bright green eyes seemed to be looking directly at him.

Crawling closer still, Nathan and his two companions froze as a young outcast walked toward them. Intent on relieving himself, the outcast stopped not a dozen paces from them and proceeded to urinate. As he did so, he tensed as if he'd seen something close to where the three men were hiding. Finishing his business, he drew out a tomahawk from his waistband and came to investigate. Behind him, none of the other outcasts noticed anything amiss.

As soon as the young outcast drew near, Joeli jumped to his feet and threw his own tomahawk at him. The weapon's blade lodged in the outcast's head, felling him. Joeli immediately dropped to the ground. He and the other two collectively held their breath, waiting for the alarm to be sounded. Miraculously, it never came. None of the other outcasts had witnessed the attack. They were too intent on preparing their meal.

But Jack had noticed. He'd been looking directly at the unlucky outcast just before Joeli had killed him. When the ratu had risen, seemingly straight up out of the earth, and thrown his tomahawk, Jack thought he must have been dreaming. It took a few moments to realize he wasn't.

It really happened!

For the first time since being captured, he sensed a glimmer of hope.

Joeli crawled forward and retrieved his tomahawk. Cries of alarm suddenly rang out. Joeli thought he'd been seen. In fact, the outcasts had seen a Qopa warrior on the other side of the campsite.

The Qopa simultaneously opened fire on all sides. So woeful was their aim that, even at near-point-blank range, only two shots found their targets.

Nathan was responsible for another two kills. Pausing to reload his musket, he felt the wind of a wayward musket ball as it all but parted his hair. Looking up, he saw he'd nearly been shot by friendly fire. The culprit, one of Joeli's trackers, flashed Nathan a guilty smile.

Fortunately, Joeli's warriors were close enough to dispatch their enemies by more traditional means, making good use of the clubs and tomahawks most of them also carried. As usual, Joeli led the way, wielding his tomahawk and massive club with devastating results.

Realizing they were outnumbered, the last two surviving outcasts made a run for it. Nathan managed to shoot one down, but the other one reached the cover of the trees unscathed. "Damn it!" Nathan cursed.

Joeli had noticed the survivor flee, also. He ordered his two trackers to hunt the man down. Rewa and Penaia immediately set off in pursuit. Not trusting them to do the job, Nathan took off after them, priming his musket as he ran.

Before disappearing into the trees, he glanced back at the European they'd set out to save and was relieved to see he was still alive.

#

After running nonstop for ten minutes, Nathan was breathing so hard he felt as if his lungs were on fire. The trackers were so far ahead of him now he could only faintly hear them crashing through the undergrowth. He wondered if they were gaining on the fleeing outcast. Two musket shots raised his hopes.

Forcing himself to run harder, Nathan finally caught up to Rewa and Penaia. They were standing at the edge of a cliff, staring resignedly down into a deep gorge. Their muskets were still smoking. Nathan immediately knew the outcast had given them the slip. Following their gaze, he saw the distant figure of the man they'd been pursuing. The outcast was running hard along the bottom of the gorge and would soon be out of sight. He was already further away than anything Nathan had previously shot.

Desperate to keep him from alerting Rambuka, Nathan dropped to the ground and lined up the fleeing outcast in his sights. The Qopa trackers looked on with interest.

Still breathing hard, Nathan knew he'd only get one shot. Even though he was a fine marksman, the outcast was so far away, he doubted he was even within range.

As he lined up his target, he forced himself to slow his breathing and remain perfectly still—not easy after his recent exertions. The target looked no bigger than an ant in his sights. Ignoring the sweat that stung his eye, Nathan tried to shut out all other thoughts as he slowly applied pressure to the trigger.

Try as he may, an image of Susannah's face kept coming to mind. Nathan forced himself to concentrate. Just before he squeezed the trigger, he breathed out slowly—as he had done a thousand times before. When his lungs were finally emptied of air, he squeezed the trigger ever so gently. The shot split the silence and echoed throughout the hills.

To Nathan's relief, his aim was true. The outcast fell to the ground and lay there, unmoving. Nathan looked up at the two trackers. They were staring at him in awe. Slowly, their faces creased into toothy smiles.

5

Returning to the outcasts' campsite, Nathan and the two trackers heard raised voices. Someone was having a heated argument. Nathan thought he recognized Joeli's voice. Emerging from the trees, he saw the ratu standing astride Jack Halliday. The Cockney was still tied up and Joeli was threatening to smash his skull with the whale bone club he was holding.

"Joeli!" Nathan called, running to his side. "What are you doing?"

When Joeli turned to face him, Nathan could see the blood lust in his eyes. Speaking Fijian, Joeli said, "This dog slept with my woman!" He paused to spit on Jack. "And he slept with two of my sisters!" He then kicked Jack in the ribs, causing him to grunt in pain.

"Speak English!" Nathan said.

"He . . . Jack Halliday," Joeli said, in English this time. "He visit Momi Bay before. He sleep with my woman . . .and my two sisters!"

"Tell him he's got the wrong man, will you?" Jack mumbled to Nathan.

The American immediately noted the other's distinctly English accent. "Who are you then?" he asked.

"I'm Jack Halliday, but I never slept with those women." Jack knew he was talking for his life. He sensed the American was his only chance if he was to escape the wrath of Joeli, whose woman and sisters he had indeed slept with. Until six months ago, he'd been a frequent visitor to Momi Bay—to trade with Joeli's father. During those visits, he estimated he'd slept with a dozen or more different women in the village. He clearly remembered seducing Joeli's woman. That had been on his last visit. He'd been found out and had only just managed to flee Momi Bay alive. Glancing at Joeli, he said, "He confused me then and he's confusing me now for another man."

"What other man?" Nathan asked.

"Me trading partner."

Nathan turned to Joeli. "He said you're confusing him with his trading partner."

In his angry state, Joeli couldn't understand what Nathan was saying—and he was running out of patience. "He die!" Joeli said, raising his club threateningly.

"No!" Nathan said, jumping between Joeli and the captive. "He can help us." Both Joeli and Jack looked bemused. Turning back to Jack, Nathan asked, "You can use a musket, can't you?"

"Of course," Jack responded eagerly.

Looking back at Joeli, Nathan said, "He can use one of the spare muskets. God knows, we need all the help we can get."

Joeli remained unconvinced.

Sensing an opportunity, Jack hurriedly added, "I have muskets."

This got Joeli's attention. "Where?"

"A few miles east of here," Jack said, quickly explaining how he'd left his horse-drawn cart earlier to strike out on foot. "I have two spare muskets and powder in the cart."

Joeli considered this. Finally, he said, "You show us."

Relief flooded through Jack. He knew he'd bought himself some time at the very least.

Joeli left Nathan to untie Jack, indicating he was anxious to get moving. Nathan produced his Bowie knife and quickly cut Jack's bonds.

"I can't thank you enough," a relieved Jack said as he painfully pushed himself to his feet.

"You'll get your chance to help us soon enough," Nathan promised. Looking around, he saw Joeli and his warriors were waiting impatiently for Jack to lead them to his cart. "Let's go."

Jack nodded then hesitated, remembering his faithful guide. He turned back to look at the remains of the native hanging over the still-flickering fire. Glancing at the Bowie knife Nathan carried on his hip, he held out his hand. "Your knife," he said.

Nathan handed the knife over without hesitating. He and the others looked on impassively as Jack cut his guide free before dragging the body away from the fire and covering it with branches that were lying nearby.

"May you find peace in the Afterworld," Jack murmured in fluent Fijian before returning the knife to Nathan and setting off to find his cart. The others followed. Fortunately, the cart had been left close to their intended route, so they wouldn't have to go far out of their way.

Before leaving the campsite, Nathan noticed the Qopa warriors had helped themselves to sizable morsels of pork from one of the pig carcasses to supplement their rations. All that was left of it was the head and hind legs. Taking their lead, he sliced off some portions from another carcass for himself and stuffed them into his backpack before hurrying to catch up to the others.

#

An hour later, they located the cart exactly where Jack said it would be. The two horses were still patiently waiting, grazing on the grass beneath their hooves. Throwing back the covers, Jack produced two muskets and a bag of powder. Placing one musket over his shoulder, he held the other one out to Joeli, saying, "It's yours."

Joeli snatched it from him and handed it to Nathan. The American willingly accepted it. Although he already had a musket, he had a feeling he'd soon be thankful for the extra one.

"We go now," Joeli announced. He set off at a fast trot, keen to make up for lost time. His warriors followed.

Anxious not to get left behind, Nathan turned to Jack. "Hurry!" He turned to leave.

"Wait," Jack said. He immediately untied his horses. "I can't leave these beauties to starve." He whacked the nearest horse on the rump, sending her scampering away. The other horse reared up and followed her mate. Looking at Nathan, Jack said, "Ready now, me ol' china."

The two men set off. Nathan set a fast pace, determined to catch up to the others as quickly as possible. As they ran, Nathan noted his companion was having no trouble keeping up. He obviously kept fit.

Running at Nathan's shoulder, Jack wondered where they were heading and what the urgency was. He guessed it had something to do with the cannibals who had captured his guide and himself. "Where are we going?" he called out.

"Save your breath," Nathan responded. "I'll tell you later."

#

It took the pair some time to catch up to the others. As soon as the Qopa warriors noticed them, they pulled up. Several rounded on Jack. Weapons raised, they looked like they wanted to kill him. Joeli stood back, content to let his men have their way.

Turning to Nathan, a bemused Jack asked, "What now?"

Before Nathan could inquire, a warrior struck the Cockney a glancing blow with the stock of his musket, felling him. The others closed in. There was murder in their eyes. Only the intervention of Waisale prevented further harm being done to Jack. While Waisale held the others at bay, Nathan looked at Joeli inquiringly.

"Some of men say Jack Halliday sleep with their women, also," the ratu said accusingly. He pointed out two young warriors who were betrothed to his sisters. "They want kill the White-Face, too." He then pointed to an older warrior. "And he angry. He say Jack Halliday sleep with his daughter."

Nathan looked back to Jack, who was only now recovering his senses from the blow he'd received. The American realized he needed to do something to prevent the irate warriors from killing Jack.

Stepping between the Cockney and the others, Nathan looked directly at Joeli. "Jack Halliday can help us get the golden tabua back," he said. "When it is back where it belongs then you can discipline him."

Joeli thought about this. He quickly saw the wisdom in Nathan's words. Firing orders at his warriors, the ratu turned and resumed walking. His warriors glared at Jack before following their leader.

Jack turned to Nathan. "That's another one I owe you."

Without another word, Nathan resumed walking. Jack hurried to catch up to him. They walked in silence for the next little while, each man lost in his thoughts. Finally, Nathan asked, "So who else have you slept with?"

Jack chuckled. "Your friends were exaggerating," he said. "I'm a happily married man." They walked a little further in silence then Jack asked, "Who can I thank for saving me back there?"

"Nathan Johnson."

"Well, I'm grateful to you, Nathan Johnson."

"So, when did you sleep with Joeli's woman?" Nathan asked, making it clear he didn't believe his companion's earlier lies.

Grinning sheepishly, Jack said, "On me last visit to Momi Bay...about six months ago."

"And his sisters?"

"That was the previous visit."

"What did you trade at Momi Bay, or didn't you have time for that?"

Ignoring Nathan's sarcasm, Jack said, "Mainly tools and clothing."

"For what?"

"Sandalwood . . . until the timber ran out." Jack went on to tell Nathan about his new venture, trading muskets for cutting rights to the kauri forests around Tomanivi.

In turn, Nathan told Jack about himself and the reason they were heading for Tomanivi. As the day progressed, the Cockney and his American savior found they had much in common. Each recognized a kindred spirit in the other. Like it or not, Nathan knew a bond was developing between them.

6

In less than two days, despite being slowed down by his hostage, Rambuka had put nearly a day on his pursuers. In addition to his superior knowledge of the Nausori Highlands and most, if not all, the shortcuts over, through, and around them, he'd been receiving help from friendly villagers along the way.

Most recently, the Outcast and Susannah had been ferried by canoe from one friendly village to a point not two miles from his hideout at Tomanivi. Now, as they trekked the final leg to his hideout, he knew there was no stopping him.

Rambuka was having second thoughts about whether Joeli was coming after him. There had been no sightings of a Qopa raiding party reported by villagers—or by his men whom he believed were hunting west of his current position. He was convinced if Joeli and his warriors were on the warpath, one of his hunters would have seen them, or heard about them at least, and got word to him. For the first time since abducting the white woman, he was starting to relax.

Susannah, however, was more fearful than ever. Although her abductor hadn't had his way with her yet, she knew it was only a matter of time. The frightened Englishwoman wasn't quite sure why Rambuka hadn't already raped her.

God knows, he's had plenty of opportunity.

#

By the time they arrived at the outcasts' hideout at Tomanivi, Susannah was so exhausted she had to be half-carried by her abductor. What remained of her dress was hanging from her in tatters and she was now covered from head to foot in scratches, bruises, and abrasions—some of which she'd received in the beating Rambuka had given her after her unsuccessful escape attempt.

When lookouts announced their arrival, Rambuka and Susannah were greeted by a hundred or more whooping and hollering outcasts. Half-naked and adorned in nose and ear bones, the outcasts looked frighteningly savage. All the men and some of the women were armed.

Susannah noticed there was almost one woman for every man. Some looked so tough they were almost indistinguishable from the men. Most of the women were slaves. They were carrying firewood and performing other mundane chores. Some would have been attractive were it not for their tattered clothes and unkempt appearance. Many bore cuts and bruises, the results of recent beatings. Some were caring for toddlers and babies. It seemed Rambuka's aim to increase his followers' numbers was working.

Susannah also noted there were a number of non-Fijian Islanders among the outcasts. They included Tongans and Samoans. Their facial features were Polynesian rather than Melanesian and their skin color more golden than dark. Susannah was able to accurately guess their origins having seen portraits of Islanders in the numerous text books she had studied.

Among the slaves was Sina, the pretty Qopa maiden Rambuka had abducted from Momi Bay earlier that year. Gone was the happy smile and carefree manner she'd once possessed. These had long since been replaced by a dejected countenance and sadness for the life she'd lost. Sina noted Susannah's arrival with interest as did several older women who drooled over her, poking her white skin and stroking her hair. Susannah recoiled from them.

Rambuka handed his latest captive over to two grinning outcasts and pointed to a large bure in the middle of the clearing. They escorted her toward it, half dragging her through the mud.

Lord, give me strength, Susannah thought as she was dragged toward the bure.

Although close to collapse, she had the presence of mind to observe her new surroundings. The outcasts' encampment was a motley collection of crude bures. It was in a valley running north to south at the foot of the forest-covered Tomanivi—just as the captured outcast had told Joeli back at Momi Bay. Human bones in and around cooking pots outside some huts pointed to cannibalistic practices. Skulls and the grotesque shrunken heads of former enemies and slaves were displayed outside almost every dwelling.

Susannah couldn't believe her eyes when a middle-aged midget around four feet tall suddenly appeared from within a dwelling and walked right up to her. The very sight of him made her skin crawl. Wearing snakeskin garments and a lizard skin turban adorned with the heads of dead snakes and lizards, the midget stopped in front of Susannah and clapped his hands half a dozen times as if to clear the air around her. He then made some strange clicking noises with his tongue before walking away.

The young woman guessed, correctly, the midget was some kind of barau, or sorcerer. In fact, he was one of several barau who had joined Rambuka's outcasts after being cast out from other clans around Viti Levu. In most cases, they'd become outcasts because their considerable powers were feared by the common people. In the midget's case, the other members of his clan had rightly believed him to be evil. Rambuka had taken him and the other barau in, in the hope they would give him some kind of supernatural advantage over his enemies.

Susannah's escorts delivered her to the large bure, pausing only in the doorway to hand her over to a huge woman with no hair and, it seemed, no teeth. Apparently used to the routine, the woman took Susannah inside, forcibly sat her down on the dirt floor in the center of the bure and tied her to a pole that extended all the way up to the high thatched roof.

Despite her fear and discomfort, Susannah fell into an exhausted sleep almost immediately.

#

Later, Sina entered the bure carrying a calabash of berries. She knelt down in front of Susannah and shook her gently, waking her with a start. Speaking passable English, Sina said, "Do not be frightened."

Susannah registered surprise at being addressed in English. "You speak English!" She wasn't to know Sina had been taught English by the Wesley Methodist missionary couple the Drakes had taken over from at Momi Bay. "Who are you?"

Sina smiled and began hand-feeding Susannah who gulped the berries down hungrily. "I am Sina, of the Qopa. Iremaia is my ratu—"

Interjecting, Susannah asked, "You are from Momi Bay?" Sina nodded. The Englishwoman continued, "I am from the mission station at Momi Bay. I arrived there recently. Iremaia is now dead. Joeli is the ratu."

Sina quickly accepted this news in the manner of one who has experienced much sadness in her short life. "You know Waisale?" she asked hopefully.

Susannah racked her brains. "Yes, I think so." She was in such a wretched state she was having difficulty marshalling her thoughts. However, she eventually managed to put a face to the name. "Waisale is the fine-looking young man with a birthmark . . . here?" she asked, pointing to her forehead.

Sina smiled. "Yes. That him." A look of pain and happiness simultaneously registered in her eyes. She looked down and whispered, "He my man." After a painful pause, the young maiden continued, "Rambuka take me as slave." She touched Susannah affectionately. "You also slave now."

Susannah shook her head. "No, I am not a slave."

"We slave for life. There nowhere to go for escape."

"No, Nathan will come for me," Susannah assured her.

Sina looked bemused. "Who Nay-than?"

"He . . . he's . . . my friend." Looking into Sina's eyes, Susannah could see the girl didn't believe that Nathan, or anyone, was coming for her. It suddenly hit her, Sina was probably right. She knew the Qopa had been trying to track down the outcasts for years.

Even if Nathan is looking for me, why would he have any more luck than the others?

As the hopelessness of her situation sank in, Susannah dissolved into tears.

#

With dusk approaching and light rain beginning to fall, Joeli ordered his trackers to find a suitable site for his party to overnight at.

185

Just as Waisale had the previous evening, the trackers found a cave—this time in the side of a hill. Fortunately, there was no shortage of caves in the interior of Viti Levu.

Thanks to their foresight in taking pork morsels from the outcasts' campsite earlier in the day, all except Jack enjoyed a fine meal of roast pork. Joeli had banned Jack from eating with them, or from sleeping in the cave. He and the other aggrieved warriors were adamant the womanizing white man stay as far away from them as possible. They were still furious he was in their midst. It was only the realization they may need him and his muskets in the days ahead that was keeping him alive.

Feeling sorry for his new friend, Nathan smuggled some roasted pork slithers out to a grateful Jack, who was doing his best to make himself comfortable on a damp bed of ferns just outside the cave entrance. "Don't let them see you eating this, or that'll be the last straw," Nathan warned.

Grinning his cheeky grin, Jack said, "Thanks, mate. That's another one I owe ya."

The American was about to head back inside the cave, when he noticed Jack's back was criss-crossed by numerous scars. The high humidity had prompted the Cockney to remove his shirt. Even in the gloom, the unsightly welts were noticeable. Nathan knew they could only have been caused by floggings. He also knew the Pacific Islands were a magnet for escaped convicts and many of them ended up in Fiji at some point.

"Why didn't you tell me you were a convict?" Nathan asked.

Surprised, Jack spun around to face the American. He'd momentarily forgotten about the telltale marks on his back. "Me convict days ain't somethin' I like to brag about," he eventually replied. "Besides, it was so long ago it seems like it never happened."

Nathan nodded. He understood exactly what it felt like to want to leave the past behind and try to become a different person.

The rain began pelting down, prompting Nathan to retreat to the relative comfort of the cave, leaving the Cockney suddenly feeling very alone. With nothing but leaves and branches covering him, Jack was wet and miserable. His thoughts immediately turned to self preservation.

Jack deduced there was nothing to stop him heading back to his own village on the Coral Coast. He knew exactly where it was and guessed he'd be halfway there before he was even missed. But something was holding him back. Nathan's predicament, or, more correctly, the predicament Nathan's English friend had found herself in, had touched him. Jack genuinely wanted to help Nathan rescue the woman he so obviously loved.

Besides, he saved me life. I owe him.

Thunder and lightning announced the arrival of a storm. Suddenly cold, Jack quickly donned his shirt, pulled the branches back over him, and settled down for what he expected would be a long night.

Inside the cave, Nathan was in for a long night, too, but for different reasons: looking into the flames of the nearby fire, he was consumed by worry for Susannah. He wondered how she was faring and whether Rambuka had had his way with her yet.

7

That night, a frightened Susannah sat in the corner of the same bure she'd been interned in since arriving in the outcasts' encampment. She wasn't yet aware this was Rambuka's residence.

The same huge, bald, toothless woman who had greeted her earlier was now trying to feed her some taro. Gagging, Susannah refused the food.

This only angered the woman, who then proceeded to forcefeed her. She stopped as several outcasts suddenly entered the bure. Rambuka was among them.

Ignoring the two women, the outcasts sat down and, as they did most nights, began drinking kava. None of them observed the traditional rituals normally associated with the sacred kava ceremony: they drank greedily from a large bowl. While they were drinking, Susannah surreptitiously observed them.

A disfigured outcast leered at Susannah. To nobody in particular, he said, "I want to be first to plant my seed in her." The others laughed.

Another outcast turned to Rambuka, asking, "What are you going to do with this red-haired White-Face?"

Rambuka said, "When it is time, we will ravage her until we tire of her. Then we will deliver her shrunken head to our enemies."

Susannah shuddered. She understood the gist of what Rambuka was saying.

A pockmarked outcast asked, "And what of our Qopa enemies?"

Rambuka scooped up a large insect from the dirt floor. He crushed it then opened his hand, displaying its mangled remains. "We are going to crush them like the insects they are." The others smiled in anticipation as they helped themselves to more kava.

Susannah found she was trembling violently. She'd always known she'd be mistreated by these cannibals, but it was chilling to hear them articulate what they were planning to do. She looked wildly around the bure's interior, as if searching for an escape route. Her eyes were drawn to the golden tabua Rambuka had seized during the raid on the village at Momi Bay. It now occupied pride of place on the far wall.

The young woman instinctively knew the sacred whale's tooth was the one that rightfully belonged to the Qopa. They'd talked about little else since the raid. While she didn't fully appreciate what the golden tabua meant to them, she could appreciate its beauty. It seemed to have an ethereal aura around it that vaguely reminded her of the colorful stained-glass windows of English churches.

Rambuka caught Susannah staring at the golden tabua. She hurriedly looked away. The Outcast walked over to her, knelt down beside her, and grabbed her by the hair. Speaking English, he asked, "How many muskets my enemies have?"

Susannah shook her head. "I don't know."

"How many?" Rambuka repeated.

"I told you . . . I don't know."

Rambuka slapped her face hard. "How many muskets?"

Tears stream down Susannah's cheeks. "I don't know," she sobbed. "Twenty . . . maybe thirty."

Rambuka slapped her again, harder this time. The blow drew blood from her upper lip. "Woman lie! How many?"

"Fifty," Susannah sobbed. While she was telling the truth, she didn't mention that the Qopa had less than half that number of ablebodied warriors left.

Satisfied, Rambuka turned to the other outcasts. In Fijian, he said, "As I thought. Fifty muskets." Rambuka studied Susannah's face for a moment. He suddenly pulled her to him and began fondling her breasts. Susannah resisted futilely, crying out in pain as her tormentor squeezed her nipples between his probing fingers. When Rambuka finally stopped, he put his face close to Susannah's. Reverting to English again, he said, "When I see the White-Face, I cut out his heart."

Susannah knew he was referring to Nathan. Smiling cruelly, Rambuka was about to say something else when he was interrupted by shouts from outside the bure. He and the other men jumped up and hurried outside to investigate.

Outside, they saw several outcasts pulling two male slaves out of a pit in the middle of the encampment. The pit, which was open to the elements, served as home for a dozen or more male slaves. The slaves being pulled out were resisting as they knew full well what was in store for them. This was part of a regular, gruesome ritual that saw the need for a constant supply of slaves at the encampment.

Despite their incarceration, these slaves were in remarkably good condition. They appeared well fed, even overweight. Unlike the female slaves, the males were rarely used for work. Rather, they were used to supplement their masters' food supply and keep the outcasts supplied with the precious protein human flesh provided.

Looking on, Rambuka smiled to himself and returned inside as the two slaves were hauled out of the pit and clubbed to death. Stripped naked, they were then dragged over to a lovo just outside Rambuka's bure. There, willing hands lay the fresh carcasses on the lovo where they were roasted on red-hot rocks. The excited outcasts attending the lovo uttered savage war cries as the prospect of another meal of human flesh drew closer.

Inside the bure, Susannah was aware something was happening. The sickly odor of human flesh filled her nostrils, but she'd never smelled it before so could not connect the smell with the ghastly reality.

Susannah's thoughts returned to her father. She still couldn't believe he'd been taken from her so violently. A vision of the spear's serrated tip protruding from the back of his neck kept coming to her. *Papa!* She was suddenly consumed by a feeling of helplessness.

The earlier thoughts of suicide she'd had returned. She closed her eyes and whispered a passionate but silent prayer.

Dear Lord, let me die quickly and painlessly so that I can join my dearest papa in heaven and be spared the abuse of these savages.

Then she remembered Nathan and suddenly knew she didn't want to die.

#

Later, outside Rambuka's bure, a portly outcast who clearly enjoyed food more than most, poked the nearest of the two human carcasses with a stick and gleefully pronounced it ready to eat. More war cries were uttered as the carcass was removed from the lovo.

The cries alerted the others and soon men from throughout the encampment were wandering over and queuing up to receive their share of the flesh. Women weren't involved in this ritual. Nor would they get to taste the meat. The portly outcast officiated. Starting on the thighs, he carved off juicy portions with a hunting knife and dished them out. As usual, the best portions, along with the heart and other vital organs, were saved for Rambuka. Almost every part of the unfortunate slave's body would be used—either for eating or for decoration.

Even the penis and testicles would be used: these would be crushed then mixed with coconut milk and taken as an aphrodisiac. Again, these valued body parts would be saved exclusively for Rambuka.

A boy slave carried a steaming bowl of flesh inside to Rambuka, who took it from him. Staring at Susannah, the Outcast stuffed a large slither of meat into his mouth.

Susannah could only wonder at what he was eating. Any uncertainty was abruptly ended when the portly outcast walked in holding the dead slave's head. He placed it on a floor mat in front of Rambuka, who eyed it gleefully. The crown of the head had been carved off, exposing the slave's brain. The brain was considered a delicacy and was also reserved for Rambuka. Susannah's eyes opened wide at the gruesome sight. Try as she may, she couldn't look away.

Relishing the fact he had her attention, Rambuka smiled as he picked up the head and rested it on his lap. Using a fork fashioned from a strong twig, he began scooping the brains out of their encasement and into his mouth. Leering at Susannah, he said, "This what Rambuka do to the White-Face."

Horrified, Susannah watched as segments of brain dribbled out of the corners of Rambuka's mouth. A feeling of faintness came over her. She tried to fight it, but it consumed her. She collapsed face-down on the floor. The huge woman who had been watching over her hurried to assist her, but Rambuka waved her away. He and the other outcasts proceeded to eat their fill. In keeping with their tradition, this would be the last food they'd touch for the next week. Then, after seven days, they'd each have their way with Susannah. As usual, Rambuka would have first use of her.

8

Next day, Susannah found herself standing knee-deep in water washing dirty clothes alongside half a dozen other female slaves in a river near the outcasts' encampment. She was thankful she hadn't yet been raped. Sina had told her earlier how the outcasts usually treated their newly acquired women, so she now understood why they'd largely left her alone so far.

Although she remained fearful, Susannah was breathing a little easier knowing she'd remain unmolested for the next week. *If* Nathan was coming for her, he'd be here by then, she hoped.

Susannah noticed that the pockmarked outcast who had been in Rambuka's bure the previous night was watching over them now. She could see he was still leering at her. Filled with revulsion, she busied herself with her washing, pretending she hadn't noticed him. Around her, the other women toiled as if they were in a trance. Susannah realized they seemed totally resigned to their fate. She found this more depressing than anything else she'd seen since her arrival.

The splash of paddles announced the approach of a canoe from upstream. Looking up, Susannah was amazed to see its three occupants included a boyishly handsome white man sitting in the bow. Behind him, his two native guides were doing the paddling.

Susannah felt her prayers had been answered.

A European!

She guessed the man was in his late twenties and immediately wondered who he was and whether he had in fact come for her. It was then she noticed he was wearing the white collar of a priest. She would soon learn he was Father Montrose, a French priest whose remote Catholic parish included Tomanivi.

A musket shot suddenly boomed out, making Susannah and the other women jump. Looking around, they saw their pockmarked guard had just fired his musket to alert his fellow outcasts to the visitors' arrival. Other outcasts soon came running, their muskets at the ready.

As the visitors' canoe neared the bank, Susannah immediately ran toward it to ensure she was first to greet the new arrivals. The pockmarked outcast tried to stop her, but she ducked around him and rushed up to the priest. Breathless, she gasped, "Thank God, Father. I am Susannah Drake, from the Wesley Methodist mission at Momi Bay."

Only now did Father Montrose notice Susannah. He was as surprised as her to see another European in Rambuka's territory. "Good Lord!" he exclaimed in French.

Susannah gabbled, "They're holding me here. You must help me!"

The pockmarked guard grabbed Susannah and dragged her away. Alarmed, Father Montrose looked strangely at the young English-woman.

Susannah could tell by the guard's reaction the priest was no stranger here. As she was dragged away, she shouted, "I am a slave here! They killed my father!" The guard clamped his hand over her mouth to quieten her while other outcasts escorted the priest to their encampment. She could only watch as the priest was led away.

Entering the encampment, Father Montrose's mind was racing. It had long concerned him and his fellow priests that Rambuka regularly abducted women to serve as slaves. While he lectured the outcasts on the evils of slavery, he'd never reported the location of their hideouts to anyone else for he knew that would destroy the trust he'd painstakingly built up over the last few years. And that, in turn, would end any chance he had of converting Rambuka and his followers to Christianity.

However, the abduction of a white woman had taken things to a new level. He knew he could no longer turn a blind eye. God would not allow it.

Father Montrose found Rambuka waiting for him outside his bure. Speaking fluent Fijian, the priest respectfully said, "I see you, great Rambuka."

An unwelcoming Rambuka stepped forward and stood with his face inches away from the priest's. "And I see you, little priest," he grumbled disparagingly. "Why do you keep coming to my home to fill me with troubling thoughts about the white man's god?"

"As always, I come to spread the true Word of the true God."

Rambuka laughed in the priest's face. He pointed skyward. "You know the great Degei?" he asked, referring to the Fijian god of war.

"Yes, I know of your god."

Rambuka motioned to his visitor to follow him and retired inside his bure. Father Montrose followed. Inside, the two sat down cross-legged, facing each other. A kava bowl rested between them. As a slave boy dispensed servings of kava to each of them, the priest studied a shrunken head on the near wall. A shrunken head had occupied the same position on the wall when he was last here, but he was sure that head was different to the one he was looking at now.

Finally, an impatient Rambuka shooed the slave away then turned to the priest, asking, "You speak for the new god?"

"Yes, for our Lord Jesus Christ."

Leaning forward, Rambuka reached out and touched the bronze crucifix he'd noticed hanging from Father Montrose's neck. While he studied it, the priest looked around the hut and saw more shrunken heads and skulls hanging from the roof. Turning back to his host, his attention was drawn to several dried fingers hanging from a cord around Rambuka's waist. He wondered who they'd belonged to.

After a long silence, Father Montrose said, "The Lord Jesus Christ has instructed me to bring his Word to your lands."

Rambuka laughed aloud once again. "My people will listen to this new god if his disciples bring rum, women and muskets."

Father Montrose swallowed hard as the Outcast tapped his forefinger on the dried fingers hanging from his waist.

Rambuka said accusingly, "You come empty-handed and we

remain deaf to your ways. You bring gifts and we hear your god very clearly."

The priest nodded, but he wasn't listening to Rambuka. His mind was elsewhere – on the white woman outside.

#

Susannah was collecting firewood with Sina when Father Montrose and Rambuka finally emerged from the bure. The priest deliberately didn't look in her direction as the Outcast escorted him back to his waiting canoe. He didn't want Rambuka to know he'd seen her. The young Englishwoman looked at him imploringly, willing him to look at her. She silently mouthed the words, *Help me,* but he didn't see her. However, Rambuka did.

Down at the riverbank, a thoughtful Rambuka saw Father Montrose and his guides off as they headed upriver. The Outcast began walking back toward the encampment. As he walked, he knew he had a decision to make. He'd been tolerating Father Montrose's visits on the off-chance he would one day prove useful to him, but now that the priest had seen the white woman, that put a new complexion on things. The more he thought about it, the more certain he was Father Montrose would reveal to others what he'd seen.

After much deliberation, Rambuka sought out Serevi, a menacing-looking outcast. "The white priest knows too much. See that he does not talk."

Serevi nodded and quickly recruited four others to assist him. They ran to the river and set about launching one of several canoes that rested on the bank.

#

Serevi and his companions had been paddling for about an hour when they saw the priest's canoe tethered to the overhanging branch of a tree on the far bank. A column of smoke rose above the treetops just beyond it. They quietly paddled over to the other canoe, tethered their craft to it, and climbed onto the riverbank.

A quick reconnoiter of the area found Father Montrose reading his Bible beneath a tree while his two guides cooked freshly caught fish over a campfire.

From the cover of the trees, Serevi aimed his musket at the nearest guide. The shot shattered the silence and the guide died the moment the musket ball struck his heart.

The second guide grabbed his club and turned to face the unseen threat. Another shot boomed out and he fell face down, mortally wounded.

A fearful Father Montrose could only watch as an outcast ran forward and savagely clubbed the wounded guide, killing him. Just as the priest began to stand, yet another outcast clubbed him from behind, knocking him out.

#

As Father Montrose slowly came to, the first thing he heard was laughter. Opening his eyes, he saw the laughter was directed at him. The five outcasts were standing around him in a circle, looking down at him. He suddenly realized he couldn't move. Dazed and unable to comprehend where he was or what was happening, his gaze settled on a pile of stones beside him.

The realization of what awaited him suddenly registered. In French, Father Montrose implored, "Dear God, not this way!" Aware his captors couldn't understand him, he began pleading for his life in Fijian.

The outcasts had buried him up to his neck so that only his head was visible. They'd then gathered up some stones and waited for their victim to come round.

Now that Father Montrose was conscious and fully aware of what was happening, Serevi nodded to a stocky outcast who forcibly prized the terrified priest's mouth open. Picking up a stone from the pile, Serevi dropped it into his victim's mouth. The others took turns to force the stones down the priest's throat. Father Montrose's eyes bulged as he struggled for air. He was beginning to suffocate.

A few agonizing moments later, Serevi asked, "Where is your god now, priest?"

Father Montrose couldn't have answered even if he'd wanted to. He was now only moments from death. As yet another stone was forced down his throat, he convulsed once then died, his face forever frozen in fear, his eyes wide open.

#

Oblivious to the priest's demise, Susannah and Sina discussed his visit while resting in the company of three other women in one of several huts that had been designated for female slaves.

Leaning over to Sina, Susannah whispered, "The priest will get word out about our situation. We will be rescued soon, I am sure."

Sina looked doubtful. Susannah continued, "The Lord has answered our prayers. Have faith, it is only a matter of time now."

The two stretched out as they prepared to have an afternoon nap. The bure wasn't conducive to sleeping in. Water dripped down from the roof onto the bure's occupants whenever it was raining—as it was now. Despite this, Sina quickly fell asleep. Susannah marveled at her companion's ability to accept their dire situation so easily. Looking around, she saw the other women were now sleeping, too.

Noises outside alerted Susannah to the return of Serevi's party from upriver. Standing up, she hurried to investigate. From the open doorway, she saw Rambuka and Serevi in deep discussion.

Susannah wondered what they were talking about. The feelings of dread she'd experienced earlier returned.

9

West of Tomanivi, on the Nadrau Plateau, Joeli's raiding party skirted around the edge of a small lake. The surrounding hills were reflected in the lake's still waters. So, too, was a flock of doves flying overhead, albeit fleetingly.

Nathan was growing impatient. To him, it felt like they'd been on the trail for three weeks, not three days.

Following just behind him, Jack could sense his companion's frustration. "We'll soon be there," Jack assured him.

"How do you know?"

"Trust me, mate. I know this area." Rain began falling as they ventured into the hills bordering the eastern edge of the plateau. "This proves me point," Jack added. "It always rains around Tomanivi."

Since Jack had joined Joeli's party, an uneasy truce had evolved between the warriors and the Cockney whom they suspected of having slept with half the women in their village. Even so, Nathan had had to intervene more than once to defuse potentially explosive situations that had arisen as certain warriors had been reminded of Jack's indiscretions with women who, one way or another, were close to them.

For his part, Jack was just pleased to be alive. He knew he'd come close to dying the previous day, so he considered every breath he drew as a bonus. As the trackers led the way through a valley, Jack pointed to a nearby hill. "You can see Tomanivi from up there," he said.

"You sure?" Nathan asked.

"Do chickens have lips?"

Not bothering to respond to Jack's attempt at humor, Nathan ran forward to alert Joeli. Reaching the ratu's side, he said, "Jack says you can see Tomanivi from up there."

Joeli looked up at the hill Nathan was referring to. After conferring with his trackers, he began climbing the hill. The others followed.

#

After a hard climb, the men found themselves on the summit. Looking eastward, they were relieved to see Tomanivi. The four-thousand-odd-foot-high mountain was partially concealed by rain clouds.

Standing away from the others, studying the rain-shrouded Tomanivi, Nathan experienced inexplicable feelings of dread. The sacred mountain seemed forbidding. Nathan felt like it was telling him that Man should not venture there. As always, his thoughts turned to Susannah.

Are you still alive?

Looking over at Waisale, he wondered if he was having similar thoughts.

Joeli noticed Nathan standing alone and wandered over to join him. Nodding toward Tomanivi, he said, "That . . . Land of Red Rain." Still Nathan didn't understand the meaning behind the ratu's words. Then, as if he'd been reading Nathan's mind, Joeli said, "We find your woman."

Turning back to his warriors, Joeli rallied them for one final push then began striding down the hill. The others followed, slipping and sliding in the mud. The pace was noticeably more urgent now.

At the foot of the hill, they ran along a shallow stream for some distance before clambering out of it and following a track through a rainforest. Faced with fording a swollen river or finding a safer crossing, they forded it, holding their muskets above their heads. All the while, Tomanivi drew ever closer.

As they neared their destination, Jack wondered what he was

getting himself into. Nathan had explained to him what they were planning to do. Jack had told him even if they managed to find the two women and uplift the golden tabua, he doubted they could outrun the outcasts and survive the return journey to Momi Bay. After all, they were now in Rambuka's territory and badly outnumbered.

Nathan hadn't commented, but Jack knew deep down he agreed with him. *The fool's in love,* Jack decided. He knew better than to try to dissuade a man in love.

#

It was late afternoon and still raining when Joeli's party reached Tomanivi. Although their enemies couldn't be seen from the present position, smoke could be seen rising from the floor of a valley below them. It merged with the mist that clung to the treetops.

Joeli ordered Rewa, the tracker, up a tree. From its upper branches, Rewa flashed a signal, confirming he could see the outcasts' encampment.

Nathan breathed a sigh of relief. There had always been a suspicion that the outcast they'd interrogated back at Momi Bay had lied regarding the whereabouts of Rambuka's hideout. Now the location had been confirmed, he and the others could give their full attention to the task of recovering the golden tabua and, more important, the two women.

Joeli turned to his men. "We are here," he said simply. "Tonight we make our move."

Meanwhile, up in the tree, Rewa's keen eyes took in everything in the encampment below as the outcasts went about their everyday business. He took special notice of the armed lookouts patrolling the camp perimeter. Climbing down, he immediately reported to Joeli. "All is quiet," he said. "Rambuka's men suspect nothing."

Joeli grunted his satisfaction at hearing this. "Did you see the two women?"

"No."

Joeli turned to see both Nathan and Waisale looking at him inquiringly. He shook his head, indicating the tracker hadn't seen either Susannah or Sina. The two young men looked at each other. Each knew what the other was thinking and how the other felt. Keen to find a vantage point from where they could all observe their enemies, Joeli led the others along a ridge, which his trackers indicated should take them to a point directly above the encampment.

10

While his enemies were positioning themselves on the hillside above, Rambuka was having his way with a shapely slave girl on a flax mat in the corner of his bure. Almost satiated after an afternoon of near nonstop coupling with his favorite maidens, the Outcast treated this particular girl roughly and satisfied himself quickly.

Nearby, two fellow outcasts lay snoring in the arms of three women. All the women had seen better days. The biggest of them snored even louder than did her male companions, her open mouth revealing several missing teeth.

Looking at the women, Rambuka reminded himself to replace them with more attractive maidens as soon as he could. Before drifting off to sleep, he looked at the golden tabua hanging from the wall. Despite the bure's gloomy interior, its golden aura seemed brighter than ever.

#

Nearby, in the slaves' quarters, Susannah woke Sina to advise her she had a premonition something bad had happened to the French priest. She was interrupted by the arrival of the pockmarked outcast. He was accompanied by the shapely slave girl Rambuka had just had his way with.

The outcast threw the girl down onto the floor beside Susannah.

202

Then he looked around at the other maidens. His eyes rested on Susannah longingly but, knowing she was off limits until Rambuka had his way with her, he settled on Sina. Grabbing her by her wrists, he pulled her toward the doorway.

Susannah cried, "Sina!"

Sina didn't struggle. Having been through this many times before, she stoically allowed herself to be led away.

Susannah wondered how she'd be when her turn came. She knew it was only a matter of time. Her thoughts turned to Nathan. Something told her that he was her only hope. Yet she seriously doubted he would risk his life for her.

As the doubts resurfaced in her mind, she began to think of suicide once more. If it was a choice between being Rambuka's sexual slave for the rest of her life and joining her papa in heaven, she would willingly choose death, she decided.

#

With the approach of dusk, the rain eased and finally disappeared altogether. In a forest clearing high above the outcasts' hideout, Joeli and his men studied the encampment below. It was a hive of activity as female slaves tended cooking fires and helped the other women prepare evening meals while the outcasts themselves sat around drinking kava.

By now, Nathan and Waisale were becoming increasingly worried. Neither had seen any sign of the women they'd come for.

Nathan was currently studying the encampment through a telescope he'd brought in his backpack.

Where are you?

He hoped Susannah had survived the journey from Momi Bay.

Noting Nathan's concern, Jack sidled up to him. "I'm sure she's here," he said. "She'll be in one of the bures."

"Maybe," Nathan replied non-committedly.

"If she's anywhere near as beautiful as you say she is, then Rambuka will keep her alive so he can . . . ." Jack's voice trailed off when he noticed Nathan seemed to be growing agitated.

Watching the two whites together, Joeli realized their pale skin would stand out like lanterns at night, especially if there was a moon. Approaching the pair, he scooped up a handful of mud and held it out to them. "For you," he said, motioning to them to use mud to darken their skin.

Nathan and Jack immediately rubbed mud over their faces and over the back of their hands until there was no white skin visible.

Satisfied, Joeli turned away. Addressing several nearby warriors in Fijian, he whispered, "The White-Faces try to look like us." The warriors chuckled.

Nathan and Jack suspected the Qopa considered them a source of amusement. Ignoring the others, Nathan returned his attention to the encampment below.

Just along from him, Waisale suddenly tensed. Turning around to Nathan, the handsome young warrior extended his hand. Nathan guessed he wanted his telescope so handed it to him. Raising the scope to his eye, Waisale focused it on what it was that had caught his attention. Suddenly, through the lens, he saw the magnified form of Sina. She was walking from one bure to another.

Waisale whispered aloud, "Sina!" A hundred intimate memories flashed through his mind as he watched her. Something else caught his eye. He handed the scope to Nathan and pointed.

The American raised the scope in the direction Waisale had indicated. Through the lens a blurred image came into view.

Let it be her.

As he focused the lenses, the blurred image evolved into Susannah.

She's alive!

Nathan felt like whooping for joy, but he contained himself.

Studying Susannah, he noted how dirty and unkempt she looked. He watched as she walked, zombie-like, to a campfire where an elderly woman handed her a morsel of food. Susannah stuffed the food into her mouth and reached out for more. The elderly woman hit her with a stick and sent her away.

Susannah retired to the large bure that served as her quarters. As she entered it, Rambuka emerged. He leered at her and stroked her hair as they passed each other in the doorway.

As soon as Susannah disappeared from sight, Nathan focused the scope on Rambuka. His hatred for the Outcast was matched only by the relief he felt knowing Susannah was alive. Returning the scope to his backpack, he could hardly contain his excitement. Looking at Waisale, he saw the young warrior was experiencing similar feelings. Nathan fingered the whale bone pendant around his neck as he pondered their chances of freeing the two women they'd come for.

11

Night couldn't come quick enough for Nathan. When it finally arrived, it was accompanied by a starry sky and a full moon, which, he knew, would not assist what he and his companions were planning to do.

Waiting in a forest clearing on the hillside above the outcasts' encampment, Nathan and Jack looked on as the Qopa warriors stood in a circle around their ratu. Listening to Joeli issue whispered instructions to his men, the two whites could feel the tension in the still night air.

Joeli looked at the one-eyed Babitu. "Take three men and silence the lookouts," he whispered. Babitu nodded and quietly selected three seasoned warriors. Joeli added, "Do it quietly." He pointed to his club, making it clear to the men they must not fire their muskets. The warriors nodded and melted into the surrounding trees.

Joeli walked over to Nathan. Addressing him in English, he whispered, "You and Waisale stay with me. We rescue the two women."

"What about him?" Nathan asked, looking at Jack.

Joeli looked at Jack disdainfully. "He look out for our backs." The ratu then began making his way silently down the hill. His warriors followed with Nathan and Jack bringing up the rear.

Near the valley floor, the two whites found Joeli and Waisale waiting for them. The other warriors had vanished.

Approaching the two Fijians, Nathan asked, "What now?"

"Now we sleep," Joeli said.

Nathan thought he was hearing things until Joeli and Waisale sat down, their backs against a tree, and closed their eyes. He looked at Jack, who just shrugged.

"These people have their own way of doing things," Jack whispered. The Cockney added, "I best be getting into position."

Before Jack could depart, Nathan handed him his spare musket. "You'll have more use for two muskets than me," he said, knowing—or hoping—he'd soon have his hands full looking after Susannah.

Jack took the spare musket from him. The two looked at each other for a moment. Finally, Nathan whispered, "Thanks, Jack."

"For what?"

"For sticking around."

"I wouldn't miss this for the world, me ol' china." Jack grinned before disappearing into the darkness.

As Jack made his way down the hillside, his thoughts once more turned to his own survival. Weighing up what Nathan and the others were planning, the Cockney knew the odds were very much stacked against them. Even if they managed to snatch the two women, they would then have to get back to Momi Bay before the outcasts could catch them.

Very unlikely.

Jack's thoughts turned to the village he and his doomed guide had based themselves at while mapping the kauri forests around Tomanivi. He knew it was only a day's trek at most from Tomanivi and his latest concubine would be there anxiously awaiting his return. Images of her, and of his wife and children waiting for him back on the Coral Coast, sprang to mind, overriding feelings of loyalty he had for Nathan.

I hardly even know the guy.

In an instant, his mind was made up. He'd worry about his own well-being from here on in. *I owe the wife and kids that much,* he reasoned.

Shaking off any feelings of guilt, Jack veered off the path he'd been following, determined to put as much distance between himself and the outcasts' encampment as possible. He avoided forest trails so as not to bump into any of Joeli's warriors or, worse, any of Rambuka's lookouts.

#

Later, as the moon moved around the night sky, Nathan wondered whether he should wake Joeli and Waisale. Just then, almost as if they'd read his mind, they woke up. Refreshed after their nap, they jumped to their feet and immediately began making their way down to the valley floor.

Following close behind, Nathan regretted he hadn't slept. He knew he was operating on adrenalin and nervous energy, and was already feeling strung out. Creeping down the hillside, he wondered where Jack was hiding. Just knowing he was somewhere out there in the darkness gave him comfort. He had a feeling the Cockney would prove a handy ally in what was to come.

Walking through a patch of mud, Joeli caught Nathan's eye and looked pointedly at the ground. Nathan knew exactly what he was suggesting. He immediately bent down, scooped up a handful of mud and applied it to his face and hands—as he had earlier. Satisfied Nathan's white skin was covered once more, Joeli continued on.

When they'd ventured as close as they dared to the outcasts' encampment, the three studied the bures from within the trees. Aside from the glow from the embers of cooking fires that still smoldered in and around some of the dwellings, the encampment was in darkness.

Picking his moment, Joeli mimicked the squawk of a masked parrot. An answering squawk came from the trees nearby. The ratu looked at Waisale and nodded then, turning to Nathan, whispered, "We go."

Tomahawk in hand, Joeli led Nathan and Waisale out of the cover of the trees. The American was holding his Bowie knife and Waisale his club. Their muskets were slung over their shoulders.

The three were unchallenged as they slunk into the encampment. Their target was the same bure they'd observed Susannah and Sina coming and going from earlier.

12

Approaching the slaves' quarters, the trio froze when a scar-faced outcast emerged from a nearby bure. Half-asleep, the man walked behind his dwelling and urinated against its outer wall. He seemed to take an eternity. While urinating, he sang softly to himself. Finally, he finished his business and retired to his bure.

The three intruders resumed moving forward.

Nearing the slaves' bure, Joeli suddenly nodded to Waisale and ran off alone into the darkness. Nathan knew the ratu would be looking for the golden tabua. Joeli had been obsessed with recovering the sacred whale's tooth ever since Rambuka had taken it. The American guessed, correctly, Joeli would willingly sacrifice the two women they'd come to save if it meant recovering the golden tabua.

Circling around to the rear of the slaves' quarters, Nathan and Waisale could see a faint glow coming from inside it. It came from a hole in the bure's wall. Waisale started moving toward it, but Nathan restrained him. Wanting to do this himself, he crept toward the hole while Waisale kept watch.

Reaching the hole, which was just big enough for him to crawl through, Nathan cautiously poked his head through it. He immediately saw the bure's interior was illuminated by a small fire that was flickering on the dirt floor in the middle of the hut. Beyond the fire, he saw Susannah. She was awake and seemed to be looking directly at him.

Sina and several other slave girls lay sleeping nearby. They were exhausted after a long day of chores, which had included entertaining Rambuka and his men.

Susannah had been trying to get to sleep when Nathan's head appeared through the hole in the wall opposite. Through the flames of the fire, his mud-covered face was distorted. She didn't recognize him at first and wondered if she was dreaming. It was only when she saw his startling blue eyes she knew for sure it was him. Her heart leapt.

Nathan placed his forefinger to his lips, urging her to remain silent. As he prepared to crawl through the hole, Susannah looked at him sharply and shook her head once, ever so faintly. Nathan stared at her inquiringly. She looked pointedly to her left.

The American cautiously poked his head further through the hole, glanced to his right and saw a Tongan guard was watching over the slaves—or he would have been were he still awake. The Tongan was asleep sitting upright, his back against the bure's near wall.

Nathan pulled his head back quickly and looked at Susannah, as if for inspiration. She looked thoughtfully at the guard for a few moments. The young woman appeared to steel herself then coughed once.

The Tongan woke with a start. Susannah looked at him and suggestively ran her tongue over her lips. The guard's eyes opened wide as Susannah suddenly unbuttoned her cotton dress, partially exposing her breasts. She motioned to him to come to her. The Tongan hesitated.

Taking care not to wake the other women, Susannah addressed him quietly in Fijian. "Rambuka will never know," she whispered seductively.

The Tongan considered this for a moment. Leering at Susannah, he pushed himself to his feet and hurried over to her.

Susannah reclined on a flax mat as her smiling, would-be lover removed his grass skirt and lowered himself onto her. Susannah immediately encircled his waist with her legs.

As the excited, now-naked Tongan prepared to enter her, his moment of passion was interrupted by the blade of Nathan's knife as it sliced through his windpipe. Nathan placed one hand over his victim's mouth to stifle the noise as his victim fought for air. Blood spurted over Susannah's face. As the life ebbed out of the Tongan guard, Susannah rolled out from beneath him. The Tongan breathed his last and Nathan pushed him aside.

A bloodied Susannah threw her arms around Nathan. They held each other tight while Sina and the others slept on. Nathan wanted to hold Susannah like this forever. He also wanted to tell her his true feelings for her right there and then, but knowing of the danger they were in, he lifted her to her feet, saying, "We must hurry."

Susannah quickly dressed. She was experiencing a flood of emotions: horror at the sight of the bloodied corpse at her feet, relief that help had come, fear at the thought of what would happen to her if they were discovered, and joy at being reunited with Nathan.

Seeing the handsome American suddenly appear as if in a dream had confirmed something for Susannah: she really did love him. *There, I've said it,* she told herself. *I love him.*

Looking at Nathan now, she couldn't be sure if he'd come for her because he really did love her as she loved him or because he was helping the Qopa out of some loyalty to them or to Joeli. His tense body language and cold expression made him impossible to read. He remained an enigma to her.

Nathan was consciously trying to remain detached and business-like. He knew the next little while could well determine whether they lived or died, and he didn't want emotions getting in the way. However, although he didn't show it, he was asking himself the exact same questions about Susannah that she was about him.

Is she happy to see me because she's desperate to be rescued or does she really love me?

Susannah suddenly gasped when she saw Waisale's face appear through the hole in the wall.

"It's only Waisale," Nathan whispered.

The young warrior entered the hut and immediately went to Sina. Placing one hand over her mouth, he gently woke her. Sina's surprise quickly turned to delight. She smiled as she recognized her former lover. Waisale touched her cheek affectionately.

Nathan urgently motioned to Susannah and the others to follow him outside. They silently departed and still the other slave girls slept on.

Waiting for them outside was an impatient Joeli. He gave a quick nod of acknowledgment to the two women then led the small group into the cover of the nearby trees. The men were relieved they'd come this far without alerting the outcasts to their presence.

The small group moved quietly, taking care not to stand on twigs or make any sound. As they retreated deeper into the rainforest, they were joined by the Qopa warriors who appeared like spirits out of the darkness.

Nathan noted Jack was not among them. He wondered where the Cockney was. Joeli also noticed Jack was missing. The ratu assumed he'd made a run for it while he could. Joeli thought Jack must have read his mind: he'd intended to kill the womanizing White-Face if they made it back to Momi Bay alive.

As soon as they were out of earshot of the encampment, they started running. They ran as fast as the slowest person would allow. That was Susannah, who was still exhausted from her forced march from Momi Bay. Nathan assisted her over the muddy terrain while Waisale also stayed close to Sina.

Leading the way, Joeli continuously glanced over his shoulder. His worried look told the others he knew Rambuka's outcasts would be coming for them sooner or later. He was anxious to put as much distance between themselves and Tomanivi as possible.

Despite the precariousness of their situation, Joeli felt elated. While Nathan and Waisale had been rescuing the women, he'd entered Rambuka's bure and retrieved the golden tabua. Earlier reconnaissance had determined which bure was Rambuka's. Joeli had reasoned that his deceitful half-brother would keep the sacred whale's tooth there. And he was right: as soon as he'd entered the bure, he had seen the golden tabua hanging on the far wall.

Retrieving the object had been no mean feat. Joeli had had to walk within a few feet of a sleeping Rambuka and half a dozen slave girls who were sleeping with him. He had been sorely tempted to kill Rambuka where he slept, but he knew he'd have risked waking the slaves.

When the moon disappeared behind clouds and light rain began falling, Joeli took this as a sign the gods of the forest were smiling on him. Now that he had the golden tabua once more in his possession, the ratu knew all would be well. His heart felt at peace.

13

At dawn, a soft drizzle cast a watery curtain over Tomanivi and its surrounds. In the outcasts' encampment, Rambuka's cousin, Uraia, walked toward the slaves' quarters. A more youthful version of Rambuka, he shared the same fierce features.

Entering the slaves' bure, Uraia saw at a glance Susannah and Sina were missing. The remaining slave girls were still asleep. Then he noticed the dead Tongan guard. Rolling him onto his back, he grimaced at the sight of the ugly knife wound around his comrade's throat.

Uraia hurriedly backed out of the bure and sprinted to Rambuka's bure.

Behind him, screams rang out from the slaves' quarters when the remaining slave girls woke and saw the dead guard.

Uraia burst in to Rambuka's bure, waking his cousin. "They have killed Tefolaha!" he shouted. "And they have taken the White-Face and the Qopa slave girl!"

Wiping sleep from his eyes, Rambuka looked at his cousin, his expression one of fury. He turned around and immediately saw the golden tabua was missing from its usual place on the wall. Rambuka knew it could have only been Joeli.

Springing to his feet, he grabbed the musket, tomahawk, and

hunting knife he kept by his bed mat. "Assemble a war party," he commanded.

#

Five miles to the west, Nathan was dragging Susannah by the arm through driving rain in the dense rainforest. Other than an urgent word here or there, there had been no time for discussion. Even breathing was an effort.

Though he still hadn't given Susannah any indication as to how he felt about her, the American's entire being was focused on her wellbeing. He knew now beyond a shadow of a doubt he loved the Englishwoman. And he realized it wasn't just her beauty; it was her spirit. Looking at her now, he could see the will to live was as strong in her as it was in him.

Nathan wanted to stop and hug her right then, but he couldn't. It wasn't just the fact that they had to keep moving; he still wasn't sure if the deep feelings he had for her were mutual.

Exhausted though she was, Susannah was feeling as though she'd been given a second chance at life. It wasn't that long ago, she'd been contemplating death. Now she believed she knew how Lazarus must have felt after Jesus raised him from the dead.

Holding on to Nathan's strong hand and surrounded by brave Qopa warriors, she could feel life throbbing through her veins.

I am alive!

Full of hope once more, Susannah allowed herself to dare to fantasize about the things she wanted most out of life: love, passion, a family of her own.

As she pictured this future, she looked at Nathan running beside her. He briefly glanced into her eyes. Things suddenly became clear to Susannah.

Yes, this is the man I wish to spend the rest of my life with. Please, God, let it be.

Then doubts began to invade her mind once more. She knew she still wasn't sure how he really felt about her.

Do his feelings mirror mine or am I just fooling myself that such a worldly man would care for a naïve young woman like me? I wish he'd give me a sign.

A frank discussion would have answered the doubts that were simultaneously running through the minds of each, but there was no time for that now.

Peering through the driving rain, they noticed Joeli and the others had stopped to inspect something in a forest clearing beside a river.

As the couple drew closer, they saw the object of the Qopas' attention: the head of a man who had been buried up to his neck.

Susannah screamed when she recognized Father Montrose. The dead priest's eyes were wide open, his mouth stuffed with stones. It was a macabre sight. Nathan tried to shield Susannah from the gruesome spectacle, but was too late. The young woman doubled over and began dry-retching.

Joeli exhorted the party to keep moving. He knew Rambuka's outcasts would most certainly be coming for them by now.

#

Joeli was right. Rambuka was leading some thirty musketbearing men out from Tomanivi at a fast trot. His cousin, Uraia, was among them. Heavy rain reduced their visibility to a few yards, and they also struggled to keep their footing in the muddy conditions. Despite this, they were closing on their quarry.

Although the rain had washed away his enemies' tracks, Rambuka knew roughly which course they would follow. He guessed it was his half-brother Joeli who had led the raid on his encampment, and he strongly suspected Nathan was with him.

Putting himself in Joeli's position, he knew his enemies would head straight for Momi Bay. To deviate from that course would be to invite disaster. The longer they took to reach the safety of their fortified village, the more time the outcasts would have to hunt them down.

The only question in Rambuka's mind was how many of them there were and how much of a start they had. Desperate to kill Joeli, recover the golden tabua, and crush his Qopa enemies once and for all, he exhorted his men to run harder.

#

Further west, in a valley that dissected the Nadrau Plateau, Joeli's party battled the conditions as they tried to distance themselves from Tomanivi. The heavy rain and mud combined to slow them down.

Susannah slowed them down even more. She was tiring rapidly, and Nathan now had to virtually carry her.

With Joeli still leading the way, they plunged through swamps and heavy undergrowth, forded streams, and scrambled up and down hills. Slipping and sliding in the mud, Susannah in particular was finding the going tough.

Joeli continuously looked over his shoulder. "Faster!" he called. "Rambuka's dogs will be coming now!"

Struggling to support Susannah's weight and stay on his feet, Nathan wondered again where Jack was. For the first time, he began to believe his Cockney friend may have deserted them. Having saved the Cockney's life, Nathan felt some resentment toward him for his apparent cowardice, but he had no time to dwell on it. Besides, he couldn't be sure what had become of Jack.

At the foot of a hill, they came to a flood-swollen river, which they judged was too fast-flowing to ford. They ran along its bank and soon found themselves in a deep gorge. High cliffs rose up on either side of them as the gorge narrowed, turning the river into a series of treacherous rapids. Joeli's party scrambled over and around large boulders. In places they were forced to wade along the edge of the raging torrent.

Manasa, the warrior who helped strangle his sister, Adi, so her spirit could accompany Iremaia's on its journey to the Afterlife, lost his footing and fell in. Only the quick reactions of the one-eyed Babitu saved him from being swept away.

#

With no tracks to follow in the heavy rain, Rambuka took a slightly different course to that of his quarry. The route he followed brought him to a cliff top above the same gorge Joeli's party had ventured into a short time earlier.

Running hard at the head of his men, Rambuka had to pull up quickly to avoid falling over the cliff edge. Uraia was first to reach his side. Together, the cousins peered through the rain into the gorge.

The rain eased momentarily to reveal their enemies making their way along the bottom of the gorge. Uraia pointed at them. Rambuka nodded and immediately began climbing down the cliff face. Uraia and the others followed.

Down in the gorge, Nathan and Waisale were helping the two women scramble over a large boulder when Waisale looked up at the cliff top just in time to see an outcast framed against the skyline. He immediately signaled to Joeli, who looked up and saw the outcast just before he disappeared from view. The ratu alerted his warriors. They immediately dispersed and began setting up ambush positions among the rocks.

Nathan turned to Susannah. "You and Sina go with Waisale," he ordered. Susannah clung to Nathan, indicating she wanted to remain with him. The American pushed her firmly toward Waisale. "Go," he commanded. He nodded to Waisale, who took Susannah and Sina each by an arm and led them away.

Nathan hurried to Joeli's side. He noted the ratu was now holding a musket instead of his huge whale bone club. Looking pointedly at the musket, he asked, "Don't tell me the great Joeli now uses the dreaded white man's weapons?"

"A wise leader use anything to kill Rambuka's dogs," Joeli said defensively. He busied himself as he practised priming the weapon.

Noting his clumsy efforts, Nathan quickly showed him how to prime the musket correctly. Joeli then circulated among his warriors, issuing orders. By now, the warriors were well hidden among the rocks and seemed resigned to the fight that was coming their way.

Nathan scouted around for a good vantage point for himself. He soon found one: a narrow gap between two boulders. The gap was just wide enough to cradle the barrel of his musket and provide an uninterrupted view of the terrain ahead. Settling down to await the outcasts, he scanned the cliff tops above, looking for some sign of Jack.

The possibility that the Cockney had deserted them was rapidly becoming a certainty in Nathan's mind.

Damn you, Jack!

Looking behind him, Nathan saw that Waisale was still leading the two women away from the immediate danger zone. Their progress seemed painfully slow.

#

The outcasts soon reached the foot of the cliff and, with Rambuka still leading the way, soon caught up with their quarry. They were met by a barrage of musket fire, which echoed up and down the gorge like rolling thunder.

Despite the deafening noise, the results were less impressive. Joeli's warriors were using muskets for only the second time in anger, and their shots were way off target. Only Nathan found his mark, killing two outcasts. His accuracy was sufficient to prompt the outcasts to take cover.

Then, in a classic rearguard action, Nathan, Joeli, and four others lay down cover fire from the protection of the rocks to allow their fellow warriors to retreat along the gorge. Outnumbered and in danger of being overrun, Joeli was employing advice Nathan had given to him earlier, ordering those closest to their pursuers to retreat while others lay down cover fire for them.

As they continued this strategy along the length of the gorge, the retreating warriors slowly became more confident with their muskets. Four more outcasts were felled. Another slipped into the river and disappeared beneath the swirling waters. The rearguard tactic was proving effective.

Babitu suddenly became isolated from the others. While trying to catch up to his fellow warriors, he was shot in the leg. Babitu was quickly overtaken by two outcasts who hacked him to death. Adi's brother, Manasa, and another Qopa warrior were wounded too severely to even try to escape and were shot where they lay.

Further up the gorge, Waisale was pushing the two women in his charge to run faster along the riverbank. Spurred on by the sounds of battle behind them, Susannah and Sina ran for their lives.

14

In the gorge, as the rain abated, Rambuka took stock of the situation. Recognizing his enemies had the advantage of superior cover, he signaled to his men to pull back and regroup. A quick headcount showed he'd suffered eight casualties—five dead and another three seriously wounded. That left him with twenty-three able-bodied men.

Cursing his enemies, Rambuka conferred with his senior warriors. They quickly concluded their enemies could not remain in the gorge forever. Sooner or later, they'd have to move on. That was when they'd be vulnerable.

"We wait for them to make the next move," Rambuka said.

Joeli's men took advantage of the lull in fighting to retreat to the foot of a steep hill at the far end of the gorge. There, they found Waisale and the two women resting.

Seeing Nathan, Susannah rushed over to him. "Thank God you're alive," she whispered. She immediately regretted expressing her innermost emotions. Still unsure whether he felt the same as she did, she didn't want to make herself any more vulnerable than she was.

"It's not God you should be thanking," Nathan said, raising his musket. "It's this."

Susannah smiled patiently and shook her head. "No, Nathan. It's God."

Nathan chuckled then grew serious. Looking into Susannah's hazel-flecked eyes, he wondered again if she was experiencing the same strong feelings he had for her. He sensed she was. Nathan longed to pull her to him and kiss her, but still something made him hesitate.

Not usually one to hesitate, he didn't know what it was that was stopping him being spontaneous now. Maybe the timing wasn't right, he reasoned. Whatever it was, he despised himself for not revealing his true feelings.

You don't even know if you're going to survive this little excursion, and yet here you are afraid of being rejected by a missionary's daughter!

Nathan became aware of Joeli firing orders at his warriors. Moments later, a Qopa warrior ran past them, accidentally nudging Susannah.

She nearly lost her footing and suddenly found herself in Nathan's arms, her face less than an inch from his.

The American went to release her. To his surprise, Susannah kept hold of him for a moment.

What's she playing at?

Again, he looked into her eyes. Not for the first time, he felt as though he were drowning in them. He wanted to kiss her, but again he froze.

As Susannah looked up at Nathan, she felt as though she was losing control of her senses. Everything seemed to be whirling around her and her heart was hammering away in her chest.

In Nathan's powerful masculine presence, Susannah had an overwhelming sense that God had created him just for her. She knew that was irrational, but she clung to that thought as everything began spinning around her.

Fearing she was about to faint, she pushed Nathan away and took a step back.

Nathan thought he'd upset her. Embarrassed, he mumbled, "I'll be back shortly." He hurried over to where Joeli was standing.

Watching him go, Susannah was upset, but not for the reason Nathan thought she was. She was upset he hadn't kissed her. She'd seen him looking longingly at her, yet nothing had happened.

Susannah wanted so desperately to feel his kiss. She recognized her intense feelings for Nathan were growing ever stronger—hastened no doubt by the dangerous situation they found themselves in.

It was then Susannah realized she didn't want to die before she'd made love to Nathan. *To die without ever feeling that intimacy with another soul,* she decided, *would be an injustice of the highest order.* Susannah uttered a silent prayer to God that he would not allow her to die a virgin. She knew if she died after she'd made love to Nathan, she would at least feel she'd reached fulfillment as a woman.

Nathan arrived at Joeli's side as the ratu was doing a headcount. Joeli quickly determined their numbers had been reduced to seventeen. He'd lost three men and several others had been wounded.

Grim-faced, the ratu turned to Nathan. "Where Jack Halliday?" he asked. Nathan shrugged, indicating he didn't know. Joeli added, "We could use his muskets."

Like Joeli, Nathan was now convinced Jack had fled. In a way, he couldn't really blame him. The Cockney had probably reached the conclusion this was a suicide mission. Even if he survived it, it was likely Joeli or one of his warriors would kill him for having seduced their women.

Despite this, Nathan was angry he'd misread Jack. He'd picked him to be a man of his word and now felt let down.

Looking at Joeli, Nathan asked, "What do you want to do?"

"We cannot outrun outcasts," Joeli said resignedly. "We make stand here."

Nathan saw Joeli was looking at the steep hill that rose up directly in front of them. He assessed it was at least one thousand feet high. Although strangely devoid of vegetation, it offered plenty of cover in the form of large rocks and boulders. It was a natural fortress. "This looks like a good killing ground," he agreed.

Joeli nodded. Turning to Waisale and pointing to the hill's summit, he said, "Take the women up there."

Again, Waisale took the two women each by the hand and started dragging them up the hill. As they began climbing, Susannah looked back at Nathan. Their eyes locked knowingly for a few moments. Nathan felt his heart go out to her. He prayed she'd be safe.

Just then, shouts came from upriver. Joeli turned to see one of his trackers, Penaia, running toward them. Shouting as he ran, Penaia called, "Rambuka's dogs are coming again!"

"How many?" Joeli asked. He guessed the outcasts had seen Waisale and the women setting off up the hill.

"I count twenty-three," Penaia responded.

Joeli signaled to his warriors to follow him up the hill. They strode out after him, carrying their wounded with them.

Nathan lingered behind. He absentmindedly touched his whale bone pendant as he waited. Moments later, Rambuka and Uraia rounded a bend not a hundred yards upriver. They were closely followed by the other outcasts.

Seeing the American standing his ground, Rambuka stopped and looked directly at him. Uraia and the others pulled up beside their leader. Behind Nathan, the figures of Joeli and his warriors could be seen scrambling up the steep hill. Not taking his eyes off Nathan, Rambuka said, "The White-Face is mine." Uraia nodded.

Nathan looked directly at Rambuka for a moment longer then turned and started running up the hill. He zigzagged as he ran, to make the uphill journey easier and to make it harder for anyone to shoot him if they were so inclined. No shots came.

Behind him, Uraia surveyed the steep hill. "The Qopa pigs will make their stand there," he predicted.

Rambuka studied the terrain. "They have chosen well," he conceded. He then gathered his followers around him to discuss tactics.

#

It was late morning before the outcasts made their move. It hadn't surprised Nathan that they were in no hurry. The outcasts would know the hill their enemies now occupied offered their best chance of survival, so it was obvious they would make their stand here.

Now, as Rambuka led his followers up the hill, Nathan and Joeli watched them from behind a small boulder near the summit. Nathan focused his scope on Rambuka. The Outcast's menacing features were magnified dramatically by the scope's lenses. Nathan handed the scope to Joeli, who immediately put it up to his eye. "We need to hold this hill or we're dead," the American said.

Joeli grunted once as he studied his enemy through the scope. "We have the high ground," he said. "Rambuka soon feel power of Joeli."

"As long as our ammunition holds," Nathan cautioned. His

concern was shared by Joeli. Nathan looked around as Waisale joined them. "Are the women okay?"

Not comprehending the question, Waisale looked at Joeli.

"He asks if the women are safe," the ratu translated.

The handsome young warrior looked at Nathan and nodded. Nathan knew Waisale had hidden Susannah and Sina behind a large boulder on the summit, which was only a few yards away.

For no apparent reason, and despite the severity of their situation, Joeli found himself thinking about the secret dye Waisale had used to turn his hair pink. Although the warriors had all washed the dye from their hair before setting out from Momi Bay, Joeli hadn't forgotten Waisale's promise to divulge the ingredients he used to dye his hair pink if Sina was rescued from the outcasts. Joeli and his warriors had spent many long hours speculating on the various natural ingredients that could have been used. The thought suddenly occurred to him that if Waisale was killed in the coming battle, his secret would die with him. Looking at his friend, he asked, "Do you remember your promise?"

Waisale immediately knew what Joeli was talking about. He was aware that Joeli and the others had been highly jealous of his uniquely colored hair. Grinning sheepishly, he said, "I traded fish for some dyes of the White-Face when one of the tall ships visited."

For the first time in days, Joeli laughed aloud. After so much speculation, it struck him as amusing that the so-called secret ingredients Waisale used was something as mundane as European dyes. Waisale joined in the laughter.

Looking on, Nathan could only guess as to what had amused them. The trio returned their attention to their enemies below. The outcasts were already a third of the way up the hill. They were zigzagging their way up the hill, using boulders for cover.

Turning to Joeli, Nathan said, "You should tell the others to wait for your signal before they start shooting. We must save ammunition."

Joeli immediately relayed instructions to Waisale. The young warrior nodded and scampered away to pass on Joeli's orders to the other warriors who had taken up defensive positions among the rocks.

15

As the outcasts continued climbing up the hill, a frightened Susannah and Sina sat resting, their backs against the large boulder on the summit. A broad, grassy valley stretched out before them. It extended all the way to a range of forest-covered hills far to the west.

Holding hands for comfort, the two women were exhausted after a morning of non-stop activity. Susannah, in particular, was in bad shape. Having survived her abduction from Momi Bay and then the morning's flight from Tomanivi, being dragged up the hill had been the last straw for her. She was physically, mentally, and emotionally spent.

Sina nodded toward the distant hills. "Momi Bay that way," she said wistfully.

Susannah smiled. She could only guess at how much Sina missed her home and loved ones. Nathan suddenly appeared at her side. "Nathan!" She couldn't disguise how relieved she was to see him.

"Are you all right?" he asked, kneeling down beside her.

Susannah nodded. "Where are they now?" she asked, referring to the outcasts.

"They're coming," Nathan said, scanning the valley below. He lingered a moment, keen to spend as much time as he could in Susannah's presence, but more unsure than ever what to say to her.

Looking at him as he studied the valley floor, Susannah wished she had more time with Nathan so they could just get to know each other. Everything seemed so rushed and out of control. The young woman sensed that behind Nathan's confident exterior, there was uncertainty. Suddenly fearful, she leaned closer to him and whispered, "I don't want to die here, Nathan."

"That's not going to happen, Susannah," Nathan said adamantly. He tried to sound as convincing as he could even if he didn't fully believe what he was saying. "Our Qopa friends are great fighters, and they will defend us just as they did when the outcasts attacked us at Momi Bay."

He purposefully omitted the fact that this battle was in Rambuka's territory and the outcasts were numerically superior. Nor did he mention the Qopa didn't have the sophisticated palisades and trenches that protected their village.

Susannah looked at him intently. "How did we ever get caught up in all this?"

"I don't know," Nathan said, sitting down beside her.

Susannah rested her head against Nathan's shoulder. It felt so natural, she didn't even notice the light rain that was beginning to fall. For some unfathomable reason, the memory of her father's gruesome death came to her. Slowly, inevitably, the emotions she'd been storing up since her abduction bubbled to the surface. Giving in to her grief, she buried her face in Nathan's chest and cried until she had no tears left.

As he held her tight, Nathan glanced at Sina, who stared back at him gravely. She could relate to how he and Susannah felt. After all, she had just been reunited with Waisale and they were both experiencing similar emotions. She smiled understandingly at Nathan.

Finally, Susannah looked up at Nathan. "I miss my father," she whispered.

"I know." He wished he could help her through her pain. All he could do was hold her. Forcing himself to focus on their present situation, he suddenly stood up and addressed both women. "You must flee while you can." He spoke with urgency now. "There's no guarantee we can hold these savages off. Do you understand?"

The women looked at each other then back at Nathan and shook their heads in unison.

Sina said, "No . . . our place here."

Nathan became angry. "Look—"

Susannah interjected, saying, "No, Nathan. We stay."

Nathan was momentarily dumbfounded. He stood staring down at the stubborn pair.

The silence was shattered by a musket shot and all three jumped. The shot was immediately followed by a crescendo of musket fire.

Nathan looked around the boulder and saw that the outcasts were nearing the summit. He turned back to Susannah. Grabbing her by both shoulders, he said, "If we look like we're gonna be overrun, you get down there to safety." He pointed to the valley below. "Find a place to hide and stay there."

Susannah nodded. Their eyes locked once more. Nathan then hurried off to rejoin the others.

Crawling down to Joeli, he could see the outcasts were very close now. They were dashing from rock to rock, priming and firing their muskets as they ran. The light rain ensured conditions underfoot remained treacherous, slowing them, but still they kept coming, inching toward their enemies at the top of the hill.

The outcasts were inspired by their leader, Rambuka, who suddenly decided to ignore the available cover and run straight up the hill. Other outcasts fell in behind him.

Joeli shouted, "Kill Rambuka!

Waisale and several other warriors aimed their muskets at the outcast leader. All shots missed their mark. Noting their intentions, Nathan raised his musket. Looking down the barrel, he lined up Rambuka in his sights. Rambuka was fifty yards away and closing fast. A Samoan outcast followed hard on his heels.

Just as Nathan squeezed the trigger, Rambuka slipped and fell. Nathan's shot hit the Samoan between the eyes, felling him. Oblivious to the near miss, Rambuka jumped up and continued running.

Cursing, Nathan primed his musket for another shot. He looked up just in time to see Rambuka dive for cover behind rocks some thirty yards away.

At the same time, a musket shot boomed out from a nearby hillside, felling an outcast. Nathan scanned the terrain, looking for a glimpse of the marksman.

It could only be Jack.

Over the next minute, three more shots came from the direction of the adjoining hill and three more outcasts fell.

Finally, Nathan saw him.

It is Jack!

The Cockney was lying prone on a rock ledge near the top of the adjoining hill. From where he was, Jack had a clear view of the outcasts. He fired again and yet another outcast fell.

Cheering erupted among Joeli's warriors.

Below them, Rambuka's outcasts were forced to take cover to avoid Jack's sharpshooting.

Realizing the danger, Rambuka led his followers along a ridge to remove themselves from Jack's line of fire. Behind them, the bodies of their fellow outcasts lay strewn over the hillside.

In the preceding firefight, the defenders had also taken casualties. Two more warriors lay dead and another two wounded. Waisale was among the latter. He was nursing a shoulder wound.

Fleeing Tomanivi the previous night, Jack had had second thoughts about deserting the very people who had rescued him from the cannibals' cooking pot. He was nearly halfway to the village he'd been using as his base when his conscience had finally gotten the better of him; he'd turned back and retraced his steps to Tomanivi, eventually catching up with Joeli's party in the gorge. By then, the outcasts had also caught up to them, so he'd looked for a vantage point from where he could inflict some damage with the two muskets he still carried. He'd soon found a good spot on the hillside that adjoined the hill Nathan and the others were making their stand on.

The shooting faded then died, heralding another lull in the fighting. For the moment, both camps lay low as light rain continued to fall.

Casualties were mounting. The Qopas' numbers had been reduced to fifteen, the outcasts seventeen. Although only slightly fewer in number, and holding the high ground advantage, Joeli's men were running dangerously low on ammunition.

16

Nathan sensed it would only be a matter of time before he and the others were overrun. Behind the big boulder at the summit, he could hear Susannah reciting the Lord's Prayer. He wished she and Sina would save themselves and flee.

Sina suddenly appeared from behind the boulder. Noticing that Waisale had been wounded, she rushed to his side. The young warrior frowned at her, annoyed that she was exposing herself to danger. Ignoring him, she hurriedly applied a makeshift dressing to his shoulder. "I never thought I would see you again," Sina confided.

"I never lost hope," Waisale smiled. "I thought about you every day." He touched her face affectionately.

Nathan looked back to see what Jack was doing. There was no sign of him. The American guessed he was looking for a better vantage point. Nathan suddenly felt guilty he'd ever doubted Jack. He made a mental note to buy him a drink if they ever made it back to civilization.

While Nathan was thinking about Jack, the Cockney was making his way up the other side of the same hill the warring parties occupied. As soon as the outcasts had moved out of his line of fire, he'd decided to join Joeli's party and had crossed over via a ridge connecting the two hills. He carried a musket over each shoulder as he hurried up toward the boulder where Susannah was sitting.

At that moment, Susannah was the only one who could see Jack. Not expecting to find another white man in the area, she was, to put it mildly, surprised.

Unsure of his intentions, she stood up and prepared to alert the others.

"Morning, sunshine," Jack called out breathlessly, flashing a cheeky grin. "Lovely day for a war, ain't it?"

"And who are you?" Susannah asked, mystified.

"You know, I've been asking meself that same question for years, Miss," Jack laughed, stopping in front of the young woman. "Me friends call me Jack Halliday," he said, "so I guess that's who I am." His green eyes twinkled as he flirted with Susannah. "You can call me Jack."

Warming to the irrepressible Cockney, Susannah said, "Well, I am sure my friends will be pleased to see you, Jack. They need all the help they can get at present."

"I gathered that," Jack chuckled. Looking Susannah up and down admiringly, he added, "If ya don't mind me sayin' so, I can see why Nathan risked his life for you."

"You know Nathan?"

"Know 'im? If we was any closer we'd be lovers, Miss." Susannah smiled at the other's choice of words. Jack added, "Well, I best be makin' meself useful." He walked off to join the others.

The first Nathan knew Jack had crossed over from the adjoining hillside was when the Cockney flopped down on the ground next to him. Hiding his surprise, Nathan asked, "What took you so long?"

"Why, did you miss me smiling face?"

"Not really. We were enjoying the break." As an afterthought, he added, "You weren't making a pass at the Englishwoman, I hope."

"Who, me?" Jack grinned. "Now that you mention it, I should've. Think she was pretty taken with me."

Nathan hid a smile. Jack could tell the young American was pleased to see him. He appreciated the fact Nathan didn't interrogate him about where he'd been since the previous night. Looking around, Jack saw that even Joeli's warriors appeared pleased he'd returned. He noticed Joeli was still glaring at him, but even his glares didn't seem as menacing as before.

"I wasn't gonna come back till I remembered what lousy shooters you lot are," Jack mumbled.

"Well, I'm glad you did," Nathan smiled, eyeing Jack's two muskets. "We can sure use the extra fire power."

"You got any more powder 'n shot?" Jack asked hopefully.

Nathan shook his head. "We're nearly out."

"Oh shite. I'm nearly out, too." Jack discarded one of his two muskets. "Guess I won't be needing that."

"Where'd you learn to shoot?" Nathan asked.

"Back at Koroi . . . my village. I hadn't even touched a musket before I arrived there some years back. I soon realized my wife's people had their share of enemies so I supplied 'em with muskets to help 'em out. That's when I learned."

"You got a family, Jack?"

"Oh, yeah," Jack smiled as he thought of his beautiful Fijian wife, Namosi, and their two young children. "Me 'n Namosi have two kids and another on the—"

Jack was interrupted by a shout from one of Joeli's warriors alerting them to signs of movement on the hillside below. It seemed Rambuka's followers were preparing for one final push.

"Here we go again," Nathan said resignedly.

The silence was broken by musket fire as the outcasts resumed their attack, firing as they came. The defenders kept their heads down for the moment. They were under strict orders to conserve their rapidly dwindling ammunition supplies.

Waiting for the outcasts to come closer, Nathan felt Jack's hand on his shoulder. He turned to see his friend grinning at him.

"Just wanted to say it's been a pleasure knowing ya," Jack said in recognition of the fact they may not survive what was to follow.

"Likewise," Nathan said, shaking the other's outstretched hand.

The pair aimed their muskets at the approaching outcasts who were now closing fast. Just below them, Nathan saw Joeli preparing to fire his musket. Under his breath Nathan said, "Not yet, Joeli. Not yet." Not taking his eyes off the outcasts, Nathan asked, "So why did you really come back, Jack?"

Jack chuckled. "Damned if I know. I must be two farthings short of a penny."

The outcasts were within ten yards of the defenders when Joeli finally fired his musket. This was the signal for the defenders to open fire. Nathan and Jack fired in unison and a dozen other shots rang out.

Six outcasts fell in the first volley. It wasn't totally one-sided: three Qopa defenders were also killed in the exchange.

Despite their losses, the outcasts kept coming. As they overran the Qopas' front lines, vicious hand-to-hand fighting ensued. Rambuka was to the fore. Using his musket as a club, he dispatched two defenders in his path. Uraia fought alongside his cousin with equal fury.

Joeli spotted Rambuka and swung his musket around in the Outcast's direction. In his excitement, he accidentally discharged the weapon as he was still raising it to his shoulder. Throwing the musket aside, Joeli charged Rambuka, whale bone club in one hand and tomahawk in the other.

Rambuka saw Joeli coming and picked up the loaded musket of a fallen outcast. Firing from the hip, he shot Joeli at point-blank range. The impact of the shot knocked Joeli backward. The ratu rolled a short distance until his journey was brought to an abrupt halt by a protruding rock. Joeli lay motionless, clutching a gut wound. He knew instinctively he'd been mortally wounded.

In half a dozen strides, Rambuka reached Joeli. Standing astride his half-brother as the fighting raged around them, the Outcast raised one arm above his head triumphantly. "Joeli is mine!" he shouted before uttering a blood-curdling war cry.

17

Drawing his hunting knife, Rambuka bent down to cut Joeli's throat. He looked up just in time to see Waisale almost upon him. Now out of ammunition, the handsome young Qopa warrior had swapped his musket for a tomahawk.

Waisale was desperate to save his friend and ratu. He swung his tomahawk at Rambuka. The Outcast ducked beneath the swinging weapon, stepped forward, and thrust his knife upwards, burying it up to its hilt in Waisale's chest. The young warrior sank to his knees, staring up at Rambuka. He died like that, still kneeling.

A woman's screams attracted Rambuka's attention. He looked up to see Sina staring down from the large boulder above. Susannah appeared next to her. Grinning at the two women, Rambuka pulled his knife from Waisale's chest. The young warrior toppled forward and lay unmoving, face down in the mud.

Still screaming, Sina started running toward Waisale. Susannah grabbed her arm and tried to restrain her. "Sina, no!" Susannah cried as she struggled to hold her friend. She looked around for help and saw Nathan. "Nathan!" she shouted.

Nathan, who had witnessed Waisale's death, rushed to Susannah's assistance and helped pull Sina back behind the large boulder. "Stay here!" he said harshly to Sina, pushing her back. The young woman collapsed into Susannah's arms, sobbing. "Keep her here," Nathan ordered.

Meanwhile, Rambuka was anxious to finish Joeli off and recover the golden tabua he was sure his half-brother had in his possession. Turning back to Joeli, Rambuka suddenly found himself confronted by two warriors intent on protecting their ratu. They, too, had been reduced to using their muskets as clubs. The Outcast was forced backward before their onslaught. Priming his borrowed musket as he backpeddled, Rambuka shot one of his attackers dead then grappled with the second. The two rolled down the hill in a life-and-death struggle.

Near death, Joeli could only watch the mayhem happening around him.

Nathan returned to the fray in time to see Rambuka stab the warrior he'd been grappling with. Looking around, the American also saw that Jack was making good use of the last of his ammunition. The Cockney's hands were a blur as he fired, primed his musket, and fired again, killing two more outcasts.

However, Nathan's immediate concern was for Joeli. He rushed to the ratu's side and dragged him to the temporary safety afforded by the large boulder that Susannah and Sina were sheltering behind.

The women looked on as Nathan cradled Joeli in his arms. Blood flowing from the ratu's gaping stomach wound now covered both men.

Oblivious to the rain that fell, Joeli looked up at Nathan through pain-filled eyes. Speaking English, he gasped, "Nathan Johnson...we are brothers." Nathan nodded. Joeli reached down into his rations pouch and drew out the precious golden tabua he'd retrieved from Rambuka's hut. He handed it to Nathan, saying, "This belong to my people."

Nathan took the golden tabua from Joeli and placed it in his backpack. "I will see they get it," Nathan assured him.

Joeli then looked at Susannah and Sina. His eyes began to glaze over as the life slowly ebbed out of him. "You must take women to safety." Joeli touched the open wound in his stomach then lifted his bloodied hand skyward. Rain drops mingled with blood, splattering his face. "Red rain," he said, studying the blood-red raindrops.

"Red . . . rain."

18

As Joeli died in Nathan's arms, the rain intensified, as if on cue, washing the blood from the young ratu's face. The American now understood why the Qopa referred to this region as the Land of Red Rain.

Nathan was more deeply affected by Joeli's death than he would have believed possible. Looking into the ratu's open but unseeing eyes, he knew he would always remember Joeli as a true and loyal friend.

Susannah leaned forward and closed Joeli's eyes. Next to her, Sina sobbed uncontrollably, but the Englishwoman appeared to have found a new inner strength. She recognized she needed to be strong for Sina and herself.

Nathan couldn't believe how much courage Susannah was showing in the face of death. As he looked into her eyes, he wondered if he was the reason she was being so strong just as she was the reason he was remaining staunch.

With the sounds of fighting drawing closer, Nathan tore himself away from Joeli's lifeless body and looked around the boulder. At a glance he saw that Jack and the other defenders were in danger of being overwhelmed by the outcasts.

Both sides had sustained heavy casualties, but the Qopa had

fared worst. The remaining five defenders were now outnumbered two to one and all except Jack had run out of ammunition. The fighting was now entirely being conducted at close quarters, and the weapons being used were mainly clubs, knives, and tomahawks.

Rambuka, with his cousin Uraia by his side, was fighting with a fury that inspired the remaining outcasts, whereas the Qopa, without their ratu, were becoming dispirited—as if they could sense they were fighting a losing battle.

Nathan's fingers strayed to the whale bone pendant hanging from his neck. Thinking through his options, his fingertips subconsciously traced the carvings that ran the full length of the pendant, from its rounded end all the way down to its sharp, dagger-like tip.

The American looked back at Susannah and Sina and immediately experienced conflicting emotions: he wanted to help Jack out and remain loyal to Joeli's warriors, but he also wanted to save the two women in his charge. Looking around the boulder again, he saw Jack staring directly at him.

"Run for it!" Jack yelled.

Nathan hesitated. He couldn't believe this man he hardly even knew was willing to sacrifice his life for him.

"Run, damn you!" the Cockney shouted.

Their eyes locked for what seemed an eternity, but was in fact only the briefest of moments. In that instant, Nathan sensed they were kindred souls. He looked at Jack then back to the two women in his charge. The women's safety was paramount in his mind. So, too, was Joeli's dying wish. Yet the loyalty he felt toward Jack and the surviving Qopa could not be denied. A thousand conflicting emotions gripped him, momentarily paralyzing him.

Returning his attention to the battlefield, Nathan saw it was now seven against three—Rambuka, Uraia, and five other outcasts against Jack and the two Qopa trackers, Penaia and Rewa. To make matters worse, the three defenders had all been wounded. Jack had a minor flesh wound, but his two Qopa companions were both gravely wounded and were so exhausted they could hardly defend themselves.

Nathan's mind was made up: he couldn't desert Jack and the others. Turning to Susannah and Sina, he snapped, "Stay out of sight!"

Both women nodded, wide-eyed. They were too frightened even to speak.

Without another word, Nathan left the cover of the boulder and scrambled to join the others. The Cockney saw him coming and shook his head disparagingly, making it clear he considered the American crazy. Jack was too busy to say anything: he was frantically priming his musket as a disfigured outcast ran at him, knife in hand. Nathan shot the outcast dead just before he could reach the Cockney. Jack flashed a look of gratitude Nathan's way.

Not ten feet away, Rambuka and Uraia were hacking at the wounded Qopa trackers with their tomahawks. It was clearly only a matter of time before Rewa and Penaia succumbed to the cousins' fury.

Uraia was the first to strike, clubbing Rewa to the ground then burying his tomahawk in his victim's chest; then Rambuka brought his tomahawk savagely down on the head of Penaia. The tracker was dead before he hit the ground but, with another swing of his tomahawk, Rambuka decapitated him to make doubly sure.

As Nathan tried to prime his musket, he was hit by the sickening realization he was out of powder. Throwing the musket aside, he drew out his pistol from beneath his shirt just as two outcasts ran at him, their weapons raised. Nathan shot one dead while Jack dispatched the other with a well-aimed musket ball.

The two whites took stock of their situation; it didn't look good. They were the last remaining defenders. Outnumbered four to two, and almost out of ammunition, it seemed only a question of time before they were overpowered.

Nathan's thoughts returned to the two women whose lives, he knew, depended on him.

Jack looked at him. "We have to run for it!"

It was as if the Cockney had read his mind. Nathan needed no second bidding. "Let's go!"

The pair retreated behind the boulder where they found Susannah and Sina waiting, ready to flee. Without a word, Nathan grabbed the two women and began dragging them down the hill. He assumed Jack was following.

Jack never had any intention of fleeing. He knew they'd soon be chased down by the fleetfooted outcasts, so decided to stay and try to buy the trio some time.

Through the rain, Rambuka caught a glimpse of the American fleeing with the two women. The Outcast guessed that Nathan now had possession of the golden tabua. He vowed to hunt the White-Face down.

A quarter way down the hill, Nathan looked behind and was alarmed to see Jack was still on the summit. The Cockney flashed a cheeky grin Nathan's way then disappeared from view. *What's he playing at?* Nathan asked himself. It dawned on him the Cockney never had any intention of fleeing. Jack was sacrificing himself to give him and the women a chance to survive.

Nathan's heart went out to Jack and feelings of gratitude coursed through him. His heart also went out to Joeli, Waisale, and the others he was leaving behind. He realized, without a shadow of a doubt, they were true friends. It was a bitter-sweet realization: for the first time in his life, he'd finally made friends.

On the summit, Jack stepped out from behind the boulder to see the four remaining outcasts coming at him. At the sight of the musket in his hands, they dived for cover behind rocks. Jack smiled grimly to himself. He was aware he was down to his last musket ball, so knew he would need to find creative ways to stall his enemies.

After several long minutes, a squat, bearded outcast with a spear in each hand suddenly showed himself and hurled one of his spears at Jack. His aim was off and he paid the price: Jack shot him dead.

As one, the other outcasts ran at their enemy. Now out of powder, Jack hurled his musket at the nearest outcast, an especially ugly individual, then drew his hunting knife and stabbed him in the chest, killing him. It was now two against one: Rambuka and Uraia against the Cockney.

Aware he was on borrowed time, Jack resolved he'd hold out as long as he could to give his friends more time to make good their escape. As the two surviving outcasts came at him, he bent down and scooped up a huge whale bone club lying at his feet. He wasn't to know the weapon had belonged to Joeli. Jack whirled it about his head, forcing Rambuka and Uraia to remain out of reach.

The cousins bided their time. They knew if they weren't careful they could both be taken out with one swing of the huge club. Jack waited for them. Rambuka finally came at him head on while Uraia approached from an angle.

Realizing he would have to deal with Rambuka first, Jack swung at him. Rambuka pulled up and the edge of the club missed his head by a whisker. At the same time, the Outcast lashed out with his tomahawk, shattering Jack's left arm. Jack screamed in agony. The pain coursed through his body like hot irons, and he thought he was going to faint. With his shattered left arm now hanging uselessly at his side, he steeled himself for the end.

As the cousins closed in for the kill, Jack's thoughts went to his Fijian wife, Namosi, and their two children back at Koroi. At that moment, he knew he'd never see them again. Nor would he see the baby his wife was due to have soon.

Rather than wait for death to come, Jack charged the outcasts, swinging Joeli's club around his head. Rambuka met him head on, parrying a blow with his tomahawk. At the same time, Uraia brought his tomahawk down on Jack's skull, killing him instantly.

The Cockney's broken body rolled down the hill until it stopped against the body of Waisale. By chance, his broken arm ended up flung out over the young warrior's chest, as if he were comforting him in death.

Rambuka and Uraia looked around them. The realization set in that they were the last men standing; the bodies of the fallen were strewn all the way down the hillside. Both sides had paid a terrible price.

Although they'd prevailed, neither cousin was happy. They knew there would be no victory until they'd reclaimed the golden tabua. With that in mind, they hurried to the summit to try to catch a glimpse of Nathan and the two women.

Rambuka was first to round the boulder at the summit. Looking out over the valley below, he was perturbed to see there was no sign of the trio. Uraia joined him. The two studied every possible hiding place from their vantage point.

As the rain eased, Rambuka suddenly pointed at a stand of kauri trees on the valley floor a hundred yards or so distant. "The White-Face and his women are there," he said with certainty.

Uraia nodded. There were no other hiding places nearby; in the time that had elapsed since the trio had fled the hilltop, the kauri trees offered the only possible hiding place. The cousins immediately began jogging down the hill toward the valley floor.

19

The cousins were right about where their quarry were hiding. Nathan and the two women were indeed hiding in the small stand of kauri trees. The American had ascertained the trees offered the only opportunity for concealment before the outcasts came after them.

Once the defenders had run out of powder and shot, defeat had been the only feasible outcome in Nathan's mind. He had realized if he and the two women were still out in the open when the fighting ended, they'd immediately be seen and would quickly be run down. So he'd opted to hide among the trees even though he knew the outcasts would probably guess that's where they were.

Nathan was under no illusions if Rambuka survived, he'd come after them, or his men would come in his place. *They'll want the women back*, he thought, *but they'll want the golden tabua even more*. Nathan looked at Susannah and Sina. "That's it," he announced. "Now they'll come for us." Nathan saw the fear in the women's eyes. He smiled encouragingly to try and instill a degree of confidence in them that he didn't feel himself.

Susannah asked, "What will we do?"

Nathan pulled his pistol from his belt, primed it then returned it to his belt. Pointing to some dense undergrowth nearby, he said, "You wait there. Make sure you keep quiet and don't move."

Nathan touched Susannah's hand briefly to comfort her. As he looked into her eyes he sensed she feared for his safety as much as he did hers. Nathan wanted to say so much more, but he knew there wasn't time. He withdrew his hand and strode off through the undergrowth.

Suddenly alone, Susannah and Sina looked at each other. Holding onto each other for comfort, they retreated into some dense foliage and made themselves as small as possible.

#

From the cover of the trees, Nathan watched as the two outcasts came running directly toward his hiding place. He frowned as he realized they were onto him. "Damn," he swore to himself. He drew his pistol and prepared to meet the approaching threat.

Tomahawks in hand, Rambuka and Uraia neared the stand of kauri trees. From the cover of the trees, Nathan watched as Rambuka signaled to his cousin to indicate he'd circle around behind. Uraia nodded. Rambuka ran off to his left, disappearing from sight.

Uraia walked directly toward Nathan's hiding place. The American withdrew deeper into the trees then stood dead still, straining his eyes and ears to pick up any foreign sight or sound. There was only silence. He tiptoed forward, trying to second-guess where Uraia was.

Nathan froze when he heard ferns rustle close by. Unseen, Uraia was coming toward him through the undergrowth. Nathan nervously fingered the whale bone pendant hanging around his neck. As the outcast passed unknowingly within a few feet of him, Nathan stepped out behind him, his pistol raised. Uraia spun around, but he was too slow. Nathan shot him in the chest. The outcast fell face-down, dead.

Elsewhere in the stand of kauri trees, Rambuka ducked reflexively when he heard the shot. He began running toward the direction of the sound.

In the undergrowth, Susannah and Sina cowered behind the large fern fronds as Rambuka crashed past them. They remained undiscovered.

Meanwhile, Nathan used his foot to cautiously roll Uraia over onto his back. The outcast's sightless eyes stared directly at him. Nathan heard Rambuka crashing through the ferns behind him. This presented a new problem for him as there was no ammunition left for his pistol.

As Rambuka approached, Nathan hid in the undergrowth, hoping the Outcast would fail to find him, or the women, and simply go home.

Something tells me that's too much to hope for.

Nathan held his breath as Rambuka stumbled across the body of his cousin.

Rambuka spun around, looking for Nathan. For some unfathomable reason, his eyes locked onto Nathan's hiding place.

20

Aware he'd been discovered, Nathan threw away his empty pistol, picked up a fallen branch, and emerged from the undergrowth. Legs astride, he stood facing Rambuka, who was about fifteen yards away.

The Outcast looked back at Nathan, his eyes full of hate. Furious, he charged the American, his tomahawk raised.

Nathan swung the branch he was holding. The blow knocked the tomahawk from the other's hand. Rambuka drew a knife and immediately dropped into the crouch of a seasoned knife fighter. Nathan drew his Bowie knife and went forward to meet him. They clashed head-on. Each managed to secure a firm grip on the other's right wrist, thereby preventing his opposite from using his weapon. Nathan was as tall as his opponent, but lighter. They crashed through the ferns as the stronger Rambuka forced Nathan backward.

Susannah and Sina suddenly appeared behind Rambuka. As soon as they had heard the pistol shot, they'd run to see how Nathan was faring.

Susannah was hobbling badly: she'd fallen and sprained her ankle in her haste to reach Nathan's side.

Noticing the women over his opponent's shoulder, Nathan shouted, "Get out of here!"

Neither woman moved. They seemed mesmerized, their eyes transfixed on the deadly dual unfolding before them.

Rambuka glanced over his shoulder and leered at Susannah. Turning his attention back to Nathan, he brought his knee up into his opponent's stomach, forcing him to release his grip on his wrist. Nathan rolled away, but was not quick enough to avoid the blade of Rambuka's knife. It slashed his forehead, leaving a nasty gash. Susannah screamed.

Blood flowed freely down Nathan's forehead and into his eyes. He blinked repeatedly, trying to clear his vision. Again, Rambuka came at him. Nathan lunged at him with his knife. Rambuka parried the blow and slashed his opponent's arm with his own knife, causing Nathan to drop his weapon. Nathan cried out in agony. Susannah screamed again.

Sizing up the situation, Sina picked up a rock and hurled it at Rambuka, striking him on the side of his head and causing him to drop his knife. The Outcast was momentarily stunned. Nathan reached for the knife, but Rambuka recovered quickly and kicked it away into the ferns. Both men were now unarmed.

The American made a desperate lunge at his opponent. Rambuka easily threw him aside. Crashing backward through the ferns, Nathan landed in a pond and found himself waist-deep in water. The Outcast pounced on him, grabbing him in a headlock and forcing his head under the water. He held him there for several terrifying moments.

Nathan came up for air, gasping. Again, Rambuka forced him underwater. Nathan frantically struggled to free himself from his opponent's iron grip.

At the pond edge, Susannah could only look on as the drama was being played out in front of her. "Nathan!" she cried out. Susannah desperately wanted to help him, but felt rooted to the spot. She and Sina watched, horrified, as air escaping from Nathan's mouth bubbled to the water's surface.

Beneath the water, Nathan knew he was close to drowning. His fingers closed around Rambuka's, but still he couldn't break the other's grip.

Can't breathe!

As the seconds passed, he became more desperate; he began to feel drowsy; everything seemed to be happening in slow motion;

terror was slowly replaced by an overwhelming sadness as he remembered Susannah and how he'd never expressed his love for her.

Is this what it has come to? My whole life has been a failure and now it has to end like this.

Nathan stopped struggling as he felt death approaching. It wasn't as bad as he'd feared. In fact, it was almost pleasant . . . like falling asleep. Everything was becoming foggy.

The American removed his hand from Rambuka's and subconsciously let it stray to the whale bone pendant hanging around his neck. His fingers caressed the pendant as they always did when he was stressed.

The pendant!

Nathan tried to marshal his thoughts. An idea was forming in his mind, but his brain was so starved of oxygen he was having trouble converting the idea to a plan of action.

Now beyond thought, he instinctively tore the pendant free and, holding its sharp end up, thrust it directly upward. The pendant's dagger-like point lodged in Rambuka's neck, piercing the left carotid artery and forcing him to release his grip on Nathan. Blood immediately gushed from the wound.

Nathan's head broke the surface of the water. Gasping for air, he threw himself to one side, afraid Rambuka would launch himself at him. The attack never came. Looking around, he saw the Outcast was on his knees, holding both hands to his neck as he tried to stem the flow of blood.

Disbelief registered in Rambuka's eyes. Nathan had seen that look once before—on safari in Kenya when he'd witnessed an antelope turn on a lion, mortally piercing it through the heart with one of its horns as the lion went for the kill.

Using the last of his remaining strength, Nathan jumped on top of Rambuka and forced his head beneath the water. The Outcast resisted violently, but Nathan managed to maintain his death grip on him.

Rambuka's efforts grew feebler. Eventually, all resistance ceased. Nathan released his grip on his victim and left him lying face down in the water.

Looking on from the side of the pond, a relieved Susannah wanted to wade through the water and throw her arms around Nathan, but she was too emotionally spent even to do that. All she could do was sob.

Near collapse, Nathan looked down and saw his pendant on the bottom of the pond. Reaching down, he retrieved it and clasped it firmly in his hand. For some reason, the feel of it against his skin reminded him of Joeli's father, Iremaia, the pendant's original owner. Strangely, the memory brought him comfort. It was as if the spirit of the old ratu was with him now. He touched the pendant to his lips before staggering to the edge of the pond and collapsing into Susannah's arms.

"Help me!" Susannah ordered Sina.

The two women dragged Nathan from the water and lay him down among the ferns. Susannah was alarmed to see blood flowing from the gash in his arm and from a number of cuts he'd received to his head and upper body. She and Sina immediately began tending his wounds. They could see he was close to losing consciousness.

"Stay with us, Nathan!" Susannah shouted at him.

As the two women fussed over him, Nathan struggled to stay conscious by reviewing recent events in his mind. He found it hard to reconcile the fact that, of all the men involved in the recent hostilities, he alone had survived.

Why me?

Nathan couldn't begin to fathom the odds of his surviving such mayhem. He'd never heard of a battle in which only one man survived. For the first time, he began to think someone, or something, may be watching over him.

That was the last thought he had before he finally lost consciousness.

#

When Nathan came to, he became aware of something soft on his chest and a warm feeling over his heart. He glanced down and saw Susannah's hand was resting on his chest. Looking up, he realized she was smiling at him. Her smile seemed one of immense relief.

"Welcome back," she smiled.

"How long was I gone?"

"Long enough to have us worried."

In fact, he'd been out to it for some time, though Susannah didn't mention that. She was just happy to have him back in the land of the living. Susannah left her hand on Nathan's chest. Beneath it, she could feel Nathan's heart beating. She imagined it was beating in time with her own. That thought reassured her.

Feeling Susannah's hand over his heart reassured Nathan, too. He thought it was fitting.

She owns my heart now. Without her, it could no longer continue to beat.

Looking around, Nathan noticed the rain clouds had gone and dusk was approaching. His head was throbbing. Lifting his hand to his forehead, he realized a shirt sleeve served as a bandage around his head wound. Leaf dressings covered the wounds on his arm and upper body.

"Sina worked some of her healing magic on you," Susannah informed him.

Glancing at Sina, Nathan smiled. She smiled back, but Nathan could see the pain behind her smile. He knew she was missing Waisale.

Nathan looked up at Susannah. He managed another weary smile before exhaustion overtook him and he drifted back to sleep.

21

Next day, Nathan was feeling considerably stronger as he led Susannah and Sina up a steep bush track in the Nausori Highlands. Every part of him hurt following his fight with Rambuka, but he didn't mind that too much. At least he was still breathing.

Susannah was hobbling badly as a result of her sprained ankle, which was now heavily bound, while Sina was in the best shape of all three. However, even she was moving slowly, exhausted by the events of the previous day.

The three survivors had spent the night out in the open, on the valley floor, before resuming their homeward trek at first light.

One painful step at a time, the trio walked in silence as they doggedly followed the trail leading back to Momi Bay. They didn't talk: they felt numbed by recent events. The stench of death still filled their nostrils.

Susannah was still mourning the horrible death of her father while Sina hadn't yet come to grips with losing Waisale in such cruel fashion so soon after they'd been reunited. And Nathan was feeling the loss of new friends—in particular, Jack and Joeli.

As they walked, Nathan wondered whether any of Rambuka's outcasts would be following them. He knew that was always a possibility as, sooner or later, the outcasts who had remained at

Tomanivi would come to investigate after Rambuka and the others failed to return.

The question is, will they realize anyone survived the carnage?

Nathan knew full well when they failed to find Susannah and Sina, they would suspect the pair had escaped. And when they couldn't find the golden tabua, he feared that could prompt them to hunt down any survivors. For the moment, he kept these thoughts to himself.

It was Susannah who finally broke the silence. Turning to Nathan, she said, "That man back there on the hill . . . Jack . . ."

"Jack Halliday," Nathan said.

"Was he a friend of yours?"

"No . . . yes," Nathan corrected himself. Struggling to find the words to explain his relationship with the Cockney who gave his life for them on the hill, he said, "I hardly knew him . . .yet it felt like I'd known him all my life. It was almost as if he was sent to help us . . . like a guardian angel."

"He may well have been," Susannah smiled.

"Not that I really believe in things like angels—" Nathan suddenly froze as two fierce-looking Fijian warriors materialized, as if by magic, out of the forest ahead of them.

Susannah screamed as more warriors appeared, brandishing spears and clubs.

Sina was unworried. "It all right," she assured her companions. "They our friends, the Mamanucans."

Nathan and Susannah relaxed when Joeli's friend Lemeki, the impressive, scar-faced ratu of the Mamanucans, stepped forward from the warriors' ranks. The couple recognized him immediately. They also recognized other familiar faces dating back to the Mamanucans' recent visit to Momi Bay. Likewise, the warriors recognized the white couple. They looked at Nathan with respect, having heard firsthand of his exploits during the outcasts' attack on the village at Momi Bay.

Lemeki immediately began questioning Sina. Watching the ratu, Nathan noticed he looked increasingly concerned as he learned of the tragic events of the past few days. When Sina had finished talking, Lemeki barked orders at his warriors. They immediately attended to the needs of the weary trio, cleaning and dressing their wounds and sharing rations with them.

As soon as he could get her alone, Nathan questioned Sina. "What are these people doing here?" he asked.

"Elders at my village get word to them," she said. "Tell them Qopa warriors need help. Now they go help."

"Didn't you tell him Joeli and the others are dead?"

Sina shook her head vehemently. "No . . . their spirits live. Lemeki find Joeli and pray for safe journey for his spirit. And for Waisale and others, too."

Nathan said, "I wish to speak to Lemeki."

Sina led him to the Mamanucans' ratu. "The White-Face wishes to speak to you," she advised Lemeki.

Seeing that he had Lemeki's attention, Nathan said, "I left a friend behind . . . on the killing field . . . another vulagi, like me. His name was Jack." He continued as Sina translated for him. "He deserves a burial."

Lemeki nodded. "I will see to it." The ratu meant what he said. Nathan had gone up further in his estimation following Sina's description of the American's exploits the previous day.

After Sina translated the ratu's response, Nathan thanked him and returned to Susannah's side.

When the Mamanucans had done all they could for the trio, they resumed their trek east toward Tomanivi. A grateful Nathan, Susannah, and Sina waved them off. The Mamanucans disappeared into the forest as quickly as they had appeared.

\#

Later that day, Lemeki's warriors intercepted half a dozen outcasts who had been sent ahead to track down the survivors of the previous day's carnage. Although not in possession of muskets, the element of surprise and superiority of numbers meant that the Mamanucans were able to kill the outcasts before they knew what hit them. In a few bloody minutes, the threat they posed to Nathan, Susannah, and Sina was snuffed out once and for all.

\#

The following day, Lemeki and his warriors stood on the summit of the hill where the members of Joeli's party had made their stand. Only their bodies remained; the bodies of their enemies had already been removed by outcasts who had come looking for their comrades.

Studying the bloated, fly-blown bodies of their Qopa friends, the

Mamanucans were filled with sorrow. The two peoples had been allies for many generations. Lemeki soon found the body of his old friend, Joeli. Devastated, he fell down to his knees beside the body, cradled it in his arms, and offered a chant to the spirits while his men began burying the other warriors where they lay.

Then Lemeki saw the body of Jack Halliday. Jack's arm still lay protectively over Waisale's body. Releasing Joeli, he walked over to inspect the white man. Jack's green eyes stared, unseeing, back at him. Lemeki knelt down and respectfully closed Jack's eyes. "May your journey to the Afterworld be speedy, White-Face," he whispered.

Honoring his promise to Nathan, Lemeki personally dug a grave for Jack and saw to it that the Cockney received a fitting burial. The ratu whispered a prayer for his spirit and honored him as he would one of his own. Waisale, Joeli, and the others were given similar sendoffs.

As the last of the warriors was buried, the heavens opened and heavy rain lashed the hillside, drenching everyone on it and threatening to wash the newly dug graves away. Lemeki waited for the rain to ease.

After a long wait, the rain eased almost as quickly as it had arrived. Lemeki was relieved to see the graves were still intact. Raising his right hand skyward, he shouted, "We the Mamanucans honor you, Qopa warriors!"

His warriors repeated the traditional Mamanucan salutation then, without a backward glance, began retracing their steps to Momi Bay.

Before leaving the Land of Red Rain, Lemeki thrust a spear in the ground. It would serve as a warning to others not to walk on the burial site or interfere with the Afterlife journey of the Qopa spirits.

22

Nathan, Susannah, and Sina were exhausted by the time they finally reached Momi Bay. Qopa villagers rushed out to greet them as they emerged from the rain forest. The villagers all talked at once as they plied the trio with questions.

Women and children glanced around expectantly, looking for their loved ones. Their smiles quickly turned to dismay when they realized Joeli and his warriors wouldn't be returning. A black mood descended over the village and women began wailing.

One young woman who wasn't wailing was Selaima, the slave girl. Rather, she was staring at Susannah in disbelief. While she was relieved to see Nathan had been safely returned to her, she was mortified to see that the white woman had also returned safe and sound. However, for the moment she focused her attention on Nathan. The spirits had listened to her plea that the American return to her and for that she was grateful.

Looking around, Nathan was reminded that the Qopa clan was now almost devoid of men of fighting age. The latest clash with the outcasts had seen to that. The village's reserves of warriors had been decimated. Now, apart from a few warriors who had been wounded in the outcasts' earlier raid, there were only women, children, and elderly men left. Nathan feared for the future of these people for without a fighting force of able-bodied men, they would fall prey to even the weakest of enemies.

Sina's parents simultaneously laughed and cried as they greeted the daughter they had never expected to see again. Sina pointed to Nathan as she relayed the events of the past few days to them and to other family members. They and other villagers were impressed by Nathan's exploits.

Sina did not mention that Nathan had the golden tabua in his possession. In her own unselfish way, she decided to let the American divulge that piece of good news in his own time and receive full credit for it.

As the villagers escorted the trio into the village, an elderly woman wept on Susannah's shoulder. The woman was the mother of Rewa, one of Joeli's trackers. Speaking Fijian, Susannah tried to comfort her. "Your son died an honorable death," she assured the woman.

The elderly woman began to wail. Chanting, she turned away and walked toward the cliff top on the headland above the village. Susannah tried to hold her back, but the woman shook her off and kept walking. Susannah cried out. Her cries fell on deaf ears. Still chanting, the woman stepped out into space and disappeared over the edge of the cliff, just as Joeli's mother had done after losing her husband.

Susannah turned away and buried her face in Nathan's chest.

Watching this display of intimacy, Selaima was consumed by jealousy toward, and hatred for, Susannah. She vowed that she would place a far more powerful curse on the white woman than she did previously. This time, she swore, not only would Susannah be removed from Nathan's reach, she would be removed from the physical world.

Kamisese, the respected toreni koro, or headman, walked up to Nathan and touched him on the shoulder. Looking into Kamisese's all-knowing eyes, the American felt as if the old man could see right through him.

The toreni koro inspected the bloodied bandage that still covered the wound on Nathan's forehead then studied Nathan's face for a long time before addressing him in his native tongue. "The red rain has come," he intoned. "It has drenched our land and swept away all our warriors."

Nathan didn't understand a word, but listened patiently neverthe-less. Nearby, Susannah turned her attention to what the old man was saying.

Kamisese continued, "Yet somehow you have survived the storm. As the last surviving warrior, you must stay and help us grow strong again."

Surprised, Susannah translated for Nathan. "Kamisese says he wants you to stay and help his people grow strong again."

"But I am not one of them." Nathan pointed out.

Kamisese said, "You fought bravely alongside our sons and brothers. You are now Qopa."

While Susannah translated, Kamisese turned around to address what was left of the tribe. "Nathan Johnson is the only warrior to survive the torrent of the red rain. He is a great warrior. He will stay to help us become great again!"

The villagers crowded around Nathan and cheered. They seemed to immediately accept him as their savior.

Nathan looked at Susannah. He had to shout to make himself heard. "Tell them I cannot—" His words were drowned out as he was swept away in the crowd.

The villagers began to worship him as if he were a god. In unison, they chanted, "Nathan Johnson! Nathan Johnson!" Smiling women and children reached out to touch him. Boys performed impromptu mock battles to show their respect for the man before them.

Kamisese stood back and admired the occasion. He looked well satisfied with himself.

Nathan felt strangely humbled—and emotional. Despite himself, he couldn't stem the tears as the Qopa lifted him onto their shoul-ders and began singing a traditional tribal song. Their singing was powerful and in perfect harmony.

The American's tears were prompted by a mix of emotions—partly sadness at losing newfound, close friends, partly relief at having rescued Susannah and survived the battle in the Land of Red Rain, but more than anything it was the realization that he'd evolved as a human being.

The antipathy he once felt toward Fijians, and indeed all native peoples, had been completely washed away. He no longer felt anything but love toward the Qopa and, in return, he felt nothing but love coming from them. He had truly been touched by the warmth and openness of these indomitable islanders.

For the remainder of the day, the villagers plied the three survivors with questions about their ordeal. Family and friends of the Qopa warriors demanded to know every detail about how their men had acquitted themselves on the battlefield. The old men basked in the reflected glory of the young warriors' exploits.

That night, Nathan slept in the bure he'd occupied previously, while Susannah was accommodated with Sina and her family. The returned trio were so exhausted they would sleep until well after sunup.

23

Later the following day, as the shadows lengthened, Nathan and Susannah approached the mission station. A thin dressing now covered Nathan's head wound and Susannah was still limping, though not as badly as before. She carried a small posy of wildflowers.

Susannah could hardly bring herself to look at the rebuilt mission house: it looked so empty and forlorn. While she and Nathan were happy to be alive, there were reminders everywhere of the despondency that hung over Momi Bay like a black veil. Villagers continued to mourn for their loved ones; a number of new widows had chosen strangulation to be reunited with their husbands; and the sound of wailing and chanting continued without let-up.

On top of this, the Qopa believed the spirits of their ancestors were mourning, also, compounding the oppressive feeling of sadness that embraced the entire village and its occupants.

Adding to their own despondency, Nathan was mourning the loss of friends, while Susannah was mourning the loss of her father. In a way, it felt as if they themselves had crossed over to the land of the dead.

The morbid atmosphere and the bloody events of the past few weeks reminded Susannah of an old saying she'd heard on her arrival in Fiji:

All things in Fiji are paid for in blood.

She hadn't believed it at the time. Now she did.

Outside the mission station chapel, the couple stopped before a simple wooden cross Nathan had constructed. It marked the place where Drake Senior had been buried. The villagers had taken it upon themselves to bury the reverend the day after he'd died at Rambuka's hands. Visiting his grave had filled Susannah with an unbearable sadness.

Nevertheless, it had given her some sort of closure.

Now, as she placed the posy of flowers at the foot of the cross and whispered a silent prayer, she studied the words on the cross. They read:

REV. BRIAN DRAKE 1793-1848
Beloved husband of Jeanette
Father of Susannah
And friend of the Qopa

Thinking of her father caused her to start crying. "He was such a good man, Nathan," she sobbed. Nathan pulled her to him and held her tight. "I can't believe he is gone."

"I know," Nathan agreed.

The two stood in silence, looking down at the cross. Susannah was feeling more at peace now. She'd finally come to accept her father's death and felt ready to move on. "I still half expect Papa to walk out of the chapel at any moment," she murmured.

"I feel he is still here in spirit," Nathan said.

Susannah looked at Nathan in mock surprise. "Nathan Johnson, I do believe you are becoming religious!"

Nathan smiled, shaking his head in denial. With both of them still unsure how each really felt about the other, they began walking back toward the village. Neither spoke, yet each felt they were communicating.

Nearing the village, Susannah turned to Nathan, saying, "They want you to stay, you know. The villagers." Nathan nodded. "They believe you possess supernatural powers because you are the only man from Momi Bay ever to survive a journey to the Land of Red Rain." She hesitated. "Will you stay?" Nathan shook his head, indicating he wouldn't. Susannah said, "I understand. But the Qopa will be disappointed."

Nathan knew the *Rendezvous* would be calling back into the bay any day now en route to Suva, on the other side of Viti Levu. It had always been his intention to continue on to Suva, but there were other things to consider now. Having not yet inquired, he wasn't sure of Susannah's plans—and he couldn't bear the thought of leaving without her. He suddenly realized he hadn't inquired because he was frightened of the answer she may give him.

"What about you? Where will you live now that your father is gone?" Nathan held his breath.

This is it. This is my future right here.

Doing his best to appear casual, he nervously awaited her response.

Susannah stopped and looked up at him. She thought long and hard before answering. "I don't know," she whispered. "Perhaps I should carry out my father's last wish, which was for me to return to England."

Nathan suddenly felt a deep sadness welling inside him. He hated the thought of being parted from Susannah, but he still couldn't bring himself to reveal his true feelings. Something inside him prevented him from expressing his love for her.

Nearby, some village girls called out to Susannah. They were weaving flax baskets and wanted to show off their handiwork.

Susannah smiled at them then turned back to Nathan. They stared deeply into each other's eyes for a moment.

After another uncomfortable silence, Nathan ventured, "I guess I'll see you later." The American wondered if this was the right time to kiss her. How he longed to kiss her.

To hell with it!

Taking a deep breath, he leaned toward her, but then he hesitated and simply kissed her on the cheek. Nathan felt more awkward than ever.

Susannah misinterpreted his nervousness for coldness. Upset, but hiding her feelings, she quickly pulled away from him and began walking toward the girls.

Nathan was angry with himself as he watched her walk away. He questioned what the blockage was inside him. Deep down he knew he was afraid of rejection. As he searched his mind, he suddenly realized the fear of being rejected by the only woman he'd ever loved would be nothing compared to losing her forever. If he didn't risk rejection then there was no chance of winning her.

If you don't at least try, then you may as well just shoot yourself because a life without Susannah would be akin to death anyway.

Nathan took a deep breath. "Susannah!" he called.

Susannah pulled up and turned around expectantly. She sensed something in Nathan's voice. Now, as he approached her, she noticed the intensity in his startlingly blue eyes. "What is it?"

Before she realized what was happening, Nathan pulled her to him and kissed her full on the lips. She responded fervently.

Each could feel the sexual tension in the other. It was clear to both they wanted each other badly. They kissed again, stopping only when they became aware they were being watched. To their embarrassment, they noticed the Qopa girls and other villagers in the vicinity were smiling at them.

The couple didn't realize it, but the Qopa had known from the outset that they were meant for each other. Nathan and Susannah laughed self-consciously when they saw they'd become the center of attention.

Something else they didn't realize was that they were also being observed by Selaima. The slave girl was consumed by jealousy as she watched the Englishwoman coming between her and the man of her dreams. Selaima reminded herself she needed to be patient. The time wasn't quite right to place another curse on her rival, but it would be soon.

As he held Susannah close, Nathan felt at peace for the first time in his life. In a world full of chaos, he'd now found something that made sense to him. Alone, he'd felt lost. With Susannah at his side, he felt as though he'd found his place in the universe. He knew now he wanted to spend the rest of his life with this woman and was so relieved he'd finally found the courage to express his true feelings. He kissed her again.

For the life of him, Nathan didn't know what had stopped him from kissing her weeks earlier. It now felt so comfortable and effortless. His mind was racing.

So many unanswered questions.

"What about the mission station?" he suddenly asked. "What about your calling to spread God's Word?"

Susannah looked away. "The calling I felt has gone," she confided. "If I'm honest with myself, I don't think it was ever my calling to be a missionary. It was my father's. I did it to please him."

After a few moments, they resumed walking. There was a spring in their step now. A barrier had been swept aside and they felt content.

Dusk was approaching as they walked through the village. Villagers tending their lovos in preparation for their evening meals smiled or waved as the couple strolled by.

Elders greeted Nathan with the respect usually reserved for ratus. He wondered if Sina had told them he had the golden tabua. The American didn't dwell on that for long. Right now he had more pressing matters on his mind—like Susannah. He wanted to bed her more than anything he'd ever wanted before.

Approaching the small bure that had served as his home since arriving in Momi Bay, Nathan announced, "Well, this is my place." After an awkward silence, he asked, "Which is your hut?" He knew full well which bure was hers.

Suspecting Nathan already knew, Susannah pointed to the bure she shared with Sina and her family. It was some distance away. Sina was standing outside it at that moment. The maiden waved when she saw Susannah and Nathan. They returned the wave.

Susannah smiled at Nathan and began walking toward Sina. As she walked, she tried to ignore the pounding of her heart and the feeling of faintness that threatened to engulf her.

I must have him!

No longer in control of herself, she stopped walking and slowly turned around. Looking at the handsome man before her, she suddenly felt incapable of logical thought. All she could think of was Nathan's body fused with hers.

A part of her wanted to stay true to her puritanical upbringing and remain a virgin until she was married; another part of her demanded that she connect intimately with Nathan.

She knew this was a result of coming face to face with death in recent days. That had served to remind her how fleeting life could be and how she should live every moment of every day as if it were her last.

Susannah now felt an extreme sense of urgency. Her desire for Nathan was just too strong now and it completely overpowered her religious morals. Deep down, she also knew she'd never be able to banish the sexual fantasies that raged within her mind. They were far too vivid and prolific. Susannah sensed the only way to quell them was to give herself to Nathan. She felt she'd go insane if she didn't have him right now.

Fighting against the feeling of light-headedness that still persisted, she walked slowly back to him, pausing only to take his hand before leading him inside his bure. Behind them, Sina smiled to herself as she watched her friends disappear from sight. It was a bitter-sweet smile as she remembered she had once shared similar times with Waisale.

Watching from afar, Selaima was still observing the couple. The jealousy raging inside her was at boiling point now.

Inside the bure's gloomy interior, Nathan looked at Susannah. "Are you sure about this?"

Susannah took his face in both hands and smiled. "I've never been more sure of anything in my life."

They kissed again, this time with undisguised lust. Nathan scooped her up and carried her to a pandanus mat in the far corner of the bure. He lowered her down onto it then lay on top of her. They resumed kissing, with even more urgency now.

Nathan resisted the urge to tear Susannah's clothes off. Instead, he slowly and tantalizingly undressed her then proceeded to make love to her gently and lovingly. He was mindful this was her first time and didn't want to hurt her.

Susannah moaned with a desire she never knew she possessed as she gave herself fully to him. Rocking urgently beneath him, she urged Nathan not to hold back. Nathan's gentle approach quickly gave way to full-blown lust as he buried himself deep inside her and matched her rhythmical movements.

She cried out, "I love you, Nathan!"

Susannah's words struck Nathan to the core. He knew then he wanted this woman to bear his children. Nathan lost all control and climaxed in a frenzy of passion.

They would make love several more times this night, but for the moment they were totally satiated.

#

Later, as she lay on the floor staring at the bure's roof, Susannah was surprised she no longer felt any conflict between her spiritual and sexual selves. She now understood they were one and the same. The division was something that had been imposed on her, albeit unintentionally, by her father's teachings and by the church. She felt at peace now that the war that had been going on inside her mind all these years was finally over.

In many ways it was a coming of age for Nathan, too. Not in the same way as it was for Susannah, as he was older and more experienced. His evolution was more an emotional one. He'd finally grown up to the point where he could put others—or *another* at least—before himself. He now understood that a man's life was fleeting and, in the end, the only thing that mattered was his relationships with loved ones.

From now on, he vowed he would do the right thing by Susannah.

Her happiness is my happiness.

24

While Nathan and Susannah, and most of the villagers, were sleeping, Selaima crept out of the bure she shared with the other female slaves and walked quickly toward the nearby rainforest. She carried the small flax bag that was never far from her side.

Her way was conveniently lit by a full moon. She was thankful for it as the powerful curse she intended to place on the white woman demanded there be a full moon.

Selaima suddenly stopped, as if she'd forgotten something, and doubled back to Nathan's bure. Pausing in the bure's open doorway, she tiptoed inside.

In the moonlight, she saw that Nathan and Susannah were fast asleep in each other's arms. Staring at the two lovers, she realized she'd never experienced such deep and conflicting emotions: her love for Nathan was so powerful she felt as though she was already in the Afterlife's paradise, while her hatred for Susannah knew no bounds.

More convinced than ever that what she was about to do was justifiable, she backed out of the bure and once again struck off toward the forest. After quickly locating the track she knew would lead her to her cave, she began jogging, so keen was she to execute her plan.

#

On her arrival at the cave, Selaima had found the full moon's position was perfect: it was almost directly above the cave. Moonlight flooded in through the small opening in the roof, illuminating her as she stood naked by the fire she'd lit moments earlier.

Selaima had already sprinkled the special herbs and potions she carried in her bag onto the fire, and the flames were leaping skyward. The resulting aromas had quickly taken effect and she was already in a trance. She began dancing and her sensuous body was soon covered in perspiration.

Chanting, she called on her Bauan ancestors to protect her from the dark spirits she planned to summon. She'd neglected to do that last time she'd summoned the dark forces and the memory of that harrowing experience was still with her. She wanted to have allies present this time around.

The Bauan ancestors appeared to her as bright shadows. These shadows were so bright, they almost blinded her, making identification possible. However, Selaima was certain they included her mother and her mother's mother—the two people she'd been closest to before illness had taken them from her.

When she was satisfied her spiritual allies were present, Selaima summoned the darker spirits. A fluttering sound alerted her to their presence. As always, they were invisible to her until she closed her eyes. When she did so, the familiar bat-like creatures immediately appeared to her—moving too fast to see clearly. On this occasion their movements were so fast they seemed violent. It was as if they sensed Selaima was about to place a dreadful curse on someone.

Selaima worked herself into a heightened state, grunting and frothing at the mouth as usual. The feeling of faintness that always descended on her about now was strangely absent on this occasion. Selaima was feeling stronger and more in command than ever before.

Screaming in a voice that wasn't hers, she shouted, "Dark Spirits, I command you to kill the white woman who has come between me and Nathan Johnson!" The spirits were now moving so rapidly they came in and out of Selaima's vision. "Let her be visited by a fatal illness this very night," she continued, "and let her not see another sunrise!"

The feeling of faintness that had held off now arrived with a vengeance. This didn't worry Selaima. She'd placed her curse and the dark spirits had listened. She happily gave in to the feeling and collapsed beside the fire.

#

While Selaima lay unconscious in the cave, Nathan and Susannah were making love for the third or maybe fourth time that night: they'd lost count. Their lovemaking merged into one long, wonderful experience that neither wanted to end.

They came in each other's arms and lay there, smiling at each other. In the moonlight, they could just make out the expression on the other's face.

"Where have you been all my life, Nathan Johnson?" Susannah asked.

"I could ask the same about you."

"I asked first."

"Well, I—"

Susannah suddenly began coughing. "Sorry. Carry on."

Before Nathan could continue, Susannah resumed coughing. This time she couldn't stop.

"Are you okay?" Nathan asked, concerned.

Susannah nodded as the coughing gradually subsided. However, she suddenly had difficulty breathing. "I can't breathe!" she gasped, sitting up.

More concerned than ever, Nathan placed his arm around her. "What's wrong?"

Susannah shook her head. "I don't know!" She was becoming more frightened as her airways constricted. Soon, she was having to fight for each breath.

Realizing something was badly wrong, Nathan picked her up in her arms and carried her outside. "Inoki! Inoki!" he shouted as he carried her toward the old healer's bure. In the absence of modern medical practitioners, Inoki was the first person Nathan thought of. Looking at Susannah, he was alarmed to see she'd lost consciousness. "Susannah!"

Alerted by the shouting, villagers emerged from their bures to see what the problem was. Worried out of his mind, Nathan barged into Inoki just as the old man was emerging from his bure. Inoki took one look at Susannah and motioned to Nathan to bring her inside. Concerned villagers followed them into the bure.

Inside, Nathan lay Susannah down on the same bed mat he'd

occupied while Inoki had nursed him just a few weeks earlier. Looking at Susannah, he was alarmed to see she was still unconscious. "Susannah!" he cried out.

Inoki immediately went to work, chanting while orally administering herbs and potions to his unconscious patient. Nathan instinctively knew the healer was wasting his time, but he had no answer for Susannah's condition so he sat by helplessly and watched.

#

Despite his best efforts, Inoki realized Susannah wasn't responding. If anything, her condition was deteriorating. Ignoring the desperate looks being directed his way by Nathan, Inoki studied Susannah's face. He began to suspect foul play. The healer sensed his patient had fallen prey to evil spirits.

Inoki immediately thought of Selaima. Turning to one of the women in attendance, he ordered her to fetch the slave girl. The woman hurried out of the bure and returned moments later to advise Inoki the girl was not in the slaves' quarters.

This news confirmed Inoki's suspicions. Speaking quickly to the same woman, he gathered up some herbs and potions then hurried from the bure, leaving a bemused Nathan behind. Nathan went to follow when the woman restrained him.

"Inoki say you stay here," the woman said in faltering English.

"Where'd he go?" an anxious Nathan asked.

"He go to help missionary woman."

More confused than ever, Nathan checked Susannah's pulse. It was so weak he could hardly detect it. A feeling of dread came over him.

Dear God, don't let her die!

Outside, Inoki headed straight for the rainforest. He'd long suspected the Bauan slave girl was evil and was convinced she'd placed a curse on the white woman. Inoki had seen the way Selaima looked at Susannah. And he'd seen how she lusted after Nathan.

Inoki quickly found the track he knew led to the cave Selaima frequented. He knew because he'd found the cave since his earlier unsuccessful search. Not only that, but he'd secretly observed the slave girl communicating with the spirits. He hadn't confronted her because he feared her powers. Now, with the white woman's life in the balance, he felt he had no choice.

In no time, he reached the cave. Entering it stealthily via its narrow opening, he found Selaima dancing naked. She was illuminated by a beam of moonlight that pierced the darkness courtesy of the small opening in the cave roof. Inoki immediately saw that Selaima was performing a meke ni vula, or dance to the moon. This confirmed his fears: the dance was a traditional expression of thanks to the spirits for answering a wish for someone to die.

Steeling himself for the showdown he knew would follow, the old healer swallowed a potion and, holding the herbs he'd brought, approached Selaima from behind.

Although her back was to Inoki, she knew someone was there and she knew who it was. "Stay back, old man!" she warned.

Shaken but not deterred, Inoki kept shuffling forward. At the same time, he began chanting, calling on the warrior ancestors of the Qopa to protect him.

Enraged, Selaima spun around to face the old man. She was still frothing at the mouth and her eyes had turned up so that only their whites were visible. The slave girl called on the dark spirits to overcome the spiritual forces that Inoki had summoned.

Inoki's eardrums were assaulted by ghoulish noises that were so loud they were deafening, yet he couldn't see what was making the noise. He closed his eyes and immediately saw the cause: the spirits were at war. The shadowy creatures were moving so fast, he couldn't even identify their individual shapes. However, he could distinguish between good and evil: his spiritual allies were golden in color and as bright as the golden tabua Rambuka had stolen from the village, while the dark spirits opposing them were grotesque and bat-like.

Despite Inoki's fears, the forces of good prevailed, overpowering the dark spirits. All but one of the opposing spirits were destroyed; one escaped by entering and possessing Selaima.

Snapping out of her trance, the slave girl immediately knew what fate awaited her. Her former bravado was replaced by terror. "Inoki, wise healer, cast out the dark spirit from me!" she pleaded, throwing herself at the old man's feet.

Selaima was aware that, as the person who had been possessed, she did not have the power to exorcize the dark spirit from her soul. Only Inoki had that power.

Inoki knew it, too. He looked at her knowingly for a while before turning his back on her and shuffling out of the cave. As he went, he ignored Selaima's pleas for help.

#

As Inoki retraced his steps to the village, Nathan was beside himself with worry over Susannah. Her pulse was hardly detectable now and he was convinced she was near death. "Where's Inoki?" he asked no one in particular.

The Qopa women with him looked at each other and shrugged. They were wondering the same thing.

Nathan was debating whether to go and look for Inoki when Susannah suddenly opened her eyes.

"Susannah!" Nathan gasped. He reached out and touched her face tenderly, unsure whether to laugh or cry.

Susannah managed a smile. "Where am I?" she asked weakly.

Laughing, Nathan hugged her. "You're in Inoki's hut."

At the mention of his name, Inoki himself appeared in the doorway. He beamed when he saw Susannah.

Nathan saw the pleasure on the old healer's face, but he also noted Inoki didn't appear overly surprised to see Susannah back in the land of the living. He suspected him of having something to do with Susannah's recovery, but knew he'd probably never know for sure.

While Nathan and the others celebrated Susannah's recovery, Selaima was at that very moment approaching the cliff edge on the headland beyond the village. She began chanting as she reached the edge. The voice coming from her mouth was not hers. It was harsh and vulgar and sounded more male than female. Selaima was still chanting as she fell toward the rocks below.

25

In the village meeting house next day, headman Kamisese sat cross-
legged drinking kava with other matagali. Kamisese had taken
charge since the loss of Joeli. All the elders deferred to him.

There was a hum of conversation as the Qopa discussed the
weather, the fishing, the achievements of their grandchildren, and
other things that were important to them.

Listening in to the various conversations, Kamisese marveled at
how easily men could forget about death and destruction and
concern themselves about such mundane things as whether the sun
was shining or the fish were biting.

Conversation momentarily ceased when Nathan suddenly entered
the meeting house. Kamisese motioned to him to sit next to him.
The American willingly obliged.

Nathan was feeling deeply contented. The woman he loved more
than anyone else or anything had been brought back to him from
the dead; he now knew what he wanted to do with his life—and,
more importantly, who he wanted to share the rest of his life with.

Kamisese noted Nathan carried an object wrapped in cloth. His
heart skipped a beat. He wondered if the object was the golden
tabua Rambuka had stolen from the village. Kamisese had wanted to
ask Nathan if Joeli had recovered the sacred whale's tooth, but he

dared not: to have asked and been told Joeli had failed in his quest would have been to invite disaster on the golden tabua's rightful owners. He could only hope Nathan would tell him in his own time.

A slave boy appeared and handed Nathan a drinking bowl filled with kava. The American gravely clapped his hands together three times. He took the bowl, drank the kava, and clapped again. Kamisese and the other matagali looked on, impressed by how quickly he had picked up their customs.

A moment later they were even more impressed when Nathan unfolded the cloth he was holding and proudly displayed the golden tabua Joeli had given him. He handed it to an astounded Kamisese, who snatched it from him in disbelief.

"The golden tabua!" Kamisese shouted triumphantly, holding the sacred whale's tooth above his head.

The other matagali began chanting praises to their gods when they realized what Kamisese was holding. Scarcely able to believe their most precious possession had been returned to them, they couldn't contain themselves.

When the celebrations died down, a delighted Kamisese and the other matagali fired questions at Nathan in Fijian. They demanded to know how he had come by the golden tabua.

Nathan tried to explain, but of course the language barrier prevented this.

The blast of a lookout's conch, or seashell horn, outside warned of the approach of visitors. It was quickly followed by shouts of alarm from the villagers. Nathan and the others hurried outside in time to see the scar-faced Lemeki and his Mamanucan warriors emerging from the rainforest. The Qopa relaxed when they recognized the visitors.

To demonstrate he came in peace, Lemeki immediately placed his club on the ground and motioned to his warriors to do the same. They, too, lay down their weapons.

Kamisese walked forward to greet them. He placed his hand on Lemeki's shoulder in a gesture of friendship. Lemeki reciprocated in kind. "I see you, great Lemeki," Kamisese said.

"I see you, Kamisese, worthy headman," Lemeki responded. "I have buried the bodies of your great Qopa warriors. They died bravely in the Land of Red Rain."

Kamisese nodded gravely. He said, "The spirits will be well

pleased you farewelled your brothers." He then led Lemeki and his warriors back to the meeting house.

As he followed Kamisese, Lemeki looked around him. His eyes settled on Nathan. The Mamanucan chief inclined his head briefly toward the American. Nathan knew immediately he'd kept his word and given Jack a fitting burial.

#

Later, the meeting house was overflowing with villagers and their Mamanucan guests as they celebrated the return of the golden tabua with an impromptu feast. The sacred possession now occupied pride of place on the meeting house wall. Kamisese and the other matagali kept touching it. They couldn't help themselves, so relieved were they to see it back where it rightfully belonged.

Several Mamanucans were busy courting Qopa women who had lost their men in the recent hostilities. The women appeared receptive to the visitors' advances. Kamisese's wise old eyes surveyed the developing intertribal relationships with interest.

Nathan and Susannah were also in attendance. Susannah was a picture of health after her near-fatal experience.

Kamisese's gaze settled on the young white couple who were smiling at each other as they ate in silence. The two lovers sat close together, their knees and shoulders touching, and were clearly a couple now.

The elder nodded to himself knowingly. Kamisese pushed himself to his feet as fast as his arthritic knees would allow and approached the couple, indicating to them they should follow him outside. He led them down to the beach and stopped alongside three canoes that were being watched over by a toothless matagali who stood guard over them. The old man was armed with one of the muskets Nathan had supplied.

Nathan noticed the canoes were laden down with something that was hidden beneath pandanus mats. Kamisese motioned to the American to inspect the contents of the nearest canoe.

Lifting the mat from the bow of the canoe, Nathan was stunned to see the craft was full of dried sea slugs. "Beche-de-mer," he murmured. A huge smile crossed his face.

Kamisese was delighted by the young man's reaction. Using Susannah to translate, he told Nathan that Joeli's last instructions to him had been to fill two canoes with the precious sea slugs in return for the muskets. Because Nathan had returned the golden tabua safely, Kamisese had taken it upon himself to throw in the extra canoe-load.

Nathan was delighted to hear this. With Joeli and his warriors gone, he'd given up on ever being recompensed for his muskets. Now, he'd been more than compensated. The profits from this would set him up nicely. He looked at Susannah and smiled. She could see he was pleased.

"It is good?" she asked.

"It is good." He would tell her later the ramifications of the villagers' generosity. This was not the time. Right now, his delight was tempered by the sadness at having lost so many friends and by Susannah's loss. Material success somehow seemed unimportant now, but at the same time he wasn't going to turn his back on it.

Nathan had never been into self-analysis, but he realized he'd grown over the past few weeks. Things that not so long ago had meant everything to him—like money and riches—suddenly weren't so important.

I've changed!

The realization hit him like a lightning bolt. Suddenly, family and loved ones were all that mattered to him.

Susannah could see a change in him, too—and she liked it. She put her arms around Nathan's neck, pulled his head down toward hers, and kissed him. Kamisese and the toothless matagali looked on, smiling.

26

Two days later, the *Rendezvous* arrived at Momi Bay as scheduled. As it anchored offshore not long after sunrise, Nathan and Susannah joined others on the beach to welcome the schooner's master and first mate ashore.

Nathan noticed Lemeki and some of his warriors mingling with the Qopa. The Mamanucans had remained in the village and were showing no signs of leaving any time soon. Nathan thought this promising. He believed the impressive ratu and his followers could be the salvation of the Qopa and was confident Joeli would approve were he still alive.

As they were being rowed ashore in the schooner's longboat, Captain McTavish and the Irishman Eric Foley smiled when they saw the white couple in the reception party on the beach. When the *Rendezvous* had left Momi Bay, Nathan had been close to death after being wounded in the outcasts' raid on the village. Now they could see he was a picture of health apart from the dressing that still covered his recent head wound. And they couldn't help but notice he had his arm around Susannah.

"I see ye lived to fight another day, Nathan," Foley shouted as the longboat nosed up onto the beach.

Nathan greeted Foley with a firm handshake and a hug as soon as the hardcase Irishman stepped down onto the sand. "Yes, I wanted to see your ugly mug again," Nathan laughed. Looking at Susannah, he added, "And I had the best nurse in the world caring for me."

Susannah smiled.

Foley and McTavish glanced at each other knowingly. McTavish looked at Susannah and doffed his cap in her direction. "Ma'am."

"Hello, captain," Susannah responded.

Addressing Nathan and Susannah, Foley cheekily said, "Last time we saw you two together, you weren't talkin' to each other."

Nathan and Susannah both laughed. "Things have changed, Mr. Foley," Susannah said.

"So I see," said Foley, winking at her.

Leaving Susannah to talk to Foley, Nathan took McTavish aside. He quickly filled him in on the events of the past few weeks and negotiated a berth for himself and Susannah to Suva. Arrangements were also made to ship his stockpile of beche-de-mer. Terms were quickly agreed on and arrangements were made for an immediate departure.

Nathan then sought out Kamisese and, with Susannah translating, advised the matagali he and Susannah would be leaving aboard the *Rendezvous*.

This came as no surprise to Kamisese. He had already sensed the American and his Englishwoman had decided to depart their village. They were still on a journey, he realized, and Momi Bay was only ever going to be a stopover on that journey, not a final destination.

"We must drink kava," Kamisese insisted. Without waiting for a response, he turned and shuffled slowly back toward the village.

"Apparently, you are to drink kava," Susanna advised Nathan. "He insists."

Nathan rolled his eyes and followed Kamisese, pulling Susannah after him.

"Women are not allowed to participate in a kava ceremony!" she reminded him.

"I need a translator, remember?"

Susannah realized Nathan was right, so she followed along quietly. She didn't mind. Walking beside Nathan, holding his hand, felt so right. She was utterly content.

\#

After the first calabash of kava, Nathan's lips were already feeling numb. Now, drinking his fourth serving of the traditional drink, his cheeks were feeling numb, too.

Nathan and Kamisese drank in companionable silence on the veranda outside the meeting house. As usual during a kava ceremony, a slave boy was waiting on them. Because Susannah was present, the Qopa headman had determined they could not proceed with the ceremony inside. This suited Nathan better: sitting outside they could view Momi Bay and enjoy the sea breeze.

In the continuing silence, Susannah realized her translation services may not be required on this occasion. And they weren't. Kamisese didn't need to talk to Nathan at the moment. He just wanted to enjoy his company one last time and drink kava with the man who had returned the golden tabua to Momi Bay.

27

Later, the villagers and their Mamanucan guests congregated at the water's edge to farewell Nathan and Susannah. The young lovers were preparing to board a longboat that would take them out to the *Rendezvous*. Nathan's cargo of beche-de-mer had already been loaded into the schooner's hold.

Lemeki was also here to farewell the couple. The ratu was standing nearby with his arm around the waist of a fetching village maiden. She touched the scar on his face and giggled when he whispered something to her. This wasn't missed by Nathan and Susannah. They also noticed several other Mamanucans had paired up with Qopa girls.

"The cycle of life looks set to continue at Momi Bay," Nathan whispered. Susannah nodded in agreement.

Lemeki caught Nathan's eye. The two nodded respectfully to each other.

If Lemeki had decided to *adopt* these villagers into his clan then that augured well for the Qopa, Nathan decided.

While Foley helped Nathan load the last of his and Susannah's possessions into the longboat, Susannah stood with her arm around Sina. The young women had become close and they dreaded parting.

Susannah asked, "What will become of your people?"

"Do not fear for us," Sina said, smiling at a handsome Mamanu-can who stood openly staring at her not five yards away. "Our friends the Mamanucans will protect us."

The Mamanucan, who immediately struck Susannah as a Waisale look-alike, flashed a smile at Sina and walked away. The likeness had occurred to Sina, also.

Susannah asked, "And what of you, my dear Sina?"

Sina nodded toward the retreating Mamanucan and smiled shyly. "He will look after me."

Susannah noted there was not a shred of doubt in her voice.

Behind them, Captain McTavish announced, "We best be going now."

Susannah looked around to see McTavish beckoning to her and Nathan to board the longboat. She turned back to Sina and hugged her. "God be with you, Sina." She hurried over to Nathan, who was waiting to assist her into the boat. Nathan hesitated as he saw Kamisese approach.

The old headman studied the young American for several moments in his own unhurried way. "The Qopa people owe Nathan Johnson a debt of gratitude," he said in his native tongue. With Susannah translating for Nathan's benefit, Kamisese continued, "Without your muskets, Rambuka's dogs would have slaughtered all my people. And without your bravery, the golden tabua would have been lost forever." The headman placed his right hand on Nathan's shoulder and said, "Take this as my blessing."

Nathan was moved deeply. He placed his hand on Kamisese's shoulder. "I originally came here to seek my fortune," he said, wait-ing while Susannah translated his words. He continued, "Instead, I ended up being involved in your tribal battles." Kamisese listened intently as Susannah translated. His voice brimming with emotion, Nathan said, "I learned the meaning of loyalty, and of love," he added, looking at Susannah. "I will never forget the lessons I have learned here."

Susannah finished translating. The two men looked at each other a while longer before Nathan turned away and helped Susannah into the longboat. When everyone was aboard, oarsmen began rowing the craft out to the *Rendezvous*.

From the longboat, a subdued Nathan and Susannah looked back at the equally subdued Fijians who watched in silence as the distance between them and the boat increased. Sina and Susannah waved to each other.

Behind the Fijians, Nathan noticed rain clouds forming over Viti Levu's interior.

#

Within minutes of boarding the *Rendezvous*, the schooner was readied to sail. Sailors scrambled over her decks and riggers scaled the masts as Foley barked orders at them.

As the *Rendezvous* set sail, Nathan and Susannah stood at the stern waving at the Fijians on the distant beach. The young lovers held each other tightly and looked into each other's eyes.

Susannah was feeling sad yet content at the same time. She knew, instinctively, Nathan was her soulmate. She felt safe and secure in his arms.

A thousand different feelings coursed through Nathan. He felt sad over the loss of Jack and Joeli and others he'd become close to, but thrilled to have Susannah at his side. Although he was unsure what the future held, he knew he'd be sharing it with her. He kissed her forehead tenderly. She snuggled in closer to him.

On shore, Kamisese was leading the Qopa villagers in a chant of respect for the departing couple. It was an emotive chant.

At the same time, on the headland behind the village, a lone figure blew into a conch. Its haunting sound echoed around the bay. Nathan looked directly at the distant figure, trying to identify him. He thought it may have been Lemeki, but the man was too far away to recognize.

The conch blower was, indeed, Lemeki. Looking directly at the *Rendezvous*, the Mamanucan ratu blew into the conch once more then walked away.

As the schooner neared the reef, the thunder of the ever-present waves crashing against it drowned out all other sounds. Moments later, as the *Rendezvous* sailed through the reef and out of Momi Bay, Susannah's eyes were drawn one last time to the mission station where her beloved father lay in eternal rest.

Next to her, Nathan studied the highlands of Viti Levu's interior. Touching the whale bone pendant that once more hung from his neck, he watched the highlands until they disappeared behind a curtain of rain.

#

The following day, as the Suva-bound *Rendezvous* sailed eastward off Viti Levu's Coral Coast, Nathan stood alone at the port-side rail studying the many fishing villages dotted along the distant shore. He recalled Jack had mentioned he lived in the Coral Coast village of Koroi, but the American didn't know where that was exactly.

Thinking about Jack reminded him he probably owed his life to the cheeky Cockney. He was grateful Jack came into his life when he did and vowed he'd find out where Koroi was and ensure his friend's wife and children were looked after.

I owe him that much.

Another village caught his eye. Nathan wasn't to know, but it was Koroi, Jack's village.

#

In Koroi at that very moment, the villagers stopped what they were doing to admire the *Rendezvous* as it sailed by. Jack's wife, Namosi, now only days from giving birth, took special interest in the schooner. It reminded her of her beloved Jack. She wondered when the lovable rascal would be returning home.

The baby inside her suddenly moved. Namosi knew instinctively it was a boy. She'd already decided she would call him Jack.

#

On board the *Rendezvous*, Nathan was joined by Susannah at the port-side rail. Without a word, they kissed, then, in blissful silence, watched the Coral Coast shoreline pass by.

Alone with their thoughts, each sensed the cycle of life and death was set to continue in Fiji—as it had for centuries. However, they had yet to discuss their plans, so at this point had no idea Fiji's future and theirs would forever be intertwined.

EPILOGUE

After personally delivering his precious beche-de-mer to China and consolidating his already considerable wealth, Nathan married Susannah. They settled in Suva, Fiji's future capital.

Operating as Johnson Traders, Nathan built a trading empire, contributing in no small way to Fiji's prosperity, while Susannah returned to teaching and opened a school in memory of her father. And, of course, Nathan did ensure that Jack Halliday's wife and children were well cared for.

The Qopa villagers, of Momi Bay, rebounded in fine style and, through intermarriage with the Mamanucans and other clans, eventually became a thriving community once again. The muskets they'd inherited from Nathan helped protect them from their enemies, and the golden tabua brought them good fortune.

Without Rambuka to lead them, the surviving outcasts soon disintegrated into disorganized rabble and were never heard of again.

Had he lived, Reverend Drake would have been impressed by the efforts of successive Methodist missionaries who met with wide success as Fiji's indigenous people forsook their old ways and embraced Christianity.

By the time Fiji became a British colony in 1874, the Johnson trading empire, operating as Johnson & Sons, had expanded throughout the islands of the South Pacific. Nathan and his two sons, Daniel and Joseph, played a major role in lobbying the Fijian Government to bring in indentured Indian laborers to cut sugar cane. Little did they know that in less than a hundred years Indians would make up nearly half Fiji's population.

With the influx of Indians came a new set of problems. Indigenous Fijians resented the new arrivals; resentment soon turned to violence and bloodshed, and the Johnsons became caught up in the resulting mayhem.

Despite the upheavals, Nathan and Susannah both lived into their nineties. Their twilight years were as peaceful as their younger years were tumultuous. The proud parents of two fine sons and grandparents to five loving grandchildren, the couple died within a month of each other.

In accordance with their final wishes, they were buried in adjoining plots on the headland behind the Qopa village at Momi Bay.

THE END

If you enjoyed the writing in this book you may care to read *The Ninth Orphan*, a thriller novel also written by father-and-son writing team Lance & James Morcan.

The Ninth Orphan

How do you catch a man who is never the same man twice?

That is the question posed in *The Ninth Orphan*, a new release conspiracy thriller novel . . .

An orphan grows up to become an assassin for a highly secretive organization. When he tries to break free and live a normal life, he is hunted by his mentor and father figure, and by a female orphan he spent his childhood with. On the run, the mysterious man's life becomes entwined with his beautiful French-African hostage and a shocking past riddled with the darkest of conspiracies is revealed.

Fast-paced, totally fresh and original, filled with deep and complex characters, *The Ninth Orphan* is a controversial, high-octane thriller with an edge. Merging fact with fiction, it illuminates shadow organizations rumored to exist in the real world.

Tackling genetic selection, mind control, secret societies and a chase around the globe, *The Ninth Orphan* also has a poignant, romantic sub-plot. The story contains the kind of intimate character portraits usually associated with psychological novels.

The Ninth Orphan is the first novel in the *Orphan* Trilogy and sets the stage for a new thriller franchise. The *Orphan* Trilogy includes a prequel, *The Orphan Factory*, and a sequel, *The Orphan Uprising*. Books two and three in the series will both be published by Sterling Gate Books in 2012.

The Ninth Orphan is published by Sterling Gate Books and available now for purchase.

Made in the USA
Middletown, DE
04 February 2015